SOUTH STREET

SOUTH STREET

WILLIAM GARDNER SMITH

THE CHATHAM BOOKSELLER
CHATHAM, NEW JERSEY

Library of Congress Catalog Card No. 73-86228
ISBN 0-911860-38-X

Reissued, 1973, by The Chatham Bookseller
by arrangement with Farrar, Straus and Giroux,
Inc.

To Mary

Book One:

BOULEVARD

1.

IT WAS A HOT SATURDAY IN JULY, AND SOUTH STREET WAS crowded: people promenading, vendors with their wares, streetcars clanging, automobiles crawling slowly and honking their horns. The brown pedestrians wore, for the most part, no coats or ties; their shirts were open at the neck and their sleeves rolled up above their elbows. Slim burned in the heat, walking slowly, mopping his brow. At Seventeenth Street he stopped at Crane's Jewelry Shop, looking fondly at a gold bracelet. He chuckled: "Lil would sure like that." He moved on.

Near Fifteenth Street, he turned into the *Postal Card*. The men sitting at the bar were watching intently the baseball game on the television set, but when Slim entered nearly everyone turned to him: "What's the lead, man?" Slim held up three fingers. Most of the men groaned or swore, but one slapped his side in glee: "I'm gonna hit it today!"

Slim sat down at the bar, nodded briefly to Catherine, the proprietor, ordered a gin fizz and settled down to see what Roy Campanella was going to do. Campanella rapped a double off the left-field wall, and a cheer went up in the bar almost as loud as the one that echoed from the stands of the park. (In a thousand bars across the eastern part of the nation, similar cheers were ringing.)

"That's my boy!" shouted the man who thought he was going to hit the numbers. "Today is my lucky day! I knew it when I got up this mornin'!"

Slim sipped his gin fizz. The Dodgers were some team. They were some team because they had Don Newcombe and Roy Campanella and Jackie Robinson—that was why. Gil Hodges was good, too. And Reese, and Cox, and Snider who was death on curve balls. But Newcombe, Campanella, Robinson—the Negroes —they were the real ones, the boys who made the team!

The cute, brown waitress moved beside Slim, to give an order to the bartender. Slim looked at her and winked. "Hi, baby," he said, "when you gonna give old Slim a chance?"

She laughed. "You must be crazy, Slim. I don't want Lil stickin' a knife in me. I got more sense than *that!*"

"Lil ain't no harm," Slim said innocently.

"Yeah, I know. Don't hand that stuff to me." The waitress moved away.

Slim chuckled. Yes, Lil was some girl. Some girl. It was great being the boyfriend of the hottest woman in town.

"Hey, Slim, there're your boys out there lookin' for you!"

Through the door Slim saw the patrolmen beckon from their red patrol car. He chuckled to himself as he climbed down from the stool and went to the door.

"Hi, Pat. Hi, Harry. How's it going?"

"Okay, Slim," the first Irishman said.

Slim reached into his pocket and pulled out a roll of bills about six inches in diameter. One of the policemen whistled. "You're doin' all right, Slim!"

"Sure, sure, wish it was mine!" He counted off several of the bills and handed them to the policemen.

"Okay, Slim. Thanks. See you next week."

"Sure, sure," Slim said.

Hardly had Slim reseated himself at the bar before a boy, about twelve years old, rushed in, calling his name. "Uncle Slim, the wagon's outside!"

"Hi, Joe. Come on over here. What's cookin'?"

"The wagon's outside!"

"The wagon? The wagon?" But memory was returning swiftly.

"Uncle Slim, did you forget again?"

"Forget? Oh, no, no, 'course not. 'Course not. Sure, the wagon. Okay, let's go on out."

The boy ran ahead. He was small and chubby, with soft brown eyes like Slim's, dressed in dungarees. A horse-drawn wagon, such as vegetable vendors use, stood outside the bar. An old, skinny man held the horse's reins.

"Joe tole me you ordered the wagon, Slim," the man said.

"So I did, so I did," Slim said. He paid the man, who walked off; then he started to lift the boy, Joe, to the seat, but Joe pulled angrily away. "I told you before, Uncle Slim, I can do it myself!" he cried indignantly.

"So you did, so you did," Slim chuckled. On the seat, Slim said, "But suppose you let me take the reins, huh?—and you can handle the whip." The boy frowned, but handed the reins to Slim.

The youth and his uncle rode up South Street to Twelfth, then along Twelfth Street. They tried to follow routes with the least amount of traffic. When they came to open sections, without intersections, Slim galloped the horse; Joe wielded the whip with glee; the horse sweated and his odor came back to the drivers; the old, flimsy wagon groaned.

"Let's go over to Carpenter Street so the fellas can see me," said Joe.

"Sure, just a showoff, that's all!" laughed Slim.

As they approached Carpenter, Joe said to Slim, "Let me handle the reins!" Joe drove along Carpenter and up to the boys who had stopped playing "Deadbox" to turn and stare. Joe reared back on the reins: "Whoa! Whoa!" he said authoritatively. The wagon pulled to a halt beside the boys.

The boys, dressed in patched knickers, inspected the horse. "Got good legs." From time to time they glanced in envy at Joe. "Wagon ain't much, though."

"Can you take us for a ride?"

Joe looked warily at Slim, who grinned and winked. "Sure,"

Joe said, "Climb on." The boys scrambled into the rear of the wagon. When they were all on, Joe said to the horse, "Giddyap!" The horse did not move. "Giddyap! Giddyap!" The horse did not budge. Joe cast a sidelong glance of panic at Slim, and a glance of apprehension at the boys, who were saying, "Let's get a move on!" "Giddyap!" Joe shouted, letting the reins fall down on the horse's back; still the horse did not move.

Joe, shamed and exasperated, struck the horse hard with the whip. With a snort, the animal bolted off. "Jesus!" Joe cried, when he recovered his balance. The horse was racing furiously down Carpenter Street; the wagon's rickety wheels wobbled precariously. "Slow him down! Slow him down!" cried Slim. Joe, wide-eyed, sweating, pulled back hard on the reins, but the horse had taken the bit in his teeth and would not slacken his pace. "Whoa! Whoooooa!" cried Joe, but the horse dashed madly on toward the intersection at Eighteenth Street, and Joe, from the corner of his eyes, saw the automobiles approaching. "Look out! Look out!" Joe screamed, in unheard warning, and then, with a clattering of wheels on streetcar tracks, they were in the middle of the intersection, heralded by angry horns and screeching tires. Then they were across the street, on the asphalt again, the sweating frightened animal racing with nodding head, bit held tight, the clatter of its hoofs echoing from the walls and houses where people, wide-eyed, stared. "Whoa! Whoa! Whoa!" —and they were at Nineteenth Street, and the horse, frightened by an approaching car, jerked hard by Joe and Slim together, turned sharply at a forty-five-degree angle—tilting the wagon on two wheels—then flew up Nineteenth, hell-bent for Ellsworth, wheels caught in the streetcar tracks and frightened boys in the rear shouting at the top of their voices, "Whoa! Whoa! Whoa!" and the wheels of the wagon wobbling even more dangerously than before. Slim had by now wrested the reins from his terrified nephew. He pulled back hard, with all his strength, bracing his feet, wrapping the reins around his arms, feeling the strength of the horse's neck and teeth against his arms and hands. Gradually, the animal slowed. Near Wharton he was gently trotting. By Reed, where a streetcar blocked his path, the horse came to a halt; a hot, lardy sweat covered his body.

"Whew!" said Slim.

"I thought you could handle him, Joe," said a boy.

"Hell, you can't even drive the damn thing!" said another, contemptuously.

Joe looked from one to another. His eyes were wide with fear. His chest was heaving and he was sweating furiously.

"Can't even drive him!" The boy, repeating his statement, spat out of the side of the wagon.

"Sure I can drive him," said Joe. "He just got the bit in his teeth."

"Well, what the hell, you oughtn't a let him!"

Slim drove the wagon back to Carpenter Street, where the boys unloaded, and then to the stables, where the old keeper looked at his sweating animal and then, disapprovingly, at Slim. Slim did not say anything. With Joe, he walked back toward South Street.

Joe was sullen. He said, "What the hell that Davy mean?"

"What's up, sport?"

"What's he mean I can't drive a horse? He just got the bit in his mouth, that's all!"

"Sure, sure."

They were at South Street. Slim was going back to the *Postal Card* for awhile. "See you, sport," he said to Joe. "Yeah," said the chubby youth; he turned and walked, dejected, toward Carpenter.

2.

THE SHOWBOAT, AROUND THE CORNER, ON LOMBARD STREET:
basement night club: ceiling low, lights low; square, with, in the
center, an oval bar. In the center of the bar stood a platform, and
on the platform were the four-piece band and the Blues Singer.
The bar was filled with music, voices, and smoke.

The Blues Singer: shimmering sequins in the painted light:
voice a long low wail of pain, twisting round the bass, riding the
piano, throbbing with the drum-beats:

> *My man ain't got no money,*
> *My man ain't got no heart . . .*

Around the walls of the room at the tables, and on the raised
round stools at the bar—the people: varicolored faces, deep-
brown eyes, laughter and lonely smiles; bartenders, waitresses,
customers; sitting, standing; talking, listening.

> *My man ain't even got the brains*
> *To handle a push-cart*

"He was driving a Caddy," said the man, "and I didn't have
nothin' but this souped-up Ford. But when we got on the straight-
away I gave it the gun and the cat couldn't even see me! Couldn't
even *see* me!"

> *But I love him*

Smoke; womb; dream; safety.

> *Love him all the same.*

Slim went into the Showboat looking for Lil; she was a waitress there, and should have been around, but he could not find her. He saw the Old Man sitting at a table on the side, and went over to him. "Hi," Slim said, "anybody seen Lil?"

"Lil?" said the Old Man. "Ah, Lil. Hmmm. Lovely creature. Yes, Lil was here, young man, but she went out. Sit down. Buy us a drink."

"Went out?" Slim scratched his head. "That's funny. Didn't say where she was going, huh?"

"No, she just went out."

Slim sat down. He knew the other people at the table: Margaret and the three Bowers brothers, Philip, Michael and—Slim stared for a moment at the third brother.

"Claude!" he said. "I didn't notice you. Haven't seen you in years. When did you get back?"

"A week ago," Claude said. He was a broad man with a strong face. "This is my first visit to the 'Showboat.'"

"He's been in Africa!" Michael said; he said it as though he were making a pronouncement of great moment.

"That so?" said Slim. "What were you doing there?"

"He was fighting . . . for Africa's freedom!" Michael said.

At this, Claude turned and smiled at his younger, hawk-faced brother.

"That's great," Slim said vaguely, "that's great." He wondered where Lil was. He noticed, distantly, that Claude wore in his lapel a white carnation like those Slim had always seen in the lapels of the other two brothers. Slim had heard that there was some family story attached to the carnations, but he had never bothered to ask about it.

"As a matter of fact," the Old Man said, "we were just toasting Claude on his return among us. Two years in Africa, and before that several years spent moving all over the country, a kind of racial trouble-shooter. Nice to have you home," he said, nodding to Claude.

"Let's toast it," said Philip.

Margaret, who had been sitting quiet and lovely next to Philip, suddenly raised her glass and said, "To a hero." She was not beautiful, but when she smiled at Claude her face was amazingly sweet and gentle.

The Old Man was slender and very dapper; he wore a dark-green sport shirt, open at the neck, with beige gabardine pants. He smoked his cigaret from a long, expensive holder which he flourished, along with the gold signet ring on his finger, at every opportunity.

"Yes, yes," said the Old Man, lowering his glass. "Very delicious. Very delicious. Slim, my boy, did I ever tell you I have designs on your young lady?"

"Lil? Well, go right ahead, Old Man."

"Yes, yes. I do love the way she walks, you know."

"Nice rear action, huh?"

"Ah . . . yes. You put it crudely, but . . . precisely."

Slim laughed. The Old Man was a card. Slim said, "You got designs on everybody, Old Man. He ever proposition you, Margaret?"

Margaret laughed and looked at the Old Man. "Oh, he can do much better than me," she said. Her voice was soft and smooth, and seemed out of place in the club.

"I wouldn't say that," said the Old Man, "I wouldn't say that at all. One forms a . . . relationship, after all, with a spirit, a soul. To share this briefly would be worth a thousand sessions with a calloused movie queen. And there is an added attraction; you are somewhat . . . innocent, may I say. And the currency is increased in value, after all, the less there is in circulation."

Slim grinned and pointed a warning finger at Philip. "There you go, Phil, you see? Better watch yourself. The Old Man's got a slippery tongue; he's gonna talk you right out of a girlfriend." Philip smiled and touched Margaret's hand.

Intermission. The Blues Singer came down from the platform and walked over to Slim's table. "Hi. Hi. Hi, hero!" she said to Claude. "Jesus Christ! a hero among us! Scares me to death! Gimme a kiss!" She bent down and Claude kissed her on the mouth. "Damn!" she said. "You call that a kiss? That how they kiss in Africa? Gimme a *kiss*, man! None of that locked-up tongue stuff!"

Claude tried it again. As the Blues Singer walked around the table, to take a seat, the Old Man patted her buttocks. "Stop teasin'!" said the Blues Singer, "else I'll call your bluff and take you upstairs and kill you, so help me!" She laughed harshly. She sat down and looked around the table. "The Bowers brothers. The white-carnation boys." She laughed the raucous laugh again, and slapped the Old Man hard on the back.

"You know where Lil is?" Slim asked.

"How the hell I know?" said the Blues Singer. "Probably out with another man. That bitch ain't never here on time, wouldn't know she worked here."

"She's not a bitch."

"Oh, balls! Don't go gettin' loyal on me, you make me feel like a cynic." She looked at the Old Man. "Ain't this man a dope? He thinks Lil ain't a bitch. Jesus!" She burst into the laugh. Slim looked at her, but said nothing.

"Ah," said the Old Man, "here's our little lost lamb now!"

Slim's heart leapt when he saw Lil come in. Close behind her, however, was a man. They stood at the bar. Lil turned toward their table, smiled without waving, then turned back to her companion.

"Hah!" said the Blues Singer to Slim; she laughed loudly, the sound carrying, as always, throughout the room. Slim shrugged. From time to time he glanced at the bar, to see Lil and the man still talking.

Lil stood at the bar for about fifteen minutes. Slim looked at the line of her thick hair, the golden brown of her skin, the line of her back arcing gently to the waist, then flowing smoothly out, then in again, then down into the legs. From time to time Lil turned to glance at Slim and smile—a saucy, almost mocking smile. Finally, she turned, looked at Slim for a moment, turned back to the man she was with, kissed him on the cheek, her hand around his neck, then turned again and, still smiling, walked toward Slim. Her smiling, mocking dark eyes never left Slim.

"Oh, hello, Slim," she said sweetly, with a sugared, slightly drawled voice, "I didn't know you were coming tonight. Hello everybody. Mind if I sit down?" She sat next to Claude. Looking first at his face, then at his shoulders, then at his face again, she said, "And who is this lovely man? I don't remember ever meeting him."

"That's Claude," Michael said quickly. "That's my brother I told you about." He looked at Lil closely, as though expecting her to faint at this announcement.

Claude laughed and shook his head. "Michael, you're wonderful, but you're mighty embarrassing."

"Oh, but he has a right to be enthusiastic," Lil said, looking at Claude with wide eyes. "He has every right to be. Why, if I had a brother like you, I'd be shouting it to the world, too!"

She smiled sweetly at Claude. The Blues Singer chuckled. Michael looked at Lil happily. Slim fumed.

With every movement, Lil's body spoke softly beneath the clinging, deep-cut dress she wore. Her mouth was red and very full: she used it like a hand for gestures, curling her lips in words, in smile, or in funnel for the smoke of a cigarette. With her eyes she danced saucily among the people at the table, only occasionally looking, with a mocking assumption of shyness, at Slim.

"Oh, it's so hot, don't you think?" she said. "I feel so faint. Claude, would you see a pretty girl faint from the heat? Let me sip your drink . . . it looks so cool? May I? . . . You're so kind.

Ummm, that's *sooo* delicious! Cool and sweet. From your lips, I'll bet. They look so cool and nice . . . your lips, I mean. . . ."

"Hah!" laughed the Blues Singer. "Listen to her!"

"Why, what's the matter, darling? Something wrong?"

"Ain't nothin' wrong with *me*, sweetheart!"

"You laughed so strangely, darling." She looked at the Blues Singer. "My, you look nice! Those sequins become you."

"Yeah, yeah, sure," said the Blues Singer.

"Why, I'm sincere, darling. Sequins become you. You can get so many on."

"Ah, you little prostitute!" said the Blues Singer.

Lil sat suddenly rigid; her eyes fixed on the Blues Singer. She said, "Hold it, darling. That's nasty language. I'd watch my language if I were you."

"Oh, hell!" said the Blues Singer.

"But I'd watch it." She caught herself; she smiled sweetly and relaxed again, against Claude's shoulder, but her eyes never left the Blues Singer. "Sometimes," she said sweetly, the smile broadening, "sometimes it's . . . dangerous to talk to people like that, you know. Sometimes even gentle people don't like it, you know."

The Blues Singer grunted; but she did not say anything. For several minutes, no one said anything. Slim looked at Lil and his heart beat faster. *She's in one of* those *moods!*

Lil turned smiling to Claude again and said, "Do you have a girlfriend, Claude? Tell me. If you do, I'll scratch her eyes out. I can be savage, too, sometimes. Even gentle people can be savage sometimes, don't you think?"

"He hasn't got *time* for a girlfriend!" Michael said.

"My goodness, what on earth does he do?" Lil asked.

"He works," said Michael.

"That's horrible. You must relax sometimes, Claude. You let me know when you want to, will you?" She smiled again, and stood up. "Well, I've got to go change into clothes for work. I'll see you all in a little while. Claude, don't you dare go away! See you, Slim doll."

She went through a side door. "That bitch!" said the Blues Singer. Inside of Slim, anguish and anger were burning simultaneously. He could look at no one at the table. He knew that Lil had meant none of what she said to Claude, or what she had done at the bar; she was in a playful mood, and he was the victim of it. What he hated in particular was that *Claude* might not know, also, that Lil had only been playing. Slim lighted a cigarette and ordered a drink; he sat morosely, listening to the intermission pianist, paying no attention to the conversation going on among the others at the table.

"Well, I'm on again," said the Blues Singer. "Going to waste my genius on these ignorant bastards!" She moved away, tight-dressed, around the table. Moments later she was on the platform, with the combo, and the lights went dim.

3.

EARLY SUNDAY MORNING, DRESSED IN A DARK-BLUE SUIT, MICHAEL walked out of the small house where he lived with his two brothers, and down the street to another row house with wooden front steps and a bannister. He rang the bell twice, but did not wait for anyone to come to the door before walking in. "Mrs. Adams," he called from the hall.

The answering voice came from upstairs. "That you, Michael?"

"Yes, ma'am."

"Be right down."

Michael waited. The shutters of the windows in the front room were closed, the furniture was dark and old, pictures and small statues out of the Victorian Age were around the walls; the house was musty and oppressive. When he heard the steps of the old woman on the stairs, Michael mounted and took her hand. The short, bent woman leaned heavily against him.

"Seems t' me it gits harder and harder to git up an' down these stairs every day," she said.

"Yes, ma'am."

They walked slowly down Nineteenth Street, Mrs. Adams leaning on Michael's arm. Young pretty girls, dressed for Sunday, passed them, glancing with faint smiles at Michael.

"These young girls find you mighty attractive, Michael."

Michael laughed. He led Mrs. Adams up the gray stone steps of the Union Baptist Church, then through the aisle and into a pew. The Reverend Mr. Kirkland was delivering his sermon. Michael leaned over and got a fan for Mrs. Adams; the old woman smiled, said, "Thank you" voicelessly, with her lips, and settled comfortably back, fanning slowly, lost in the words of the minister. Michael sat quiet; around the church he saw the familiar Sunday faces, mostly old, lined, intent: these seemed to him direct descendants of the slaves. There was a sprinkling of young faces, too: of pretty girls and shiny-faced young men, who came, most of them, not for the church services themselves, but for the social life the church provided—the young people's group, with meetings, quiet parties, picnics.

The choir began to sing. Now Michael, too, leaned back, lost.

> *Oh, when I come to the end of my journey*
> *Weary of life, and the battle is won....*

Spirituals. The emotions beneath them. Michael closed his eyes and listened.

In the afternoon, Michael visited the Old Man in his big, four-story house on Christian Street. "Michael! Well, my boy, come in, come in!" They went through the familiar living room, the familiar dining room. "Well, well, care for a little drink? A little shot of pool?" They climbed down the narrow wooden stairs to the celler, which the Old Man had had made over into a pool room.

"Break 'em," said the Old Man. He opened a bottle of Old Grand Dad, poured some into two glasses and put the glasses on the rim of the pool table. "Taste that, young man, make you shoot straighter." Michael made the break, and a nine-ball fell into a pocket. "You're on today," said the Old Man. Michael dropped several other balls into the pockets; the Old Man regarded him with fascination and dismay.

"And what did you do today? Church?"

"Yes," Michael said.

"The charming Mrs. Adams. These widowed creatures. I could make time with that lady; she has eyes for me, you know. But she's too old. Too old. I like them rather fresher ... more dewy, as you might say."

Michael laughed and missed the next shot. The Old Man bent over the table and neatly angled the six-ball into a pocket. He fondled the stick, shot again. He waited until he had pocketed three more balls before asking, "Oh, by the way, my boy, how much are we betting?"

Michael grinned. "Nickel a ball."

The Old Man pocketed another ball and looked at Michael with disdain. "Oh, come, come, my boy, that's no bet. No bet at all. Make it a dime."

They played several games; the Old Man won them all. "Shall we go upstairs and relax?" he asked, beaming. They sat in the living room. All around the walls were paintings of nude, pink women, most of them reclining on furs. The Old Man, in a bright dressing gown and slippers, leaned back in his chair, feet propped up on a hassock.

"Yes, life is beautiful," he said. He caressed the glass that held his drink.

16 ·

Michael looked at the Old Man wonderingly. "Is it? Really?"

"Of course, of course. You have too grim a view, young man. Too grim a view. Life is rich, full, exciting, wonderful."

Michael did not say anything. He sat back in his chair, looking at his drink. After awhile, he looked up at the Old Man and said, "Why is life beautiful?"

"Why?"

"Yes. For you."

"Me?" The Old Man showed the palms of his hands and looked around the room as though the reasons should be self-evident. "Why, what more could I want, my boy? I have everything to make me happy. I'm a committeeman, don't have to work hard at it, just go get out the vote at election time and get a few crazy youngsters out of jail. Got a good job up at City Hall, pays nice, it's safe. Can make a little money extra here and there. Got my health. Got a home. Got friends. Have the pleasant company of young ladies. What else?"

Michael shook his head. "That's not enough."

"What else is there?"

"A purpose."

"A *what?*" The Old Man chuckled. "That's for you young people. That's for you and Claude. After awhile, you learn to take a good hard look at the real world, my boy; you see how it ticks, and you stop thinking about things like purposes and such. The world is what it is; people are what they are. Don't try to change it, you're wasting your time. First analyze the world, then find out how you can make your way inside of it. All you can do."

"How can you be happy while Negroes are so unhappy?" Michael said suddenly, looking at the Old Man with emotion.

Again, the Old Man chuckled. "Negroes are not unhappy, son. That's a myth created by Richard Wright."

When Michael sat staring at his glass again, the Old Man leaned forward. "Look here, Michael, I've been meaning to talk to you. You've got to stop trying to follow in the footsteps of Claude. You've got to learn to make your own way, find your own happiness. Ever since your father was killed————"

"*Murdered*, you mean!" Michael said sharply. Unconsciously, he touched the white carnation in his lapel.

"All right, murdered, then. Ever since they murdered your father you've been out on a vendetta. You and Claude both— Philip not so much, Philip's not built for that sort of thing. This carnation business. What's that but a vendetta? It's unhealthy going around wearing these things, reminding yourselves all the time of your hatred. You can't get revenge on the whole white race————"

"We don't want revenge. We want to fight for what's right!"

The Old Man threw up his hands. "It's revenge. There are ways to fight without all this hate, without these carnations." He shook his head and raised his glass to his lips.

Michael sat still. What was the use of talking? What good did it do? Not to the Old Man, who had achieved what he thought was success, should Michael talk, but to those lined-faced people sitting in the church, listening to the emotion beneath the spirituals. He looked around the room. Pictures of naked girls: soft, pink bodies to fill the daydreams of a wasted old man. Was it for *this*, in the end, that life was lived?

Michael saw the Old Man look at his watch. Michael stood up. "I'm meeting Claude for dinner at Horn and Hardart's. Would you like to come along?"

"Well, that's very kind of you, very kind of you," said the Old Man, "but as a matter of fact, a young lady—a very charming young lady, you don't know her—is coming over very shortly, and she has very graciously offered to cook dinner for the both of us. Sorry. Really sorry. But ask me again, won't you?"

The Old Man showed Michael to the door.

4.

PHILIP WISHED EVERY DAY WERE SUNDAY. IT WAS A DAY THAT deserved its name, it seemed to him: even in winter, or in the rainy season, it was a day usually more pleasant, warmer, bluer than other days. On Sunday people seemed to be more agreeable, more inclined to smile: rested from the week's work, they dressed up, went to church, took long walks in the park. On Sunday, people usually felt good. Philip felt good with them.

He had spent the day quietly, reading and studying—alone at home—which was the height of pleasantness, after all. Quietly, in the background, he had listened to his recordings of first the *Rasoumovsky* and then the *Fifteenth* quartet of Beethoven—the first his favorite, though it was undoubtedly a bit sentimental. Through his window, the Sunday sun had shone. Philip loved and admired his brothers, of course—immensely—but he was glad that they had left him alone. He had wanted peace and relaxation which he could not have found had they been there. The air of a house was a charged thing, the electricity of presences was a static in the atmosphere: even when they were silent, Philip could almost *hear* the violent personalities of Michael and Claude crackling in the air.

It was now late afternoon; the sun burned slanting down, and the white carnation in Philip's lapel was turning brown at the edges. He was twenty-three—three years younger than Michael and seven years younger than Claude; he had a smooth, round, clear-eyed face, a slender body, and extremely sensitive fingers. He was on his way to visit Margaret.

"Yes, I went to church this morning, and Reverend Jones preached a wonderful sermon. A beautiful sermon," Margaret's mother was saying, rocking back and forth in the rocking chair near the window in the living room. "Then I went to see Mrs. Morrissy—you remember her?—and we sat and talked most of the afternoon. Then I come on home and decided to take a rest, worked hard enough all week." She was a short, round woman who always wore black stockings; she was sewing socks from a basket piled high.

Philip went into the kitchen to sit with Margaret, while she got dinner ready. She was the oldest of the children—there were nine, in all—and she was the second mother, a kind of first sergeant, taking care of many of the mother's responsibilities. She acted as commander whenever her mother was absent (although her sisters and brothers, knowing her soft, were inclined to ignore Margaret's "commands," running off to their respective pleasures and leaving to her the tasks the mother had assigned, through Margaret, to them). Philip, looking at her, saw a plain, pleasant-looking girl, of rich brown skin, thick coarse hair and soft brown eyes. Her soft, pleasing body moved easily and slowly, conveying the calm and patience which never left her; her speech, likewise, was rather slow and soft, and she did not speak often. Philip was always amazed and pleased by Margaret's capacity for silence: she could sit for hours without saying a word, and without causing embarrassment; and yet, her silence was not the wordlessness of emptiness, but the stillness of a person whose life was lived, for the most part, inside. With Margaret, Philip felt at peace.

As nearly always on Sundays, Philip had dinner with Margaret's family. Mr. Daniels, Margaret's father, had been playing checkers in the park; seated at the head of the table, shirt open at the neck, he told Philip about the game, and about the baseball game he had watched earlier in the afternoon. Mr. Daniels seemed to like Philip, despite the fact that he could not comprehend his disinterest in sports, cards, and checkers. There were eight of them seated at the dining room table, into which a center-board had been inserted—the father and mother, Philip and Margaret and the four sons. The four other sisters ate at the table in the kitchen. Mr. Daniels began the meal by saying Grace. No one lifted a fork until Mr. Daniels had taken his first mouthful of food.

After dinner, Mr. Daniels invited Philip to go into the living room and listen to Jack Benny on the radio. The girls were occupied with clearing the table, sweeping the floors and washing the dishes; the boys had gone outside. "That man's funny, really funny," Mr. Daniels laughed, looking fondly at Philip, and puffing on a long cigar.

"I'd like to go for a walk," Margaret said when she had finished.

"We could walk to Market Street, to a movie," Philip said.

Down Seventeenth Street they walked, past silent South Street, silent Lombard Street, tree-lined Pine and Spruce Streets. There were many stars and a moon, although the coolness promised rain later in the night, or the next morning. Philip took Margaret's soft and incredibly smooth hand into his own.

Fantasia was back at the Trans-Lux. They saw it again, enjoyed it again, then walked out and to the *Crosstown* for a sundae. Someone inserted a nickel in one of the juke-box coin receivers that were over each table; Billy Eckstein's voice entered the room a few seconds later. Philip touched Margaret's hand on top of the table and smiled into her soft, brown eyes; she smiled in return, softly, but distantly.

The breeze was even balmier on the walk back. They went through Rittenhouse Square, where a flower show was being held, walking slowly under the pavillions and past the benches occupied by sundry lovers, children, people old and young. Down Nineteenth Street, past the pleasant streets, then across Lombard and South again, and on into the gloomier neighborhoods. A gentle depression flitted briefly across Philip's heart; it was banished as soon as he pressed Margaret's hand.

He did not know why it struck him at that moment, as they sat on the steps of Margaret's house before saying goodnight, to say the words. He had not meant to say them. Perhaps it was the unusual singing peace of his soul that pressed them out; perhaps it was the breeze blowing the soft coarse ends of her hair into his face, or perhaps, even—though he would doubt it—the sensitive rustling of her skirt as she crossed her soft, well-formed legs. At any rate, love for her, in that moment, rose like a melody to his throat, and he said:

"Margaret, let's be engaged."

Her relaxing body did not move. The breeze played with the ends of her hair, over her shoulders. Philip watched her, excited and frightened by his own boldness. She shook her head, and looked at him.

"I can't, Philip."

"Do you worry about money, or anything like that?" Philip asked. "I have only half a year more at school. It shouldn't take long after that to get a job. If we got engaged now, we could be married within the year."

"It's not that."

"Don't you love me, Margaret?"

She was looking past his shoulder. There was a film of tears over her eyes. "In a way, yes," she said softly. Philip waited, and then she said, in the same soft tone, almost a monotone, "It's crazy, Philip, I know you'll say so. But I'm in love with someone else. Someone I've loved for many years. He doesn't love me. He doesn't have time to love anyone, and that's as it should be. He has more important things to do than fall in love with me. But as long as I'm in love with him, I can't marry anyone else." She looked again at Philip. "Do you know who it is?"

Philip said, "I think so," in a hoarse voice.

"It's Claude."

"Yes, I thought so."

"And you see, he'll never love me, but I don't care. He hardly remembered me when he came back this time."

"That's not true."

"I think so. But, anyway, I want to love him. Without being a bother to him. Do you understand?"

"You shouldn't throw your own life away. It's a waste of time, as you said. You shouldn't throw your life away."

"I want to love him, Philip. That's all. I don't want to marry anyone else; not even you. In my mind, I'm already married to Claude, and he's married to me."

"All right. I understand it."

"I'm sorry, Philip."

"It's all right. I understand your loving Claude. You shouldn't throw your life away. But I understand it."

Then she sat quietly looking past him with the soft calm face and the soft calm eyes. Philip did not know precisely how he felt: a kind of hollow ringing in his ears, a sense that this scene, on the steps, on a balmy July night, was unreal, something that would pass away, leaving unchanged the past and tranquil the future.

Margaret was standing on the step, and was, therefore, higher than he. Philip stood on tiptoe and kissed her lightly on the cheek.

5.

CLAUDE AND MICHAEL HAD DINNER TOGETHER. AFTERWARDS, Michael slapped Claude on the shoulder and said, "Let's go for a long, long walk, like we used to. Yes?" The two brothers walked to Chestnut Street, then up the street, looking in windows, looking at passers-by. At Fifteenth they turned toward Market, looked in at Penn Station, listened to the honking cars, the shouting newsdealers, the lights of the movie theaters. They stopped at a drug store for a quick coffee, then went on up through the City Hall arch.

Michael felt good. He said, "Do you remember how we used to come up here, to the News Theater, just because we liked the way it looked like a long hall?" They laughed and chattered, remembering things. Michael never felt better than when he was with Claude.

Michael was tall and wiry, nervous, hawk-faced; his gestures were vigorous—almost violent—and, at least when he was with Claude, he talked rapidly and emphatically, the words tumbling out, often making dogmatic statements on one subject or another, but always listening carefully—and generally changing his mind —when Claude disagreed. Claude, while he was also tall, was broad, gave the impression of power. He talked more slowly than his brother; his laugh, while spontaneous, was softer, more considered; and he rarely gestured at all. His face was broad, like sculptored wood; it spoke of greater solidity, greater depth, and less rashness in making decisions than his brother.

They walked for more than an hour, aimlessly, leaving the broad thoroughfares for darker, smaller streets, walking in a great circle, talking, not noticing the time. "Tell me again about your trip to Africa." Michael was always like a child, listening. At the end, the fire burning even brighter in his eyes, he exclaimed: "The Africans will be free some day! They are fighting for it, just as we are fighting to be equal in our own country!" Claude liked Michael, liked his fire, his enthusiasm, his nervous energies and passions—even though, at times, these very things also disturbed him.

Walking now, in the dark, they passed a lonely church, surrounded by trees, through whose windows, strangely, there came the sound of music—the sound of a violin. Claude's attention was arrested. He paused, listening. Most of the church lay in darkness; the music came through the lighted window of a small room, probably a cloak room, in the rear. The rich, humming notes floated eerily on the night air; they echoed from the walls of facing buildings, sang among the trees. What was it? Claude

listened. Brahms. *Sonata in A.* He listened, rapt; the violinist
was good, marvelous! What was such a violinist doing there,
unheard, in that small room, at this strange hour of the night?
On a bulletin board, on the wall of the church, Claude read:

KRISTIN KENNEDY
Young Violinist
In Recital
Wednesday, July 20
Second Presbyterian Church

"What is it?" Michael asked.

"The sonata. That violinist is excellent!"

He listened in wonder. Something soft and warm moved inside
of him.

"Let's go," said Michael, impatiently.

Claude stood still for a moment. Then, with Michael, he
moved on.

Claude walked now in silence. Michael kept talking.

"Claude, you haven't changed at all, have you?"

"How do you mean?"

"Well, I don't know. I just wanted to ask you, to hear an
answer from your own lips. Some people think that you're not
the old, vigorous Claude, do you know what I mean? They think
you've gotten *conservative!*"

Claude smiled, but he did not look at Michael. "Is that so
serious?"

"Tell me, Claude. You haven't changed, have you?"

"No," Claude said. He looked at Michael. "I haven't changed."

Michael said, "You still wear the carnation. I wondered how
you were while you were in Africa, and then I saw the first pictures of you, in the newspapers, that they took when you got off
the boat. I saw the carnation in your lapel, and I knew that
everything was all right."

Claude said nothing, and Michael continued, "And, Claude? You still think that the greatest thing is for a man to be . . . well, dignified, proud, not afraid to fight for the things he knows are right. You still believe all those things you used to write?"

"Yes. Most of them."

Michael was, for a short while, silent. Then he said, "And, Claude?"

"Yes?"

"You never forgot the death of Pop? You never forgot how he died, you never stopped thinking about it and remembering who did it?"

"I never forgot who did it."

"You never stopped hating white people?"

Claude glanced at his brother. Michael was looking intently, almost desperately, at him; his eyes burned. Claude said, "Take it easy, pal."

"You never stopped hating them?" Michael would not move.

Claude said, "No, I never stoppped."

"Good." They moved on. "Because," said Michael, "because, Claude, I can never forget, you see, and never stop hating. I don't want to stop. But I'm not as strong as you, you know; I need you with me. I need to know you're with me."

Claude put his arm around his brother's shoulder, gripping him fondly.

"You're the greatest person in the world to me," Michael said. "Do you know that? You're the only person I know who's not weak, the only person who's not afraid, and who can't be bought. You're a hero, you know; they know your name all over the country. And you'll be an even greater hero. You'll be the greatest hero we've produced—greater than Nat Turner, greater than Douglass."

Claude laughed softly, looked at his brother and shook his head. He did not say anything. Then the smile faded again from his face, and he was away, distant, preoccupied.

When they reached their house, Michael mounted the steps, but Claude said, "Look, Michael, will you forgive me? There's something I want to do. I want to think out some things for an article. Do you mind going in alone?"

"Of course not. See you soon."

Claude walked slowly, smoking a cigarette, feeling the air. It was cool; the stars were out, but he was sure that the coolness would bring rain. *Good old Michael.* He felt a faint heaviness. *Michael. The same Michael.* The American cigarette tasted delicious; yes, and he had gotten used to the others. Two years.

And where was he now, on this street? Ahead of him, he saw the church they had passed; unconsciously, he had walked back toward it. He heard the violin on the air again, and was conscious of a great relief, as though he had walked back here on purpose, and, having arrived, feared that the music might have ceased.

6.

THERE WERE A LOT OF PEOPLE OUTSIDE THE CHURCH, OLD PEOPLE, most of them, poor, dressed in their Sunday clothes, out to hear the young violinist who their pastor had told them was good. A faint rain fell, but no one tried to escape it: it was a gentle, even pleasant, caressing rain, that brushed the cheeks lightly and did not seriously wet the clothes. "Isn't Mrs. Evans coming?" one woman asked another. "Do you think she'll be as good as that boy who played the piano last month?" They were church people; they wanted to hear what one of their own could do.

Claude's was the only brown face among the scores that smiled or looked grim as the people filed up the gray stone steps into the lobby of the church. The pastor was standing near the door, shaking hands with people he knew. He looked rather strangely, as though surprised, at Claude; but, of course, he said nothing, and Claude, after paying at the table in the lobby, went inside and took his seat.

There was a low hum of voices in the church. The seats were three-fourths filled. The pastor went up on the stage and held up his hand; the voices stopped, and the pastor made an announcement about a picnic, for the young, that would be given the following week; he also reminded the congregation that money was needed for new uniforms for the choir and new hymn books.

Then he came to the event of the evening. Miss Kennedy, he said, had always attended the Second Presbyterian Church; she had been practically raised in the church, he said, and the church had paid for part of her musical education. She was young, only twenty-five; this was to be her first public performance. She had shown great talent, and the church was proud to be the starting point of what would, one day, be a great career.

Claude was startled by the young girl's appearance. She had a clear, unsophisticated beauty: her face was rounded, her eyes, even from this distance, seemed bright, and her blonde hair was attractively worn off the face, tied at the back of her head. She looked even younger than twenty-five; her movements were girl-ish, and she seemed nervous standing on the platform. She raised the violin to her chin, nodded to the pianist, and then touched the bow to the strings.

From the first strains, Claude knew that *here* was a violinist. He felt the return of that warmth he had known the night before; he surrendered up his body to the sounds, letting them soothe him. He looked at the girl's nervous wrist, on the hand that held the bow—a wrist so strangely, so shockingly frail compared to the robust, active body. The music was strange and wonderful. She seemed to *be* the music she played. Claude had the impression, watching her, listening, that she and the music were one, of one substance, that they blended, intertwined, like embracing one-souled lovers whirling through the air. The girl, swaying, lost, was a stately Bach, an opaque Wagner, a churning Beethoven blasting ego and insensitivity jointly into the air; she was a fluid dress, a floating blonde head, a being liquefied, *become* music. . . .

Afterward, Claude went backstage. He felt strange; he had never gone backstage to congratulate a performer before. Many other people stood outside the dressing room; a few at a time were admitted, and Claude waited patiently, finally made his way in. The young girl stood radiant and breathless near her dressing table. Eyes shining with happiness, she thanked each person who congratulated her. Claude stepped forward. "You played beautifully," he said vaguely; "beautifully. . . ." It was all he could say; he felt ridiculous, and doubted that she could hear him, anyway, in the general din. Smiling, the girl thanked him. Someone pushed forward. Then he found himself in the hall outside the dressing room again, and other people were still trying to get in.

7.

DOWN THE CORNER FROM THE CHURCH WAS A SMALL DRUG STORE; Claude went in to get coffee before going home. Some boys were playing a pinball machine in a corner; they glanced at Claude, then went back to their game. Claude sat in a booth, ordered the coffee and a hamburger. He had been there only fifteen minutes when the door opened and Kristin Kennedy walked in.

She was carrying her violin case, and she was alone. Dressed now in a simple, powder-blue suit, she looked like any student of music who might have been in the neighborhood. The boys at the pinball machine turned and looked at her admiringly as she sat down at the counter, where she ordered a Coke. Claude saw her through the mirror behind the counter: he saw a face that was alive: her eyes were bright with *seeing*, wide, as though dazzled by the wonder of the world they saw. Her hands moved searchingly through space; her movements were quick and impulsive; her body was not tight, but easy and free. Then, through the mirror, she saw Claude looking at her.

"Hello," she said, turning around. "I didn't see you when I came in." She got down from her stool, picked up the violin and the Coke, and walked over toward his table. "Don't want to spill it," she said. "Precious stuff. Mind if I sit down?"

Claude was startled. For a moment, he did not speak. The young girl's skin was white; therefore, for him and his brothers, she was a stranger and an enemy. But he was moved by her naive directness and moved by the memory of the music in the church. He said, "Please."

She looked at him as though, for an instant, questioning her memory. "It was *you* who came backstage just now, wasn't it?"

"Yes," Claude said. "I liked your playing very much."

"Good. For a moment I was afraid I had made a mistake." She sat down. "You like music? Did you ever play?"

"I've never played, but I like it."

"Most wonderful thing in the world. I don't even know how to go about talking to people who don't love music. But, then, nearly all people love music, of one kind or another. Good music, too."

Coming slowly out of his astonishment, and fascinated by the impulsive girl, Claude said, "Do you always remember everybody who comes backstage to congratulate you?" He noticed, close up, that there were faint freckles on her face.

"No, not always. But I remembered you. You stood out, you know." She laughed. "The dark skin."

Claude said nothing. He looked at the girl, whose mouth was fixed in a gentle pucker around the straw. He was not used to such frankness; ordinarily, it would have disturbed him. And yet, the girl had come, of her own free will, to sit at his table.

"I'm so glad you liked my playing," she said, raising her head from the straw and turning her clear, frank blue eyes on him. "Technically, I'm not too good, I think; I have a lot still to learn. But, you know, I *feel* the music so much."

"That's obvious."

"Yes, and I'm so happy, because you can't learn that. And you can learn all the technique in the world and not be good unless you feel the music. Because to play Beethoven, for instance, do you know what you have to be?"

"What?"

"You have to *be Beethoven*! Do you know what I mean? You have to be able to feel all of Beethoven's emotions, which went into the music; you have to stretch your emotions to encompass all of his; you have to go from his extreme sensitivity, even femininity, up to his supreme arrogance. You can't interpret what you can't feel. You have to *be* Beethoven!"

Claude smiled. "Yes, I'm sure you're right." Her hand touched her glass; Claude looked again at that too-frail wrist. She came away from her straw and looked at Claude for a moment, then down at her Coke again. She fell into a silence, but not, oddly, the silence of the deep interior; her eyes were still darting around the room, drinking up the things they saw; her ears still heard every sound.

The boys at the pinball machine had turned in surprise at Kristin's first greeting to Claude; they had stared in astonishment as she moved her glass and herself to Claude's table. Since that time, their eyes had rested almost continuously on them. While one had played the pinball machine, the others had stared. The boys had whispered among themselves. Claude, noticing them, had grown tense and irritated.

"Anything wrong?" he asked, with hostility.

The boys looked at him but said nothing. They looked at each other. Claude grew more furious by the moment, and would have got up, or said something more, except that Kristin saw him and touched his arm. "What's wrong?"

"Nothing," Claude said. His eyes never left the boys; their eyes never left him.

"Don't bother about them," Kristin said.

Claude said nothing. The boys said nothing. But the air was growing thick with their mutual hostility. The man behind the counter watched them all, apprehensively.

Kristin suddenly stood up, looking at Claude, and said, "I know; I can fix everything!" Before Claude could say a word she had opened her violin case and extracted the violin. Claude, and the boys, and the man behind the counter, stared in astonishment. Bright eyes shining, Kristin looked at Claude and said, "Listen. Only listen." She struck the bow to the strings. The man behind the counter leaned on a shelf, astounded; he looked at Kristin as though she were crazy. The boys stood, with wide eyes and opened mouths, rooted to their spots near the pinball machine. Back and forth across the strings ran the bow; now softly, now strong, the music came. Kristin, smiling, eyes fixed in excitement on Claude, swayed to the music. It was impossible to resist the enchantment of that music, or the enthusiasm and spirit of the girl who played it. Claude's emotions first fought, then gradually surrendered to the chords. It was impossible, listening to that music, to indulge a petty emotion. Here, in this room, was Beethoven declaring his eternal life, and life's eternal mysteries: how could a man retain his anger against a group of callow youths?

Finished, Kristin lowered the violin. "And how do you feel now?"

Smiling in spite of himself, and glancing momentarily at the still-stupefied youths, Claude said, "Fine."

She laughed. "You see, I told you. How can you love music and be angry?" She stood near the edge of the table. "But shall we go?"

Claude stood up. He looked at the boys again; they were standing near the machine, still staring, but now, instead of hostility, there was bafflement in their eyes. Claude knew that they were thinking: "This woman is crazy!" He could not hold back a smile.

Outside, Kristin said, "By the way, what's your name?"

"Claude. Claude Bowers."

"Good. And I'm Kristin. Claude, can I drop you home? I have a car."

"No thanks." She was being polite, he was sure. *No one* could be so ignorant of the unwritten social laws. "I can get home alone."

"Nonsense. I'll drop you off."

She drove a small car. Her bright eyes darted from him to the street in front of her, from the street back to him. At one point she laughed. "What is it?" Claude said. She answered, "I was just thinking: 'I have saved a soul.'" She laughed again.

Claude got out at the corner of his street. Kristin gave him her card. "That's the address of my studio, I live there. Will you come see me sometime? Having saved your soul, I ought to guard it for awhile."

"Of course," Claude said vaguely.

"No! You don't mean it! When can you come?—Friday?"

"Friday. Yes."

"You don't mean it! But you'd better come. If not, I'll come and get you. What's your address?"

Claude told her. Kristin waved and drove off.

8.

ON FRIDAY, CLAUDE DID NOT VISIT KRISTIN, NOR HAD HE EVER intended to. Obviously, the pretty young violinist was nice, but he was sure that her invitation had been one of those made in a moment of exuberance which, if acted on, would have been embarrassing. Claude spent all of Friday afternoon, and most of the evening, in preparing an important article for a national Negro magazine.

On Saturday afternoon, Philip called upstairs to Claude, "There's someone to see you." Kristin stood in the living room, looking with interest at books in the cases along the wall. She was wearing black slacks and a black sweater, which placed in stark relief her blonde hair. When Claude came into the room, she thrust her hands on her hips.

"I suppose you know, sir, that I turned down a dinner engagement with my accompanist, waiting for you?"

Weakly, Claude made apologies. He had not wanted to disturb her; he had not taken seriously her invitation; he had spent the day in working, he said. She looked at him with false severity.

"There's only one way of atoning. You must visit the studio now!"

"Now?"

"Now! This minute!"

She drove almost to the outskirts of the city, passing the church where she had played the week before, then turned onto a narrow street that led into an open patch of knotty grass, spotted by big, barn-like houses. She stopped in front of one of these, and said, "We get out here." They went into a massive room with a stone floor, plaster walls and a peaked, sky-light ceiling at least twenty-five feet high. In the center of the room stood a grand piano, on top of which were several encased violins; on various tables were books and piles of sheet music; on the walls themselves hung portraits of the Masters of music. Claude could scarcely believe his eyes: the room was like the cellar of an old castle.

"Isn't it wonderful?" Kristin said.

"It must be cold in the winter."

"Oh, no, look, don't you see?—" She pointed to a big coal stove, in a corner; it had a slender chimney that rose straight up to the roof. "It's so nice! In the winter, I light this fire and sit beside it at night. It's wonderful! Come on! I'll show you the rest of the place."

She led him into another room, small, that had a stove, a table, some shelves and a sink; it, too, had a floor of stone and walls of plaster. "My kitchen!" she said. "Look—real gas! And look!" Adjacent stood the bedroom, only slightly larger than its double bed, with a closet and stained-glass windows. "I know it's strange, but it's wonderful, I love it here." She looked at Claude expectantly, waiting for his reaction, hands on hips, eyes open wide.

Claude looked at her a moment. "Do you *live* here?"

"Of *course!*" she said, hurt.

"Alone?"

"Why, what's wrong with that? Oh, I'm not always alone, of course. Gordon, my accompanist, comes to see me, and there are people who occupy the other studios around here—painters and sculptors, mostly. But I like being alone. Mr. Beethoven and Mr. Mozart and Mr. Mendelssohn—you saw their pictures on the walls—they keep me company. And of course, I practice. It's marvelous here!"

She was disappointed in Claude for not reacting with more enthusiasm to her studio. Back in the main room, they had coffee and talked for awhile, then Kristin said, "Look, I've got records and a record-player," and went to a corner, from which she pulled out a phonograph and some records. She played not a classic, but a George Shearing recording; "I like him," she said. She sat with legs crossed, leaning forward, her elbows on her knees and her chin on the palm of her hand, listening attentively to the music. Her startling blue eyes were fixed in space.

"How do you happen to be here?" Claude asked. "You're pretty young. Don't your parents object?"

She shrugged. "Young. What's young?" She laughed. "Oh,

Pop doesn't like it so much, my being here, and he doesn't know much about music, but he's resigned to it by now, I think. Then Jimmy—he's my brother, you'll meet him some day—he's away at school, in Miami. Only twenty-two. Strange person. Moody. Cloudy. You never know what's going on in his mind." She laughed. "Like you, I think. You two are not *direct*, you're complicated, you've got hidden passageways. Strange, to simple people like me."

"How long have you been here?"

"Now? Two years. I've worked since I finished school, you see, to pay for the music lessons and board at home, but I saved some, and when I got enough I moved here. I still work part-time, in an office—pretty boring, the people are nice though. But let's stop this nonsense. Tell me about you. What's that white carnation you've worn both times I've seen you? For the death of your mother?"

"No, my father."

"I'm sorry. Did he die recently?"

"No. Ten years ago."

She looked at him, then at the carnation, in surprise. "That's a long time. And you still wear the carnation. How strange." Then she said, "And what do you do?"

"It's hard to say," he said. "I work for an organization—a national Negro organization—and I used to go from place to place, wherever there was race trouble, to organize campaigns, resistance, things like that. Made lectures in various places on the Negro problem. Led picket lines, things like that. Just came back from Africa; I'd been hired by an organization to help build the Nationalist movement. Now, for the time being, I mostly write."

"Write?"

"Yes. Weekly article for a Negro newspaper. Articles for magazines, things like that."

"You never write about music?"

"No. I never write about music."

"How sad. Do you know what?"

"What?"

"I like you. I always do that, you know—decide almost instantly whether I like people or not. And nearly always I'm right. Can you do that?"

"Sometimes."

"I can always. And it's always right. May I play something for you?"

"I'd love it."

"Do you like Tartini?"

"Yes."

She played the Tartini *G Minor Sonata*. Afterwards, she made more coffee and they listened to more records. Before dinner, though Kristin begged him to stay and eat with her, Claude left.

9.

THE BLUES SINGER LIVED IN A LITTLE STREET JUST OFF SOUTH, in an apartment with two rooms and a bath, along with her dog, a fluffy French poodle, named Lilac. Nearly two years ago, while sitting in the *Casino*, the biggest night club in town, she had turned to Frank Palma, the owner, and said, "You got any loose waiters lying around, you don't need? I wanta take one home with me. I'm goddam sick and tired of livin' alone!" No waiters had been expendable; but two nights later, Palma had come to the Blues Singer's table carrying a wicker basket, closed on top. "For you," he had said. "What the hell is this?" the Blues Singer had asked; when she'd opened it, she'd found the French poodle, then only a puppy. She was the Blues Singer's closest companion now.

Today, the Blues Singer had, as usual, got up at noon, rinsed dishes from the night before, eaten a breakfast of fried eggs, bacon, and warmed-over coffee, put the dirty dishes back in the sink again, then climbed back in bed to read the newspapers. Afterwards, she had had a long chat with Lilac about the world in general, the perfidy of men, the bitchery of women and the over-all lousiness of the universe. Lilac had listened sympathetically, knowing that, later, she would be rewarded with food for her pains.

"You have fleas, Lilac," the Blues Singer said, with a mixture of accusation and pity, as the dog lay on its back across her legs to have its stomach rubbed. "We must do something about that."

The dog was forthwith carted into the bathroom, deposited protesting in a tub of soapy water, and thoroughly washed. Then, rubbed dry, Lilac lay down again, still trembling from the shock, beside her reclining mistress.

It was now the dinner hour. Afterwards, there would be time to read a bit, listen to the radio, and dress; at ten o'clock she would have to be, again, at the *Showboat*. Six nights a week. It seemed to the Blues Singer that her life was nothing but a series of boring delaying tactics leading eventually, inexorably, to the fateful hour of her appearance at the *Showboat*. Sunday? It was simply a re-charging point, after the accumulated exhaustion of the week.

The Blues Singer rinsed the morning dishes, rinsed the pots and pans and began to cook the light meal that would be her dinner. As her own food cooked, she prepared some food for Lilac, mixing into it a raw egg. "You eat better than I do, Lilac. Know that?"

She sat down to eat. There was a knock on the door, and the Blues Singer, swearing, said roughly, "Come the hell on in!" A gangling, pimply-faced boy, about nineteen, carrying a saxophone, walked grinning into the kitchen. The Blues Singer scowled. "What the hell do you want?"

"Hello," the youth said. He smiled broadly, looking at the Blues Singer.

"What the hell you want?"

"You know, to play. 'Member I tole you I was studying the saxophone, wanted you to hear me? Well, here I am!"

"Ain't that great!"

The boy stood looking at her, fondling the saxophone, shifting from foot to foot. The Blues Singer dipped the day-old bread into the gravy.

"Well, what the hell you standin' there for, lookin' simple? Thought you wanted to play."

"I *do!*"

"Well, go the hell on and play, then." She picked up a bone, and tore off the meat with her fingers.

The youth lifted the saxophone to his lips. He blew, and a note went sour. Grinning again, he looked at the Blues Singer and shifted to his other foot. "Little nervous," he said.

"Musicians ain't got no right to be nervous. Ain't supposed to be nervous. Go ahead and blow."

The youth blew—a rendition of *Body and Soul*, as played by Coleman Hawkins. As he played, the youth closed his eyes, leaning backwards, saxophone thrust out in front of him, as though carried away by his own music. The Blues Singer was occupied picking the meat from her bone; afterwards, she gave the bone to Lilac. "And from now on, don't beg!" she said scoldingly to the dog. "I thought I taught you better manners than that."

Finally, the youth was finished; he opened his eyes; he lowered the saxophone; he stood up straight again. Eyes wide in expectation, he looked at the Blues Singer.

"What'd you think?" he asked.

"Lousy."

"L . . . lousy?"

"Lousy. You'll never be a musician. Tried to copy Coleman

Hawkins. No originality. No feeling for the music. Lousy. Go get yourself a job selling newspapers."

"Well...but, gee!...I can't be perfect *yet*. I'm only *nineteen!* I can't be original yet."

"Well, what the hell you come up here botherin' me for, if you're not old enough to play music? Go get yourself a job sellin' newspapers till you're old enough."

The youth looked at the Blues Singer, crestfallen and a bit angry. His eyes were almost tearful. "G . . . gee. Is that all you got to say?"

"Lousy," said the Blues Singer. "That's all I got to say. Go home and sell some newspapers until you're old enough to play."

The youth stood looking at the Blues Singer, in bewilderment and pain, for a moment. Then, without a word, he turned around and walked out of the room and out of the apartment.

10.

THAT NIGHT, AT THE SHOWBOAT, THE BLUES SINGER WALKED OVER to Slim and said, "Hell, this life is killin' me, I got to have myself a little fun once in a while. Let's go over to the Elkins, pick up on the jam session there after I finish here tonight." The Blues Singer finished at two. She and Slim walked across Broad Street and down toward Catherine to the Elkins Ballroom. Upstairs, over the ballroom, there was a smaller room, where the best musicians in town met to have some musical fun and talk after their chores in the night clubs around the town. "The only real music," the Blues Singer frequently said, "is extemporaneous music. And you only get that at a jam session." The Blues Singer did not think much of night clubs.

They climbed the narrow stairway to the second floor; they

did not have to show membership cards, because everybody knew Slim and the Blues Singer. Inside, the Blues Singer called to some of the musicians already on the bandstand, "All right now let's play music! Let's play music!" The musicians, who had not yet started, laughed and waved greetings. "You gonna sing a couple tonight?" they asked her. "Naw, not me, I got my class on tonight. I'm gonna play lady and watch you sonsabitches work for a change." The initiates in the hall, some wearing goatees and horn-rimmed glasses as popularized by Dizzy Gillespie, looked at the Blues Singer, first with an air of superiority (not knowing who she was), and then with respect, as they recognized her. Some called greetings, but the Blues Singer ignored them. "Here are two seats, good ones," the Blues Singer said to Slim. "Let's take 'em." Some hundred and fifty spectators were already crowded into the room whose folding chairs were meant to accommodate slightly more than a hundred. It was a hot night, the air was heavy, smoke was dense in the room; the odor of alcohol was noticeable, for most of the people had visited night clubs before winding up the evening here, and some had brought along pint bottles or flasks. "Come on! Come on! Play some gaddam music, you sonsabitches!" said the Blues Singer. People sitting in front of her turned disapprovingly; but they saw it was the Blues Singer, so they smiled: it was all right.

"These bastards ain't in no hurry to start. Hold my seat a minute, Slim. I got to see a man about a dog." The Blues Singer walked to the back of the hall and entered a small room, dimly lighted. A group of musicians were standing or sitting around, chatting and laughing softly. The room was filled with a dense, acrid, eye-stinging smoke that smelled faintly like incense. "Yo, baby!" The Blues Singer went over to some men standing near a mantelpiece, leaning on it with their elbows, smiling sagely at the Blues Singer. She grinned. "Give me one," she said. One of the men, a trumpeter, handed her a slender cigarette that had obviously been rolled by hand; another, a saxophonist, struck a match to it. The Blues Singer inhaled, driving the smoke down as far as possible into her lungs. The musicians watched her, grinning sagely. The Blues Singer held her breath as long as she could, then slowly exhaled, and took another inhalation. The world began to slow down. The musicians watched her, grinning. "Ah, delicious!" said the Blues Singer. "Yes, yes," said the trumpeter. "Can you imagine," said the saxophonist, "there are people who don't *know!*" They all laughed at that, holders of the great secret, inhaling, holding their breath. The world slowed down, slowed down. The Blues Singer looked around at the slow-drifting blue smoke, at the men who sat smoking, talking, listening, smiling. "Yes, yes," she said, "yes, yes." She thought of Slim, sitting out in the big hall, holding their seats. "Poor dumb bastard; he don't *know!*" She laughed harshly. Through the parting of the drawn curtains at the window she saw the blinking blue light of a neon sign. The light held her eye; she was fascinated. On, off; on, off. Blinking, blinking. Blue. How cool the blue light was! How soothing, how refreshing! On, off; on, off. Secret symbol of the earth. On, off; beginning, end. Blue: what more beautiful than that color? Color of sky, color of water, color of the human soul. Electric energy: this, the element that made all night-things possible. Extender of man's living lifetime. Beautiful. The Blues Singer wanted to share it.

"Look at that; that streak of light."

They looked. The trumpeter said, "Ah, yes, that's the color of music, baby, the color of the songs you sing. That's the color of the symphonies, the color of the Tragedies, the color of the Spirituals." He studied the light a moment longer. "A blinking beacon. A warning sign. Man's Fate. Sword of the Archangel gleaming."

And the saxophonist said, "That's the color of sleep and of peace. Soft. Gentle. Unshouting. Steals softly over, like a blue Mediterranean breeze, lulling, whispering. Rest. Dream awhile."

The other musicians, standing close by, listened. They all

watched the gleaming blue light. Off, on; off, on. They all floated and smiled the smiles of great, inhuman wisdom.

The Blues Singer took her seat beside Slim, the musicians were on the platform, the pianist struck a chord; the spectators, crowded together, warm, hot, in the smoke-filled room, leaned forward, expectantly, as the musicians began to play. First, a simple song, rendered in the orthodox manner. Then, one after the other, the instrumentalists "took off": using the basic melody as anchor, they each in turn took off on riffs and dives, circling the melody, dodging in and out of it, frightening it, hiding from it, creeping up on it, whirling dizzily far away from it, closing back in on it again. Trumpeter, saxophonist, trombonist, drummer, pianist, bass. "Work! Work!" cried the spectators. The musicians grinned; sweat poured down their faces, down their open necks, soaked the thin shirts they wore. "Work! Work!" The trumpeter arched backward, shook, and made his trumpet scream; the drummer prayed to the great god noise, twirling his sticks into hysteria; the pianist darted discords between the notes of the others; the bassist marched in mellow frenzy up and down the scale. "Work! Work!" The shirt-sleeved spectators laughed, looked at one another, stared leaning at the musicians, shouted, stomped their feet. "Oh, Jesus!" thought the Blues Singer, "Oh, Jesus!" The now-dimmed sidelights, and the brighter stagelights, cast arching, abstract shadows through the smoke across the crowd, against the walls. The world whirled, shrieked, stood on end, did a tribal dance. Emotions angled outward, upward. "Play music!" shouted the Blues Singer. "Play music! Play music!" echoed the crowd. Sharp vision of the dinner hour, of the sad-faced saxophonist, flashed cutting across her mind. "Play music!" she shouted. Echo of the slamming door. "Play music! Play music!" cried the crowd. Louder and louder the Blues Singer shouted, against the booming bass. "Music! Music!" Around her, the frantic faces, the yelling feet, the sweating laughter. "Music!

Music! Music!" cried the Blues Singer, rising to her feet. "Music! Music!" cried the crowd. The music shouted on.

11.

SLIM RANG THE DOORBELL, WALKED IN, MUSSED THE HAIR OF THE boy who came running through the hall, went into the kitchen and said, "Hi, Grace."

"Hello, Slim," said the woman, bent over her wash.

"What'll it be today?"

"Lemme see. I'll take a four-forty-seven and nine-twenty-three. And gimme a seven-fifty-six in the box."

"Got you covered."

Slim went whistling along his route, ringing the doorbells, walking in, asking in each house the same question: "What'll it be today?" He called everybody by her first name. He knew all of the people very well; this had been his route for years.

In the afternoon, Slim took his slips and the money he had collected over into the Italian section. He walked into a green-fronted candy store named *Pete's*. "Hi, Angela," he said to the handsome, dark-eyed girl who stood behind the counter, leaning on her elbows over a newspaper. "Ummm hmmm," she said.

"Pete in?"

"Yeah. He's in back."

Slim pushed aside the curtain and went through the dining room, walking into a room further back in which six Italians stood or sat around a table covered with money, nearly all in small change. A short, stocky man with a turned-down lower lip was counting the money.

"Hi, Pete. Hi, fellas," said Slim.

The stocky man counted to an even number, then looked up. "Whatcha say, Slim? How'd it go today?"

"Ordinary," Slim said. He emptied his pockets and handed over his slips. Pete stopped counting to glance at Slim's totals.

"All right," he said, "not bad." He grinned at Slim. "You're all right, man. Cover that area like a blanket! Be banking it soon, I don't watch out." He laughed; a short, cut-off expiration.

Slim looked around the room. The other men were silently watching Pete, smoking, at ease. Slim still stood in the doorway. For some reason, he felt uncomfortable. He felt like a stranger, an outsider in their midst; yet they were all pickup men like him.

"Say, Pete," Slim said, "could I have a word with you?"

"Sure, go ahead." He looked up at Slim. "What is it, man?"

Slim looked at the others. His eyes fell on one of them, a slender, handsome youth whose eyes, for some reason, always seemed to be mocking Slim.

"Well, it's kind of private. I'd like to talk to you alone, in the other room."

"Well, I'm busy now, Slim. Got to get this stuff out. Some other time, huh?"

"It's important, Pete. I got to talk to you *now!*"

Slim looked again at the men around the room. They all sat smoking, silently. Slim felt that they had been talking before he came in, but now they would not bother to talk, because he was there. He was one of them, but he was not one of them; he was an outsider, an intruder.

Pete swore softly, in Italian. He waited until he had counted to an even number, wrote down the figure, then said, "Okay, Slim." He went with Slim into the dining room. "Now, what's on your mind?"

He did not look at Slim. He lowered his ear toward Slim's mouth, hands on hips. Slim hesitated; he felt the others could still hear, and he was embarrassed.

"Look, Pete, the boys asked me to talk to you. See, they know that you been givin' the other boys—you know, the white boys—

a bigger cut than you been givin' us. So they told me to ask you for a raise."

For a moment, Pete did not move; he stood still with head bent down, ear cocked toward Slim's mouth, as though waiting for him to say more. Then, glancing at Slim, he shook his head and said, "Nah, that's a lie. I ain't payin' nobody no different from nobody else. Everybody's gettin' the same. Where you guys pick up that crap?"

"Look, Pete, the boys are mad. See, they *know* you're payin' the Italian guys more."

"Nah. That ain't true."

"Look, Pete, we got the information from good sources. Catch? We *know* you're payin' the Italians more, and the boys are *mad!* They don't like it, Pete. They want a raise."

"It ain't true," Pete said, standing erect. "Where you guys get such crap? It ain't true. I ain't payin' nobody no different from nobody else; everybody gets the same. That all you had to say?" He was ready to go back into the other room.

"Pete, I'm tellin' you, the boys are mad."

"They ain't got no reason to be mad."

"They know what they're talkin' about, Pete. They *know.* They say if you don't pay them more, they're gonna go on strike."

Pete looked directly into Slim's eyes. "Okay, Slim. Tell 'em I said to go ahead and strike. I can get plenty other people be glad to do the work. If they strike, they're out, see. Tell 'em that for me. I toldja, don't nobody get paid no different from nobody else. If they strike, they're out!"

"Pete . . . why the hell don't you pay us the same? It ain't that much money. It's just the principle of the thing."

"How many times I got to tell you? Everybody's gettin' the same."

"Pete, if they go on strike, and you fire the boys . . . Well, you know; they're liable to start workin' for somebody else."

Pete laughed in choppy exhalations. "Yeah, sure, great. Glad to hear it. Don't think none of them are *that* crazy. You know what I mean? Might be some bodies floatin' down the river. You know what I mean?"

Slim looked at Pete. Pete scratched the back of his ear, beginning to turn away.

"That all you had to say?" Pete asked.

"Yeah, Pete," Slim said.

Slim was about to go but Pete called to him and came over to him. "Look here, Slim, we been friends a long time, ain't we? What the hell? Tell the boys to cut out this crap and just go along while everything's fine. What the hell? Ain't nobody gettin' no different from nobody else. Catch?"

"Sure, sure, sure."

Pete grinned and slapped Slim on the back. "Great. Knew you was my boy."

12.

THE DINNER TABLE WAS LAID FOR TWO WHEN SLIM WENT INTO his small flat, on Carpenter Street. From the other room came the sound of the radio playing softly. Slim felt lousy; he hoped that Lil was in one of her good moods. He went into the second room; Lil was lying across the studio couch, reading a magazine, her legs tilted up on the arm of an adjacent chair. When she looked up, Slim saw that her eyes were red.

"Baby! What's wrong?"

"Nothing. The usual. Poppa and momma again. How'd you make out?"

Slim shrugged. "No dice. Pete told us to screw ourself."

"It don't matter. Come kiss me, baby."

Slim shivered; he turned to nothing inside. He sat on the edge of the couch and kissed her. She snuggled close to him. Slim stroked her forehead and her hair.

"Poor baby," Slim said. "Somebody ought to horsewhip them parents of yours."

"I can't understand it," said Lil. "I never did nothing to them. Why the hell do they hate me so much?"

"That father of yours is a bastard. And when your mother gets drunk, she should be lynched. What'd they do?"

"Oh, I was sittin' in the house reading, and, you know, my dress came up over my knees. My brother was in the room, and then Poppa came in. So he called me names, said I was a whore trying to seduce my own brother, then he started beating me. Momma came in and egged him on; she was calling me the same names."

"Bastards!"

"I can't stand that, Slim. I don't mind the beatings so much, but I hate that word. Why do they call me a whore? I don't sleep with anyone except you."

"Those bastards!"

"I play around, like I'm flirting, you know. It don't mean anything, does it?"

"You ought to move out, baby. I told you before. You ought to come here and live with me. You know I want you to."

"No. Ain't nobody making no money in that house except me. Rex in jail. Joe hangs around on his rear. Mart always gets in trouble, been stealing again, but he never brings any of the money he steals home."

"You ought to move here. Let 'em shift for theirself."

Lil lay with her eyes wide open, covered by a film of tears, looking at the ceiling. More than sadness or pain, there was resentment in her eyes.

Slim said, "Do you love me, Lil?"

She nodded, still looking at the ceiling. "Uh huh."

He bent over and kissed her again. Her lips were soft, but her eyes were still upturned, toward the ceiling. Slim felt hot inside; he loved her when she was soft, loved her when she had need of him. That was when they were closest.

"How about some food?" Slim said.

Lil went into the kitchen and set the food on the table. They ate in semi-silence; it was broken only occasionally, when Slim made comments about the day, about people he had visited on his route, about the talk with Pete. Lil nodded now and again.

"You gonna help me with the dishes?"

"Sure," Slim said.

They finished the dishes and went into the living room. Slim turned on the radio again, and they sat on the turned-down studio couch. "Want to take off your clothes?" Slim said. Lil got up without a word, undressed, and got back on the bed; Slim had risen, meanwhile, and taken off his clothes. They moved under the sheet. Lil lay close to Slim, her head on his shoulder. He kissed her gently. His hand began to move.

Gradually, her body came alive. It was warm, moving. Tenderness and sympathy flowed from Slim to her; she was grateful for it, responded to it.

An hour later, Lil left. She wanted to stop at home before going to the *Showboat*, she said. Eyes of idle men followed her as her body moved along the street. She stopped at a flower shop. "Bunch of roses." She sniffed them as she walked out of the store.

Her brother, Mart, was sitting on the front steps, his arm around the waist of a young girl of the neighborhood, when Lil approached. "Well, well, ain't we something!" he said to Lil, noticing the flowers. Joe was out; so was her father. Lil was relieved. She forced a smile and went into the living room. She extended the flowers toward her mother, a sharp-eyed, squinting woman, who looked at the bouquet suspiciously without raising her hand to accept it.

"What's this?"

"For you, Momma," Lil said. "I don't want us to fight."

"What'm I supposed to do with them? Eat 'em?" said her mother. Her mother was drunk again; she sat dreamy sloppy in a chair near the window. "Can't eat them!"

Lil lowered the arm that held the flowers. "Sure," she said, "I shouldn't have bothered."

"Sure, sure, that's right. Shouldn'ta bothered! What'm I supposed to do with them? Eat 'em? Think they'll fill the pots and pans? Sure, a bunch of flowers. That make up for a lifetime of shiftlessness? Suppose that lousy boyfriend of your'n bought 'em for me, eh? That supposed to make things better?"

"Forget it, Momma." Lil started to walk away.

"Sure, sure, forget it! That all you can say? Forget it. Sure, a bunch of flowers, and I'm supposed to keep quiet, I suppose, while you go lazying around, just go sleeping around, making a lot of money and keeping it for yourself. Sure, where'd you get that new dress?"

"I don't have any new dress!"

"Sure, sure, a new dress. Think I don't notice things, eh? Sure, a new dress, new hat, suppose you'll be pullin' up soon in a new car, eh? They pay high, don't they? Pay high. None of the money comes home, though!"

Lil was walking toward the door. She had wanted to go to her room for a moment, to change her clothes, but she decided not to bother now.

"Sure, sure, walk off. That's right. Walk off! Don't like to hear the truth, do you? Bunch of flowers. That suppose to fill the pots and pans? That supposed to make up for everything? Be pulling up in a Cadillac next, bringing me a bunch of flowers. Little whore, keep the money to yourself."

Lil turned furiously. Her eyes were wide. "Don't call me that! Momma, I'm telling you, don't call me that!"

"Sure, sure, little whore, that's all you are. Don't like the truth, do you?"

"Don't call me that! Don't call me that!" Tears streamed furiously down her cheeks.

"Sure, sure, sure. Be pulling up in a Cadillac next. Can't eat flowers, you know. Little whore, keep all the money for yourself. I know you!"

Lil ran from the house. Her foot struck against her brother's arm, and she fell sprawling to the street. "Hey, what the hell! Look out, you kicked me," her brother said sourly. Lil got up; her arm was skinned. People were looking at her from all the steps of the little street; children, who had been playing, stared at her. Her mother's head bobbed out of the window. "Sure, sure, a little whore, that's all you are, a little whore!" her mother shouted. Lil walked down the street. She did not feel the pain in her arm. The people stared. "Little whore! Little whore!" her mother was screaming from the window. Her mother was leaning out, as far as she could. "Little whore! Little whore!" she shrieked, hysterically. Lil walked as straight as she could. Tears of fury stormed down her face. *Screw 'em! Screw 'em! Screw 'em! Screw 'em! Everybody!* Lil thought suddenly of Slim; a screaming streak of hatred shot up, inside herself, against him.

13.

ABOUT TWICE A WEEK, CLAUDE WENT TO SEE KRISTIN. HE HAD been afraid, at first, that his visits would interfere with her practice, but she assured him that this was not true: usually, she practiced early in the morning, and sometimes late at night. On his visits they sat and talked; they told anecdotes; Kristin made coffee, they listened to her records, and often she played for him.

For a long time, Claude met no one else at Kristin's secluded studio, but one day Gordon, her accompanist, came while he was there. Gordon was a soft-faced, blond man; he seemed to be somewhat taken aback to see Claude sitting there; Kristin made the introductions. Gordon sat down on a stool next to Claude, and, after an initial coolness, he seemed to warm up—even, in his gentle voice, taking part occasionally in the conversation.

After that, Claude encountered Gordon at Kristin's studio several times. The three of them sat on stools, drinking coffee, talking; frequently, Gordon accompanied Kristin while she played. Claude found it interesting to compare the two musicians. Kristin was energy and enthusiasm personified; she talked excitedly, moved nervously, plunged herself into the mood of the music. By comparison, Gordon was washed-out, limp, feeble. He simply played the notes as written, and Kristin had to drag him along; she sometimes chided him gently, and seemed a little impatient, at times, with his slowness of thought and movement, his delayed responses to things. "Don't you *feel* it?" she would cry; "Doesn't it *fill* you?" Before her vigor, Gordon always shrugged, rather helplessly, turning soft, smiling eyes upon Claude. Kristin would throw up her hands in exasperation, and then, elbows on knees, lose herself in whatever it was which excited her.

"Kristin is a wonderful violinist," Gordon said to Claude. "She'll be one of the greats some day—another Ginette Neveau." With his eyes, from his shy retirement, the accompanist followed Kristin's animated movements, her flashing moods. Kristin, on the other hand, said little directly to Gordon. Usually she talked to Claude, drawing out his impressions, criticisms, thoughts about the things that interested her. Gordon would listen silently, without resentment, looking at Kristin with obvious awe. It occurred to Claude that the soft-spoken accompanist was in love with the youthful violinist.

But, usually, they were alone in the studio. Claude enjoyed relaxing and allowing his emotions to be carried along by those of the spirited young woman who sat, nearly always in black slacks, across from him.

Often, on pleasant days, they went for short walks through the neighborhood. Kristin's eye would be caught suddenly by something in a show window—a carving, a doll, anything—and she would halt suddenly, without warning, and run from Claude's side (something that often annoyed, even while it delighted him), calling for him to come share the treasure she had discovered. "Isn't this beautiful! Isn't this marvelous!" Rarely was her attention arrested by the obvious things; it was not gorgeous sunsets, or beautiful landscapes, at which she stared. She would tug suddenly at Claude's arm and say, "Look! Look at that *beautiful* man!" And to Claude, at first, the man would seem anything but beautiful: gnarled, bent, ugly of face, often ridiculous of costume. But after a moment's reflection, Claude would see that the very *incongruity* of the man did have a kind of beauty: the man would be beautiful, as a painting by Cezanne might be.

She liked to share such things with Claude. "You are," she told him once, "the best friend I've ever had. I want to share everything with you, because *you can feel what I feel!*"

And that, he realized, was true. For Kristin was the *activator*. She was the pouring stream, the life-filled violinist. But receptacles were rare, and she poured herself in vain, for example, into the soft-eyed sieve of her accompanist, Gordon, ran her bow in vain against his frayed and slackened strings. Claude, calm, could listen and feel; he could respond. Deep inside himself, he held dormant all of the emotions, all of the enthusiasms that charged Kristin. All they needed was to be played upon.

Kristin had almost no capacity for abstract discussion, abstract thought. She seemed, in contrast to Claude, to be a person who lived externally, in the sights, sounds, and odors around her. Claude doubted that she had an inner life, doubted that she ever simply sat inside herself, involved with her own mind's reflections. Were it not for her music, Claude felt, she was a person whose nerves would long ago have dashed themselves to pieces. Music was her salvation, the all-fastening axle of her life. Only when she listened to music, or played it, did Claude see in her that repose, that peace, that deep floating restfulness without which her life would have been a torment.

But she relaxed, also, into Claude. Tired by her leaping sensitivity, weakened by her emotional exertions, she retired sometimes into the greater solidity of him. With him she found a peace, outside of music.

They went often to concerts in the open air; they heard orchestras, famous soloists, distinguished chamber groups. Kristin would listen, leaning forward, elbows on knees, eyes riveted to the performers. At such moments there was no disturbing her; she was lost in her favorite world, of rich full tones and surging, varicolored harmonies.

Claude found that when he was with her, at concerts, he heard the music through her ears, not his own. And he forgot that her skin was white, forgot that his was black, forgot the vendetta carnation in his lapel. *She was* the music, and his appreciation of it, he finally realized. All else, sounding from the stage, was hollow notes in geometric progression.

On a Friday evening in late August, Michael and Philip were walking down Market Street, on their way from a movie theater, when they saw a crowd in front of the hamburger stand at Seventeenth Street. In the center of the crowd stood a Negro and a white man, quarreling furiously. The crowd, all white, gathered silently around.

"Let's look at this," Michael said.

They stopped and looked. The Negro and the white man were close to blows. The cause of the argument was not important: one was accusing the other of having jostled him, in passing, on the street. And yet, a heaviness, an oppression seemed to lie thick upon all the gathered people. This was more than an argument between two people: Michael could feel it in the air. A Negro and a white man were close to blows. A spark was dancing near the never-absent powder keg.

Michael felt himself out there in the ring, at war with the gesticulating white man, and the people who watched. He felt the familiar tension in his stomach, the familiar trembling of his hands. He watched, listened; it was him, *him* out there, throwing down the gauntlet in the ring. One blow, one blow and that whole crowd would explode into a mass of hatred; one blow would release all the savagery they felt against that lonely brown-skinned man. Michael felt this. He waited. The Negro would have a brother in defeat.

The Negro's face was long and dark. Michael watched it. The mouth opened and closed; Michael did not hear the words. He saw the face; he saw beyond the face to the fears, the hatred, the anger inside, the blast compressed for—how many years? how many centuries? Brother. What did it matter *what* the argument was! Brother. *Lie down with me.*

Michael's set, narrowed, hollow eyes wandered to the face of the white antagonist. The face: broad, hard cheeks, hard jaws. Why did the face of all white men seem red? Why did their eyes seem empty? Why did their foreheads seem harsh? The eyes were wide; the mouth opened and closed, in words. What lay beyond the drawn white skin of the head? Guilt, Michael thought. It was his guilt he shouted now. Shouted into the black-faced spectre of his indictment. *No release from guilt for you! No release in hate for you!* Michael stared with hating eyes at the white hard face that shouted.

"Let's go," Philip said.

But the voices were subsiding. Had the air of the quarreler, and of the people standing around, grown less tense? The voices were subsiding; some people drifted off.

"Let's go, Michael," Philip whispered.

They walked off. Michael was trembling. Hatred set his muscles, assaulted his heart. Philip said nothing. Michael was hardly aware of his presence. At Eighteenth Street, Michael stopped to look back. The crowd had not moved. The quarrel was still going on. Without a word to Philip, Michael turned on his heel and walked back again to the edge of the group. Philip followed. The voices had risen again. The tension, for some reason, had returned.

"Why are we waiting around here?" Philip asked.

Michael did not hear him. He stood on the edge of the crowd. His eyes saw only the hard drawn face and the indicted eyes of the white man who waved his arms; his ears heard only the foul profanity of that voice, which rose, rose in anger, struck words against a Race. That white face, and Michael, were alone in the universe. The face burned sharp and dissolved, burned sharp and dissolved.

He was not conscious of his movement. Michael stepped through the crowd. He stood in front of the startled, drawn-white face and struck with all his force. The man, shocked, fell to the ground. There was a murmur from the crowd. Blood flowed from the mouth and nose of the man; he stared up, shocked, unmoving at Michael. Michael stared into the hating eyes. Behind him, the Negro was saying something; Michael did not hear him. He stared at the hating eyes. Then he looked at the crowd; he saw anger, accusation, bewilderment; but no one moved. He waited, tense, but no one moved. Then he was through the crowd again, and walked down Market Street again, Philip beside him. Philip was saying, softly, "But you know, Michael, the Negro might have been in the wrong?" Michael was conscious only of his tense and trembling hands.

14.

AND IN BED, WHAT PHILIP ASKED HIMSELF WAS: *Am I a coward?*
He had asked himself the question many times. At moments of tension. In the face of violence. Fear; always. Was he a coward?

At the first approach to the crowd, when he had seen that a Negro and a white man were involved, Philip had felt the sudden shooting fear he knew so well; he had felt the apprehension that would have led him, if alone, to cross the street, or turn the corner, do anything to avoid all contact, involvement with the crowd.

Then, standing before the gathered people, in presence of the shouted hatred, Philip had felt the extension of that fear. It had crept outward, drug-like, through his muscle fibers and veins. At the first quick move, at the first struck blow, he was sure he would have run. His whole physical being, independent of his mind, his will, had trembled violently and poised itself for instant flight.

Am I a coward? Miserably, Philip twisted in the bed. In terror he had whispered hoarsely to Michael: "Let's go," and he was sure, in that moment, that his soul's weakness had been laid bare. Had the worst occurred, had that crowd's animosity erupted upon Michael, Philip was sure his trembling legs would have gathered wings, his arms would have flailed the air, his heart would have become a pumping dynamo of Flight.

Longing: for a deserted island minus hostility, minus hate. Longing: for some secluded spot minus the premonition of violence. Violence always present. Latent. Lying crouched. Yellow-eyed beast with gleaming teeth, waiting to spring.

Light-hearted, he had walked one day down Chestnut Street, when someone had called. Friend; a girl, from the school he used to attend. She happened to be white. Conversation, light: where's so and so? How's so and so? People passing; some had stared. Philip had noticed this; and he had known the reason why. Then down the street, walking slowly, had come a shouting group of white youths. They had been loud; they had been coarse; their clothes had identified them. Philip had watched them approach, trembling. The girl had talked on, asking questions; Philip had tried to answer, but his throat had gone hoarse, his tongue gone thick. Casually, not noticing, she had laid her hand against his bare summer arm. White on black: the touch had been electric; she had laughed easily her laugh of the free, while all the time Philip had watched, waiting, the boys approach. They had approached. They had approached. They had approached. And they had passed. Not one of them had even noticed him.

Fear. Of the premonition. Of the beast that lay waiting, and might never spring. Might never spring. But the beast was *there*. Yellow eyes gleaming. Fangs bared.

15.

MICHAEL, TOO, LAY UNSLEEPING. HE HAD STRUCK A BLOW! HE lay warm, expended in the bed. He had struck a blow!

He was not without fear. (Only Claude, Michael felt, was totally without fear.) He was not without fear, but he had vowed, long ago, to ignore all fear, to command his body and let the body act. He had told himself: At the first hint of violence, at the first show of hate, strike a blow! Afterwards, die. Do not wait. Do not think. Trust the impulse. Strike the blow!

He had struck the blow. What had Philip said?—"*The Negro*

might have been in the wrong?" Judicial fallacy. Error of objective law. The crimes of two centuries lay upon white America. No Negro, no matter what his deed, could ever be "in the wrong."

For there did not exist a white man who was without guilt. And they, the white men, knew it. Not one who could look a Negro in the eye, not one who could call a Negro "friend," not one who could stand before God with unsinged hands. Land of the Senator: bloated face and bloodshot eyes: shrieking his hatred from the august chamber. Land of the Klansman: massed whip and brave white mask; fears, repressions, demons swinging from trembling, expulsive arm. Land of Babbitt: loud-laughing, back-pounding man; idiot with monied pockets; tongue calling "darkies" to shine his shoes. Land of the Hypocrite: pious smile of love; word hanging "tolerance"; eyes a recessive caress; Superiority entering through the back door. Land of the Smug and Righteous Blind: vacant eyes in clodhopper shoes; kneeling to God; treading. Nation. Bloated ugliness weighted down upon black humans. Massed hypocrisy across the clean green grass and soil, blocking the air and the rich blue sky. Portrait: sweating, lined-faced, black-faced sharecropper, victim of peonage, chained to a white-faced master for life, the new Slavery. Portrait: child with fear-struck eyes: night in a Northern Negro slums: roaches across ceiling, rats across floor. Memory: his own father, who had been a Man; whipped; his entrails cut out; then shot because, in a Southern town, he had been the first who had dared to vote. His mother: another victim; of grief, a few years later.

And this land, and this life, truly were beautiful. That Southern sun, which he had seen in childhood, truly shone; the air was fresh down by the sea, and the trees were good in blossom. But who had robbed him of his eyes and his sense of smell, blocking his vision with blood-stained hands, assaulting his nostrils with decay? Not music, but the crunching of souls and the cries of pain he heard. Because of whom?

16.

"WHAT DO YOU DO WITH YOUR SPARE TIME?" KRISTIN ASKED Claude one afternoon. "What do you do with your evenings? The time when I'm not with you?"

Claude shrugged. "Read. Go out sometimes." He told her about the *Showboat*. Kristin was excited.

"Is it nice there?"

"I like it."

"Can we go there sometime? Tonight?" she asked eagerly.

Claude hesitated a second. He thought of the people at the *Showboat* who might resent this white "intrusion." He thought of Michael, who would probably be outraged. He thought for a fleeting second of Kristin herself: would she really feel at ease? In that moment, the full absurdity of the "race problem" struck him with particular force. *To hell with it!* And he said to Kristin, "I don't see why not."

It was a cool, comfortable evening in late August. A slight fog lay over the city, and the veiled row buildings and houses passed ghost-like as they rode along. Kristin drove fast, looking at Claude more than the street in front of her. She was excited about going to the *Showboat*. What were the musicians like? What were the people who went there like? Did the same crowd go every night?

"You'll see it all," Claude laughed, enjoying her exhilaration.

Going down the stairs, they went into the low-ceilinged, low-lighted night club. Kristin stood in the doorway, staring at the circular bar and the musicians on the center bandstand; Claude, taking her arm, led her to the tables where he knew his friends would be sitting. Michael, Philip, the Old Man, and Margaret were at a table. They stared up, in surprise, as Claude introduced

Kristin. "A very good friend and a wonderful musician, a violinist," Claude said.

They sat down and ordered drinks. Kristin's face was as alive as a kitten's; her eyes darted from face to face. From behind the bar, the Bartender saw Kristin looking at him; he smiled, and mixed the drinks with exaggerated flourishes, for her entertainment. Kristin was delighted. From time to time she touched Claude's arm, to speak of something that had caught her fancy. The others at their table (particularly the Old Man) and some at adjoining tables and the bar, could not take their eyes off the unusual white girl who had come into the Negro bar. Claude had been afraid, at first, that Kristin might feel uncomfortable under the stares that were sure to greet her, but his fears had been quickly stilled: Kristin, far from feeling embarrassed, seemed oblivious to the special attention paid to her; she was completely caught up in the new and thrilling impressions.

Claude sat back, at ease, enjoying Kristin's fascination, when he happened to glance at his brother, Michael. Michael was staring intently, with a peculiar expression, at him. Claude was about to ask if anything were wrong when Philip reached across the table to offer first Kristin, then Claude a cigarette. Claude noticed the Old Man. With his eyes, he was examining Kristin speculatively, from head to toes, undressing her in his mind. Claude smiled. He looked at Margaret, who immediately lowered her eyes.

Lil, the waitress, brought the drinks. She looked at Kristin, whom Claude introduced, and then at Claude with a mischievous smile. Exaggerating her drawl, she said, "Oh, is *this* your young lady, Claude? How sweet she is! So *this* is why no one else has a chance with you?"

Kristin laughed and looked at Claude. Lil winked, running her hand through Claude's hair, then walked away.

When the Blues Singer appeared on the bandstand, the lights were dimmed and a small spot was turned on her angular, Indian face. In sequins she shimmered in the spotted light; the piano beat, and the wail came from her throat. Kristin leaned forward, elbow on the table, chin cupped in her hand; in the reflected light, her eyes, held spellbound, glistened. Claude watched her, could *feel*, inside himself, the beating of *her* heart. How well he knew, and how much he liked, her soul's easy enchantment!

"She's beautiful and she's wonderful!" Kristin whispered to Claude. And then, smiling at a joke they had, she added, "I mean, *my kind* of beautiful!"

The Blues Singer raised her voice on high. She was in rare form, and feeling good, so she sang many songs. The bass thumped. Claude looked at Michael again and saw his brother still regarding him with that peculiar, wondering stare. Following the Blues Singer, the combo went to work; with dexterity and feeling they wove their rhythms, injecting their pulsating bass into the bloodstreams of all the listeners. The Old Man, stroking his chin, hardly took his eyes off Kristin. Margaret, seated brown and attractive next to Philip, on the other side of the table, glanced occasionally at Kristin, but for the most part kept her eyes on the glass in front of her; from time to time, she looked at Claude and, if her eyes met his, turned her own quickly away, with a faint smile.

"Ah, do you like this kind of music, young lady?" the Old Man asked, looking at Kristin.

"I love it."

"I see. I see. Well, you must . . . ah, you must come down here more often. Yes, indeed. Indeed." His smiling, insinuating eyes went down from her face to her neck and shoulders, then up again to her eyes. "Yes, yes indeed," he repeated. "You are always welcome, with or without Claude." He looked at Claude and winked. "There will always, let me assure you, be someone here to protect you from our rougher frequenters."

At the word "protect," Michael's eyes shot to the Old Man with the same, peculiar expression with which they had regarded

Claude. Michael lowered his eyes to his drink, turned the glass once on the table, then looked up at Claude again, with the strange expression.

"Michael, what's wrong?" Claude asked, looking directly at his brother who, after a second's pause, dropped his eyes.

"Nothing," he said. But when he raised his eyes again, the expression was still there.

Philip leaned forward shyly and asked Kristin, "Would you like to dance, Miss?"

Michael looked at him quickly.

"I . . . do you mind? I'd rather just listen. It's so . . . so wonderful!"

For an hour, Kristin listened transfixed. During that time, the Blues Singer came to the table, and was introduced to Kristin. "Well, well, what's this?" she said, sitting down. Kristin smiled and said how much she had enjoyed the Blues Singer's singing. Then she was away again, in the world where the music was. She did not touch her drink. She did not notice the people who still stared. Her eyes darted from one to the other of the musicians; her face mirrored her complete absorption.

When the combo had finished, and the intermission pianist returned, Kristin leaned back in her chair and sighed heavily. "Oh, it's so wonderful! Claude, no wonder you come here. And I'm so angry with you, for not having brought me sooner!"

"Here, here!" said the Blues Singer, "how long has *this* been going on?"

The Old Man chuckled. "Well, you must come back again, young lady. Yes, indeed. Yes, indeed. You must come back soon."

"Claude," Kristin exclaimed, looking at him, "Negroes are so wonderful! No one else in this country could play such music; because no one else has such *feeling!*"

Michael's head shot up. His eyes narrowed as he looked at Kristin. His hands trembled on the table, and when he spoke his voice was harsh with repressed violence. "What do you mean by that?"

"By what?" Kristin asked, startled by his vehemence.

"About 'Negro' music. Do you find a difference between Negroes and other people?"

Claude looked at Michael, who did not look back; his eyes were fastened, accusingly, on Kristin. Philip seemed apprenhensive. The Old Man looked at Michael questioningly. Margaret sat calmly looking at her hands, which were in her lap.

"A difference?" Kristin said. "Why . . . yes, of course. Negroes feel more because they've been hurt more, don't you think? Music expresses an emotion toward . . . well, toward life. Negroes must feel differently about life than other Americans. The emotion of the music is stronger, deeper, and has more pain."

Michael's eyes did not lose their hostility. Voice heavy with sarcasm, he said relentlessly, "I see. And I suppose you also believe that Negroes are better athletes than anybody else, and that they can dance better than anybody else. Let's see—also, that they all like mammy jokes, and that they are dirty, and that they are natural cowards, and that they carry knives, and that they are better in bed than————"

"Michael! Watch yourself!" Claude's voice was sharp, charged. Michael recognized the threat in it. He glanced furiously at Claude, then looked at his glass. With trembling fingers, he turned the glass on the table.

"But"—Kristin looked at Claude helplessly, in bewilderment—"but, I don't understand! What did I say?"

"Nothing," Claude said. His eyes did not leave Michael. Michael glanced up, eyes narrowed, but, again, he said nothing.

"But I *must* have said something!" There were tears of pain in Kristin's eyes. "*Tell* me, Claude. What did I say?"

"Nothing. Nothing." Claude's eyes were angry and turned on Michael who sat, tense, turning slowly his glass.

"Don't worry about it, sugar," the Blues Singer said. "You

ought to have your tongue cut out, Mike, pickin' on a cute little girl like this! I always used to think Claude was bad enough on this crap, but you've got worse than him!"

Michael said nothing. Margaret sat motionless, looking at her hands in her lap; she had never once looked up. Philip, trying to smile, glanced nervously from person to person.

The Old Man cleared his throat. "Well, now, let's all just drink a toast, and forget this stuff. A toast. To charming women and to music, eh?"

The Old Man tried to laugh jovially, and raised his glass, but no one else lifted his. Kristin sat staring in teary-eyed bewilderment from Michael to Claude, from Claude to Michael. Claude saw her; his heart constricted.

"I'll take you home now," Claude said. "We can come back another time."

"I don't want to go home," Kristin said.

Claude stood up. "Another night." He looked at Michael. "We'll come back again. The air is too heavy tonight." He smiled down at Kristin, and she stood up.

"Well, I'm really sorry you're leaving, young lady," said the Old Man. "Really sorry. Yes, indeed. But you must come back. Don't forget what I said. You must come back—even without Claude. I'll look after you." He winked at Claude again.

Kristin said goodnight to everyone. She would be back soon again, she said. Michael looked neither at her, nor at Claude, as they left.

17.

IMMEDIATELY AFTER CLAUDE AND KRISTIN LEFT, MARGARET STOOD up. "Excuse me," she said, "I'm tired. I'm going home. I can make it alone."

Philip, who had brought her, stood up, but she said, "No, thank you, Philip, I can get home alone."

"Of course I'll take you," Philip began, but Margaret cut him short.

"I want to go home alone."

Philip looked at her and sat back down. The Blues Singer said, "Well, well, things are poppin' all over!" Michael looked intently at Margaret, who did not look back.

Margaret walked down the street against the cool wind. Her heels clicked loud against the pavement, echoed loud from the walls of the houses. Yellow street lights flanked her on either side; a faint, cool rain began to fall; a police patrol car wheeled slowly by. Margaret saw, heard or felt none of these things. Before her eyes danced a curtain of shimmering red; in her ears was a din.

She turned onto Nineteenth Street. For the first time, she noticed the rain. It was turning cool, and she lifted the collar of her dress. *I'll catch a cold.* For twenty minutes she walked.

Her mother stared up, from her chair in the living room, when Margaret walked in. "Home early," she said. "Where's Philip?" "I told him to stay; I came home alone," Margaret said. "Alone . . . ?" her mother began, but, without looking at her mother, without slowing her pace, Margaret had started up the stairs. She walked into her room and closed the door. She walked straight to her dressing table and stood before the mirror.

She examined herself: those eyes, that hair, that mouth, that skin. Each feature separately, analytically, critically, thoroughly. She stared with her angry eyes into her angry eyes. The total face.

She whirled from the mirror and threw off her clothes, then turned again, and stood, naked, in front of the mirror. She examined herself: the shoulders, the breasts, the thighs, the legs. With a set face; with angry eyes.

She turned from the mirror and looked ahead of her, seeing

nothing. Her eyes blazed; her face did not lose its set, strong, defiant expression.

She climbed into bed and lay on her back, chest heaving, eyes on the ceiling, unfocused.

18.

CLAUDE LOOKED THROUGH THE WINDSHIELD; HE DID NOT LOOK at Kristin, or talk to her, as she drove. She was quiet now; she sensed his mood, and held back the questions that burned in her throat. When they halted, in front of her studio, Kristin said, "Come in." She said it softly, and Claude climbed out of the car. Inside, Kristin said, "I'll make some coffee, how about that?" She smiled, but Claude was not looking at her.

When she had made the coffee, they sat on the familiar stools. Claude's eyes roamed the room: the portraits of the great musicians, the piano, the violin, the sheet music, the bows, the books, the stove. Spiritual home.

"Claude, please tell me what happened?"

"Nothing happened. Michael's an idiot." Claude snapped off the words.

"But why was he angry?"

"He felt you were prejudiced, he thought you believed in the stereotypes that all Negroes hate." The words tumbled out, wearily, in a monotone; Claude did not want to discuss it.

Kristin nodded. "I see." She watched Claude for a moment, rose and kissed him lightly on the cheek, then went to the piano. She played something softly: Debussy.

"Life is so strange and complicated," she said quietly. "Too much for me."

When she came back to the stool, and sat down, Claude was

still sitting in the position in which she had left him: solid on the stool, looking off, unseeing, into space. Kristin leaned forward and searched his face.

"Do you feel bad, Claude, because of me?"

"Yes. But that's only part of it."

"What is it, Claude? Can you tell me?"

He shook his head wearily, and closed his eyes. He opened them again and looked at her.

"Kristin."

"Claude."

"Kristin, how can I explain it? I don't think I can get it over. It's only that I'm so *tired!*"

She looked at him. She wanted to know, to understand; he wanted her to understand.

"Kristin, imagine a man who's not built for hate. But whose whole life has been built on hatred. Can you conceive of that?"

She kept looking at his eyes.

"Ten years ago—*ten years* ago—my father was killed in our home town, a little town in the South, because he went out and voted in a white primary. He was the first Negro who did it. And he was murdered for it—seized by a group of men as he walked along a road that night, and killed in the most . . . horrible manner. And on the day when we buried him, we—my two brothers and I—took three of the carnations from his casket, and we swore we'd wear them always, in memory of his death and the people who had killed him. It was like a vow of eternal hatred. And from that day, we kept the vow. I went all over this country preaching hatred. Call it what you like—it was hatred, and it was war. I spoke to shouting mobs and what I said was hate, hate, hate! And in articles I wrote hate! And in Africa I said hate! Hate! Hate the white man!

"But now I'm *tired* of it! I heard you play—that simple violin—and there were more emotions in me, responding, than that single one of hate! Listen, there's a softness! There's a sensitivity, a love of beauty! There's a song singing somewhere in my heart. Why should I let *them* win the greatest victory? Why should I let *them* rob me of myself, my *full* self, who I *could* be? I have a right to live, to read, to hear music, to sing! I have a right to take my heart out of the vise, to drop the sword from my hand! I'm *tired* of the struggle! I'm *sick* of the bitterness! I want to be a human being! I want to love!"

Kristin stared. Her lips were parted slightly; her eyes were in his words. When he finished talking, she sat still, watching his hands tremble, staring at him with the wide, astonished eyes. Then suddenly she dropped to the floor, near his feet, and buried her head in his knees.

It was several hours later when Claude returned to the *Showboat*. He walked straight to the table he had earlier occupied; Michael, Philip, and the Old Man were still there; the Blues Singer was on the bandstand.

"Michael," Claude said, "I'm making this announcement particularly for you; but the others should know it also. Kristin and I are going to be married next week. You're invited to the little wedding ceremony, if you'd like to come."

The Old Man gasped; Philip stared at Claude, dumbfounded. Michael stared at Claude and said nothing; but in his eyes burned something close to hate.

Book Two:

NEIGHBORS

1.

THROUGH THE WINDOW OF THE TRAIN, MOUNTING UP THROUGH New York State, they watched the pleasant play of blues and greens: the Hudson dark blue and clean under a light blue sky, the trees and grass a study in shades, though, for the most part, they were a lighter green than the grasses and trees of Pennsylvania and states south. At the station in Montreal they told the cab driver, "Windsor Hotel," not realizing that the hotel was directly across the street. The driver, without a word, piled in their luggage, then made the U-turn and halted in front of the hotel: the Windsor, old, dark and stately, where the Royal Family sometimes stopped. Claude and Kristin, who took one of the cheaper rooms, stared in awe at the huge, heavy key the desk clerk handed them.

They liked Montreal. Mostly, they simply walked through the city, stopping at restaurants for meals, investigating the buildings and monuments. Once, they climbed into a *calèche*—a horse and buggy—and went up the winding road to the top of Mount Royal, from which they could see over the whole city. The driver chattered incessantly in French, waited for them while they dined at the mountain-top pavillion, then chattered again incessantly as he drove them to the wax museum. Nights, they sometimes visited the clubs: *Ciro's, Rockhead's Paradise,* the *Tic-Toc.*

Over their radio, which operated on the insertion of a quarter, they listened laughing to commercials advertising American products in French: *"le linge le plus blanc du monde entier!—* Duz does Everything!" Both Claude and Kristin knew a few words of French, and they chatted with the maid who cleaned their room and the waiter who brought them snacks in the middle of the night. They were obviously the favorite clients of the waiter and maid: a black man and a white woman; romantic.

It was strange, the effect that the marriage, and the few days in Montreal, had on Claude. He relaxed, as after an unnoticed emotional strain: the bell, of which he had not been conscious, stopped ringing in his ears. Life seemed richer, more quietly full, than he had ever remembered; and the past ten years seemed absurd, unreal, a nightmare. His act—the marriage—had been a breaking with the past, a throwing off of racial shackles, a declaration for music—for universality. Now, standing on Life's sunlit, airy plain, he felt as though all his past had been lived in a damp and dimly lighted tunnel.

They stayed nine days in Montreal. In New York, they stayed several days at the Theresa, had a chat at the bar with Langston Hughes, went to the *Blue Angel* to see Pearl Bailey and Marian Bruce. Then they headed home.

2.

THE SEARCH FOR AN APARTMENT WAS IN VAIN: NO REAL ESTATE agent would rent an apartment to a Negro in a white neighborhood, and the Negro neighborhoods—those small, iron-bound areas into which Negroes were compressed by an unwritten law— were tremendously overcrowded; so much so, that some families of four and five were living in a single room at rents as high as those charged for houses.

They moved, therefore, into Kristin's studio. People visited them: Philip, the Old Man, Gordon, Kristin's accompanist. Michael refused to visit them; nor had he come to their wedding. Nor had Margaret.

Kristin had been startled by the effect her announcement of

the pending marriage had had on the people she knew, especially among those with whom she worked. Almost to a person, they expressed horror at the idea, warned her that she was doing something foolish, painted hair-raising pictures of later remorse. They had refused to come to the wedding, held in the studio, and refused, afterwards, to visit them.

This, to Kristin, had been amazing. Lost in her world of music, she had never before thought seriously about "the problem," never seen people as other than individuals. She was pained by the reactions of her friends and of Claude's brother, as she had been frightened and dismayed by the history of the white carnations. Such bitterness had never existed in her world.

From Kristin's brother, James, had come a plea for caution; he could not stop her from doing what she wished, he wrote, but he pointed out some of the possible pitfalls of such a union, urging that they be taken into consideration. Gordon, too, had urged caution, but, seeing that Kristin had made up her mind— and her heart—had said nothing more.

They lived more or less a life of solitude. After the first, new days, not so many people came; but neither of them regretted this. They both had work, the core of life; they had dinners together, music, coffee and talking, the discovery of each other. Love was a slow unclothing of the self—a slow unstripping of the walls that conceal the self, or parts of the self, from other, alien, eyes, in the sacred name of privacy. They searched the selves, the one of the other, and found them good.

Kristin was present the day when, finally, having won the inner battle, Claude drew the flower from his lapel and tossed it with a smile into the waste paper basket. For him, there would be no more white carnations.

3.

THE OLD MAN, TO HIMSELF AND THE OTHER PEOPLE OF THE neighborhood, was a "card." He was a neighborhood institution, ancient, eternal: politician, lover of young girls, charmer of old ladies, connoisseur of good whiskies—a man of many parts. A son, a brother, a husband in jail?—the Old Man was the person to see. He was always to be found during the day, in summer, on the front steps of his large house, or, in winter, indoors; and nights he was invariably at the *Showboat*, or the *Postal Card*, or at the Ward Political Club. He was the man to see: a committeeman who never lost his division, no matter what the city-wide returns; he knew all the magistrates, and if the Old Man spoke for you, you were as good as acquitted of any minor offense.

The Old Man never liked to be alone. He kept, in his living room, an expensive phonograph, and stacks upon stacks of the latest swing records, as bait for young female companions; on winter evenings the girls were nightly sprawled around his floor, romantic with hassocks and satin pillows, lights dimmed and incense faintly burning. Men visited him too, some because of the girls, most because of the pool table in the Old Man's cellar. Frequently, there were poker games in the Old Man's "den," with the Old Man, naturally, cutting the stakes.

"I love people!" the Old Man always said. "I love them around me, love to see them enjoying themselves."

To insure himself against a dearth in company, the Old Man kept a formidable card file of names and addresses of ladies he could call. He loved to cook and, whenever he found himself threatened with eating alone, he would look through his card file until he came across an intriguing name, then pick up the telephone and call on the favored one to be his guest. Refusals, of course, presented no problem. The file was endless; *somebody* would be happy to get a free meal. That person found, the Old Man would busy himself with preparation of the hassocks and pillows, prepare the meal, then relax in a chair, in his dressing gown, waiting.

After dinner, of course, and after drinks and the playing of music, the old man, drugged perhaps by the low lights and the incense, would become a bit romantic. The young ladies all knew this; they could predict his moves, deftly parry them, then escape, when it was polite, with the payment of a slight fee—a kiss on the cheek of the Old Man. They departed, always, with a hand-squeezing invitation from the Old Man to "come back soon."

One evening, the Old Man was looking through his card file, when he came across the name of a girl he could not at first remember. "Betty? Betty?" Suddenly it came to him: she was a waitress in a restaurant where he had once dined, and had been kind enough to copy down for him, on one of the cards he always carried, her name, address, and telephone. The Old Man called her. Dinner? This evening? She would be delighted.

Someone fresh! The Old Man, too, was delighted. He rushed out of the house, down the street, and came back with an armful of new flowers. Carefully, he arranged them in vases. He tested the lighting: nice and dim. The pillows: he fluffed them. Let's see . . . what next? Ah! the incense! He lighted the buddha's tray. He stood back and admired his handiwork. Wonderful. Exquisite. The young lady would be charmed.

When Betty arrived, something more than an hour later, the Old Man was in his dressing gown. He bowed low at the door, kissed her hand, swept her in. In the light of the living room, he surveyed her: nice, quite nice. The Old Man was beside himself with pleasure.

It had been some time since they had seen each other, the Old Man said, when they were seated. Was she still employed at that charming restaurant where he had met her? The girl said no.

She looked around the room, her pretty nose wrinkled: "What's that funny smell?"

"Incense, my dear." Really, the Old Man was a bit disappointed in her. "Shall we dine, my dear?"

Betty offered to wash the dishes. The Old Man would not hear of it; that would be left to his servant, James, who would be in in the morning. "Gee! You got a servant?" said the girl, wide-eyed. "Why, of course, my dear," said the Old Man. "My duties in politics would not allow me to take care of all the trivial details of running a household. You will understand that, I'm sure."

"Oh, sure."

Settled deep in one of the stuffed chairs in the living room, the girl looked around her. "You got a swell place here," she said.

"You find it so? Oh, it's modest enough. It's one of the first laws of politics, you know, not to create envy in the hearts of constituents. Would you care for a bit of music?"

"Oh, I'd *love* it!"

The Old Man put on a slow record. The girl was settled back in the chair, legs crossed, looking around her, seemingly in a dream. The Old Man looked at her legs. *Hmmmm.* "Would you care to dance, my dear?"

The Old Man was a good dancer—very light and sensitive. The girl was close. *Hmmmm.* He placed his cheek against her cheek, and she did not move hers away. They danced, this way, through three records.

"Lovely, my dear. You are a lovely dancer."

The girl was back in her chair, legs crossed. The Old Man sat at one end of the big divan. His problem: how to get the girl over on the divan with him.

"Ah ... my dear, don't you think you'd be more comfortable over here, on the divan? And it would be more convenient for talking."

"Sure," said the girl. She uncrossed her legs, pushed herself up out of the chair, and walked across the room to sit on the other end of the divan. She smiled at the Old Man. "Do you mind if I take off my shoes?"

"Not at all, not at all, my dear," said the Old Man.

She took off her shoes and curled up her legs, leaning back, dreamily, against the satin pillows. "This is so nice, being here like this, just talking intelligent and listening to the music," she sighed. "Don't you think it's nice?"

"I think it's . . . delicious, my dear." The girl closed her eyes and sighed again. The Old Man said, "I love to have a guest make herself at home, be comfortable here. Unfortunately, I rarely have guests. Generally, I'm very lonely. Very lonely.

The girl opened her eyes: they were big with a mixture of sympathy and indignation. "Is that so?"

"Oh, yes," said the Old Man. "You see, my dear, people think —they're not cruel, you understand, simply innocent, simply heartless—they think that because a man has piled up some years, grown a bit older, more mellow, if you wish—they think that because of that, the man has no need for company, no need for laughter. They think such a man has no heart."

"They really think that?"

"Oh yes. They think that such a man is to be cast off, dismissed out of hand, thrown to the dogs."

"Gee! I wouldn't think a thing like that."

"Of course you wouldn't, my dear. But not everyone is as . . . sympathetic, as understanding, as you. People assume that men like me have no heart, no soul, no passion. . . ."

Betty was leaning back, looking at him wide-eyed, legs curled under her. Her dress, the Old Man noted, was slightly above her knees.

"But," said the Old Man softly, sad-faced, "there is heart, there is passion."

"Sure," Betty said.

"And this is . . . unfortunate." The Old Man held up his hand, in a gesture of profound resignation to his lot. "For what is

the good of having heart when no heart will beat in time with it?
. . . what the good of having soul, when no soul will draw that
soul into its own? . . . what the good of having passion, my dear,
when it is a passion locked, barred, chained, leashed; passion
which cannot spend itself, cannot be satisfied? . . ."

The girl stared at him, eyes wide. The Old Man thought that
in a moment she was going to cry. "Gee," she said.

"No, my dear, passion housed is not passion at all, but an
animal wailing for its freedom, animal dying because it cannot
feed, except upon itself! Ah, my dear, the torment of it! If you
but knew! But, someday you will, when you are as old as I."

A moment of silence. The Old Man moved closer to Betty,
laying his hand, gently, upon her knee.

Betty was flooded with grief. "I wish I could help you," she
said.

"You do? Do you really, my dear?" said the Old Man, moving
still closer. "You can, you know."

"Oh, I wish I could!"

"Nothing is more easily arranged, my sweet."

"But . . . I can't."

"Why not, my love?"

She lowered her eyes. Again, for a moment, there was silence,
the Old Man's hand on the girl's knee, the smell of incense in the
room and music softly playing. Betty said, "I'm sick."

"Sick?" The Old Man raised his eyebrows.

"You know—woman's sickness. Every month."

The Old Man frowned. *Hmmmmmmmmmmm.* He looked at
the girl quizzically, decided she was telling the truth; he sat
pondering, looking at the lovely, curled-under legs. This was
incredible. This was tragedy. The soft lights, the satin pillows,
her willingness—and her announcement. Suddenly, Betty burst
into tears.

"Oh, come, come, come, my dear," said the Old Man. "It's not
that tragic."

"Oh, it's not that," Betty said, between sobs, "it's something else."

"What is it?"

"My mother."

"Your *what?*"

"My mother." Her tears were really tumbling now. The Old Man put his hand in front of his face, looked at Betty from between his fingers. Behind the hand, his brows were heavy.

"What, my dear, has your mother to do with all this?"

"She's sick."

"Her *too?*"

"Oh, not *that* way. *Real* sick. I was just . . . thinking of her right now, and I had to cry."

"I see." The Old Man screwed up his face.

"Oh, it's so sad! So *sad!*" cried the girl. "Oh, please, excuse me, I don't want to be a crybaby, but every time I think of it . . . oh, it's *so* sad!"

The Old Man said nothing. He had removed his hand from Betty's leg. Now, he sat frowning, watching her sob, watching her body tremble. Finally, he gave her his shoulder; she rested her head against it, continuing to cry. The Old Man patted her shoulder: "There, there, my dear, everything will be all right."

She shook her head, sobbing. "No, it won't be all right! That's what's so horrible! Oh! I wish I could die! I can't go on with it!"

"With what?"

"I hate him!"

"Who?"

"The doctor."

The Old Man scratched his head. "The doctor? What's wrong with the doctor?"

"I *won't* go to bed with him! I *won't!*"

The Old Man wished he had dined alone in a restaurant this evening, then tucked himself quietly in bed.

"First it was the rent, you see," Betty went on. "That did it really."

"Did what?"

"Took all my money. I'm the only one makes any money in the house, and the rent took all of it when I lost my job, and I couldn't find another, and then mother got sick, and there wasn't any money for the doctor. But I *won't* sleep with him!"

"Where does that enter the picture?"

"Well, we owe the doctor a lot of money, and he says he wants to be paid, one way or the other. I haven't got any money. So he says—" She burst into tears again. After a pause, she went on, "But I *love* mother so much! So much! She's *got* to get treatments. We can't get another doctor, and this one says he won't come any more unless I get the money to pay him, or unless—" Again, she was in tears.

The Old Man waited a long time before speaking. He was looking off, across the room, toward the buddha, whose small pile of incense had now burned out. He asked the girl, "How much do you owe the doctor, my dear?"

"A hundred dollars." Tears were running down her cheeks again. "My poor mother! My poor mother! But I *can't* sleep with that horrible doctor! But if someone doesn't help me, I'll *have* to! I can't let my mother die!"

"Is she *that* sick?"

"Oh, she's *very* sick!"

The Old Man stood up and turned off the phonograph. "Calm yourself, my dear," he said. "I'll loan you the money."

"Would you? . . . Oh, I couldn't accept it, you'd be too kind! . . . would you?"

The Old Man opened his wallet and handed the girl the money.

"Oh, you're so kind, so good, you deserve so many things in life. . . ."

"And I'll pay you back this money"—Betty was putting it in

her pocketbook—"I'll find another job, and I'll save every week, and I'll pay you, I swear I will."

"I'm sure you will."

"And I'll come visit you all the time, even before I've paid it. I'll come see you when I'm not sick." She smiled sweetly. "You're such a kind man. Such a kind man. I knew it that day when I met you, in the restaurant!"

A few minutes later, the girl stood up. "Well, I have to be going. Mother will be so happy! So happy! Oh, you're such a good man!"

The Old Man went to the door with her. She kissed him on his cheek; he kissed her hand. "Goodbye," she said, "God bless you!" The Old Man knew, watching her walk off, that he would never see her again.

4.

WHEN LIL HAD BEEN FOURTEEN, HER FATHER HAD OFTEN COME into her room, at night, as she was undressing for bed—come in "to talk," or "to fix the shade," or "to do some carpentry," or for some other reason. Lil had been an attractive girl, and had had, even then, the beautiful, swaying body that called to the eyes of all men. Lil had been shy, and perhaps even a little ashamed, of that body: the boys in the school had made too many comments about it, too many mysterious overtures toward it: they touched, grabbed, until she saw them in the end as a mass of clutching hands. It had been not only the body's form, but its movements that had attracted men, and Lil had tried hard, in vain, to make the body "behave." The body had seemed to have a life of its own, and when she had walked, even then, the men on the corners had turned, whistled, and stared.

• 83

So every time her father had come into Lil's room, at night, she had been shy, and had delayed as long as possible the undressing: she had found "homework" that needed doing, gone into the bathroom, begun to sew some clothes. Her father had waited. Finally, inevitably, she had had to get undressed and climb into her night clothes. And her father, always, had then kissed her—strangely, it seemed to her—good night.

As time went on, a silent war had developed between Lil and her father over the subject of this undressing. It had been a sad war, for Lil. Though she did not love him, she sympathized with her father. He had had a hard life: a great deal of labor for little pay, eternal debts, an unlovable wife; he had come, finally, to drink a lot. She had had sympathy for her father—a huge, loud man—but the war had developed, and one day, when she was sixteen, Lil had gone out and bought a lock and some screws and, during the day, put the lock on her door. That night she had locked her door. When her father had come, she had refused to open the door, refused even to respond to him. She had locked her door every night from then on.

The father had never mentioned this, as Lil had never mentioned it, but the war, and its echo, had been in the house with them. Mother and brothers had heard its rumblings. No one had spoken of it, though the mother had vented her choked fury in giving sharp, harsh commands to Lil.

One evening when she was seventeen, Lil had come downstairs, dressed to go out. Her father had demanded:

"Where are you going?"

"Out, Poppa. To the movies."

"Who with?"

"With Jane."

"You're lying!"

She had stared at her father. He had been sitting in his big chair, near the window. He had been drinking.

"You're lying!" he shouted again.

At the other side of the radio, knitting, watching them both, had sat the mother.

"I'm not lying, Poppa."

"You're lying! You're lying! I know you! You're going whoring with some of them boys from school! I know you! A whore! A whore!"

Lil had stared at her father as though he had been insane.

"A whore! A whore!"

At the other side of the radio her mother sat, saying nothing. She had been knitting, saying nothing, knitting.

"Poppa, honest, I'm only going to the movies with Jane."

"You're lying! Lying! A whore!" and her father had leaped suddenly from his chair and struck her across her face with his hand which was as hard as a block of wood. "Lying!" Lil had looked at her father from the floor; she had not bothered to wipe away the trickle of blood from her mouth. "Lying! A whore! Well, you won't go whoring tonight! Go up to your room and go to bed!"

It had been strange living in that house of unspoken drives and hatreds, moving between the sullen, brooding silence of the father and the serpent tongue of the mother.

She had met many men, despised them; then she had met Slim. He had seemed "different," but she had not trusted him completely. He was a man; one of the *pack*. In brief moments— moments of weakness, Lil thought—she had relaxed with him, opened all doors, let him glimpse her heart. But for brief moments only; then the doors slammed shut again . . . sometimes at a touch, sometimes at a look of lust in his eyes. In moods, she could not speak to him; in others, she enjoyed torturing him, by flirting with other men.

One day, in September, Lil came home from Slim's apartment to find her father sitting alone in the half-light of the living room. The odor of whiskey reached out to greet her. Lil walked past the living room door without saying anything, went upstairs, locked the door and changed her clothes, then came downstairs and went into the kitchen. It was the first time she had been alone in the house with her father; she felt apprehensive. From the icebox, she took out some food and began to warm it over for her supper.

Her father was in the doorway. Lil knew he was there, but did not turn around, took no notice of him. She lighted the gas, put on the pans, and stood watching the steam rise from the water. Her father spoke. "Why didn't you speak to me when you came in?"

"I'm sorry, Poppa." She looked at him. "I just didn't think, I guess."

He was silent, standing in the doorway, his eyes following her movements in the half-light of the room.

Lil said, "Would you flip on the light switch, please, Poppa?"

Her father said, "You come turn it on."

He was leaning on the doorjamb next to the light switch. Lil could not see his dim, red eyes in the semi-darkness. *Better just go ahead and do it.* She walked across the room toward her father; the odor of alcohol was overwhelming. As she reached for the light switch, her father seized her hand.

"Poppa!"

"We're home alone," her father said.

He tried to pull her toward him, toward the reeking odor and the unscrubbed teeth, and Lil, struggling against him, pushed hard until he fell, drunkenly, to the floor. The father sat on the floor, leaning against the wall, as Lil ran up the stairs; he sat staring into the half-light, thinking of a young body and sparkling legs, of breasts soft and young, of exultation long denied, of curling shadows and plaintive moans; he sat looking straight ahead of him for fifteen ticking minutes until Lil descended the stairs. She was carrying two suitcases; hazily, in shadows, he could see that. The father struggled to his feet.

"Where d'you think you're goin'?"

"Away from here," Lil said.

He moved toward her: leaden body grown old, leaden body long starved; he moved toward her, the world reeling, a cry of longing in his heart, and mumbled fiercely: "You ain't goin' nowhere! Nowhere!" His drunken body-swung blow knocked Lil off her feet. The father was upon her. She could scarcely breathe against the weight of his body; the smell of alcohol was nauseating; his clumsy fingers reached for her clothes. "Poppa! Poppa! You're *crazy!*" He did not feel, apparently, the fingernails she dug into his face; but he felt it, screaming, when she bit into the lips that sought to press against her own. She was out from under him as he swung heavily at her, striking a glancing blow. The heavy ash-stand was in Lil's hand; she swung it down with all her strength on his head. Lil picked up her suitcases and fled from the house.

5.

"BUT THE INTELLECTUAL," DECLARED THE YOUNG MAN, ABOUT twenty-six, "has *always* been detached from the mainstream of society—a point of view disputed by Fred Freeman, another of the guests, who maintained that, "In times of social stress and strain only, is the intellectual—who is obviously a man of acute sensitivity—forced to retreat into an ivory tower, as it were, to escape the convulsions and violence which so upset him."

This was said during the course of one of those frequent sessions held by Philip and his friends at one or another of their homes—friends who were, indeed, among those very "intellectuals" they now discussed, most of them being actual or aspiring writers, painters, teachers or the like. Philip, one of the two

Negroes present, leaned back, sipped his coffee and listened with interest.

Fred Freeman went on: "As a matter of fact, the periods of greatest artistic creativity have been those in which the intellectual—that is, the artist—has been one with his society, which is simply another way of saying, at one with his *audience*. Witness the great Greek period, or Elizabethan England or the France of Louis XIV. On the other hand, the *isolated* artists—Joyce, Kafka, Stravinsky, the abstractionists in painting and sculpture—represent a *turning inward* of art, directed only toward others in the field, and absolutely senseless to the main body of intelligent human beings. Future generations, I believe, will judge such artists to be gifted experimenters only—not great artists."

"On it's face," said a man with a brush moustache, "that strikes me as wrong. You can't blame the social condition for the state of the art. The genius may be born into any society, in any age; the genius is above society and above his age, dealing with truths which are eternal."

"The creative man is always isolated," Philip said, "from individuals and from society; but he is not isolated from humanity, the sum total of it, through all societies, through all ages."

"But all of you mistake, I think, the *cause* of the isolation. It's not simply greatness, but *temperament*, don't you see? The creative person is hypersensitive. He is a multiple person who must —to create the dialectic—be able to see all sides, be all people, all eyes, all ears."

They were sitting around the big table in the large, pleasant, living room, lined by books—sitting, some in chairs, some on the floor, sipping their coffee, nibbling on the sandwiches, potato chips and olives on the table. There were some eleven of them in all, the men with coats off and sleeves rolled up, the girls in wide skirts or dungarees, hair cut short.

"Most of you," said Clara Saunders, who was sitting on the floor, "are begging the point, I think. Essentially, among human beings, there exist two basic qualities—force and recession: masculinity and feminity. All humans tend, in greater or lesser degree, to one or the other side. The creative artist is unique because he stands almost in the middle: an almost perfect balance exists."

"I believe," said another man, "that something else drives the creator—a desire, a profound need, to create order out of the chaos which is Man in the Universe."

"I cannot," said Harold Cousins, "accept your vision of art as an ordering of the universe. Did Chekhov, for example, create an ordered universe? Does Hemingway? Does Faulkner? Does Kafka? Or Joyce? Their whole point is *disorder*. No, the artistic drive is a *beauty* drive—beauty in form, in style, in ebb and flow. The exquisite masks of primitive societies, their lovely works of art—did they come into being out of a desire to order the universe, or a desire to create beauty?"

"I agree," said Ben Webster, "and when you get right down to it, I suppose it's *style* which makes art. Out of style flows beauty."

"No," said Johnson, "I don't think that one can place such great, almost exclusive, emphasis on style or form. Everyone knows that many of Shakespeare's plays were faulty in form; the plays of Maxwell Anderson are better constructed. The novels of Dostoievsky and of Tolstoy are not beautiful from the standpoint of style; Henry James, by that criterion, would have been greater! No, I don't think we can say that style is the primary quality, but, rather, that the creative artist—"

6.

IN A TENEMENT HOUSE ON SOUTH STREET, A WOMAN LAY DYING of tuberculosis. She lived in a single room; on the walls were roaches. In a crib in the room, her baby lay sleeping.

The woman lay thinking of her husband: he was not yet home: he was probably drunk again. She hoped he had not spent all of his salary.

She had a sudden premonition of danger. The woman sat up quickly and looked toward the baby's crib: a rat was crawling on the blanket, near the baby's head. The woman leaped out of bed. There was an instant's fear of the filthy thing; then her arm darted and she seized the rat; for a split second of horror, she felt the hideous biting and squirming in her hand, then she dashed the rat, with all her strength, against the wall. The rat fell dead. The woman washed her hand and climbed back in bed. She lay panting, her heart palpitating. The baby, in the crib, had never waked up.

7.

ON THE NIGHT WHEN MICHAEL DISCOVERED THAT HIS GREAT GOD'S knees were made of water and his feet of clay like those of any man, he had lain in bed awake all night and cried.

Death of an idol. Claude: combination of strength and gentleness, great pride and necessary humility, intellect and passion. So he had seemed to Michael.

Their relationship had hardly been that of brother to brother; more accurately it had been, through Michael's eyes, that of subject to king. Though the murder of his father was the most significant thing in his life, Michael had hardly any emotional memory of the event itself. More dramatic, to his youthful mind, had been the conduct of Claude, who had stood fierce, trembling, but controlled, over the grave, and lifted the three carnations and placed them in the lapels. *Never forget this death! Never forget who killed him!* This act had had meaning; this gesture had fired Michael's imagination, filled his dreams, charged his emotions; it had been this which had remained with him through all the years.

Claude had written, and Michael had marked it well: "A nation throws up its heroes, in whom are concentrated all of the group ideals, the group feelings, the group courage. The hero is in himself nothing; he is a focal point, a galvanizer of the energies already latent in his people; his voice is not his voice at all, but their voices concentrated. And anything the hero does or says— it is they, his people, who do or say it. Any shame that befalls him—it is their group shame. From heroes: no shame, then. Honor, then. Courage, then. Strength and virtue, then."

Claude, the hero (in Michael's eyes); Claude the king. From a proper distance, like a proper subject, Michael had followed the activities of his sovereign. People admired Claude; they talked about him; they took courage, strength, from the things he did. Good; but to be expected of a king. And Michael? Ah, but he was only subject!

Michael had cried; but not, simply, because of the Fall. For a king might fall: a king was human, after all, and some error of judgment, some overreaching audacity, and some untempered precosity, might, in a fickle moment, bring him down.

But to crumble in indignity! To throw off the crown in shame! To desert a race of fourteen million souls for the seductive movement of a white woman's legs! Flight to *their* side!

8.

BUT PAIN ALWAYS, WITH TIME, SUBSIDED, MOVED TO A LOWER level of the consciousness. Michael cut himself off completely from his brother, avoided all places where he might run into him, would permit no conversation about Claude in his presence. After that, he settled down to the organization of his own life.

For a long time Michael had wanted to work, not at a job— he had a job—but at the thing which really interested him: the unending struggle for advancement of his race. The Negro press had, for some time, been filled with stories on two subjects: increasing incidents of violence in the "borderline" areas between Negro and white neighborhoods (particularly in a section known as "Grays Ferry"), and the brutality of the police in Negro sections of the city. Since the great influx of workers from the South to defense plants during the war, the usual Negro sections of the city had become intolerably congested: even the wholesale transformation of houses into rooming houses, and the letting out of rooms in private homes, and the building of housing projects (Government financed) on vacant ground, had done almost nothing to ease the situation. So, slowly, the Negro areas had been pushing *outward*, encroaching on territory formerly exclusively for white people; and those of the white population in this threatened area who could, hastily packed their bags and moved much further back, away from the "front lines." Some could not move. Between these, and the pressing Negroes, grew up conflict. The white home-owners drew up petitions for the mayor, formed committees to prevent the sale of houses to Negroes, and finally resorted to threats and—on a few occasions —actual violence, to keep the Negroes out. In front of one Negro home, further advanced than the rest, a cross was burned one night: symbol of the Ku Klux Klan.

As for the police—their story was familiar. The worst policemen of any city's police force were always stationed in the Negro neighborhoods; consequently, it had always seemed to Negroes that, of all the people in the American population, none were more clearly their enemies than the police. Brutality had always been a common thing; nothing in recent years, however, had equalled the pitch to which wanton violence by police against

Negroes had now risen. One day, a grocer, a white man, was killed in a Negro neighborhood; immediately, one hundred heavily-armed policemen threw a blockade around the neighborhood and arrested three hundred black citizens who were thrown roughly into jail on charges of suspicion—something that could never have happened in a white neighborhood. Some of those arrested were given the third degree to make them "talk"; as it turned out, months later, none of the arrested men had committed the crime.

A delivery boy, eleven years old, had allegedly run off one Saturday with the groceries of the wife of a policeman; the policeman, charging angrily to the store, seized the first delivery boy he saw and beat him with his pistol butt until his head was a mass of coagulated blood. In a snack bar, on South Street, a policeman, probably angry with his wife, beat a bystander to death with his club. Another Negro's car was stopped by two policemen who thought the woman with him was white; the man was dragged out and clubbed, then carted off to jail for "disorderly conduct" and "resisting arrest." As it turned out, the woman was Negro, and, incidentally, the man's wife: but she *looked* like she might have been white. A nineteen-year-old boy was beaten and kicked by two policemen because his roadster blocked the passage of their patrol car on a narrow street. Countless were the times that Negroes, who happened to be in neighborhoods where crimes had just been committed, were seized, beaten, and charged with the crimes, only to be found innocent afterwards; and countless, too, were the innocent men found *guilty* of such crimes, and sent off to jail. No questions of Justice. No questions of Rights. The victims were Negroes: the usual standards did not apply.

These things, and more, drove Michael to fury. He joined a conservative Negro organization and tried to press the leadership into action against such offenses. In vain. Like most organizations, this one was more concerned with membership campaigns, and the election of its officials, than with the actual work the organization was supposed to do.

Frustrated, Michael quit the organization. Through the Negro newspapers (since only the Negro newspapers carried the stories of these offenses), he found the names of victims of brutality, and managed to get in touch with them. They formed a loose organization pledged to act on its own, added to their membership some Negro veterans of World War II, spoke in Negro churches during Sunday services where collections were taken up to help finance them, called several meetings at which Michael spoke. They announced their program: it included counter-violence, if necessary, against police and those who attacked Negro homes. When another attack did occur against a Negro home in the borderline area, the association—which they called the "Action Society"—set up all-night, rotating guards in front of the home until the police, frightened by this display, and fearful of its consequences, posted police guards of their own. The Action Society also organized publicity campaigns, distributed pamphlets outlining the racial situation in the city and their plans for combating it, sent press releases to the Negro newspapers. Michael was elected the society's president.

In the full swing of activity, Michael paused one day with a start at the realization of something that had never before occurred to him: he, too, could lead! He could organize; he could think, plan; he could act and get response. Around him were others as enthusiastic, energetic, and resourceful as he; they worked together, talked together, planned and shared together. Consciousness of his own worth, and the worth of those around him, caused Michael to blossom.

So his days were filled: morning and afternoon, work in the factory; evenings, work with the Action Society, in the company of the new friends he had made. Only his nights were empty.

9.

What is my life to be? AND MARGARET WONDERED: *Is it to be like the life of my mother?*—*getting up mornings tired, washing, ironing, cooking, complaining, taking care of kids, gossiping, going to bed tired, getting up. . . ?*

She knew herself. She knew that this was no life for her.

Quiet. People saw only her quiet. They did not know the human being who lived underneath.

Sometimes, she looked at Philip and felt not even kindness that he loved her, but a great contempt: for the part of her that he loved was not her essential self, but a superficial, hated, outer mask, the face she turned toward the world. He saw sweetness. He saw gentleness. These were not she.

Passion. But what passion could he see who had no passion to match passion? Or who could command a passion, who had no will, no strength, no *drive* to hitch it to?

There had been many men who used to come around. Soft men, or, rather, youths; most from the church. Clean faces. Well-creased suits. Gently, they kissed her cheek. "Good night, Margaret." Gently, they touched her hand. "You're not like all these other girls, who run around. You're the old-fashioned kind, you're different, you're rare. You're sweet."

Sweet! She wanted to laugh sometimes in their faces. Sweet! If they knew the things that charged her blood! Kindling there, coals there; but who would strike the match?

One day, as she sat thinking, feeling the long-drawn-out frustration, Philip came. He sat down. Margaret was silent, across the room, looking at him. Philip talked. She listened to his soft, soft voice, looked at his slackened body, wondered idly whether he had ever been angry, or sincerely jealous, whether he had ever hated, whether any dream of glory had ever possessed his soul.

She said, "What do you want out of life, Philip?"

"I don't know. I think I'd like maybe to do something creative —though I doubt that I'd be any good. I want to marry, have children I suppose. Why do you ask?"

"Doesn't anything *push* you?"

Philip said, "No particular thing. I have my books, my records, I enjoy my friends. The exploration of art—that is to say, *all* art: music, literature, painting—is endless, after all."

She said nothing for awhile. Then: "Philip."

"Yes."

"I told you once that I was in love with Claude. Why do you keep coming to see me?"

"Because you love—or loved—him, does not change my feeling toward you. I can understand your loving Claude; I love him too, and admire him. But I love you. As Shakespeare said, 'Love is an ever-fixed mark.' " He smiled.

"And you don't feel shame, or anger?"

"Why should I? There was always, I felt, the possibility that you would change your mind, or that you'd get over Claude."

"And would you take me under those conditions?"

"I love you. Of course."

She sat silent, despising him.

"Are you still in love with Claude?" Philip asked, after awhile.

"You have no fire!" Margaret said bitterly.

Philip was taken aback. "No fire . . ."

"No fire, no soul! Perhaps I'd change my mind, you say. Do you think I could ever love a man with water in his veins?"

He started to speak, but Margaret said, "Please leave."

Philip was startled and pained. "Margaret, I—"

"Please!"

She stood with him at the door. "And Philip," she said, "I'm sorry . . . please don't come back."

10.

MIXED COUPLES—THAT WAS TO SAY, MARRIED COUPLES OF WHICH
the husband or wife was white, the other Negro—must always,
Claude realized, have tended to find each other and come together; for with almost no other combination of people could
they be completely comfortable. Claude's friends tended to be
cautious, unrelaxed in their speech, jokes, and actions when
Kristin was around, for they could not accept Kristin as "one of
them"—she had had a background on the "other side" and was
something of an alien; and as for Kristin's friends, most had
dropped her immediately it became known that she was going
to marry a Negro. The newlyweds had therefore, in recent weeks,
found themselves in a condition of semi-isolation, with only
Gordon, Kristin's accompanist, and Philip coming regularly to
see them.

It was pleasant, therefore, to make the acquaintance of another
couple in a similar situation. Dan and Suzette Johnson's had been
a war marriage; they had met in France at the time of the inva-
sion, Dan had fought with his unit into Germany, then returned,
when hostilities ceased, to marry Suzette. Dan had been sent back
to America for discharge, and Suzette had rejoined him shortly
afterwards. Dan was tall, broad, good-looking; Suzette tiny, chic,
and very French.

The two couples met at the Academy during the intermission
of a Heifitz concert; Claude and Kristin had been standing near
a wall, talking, when Dan had walked over to them and said,
"Uh huh. Fellow sufferers."

"What?"

"Fellow sufferers. I saw the rings on your fingers. Pardon me
if I'm wrong, but aren't you two married?"

"Yes. . . ."

"My name's Dan Johnson. That's my wife, Suzette. See what I mean? We ought to get together and form a union. You *must* be having the same kind of trouble with friends that we are."

Claude and Kristin had laughed, and after the concert, the couple had gone with them to their studio for some coffee and a chat. "Yes, yes," Dan said, "them people try to make life as tough as they can, but old Dan has got their number." He laughed. "Boy, if them officers on the ship that brought Suzette over had known that she was coming to marry a *boot*, they'd have thrown her overboard!"

"What does 'boot' mean?" asked Suzette.

"That's Hockway talk, baby. Very difficult language. Don't bother trying to learn it; it's beyond you." He winked at Claude.

"How long have you been married?" Claude asked.

"Seven years, old man. Seven years in the land of Bilbo. And little Suzette ain't learned to talk Hockway *yet!*" He chuckled. "You people go to a lot of concerts?"

"Yes."

"Great stuff. Hadn't done much of that stuff myself 'till I went overseas and got hep to all the culture jive. Great stuff. The education of Dan Johnson. Gonna write me a book."

So they went often to concerts and theater and the movies. People stared at them as they walked down the street, or sat in lobbies, or as they walked in and out of doors. "You're lucky," Dan said, "you got a car. Oughta be like us and have to ride the streetcars and subway; man, you ain't *seen* no stares yet! Old ladies looking religious, staring at you like you was committing a sin; young women staring at Suzette like she was dirt; old men staring like I was violating their daughter; young cats staring like they want to shoot me. It's a *blip*, man!"

"What does 'blip' mean?" asked Suzette.

"That's Hockway talk, baby. Forget it."

"Anyway, when zey stare, I want to tell zem all to go to hell!"

"Just tell 'em in your mind, baby," said Dan, "but not out loud. I don't want to make no newspaper headlines." He chuckled.

Dan smoked, leaning back long and lanky in his chair. "Ever notice," he said, "how it's impossible for most white people to believe that your wife is *really* in love with you? Say they figure out you're married, see, they see the rings and all that—ever try to figure out why they stare at you so funny sometimes? They're finding *reasons*, catch? They're trying to figure out—well, is she crazy? Is she a whore? Is she sick? Didn't no white man want her? Catch? Ain't that a blip?"

It was undoubtedly true that, more than anything else in the world, Dan loved to hear himself talk. He held forth on one subject after the other, slouched like a bent stringbean in his chair, chuckling softly, halting occasionally to allow a word from his wife or Kristin to slip in edgewise. He loved to baffle his small, cute wife, with her cute accent; loved to set her head aspin in futile efforts to comprehend the rich argot born and nourished in the black belts of the nation to baffle the surrounding, all-powerful white world.

"It is unfair that you talk in riddles!" The small, puckered French lips would pout.

"But you're ofay, *cherie;* tough, I know, but you might's well pad down with it. The jive put down by Claude and me is strictly boot stuff, got to be. You can't dig it; I can't school you; it's got to be in your bones, like the feelin' for a night club or the sound of spirituals. You Paddy-talk, you can't blow with Caldonia. Ain't my fault; Mr. Charlie invented this crap, all I can do is look what's being put down, hep myself to the play and ball the best I can."

"You are terreeeble!" said Suzette.

11.

ONE EVENING, AFTER A CONCERT (A PERFORMANCE OF THE Mendelssohn Violin Concerto; Kristin's comment was, "Miriam Solovief does it much better!"), the two couples decided to go to the *Rendezvous*, a small, cozy night club on Walnut Street, where Billie Holiday was singing. None of them noticed, as they drove along, that a big car was following them; but when they descended, in front of the club. Dan saw the car pull up behind them, saw the windows go down and saw the men—youths, really, about twenty-two—who looked out at them.

"Oh, oh," he said to Claude. Claude had noticed it, too. The men in the car did nothing, said nothing; they simply watched the two couples as they walked into the night club. "What the hell was that?" Dan wondered aloud, when they were inside; but Lee Guber, the proprietor of the club, had stepped forward smiling to shake Claude's hand, and the incident was forgotten.

They sat at one of the small tables that lined the wall, sipping drinks in the half-light, listening to the singing of "Lady Day," queen of the modern blues singers. She was singing "Gloomy Sunday"; her voiced chilled the audience, caught them, held them fascinated, pulled at their emotions. During intermission the four chatted. No one paid any particular attention to them; the *Rendezvous* was a sophisticated club, where mixed couples, while not the rule, were taken for granted.

They did not stay for the second show; just finished their drinks, paid and went outside into the cool, star-rich evening. Kristin was enthusiastic about Billie Holiday's singing. "She's wonderful! *W*onderful!"

Her exclamations were interrupted, however, by Suzette's cry of astonishment and Dan's shout of rage. Claude and Kristin looked at their car: every tire had been slashed; every window had been broken.

12.

IT WAS A SAD, A PATHETIC THING NOT TO BE ADMIRABLE IN ANY way, and to know it—and one nearly always knew it, Philip thought, if one was honest with oneself. Seen through his own eyes, Philip was not admirable; he searched himself, and could find no quality, no eccentricity even, of which he might be proud. Small wonder, then, that Margaret had contempt for him.

Evenings, Philip wandered frequently over to see Claude and Kristin, lolled about their living room, chatted, sometimes listened to Kristin play, sometimes simply watched the incredible liveliness of her movements about the room; and frequently, suddenly, he would look across the room at Claude, at the strong face, at the strong hands in motion, and he would think of Claude's fame, of all the things he had done in his life, and the question would come to him: Is he really my brother? Is Michael really my brother? *What strange combination of chromosomes led to the issuance of these three products from that one womb?*

Philip felt repulsed even—or in particular, perhaps—by that unnatural fragment of American life known as *Negro* life. Philip never felt that he was "a Negro"; he was Man-Alive, not Negro-Alive: sentiment, intellect, the esthetic sense—these were universal. He felt no particular bond with other Negroes, no particular sense of identification, no particular affection.

He would have felt no identification with Negroes at all, except that—and here was the rub—white America *forced* that identification upon him. *They* reminded him, would not let him forget, that his skin was darker than theirs: *they* segregated him on the street cars and trains of the South, *they* would not serve him in certain restaurants and bars or let him stay in certain hotels, even in the North; *they* reminded him every day, by word, by attitude, by the raising of an eyebrow, by a tone of voice, that *they* did not recognize his declaration of universality.

Because of this, the conflict: there was no world he could call his own; he was in that half world between the white and the black, participating in neither, inactive, ineffectual, unalive. The white carnation was a mockery in his lapel. He felt the truth of Margaret's indictment: there was "water" in his veins.

One evening, riding the subway, on his way to visit some friends, Philip was startled from revery by shouting voices and, near him on the train, saw a white and Negro workman in violent dispute. The cause of the quarrel was not important; the men stood shouting, making threatening gestures; the people on the subway watched. Philip sat watching, quietly and analytically noting the usual, slow, steady, chilling, filling, rising of the well-known fear and tension inside of himself; quietly noting the hint of trembling in his knees, the out-flowing of his strength; quietly noting the palpitation of his heart which brought to him, incongrouously, memories of Poe. The workmen began to fight. The subway was in uproar. When the train stopped, Philip rose on trembling legs and walked out. He stumbled against a big white man on the platform. "Watch were the hell you're going!" shouted the man, running into the train. Trembling, cold, but analyzing the trembling and the cold without panic, Philip climbed the stairs, went outside. He stood for several moments, staring into a shopwindow, analyzing himself, the man he was, and the man he perhaps would like to be. He went back down the stairs of the subway, waited for a train going back in the direction from which he had just come; he boarded it, rode to a certain stop, got off. The trembling was over, but he was still cold. There was the church and the sign: "Meeting." Philip went in, stood at the rear of the church, which was quite filled; Philip smiled, hearing, for the first time, his brother, Michael, delivering a speech from a platform. *He's really quite good.* Philip felt good about seeing his brother in such a situation, but felt no particular emotional response to the indignities Michael was reciting; Philip simply observed, then, after the meeting, walked up the aisle to the platform and called to Michael.

"Philip!" Michael was startled to see him.

"Michael, is there some kind of work I can do with your committee? I'd like to help, if I may."

Michael was for a moment speechless with amazement. Then he laughed, jumped down from the platform and embraced his brother.

13.

THE BLUES SINGER SAID, "WHERE THE HELL'S THAT KEY?", finally found it, then managed to find the lock and open the door so that she and the trumpet player could walk in. "Rest your bones," she said. "Want anything to drink?" "Sure, baby, you know ole Jeff," said the trumpet player. "Goddamn right, always lookin' for a free drink!" the Blues Singer said and laughed harshly. They were both drunk.

She poured the drinks in water glasses and put the bottle of whiskey on the floor. She sat on the bed; the trumpet player was in the soft chair.

"Jesus! that sonofabitch played some horn!" the Blues Singer said.

"Max? Oh, yeah, he plays." The trumpet player was tall, dark, lanky with long, gnarled fingers. He held the glass with three fingers and a thumb, swishing the whiskey around in the glass, studying the glass carefully.

"Well, here's to you, baby."

"Down the hatch!" said the Blues Singer. "What them goddamn Swedes say? *Skoal!*" She laughed again the usual, harsh
laugh. They drank. The room spun. The Blues Singer sat slumped
on the edge of the bed; the trumpet player was studying his glass.
The room seemed gray to the Blues Singer.

"What the hell. What the hell."

"What's the matter, baby?"

"Aw, what the hell! Know what I mean?"

"Sure, baby. I know how you feel."

"You don't know a goddamn thing! Not a goddamn thing
except whiskey!"

"Ain't nothin' wrong with whiskey," Jeff laughed.

"Naw." She pondered the wisdoms of her glass for awhile.
"Well, it don't cure everything, though."

"Naw, but it makes most things better."

The Blues Singer laughed. "You're a crazy sonofabitch." She
liked Jeff; he was a crazy sonofabitch, but he could play a horn;
he could damn sure play a horn!

"You want some music?" she asked him.

"Naw, had enough music for tonight."

"What kinda goddamn musician are you, had enough music!
Musician ain't *never* supposed to have enough music!"

"Well, I had enough." He lifted the bottle and poured some
more whiskey into his glass. "You want some more?" "Naw,"
she said. He placed the bottle carefully on the floor again and
leaned back in his chair and looked at the Blues Singer.

"Baby, you got some real fine legs."

"What's that got to do with the price of potatoes?"

"Just a compliment." He looked at her legs. "Sure got some
fine legs!"

"Just stick to your glass!"

Jeff leaned forward. "Look here, baby, ain't no needa actin' that way. You been knowin' ole Jeff for a long time. Why'nt you give ole Jeff a break?"

"Shit!"

"Ain't no needa actin' that way, baby. I'm your *friend*. You know how I feel about you. Hell, you know. . . ." He showed the palms of his hands.

"Look," said the Blues Singer, "I asked you if you wanted a nightcap, and that's all you're gonna get here, so just drink your goddamn whiskey and get the hell out."

"Aw, baby"—Jeff moved from the chair to the bed—"aw, baby, ain't no needa actin' that way. Hell, I mean, this is *Jeff*, you know? Hell, we been knowin' each other too long an' we been too close for all this kinda crap. Know what I mean? I mean, hell, I ain't one of them goddamn jitterbugs tryin' to make time in a hurry, or tryin' to jive you, or nothin' like that. Hell, baby, you and me, we're *thick*, know what I mean?"

"Shit!" said the Blues Singer, with the harsh laugh. She was looking at him and somewhere, vaguely, something was stirring, but she did not trust it, and could not surrender to it. "All you men's a bitch! Think you can smooth-talk a woman into anything. Shit, I get up too goddamn early in the mornin' to fall for *that* crap!"

"See there, baby, now when you talk like that you hurt my feelings."

The Blues Singer howled. "Ain't that a bitch! Feelings? Ain't that a bitch!"

"That's true, baby. You wound ole Jeff. I thought you and me was closer than that."

She looked directly at him and said, "Look here, Jeff, I wanta tell you something. No jive, get me? No bullshit about you love me, or you feel no goddamn burning passion for me, or nothing like that. Get me? Because I get up too early in the morning for *that* crap. You want something from me—okay. You can have it. But no bullshit about love or passion or none of that. Get me?"

"Aw, now, baby—"

"Goddammit, get me! No crap!"

"Okay, baby."

She turned off the light: she did not want to undress in front of Jeff: her body was not good, she knew, and, besides, she had a shyness about nudity. It had been a long time, and this, which was about to occur, was too intimate a thing to permit her to retain the usual mask. She felt strangely like a child, frightened, at the mercy of another, as she climbed into the bed; yet, something within her, some bitterness and some fear, rebelled against the childlike role and against the man and the act. She lay back, eyes wide open, rebellion in her. She was conscious of weight, of friction, of throated noises. A chill gripped her and her body went tight with the fear and the bitterness, even though it still moved, with effort, through force of will rather than force of passion. The ridiculous noises struck her suddenly as funny; she wanted to laugh, but the pain and the frustration cut it off.

He lay beside her in silence. The Blues Singer knew that this had been a fiasco. She was ashamed, and angry at her shame and her nakedness, and she said, "Guess I ought to go out and find me a woman." She laughed bitterly.

14.

IN THE AFTERNOON, WHEN THE OLD MAN STOPPED BY THE Thirtieth Ward Political Club, there was a message for him from Dave Clarris, city chairman of the political party to which the Old Man belonged. "From Dave Clarris," the Old Man commented casually to the boy at the desk, "wants me to drop by his office, see him this evening." The boy whistled. Dave Clarris! That was something!

The Old Man looked very dapper in a blue pin-stripe suit, glossy black shoes, maroon tie and navy blue overcoat. His hair was carefully brushed, his nails manicured and his gray hat at just the proper angle. For no particular reason, he felt in an exceptionally good mood.

For dinner the Old Man went to the *Apex Club*, meeting place of all well-to-do and influential Negroes of the city.

The waitress came to his table. "My dear," said the Old Man, "did anyone ever tell you you have beautiful legs?"

"Never," the waitress said. "Would you like the baked ham? It's very good today."

"Or that when you walk, the movement is like that of a gazelle?"

"Never." The waitress waited patiently, looking at her order slip.

"I'll take the baked ham," the Old Man said, "plus your telephone number."

"One ham," the waitress said, walking away.

The Old Man sat humming and looking at pretty young ladies who came into the club to eat. Hmmmm. He wondered what Dave Clarris wanted. Probably wanted to talk over some details of the campaign, wanted the Old Man's advice on something. It was nice, this involvement in the great game of politics, the great game of ruler and ruled.

The Steward walked by. The Old Man called, "Why, hello, Ed, how are you, how are you?"

"Fine. And you?"

"Well, things are going fine. Doing big things you know. Conference tonight with Dave Clarris, going to help him and some other big leaders map out plans for the campaign. They're placing me in charge of the South Section."

"That so?" said the Steward distantly; he was looking at some people who had just come in the door.

"Yes, I think they'll make me a magistrate after the next

election. Dave practically promised it to me, last time I saw him. Maybe a judgeship. You never know."

"Judgeship? You ever study law?"

"Well . . . Yes, of course, studied law at Harvard, in my younger days. You didn't know that? Oh, of course, I never made much use of it. Preferred politics, you know—the power game always fascinated me. Besides that, I never cared much for court-rooms, you know. From the lawyer side, that is. However, a judgeship is something else again."

"Well, I've got to get to work," said the Steward.

"Righto, Ed. See you around, eh? And give my regards to your wife," he called, as the Steward moved away.

It was wonderful having so many friends, knowing so many people, the Old Man thought, as he walked outside. Dealing with judges, police, magistrates. All knew him; he knew all of them. Could get a man out of jail. Out of jail. Politics. Great game.

He was surprised to see the circling line of Negro pickets outside the main door of City Hall. When he came closer, he could see the signs they carried: they were from the Negro Action Society, and they called on the mayor and other officials to "end brutality" on the part of the police against Negroes. Hmmmm. The Old Man was about to enter the Hall when someone called his name. He turned; it was Michael.

"Well, well, Michael, still crusading, eh? What's this all about?"

"I'm so glad to see you," Michael said. "You're just the man we need. You know the mayor and the rest of those bigshots. Help us from the inside. Tell these bastards to make a public declaration condemning police violence. Get the mayor to enforce discipline among the police, and let them know that when they assault human beings for no reason at all, they'll be punished. . . ." The words tumbled out.

A policeman came over and nudged Michael with his night-stick. "Keep moving."

"Tell them," Michael shouted to the Old Man. "Use whatever influence you've got."

"Sure, sure," called the Old Man. He said hello to the elevator operator, mounted to the fourth floor, knocked on the door of Dave Clarris' office. The city chairman was in: a short, stout, balding man, dressed in a business suit and starched white collar. "Well, well, hello, Dave. Got your note." They shook hands, the Old Man sat down, took one of the cigars the city chairman proferred him: "Don't mind if I do, don't mind at all."

They talked for awhile about politics in general, the next election; the city chairman was certain that the Old Man would, as usual, carry his division for the party; the Old Man chuckled— that was a foregone conclusion, naturally. Then the city chairman got to the point.

"Is there any truth to the rumor that you and some of the other committeemen have gotten together and been talking about voting Mike Brophy out as ward leader at the next ward committee election?"

"Well . . . well, yes, as a matter of fact, though it wasn't supposed to be generally known. . . ."

"Why?"

"Well . . ." The Old Man was a bit embarrassed; ward committee elections were supposed to be the affairs of committeemen, not the city chairman. "Well, we don't like Mike very much, as a matter of fact, Dave. . . ."

"What's wrong with Mike?"

"Well, he's—well, for one thing, he's a dictator. He treats the rest of us like we were dogs, Dave."

"I know Mike's not a dictator. Oh, he sometimes is a little gruff, but—"

"A *little* gruff!"

"But he's not a dictator. What other reason do you have?"

"Well . . . well, you know I'm not one of these oversensitive people, Dave, but he's . . . well, he's prejudiced."

"Prejudiced?"

"Sure, Dave. Mind you, I'm not oversensitive, you know that—but he's prejudiced as hell, Dave."

The city chairman laughed. "Nonsense. Mike doesn't have a prejudiced bone in his body!"

"Well, Dave, I know what you mean; I know it's hard for you to believe it, but, well, after all, you know, I'm a Negro, and I can tell you for a fact, he thinks Negroes are nothing but dirt. Says it, too. Now, you can't have a man like that leader over a Negro ward. It doesn't make sense, does it?"

"Nonsense. Really, I thought you had more sense than that. Mike prejudiced? Why, Mike likes Negroes. I happen to know for a fact. Well, if that's all you've got against him, it's plain that there's no real reason to get rid of him. Now, I'm for Mike; he's been a good lieutenant, and I want him to stay in."

"Well, Dave . . ."—the Old Man floundered—"well, of course, if he's your boy, but . . . well, the boys might not listen."

"What do you mean?"

"Well, the boys are really against him. They might not vote for him."

"Of course they will. Tell them I want them. If any have any questions, tell them to come see me. I'll talk to them. Mike's a good man. Can't let him get thrown aside like an old sock. You must understand that."

"Sure . . . sure," said the Old Man.

"You know, there are certain things. I've got to be loyal to Mike."

"Well . . . but what about the rest of us, Dave?"

"You'd be making a great mistake. I want Mike in. Get the word to the rest of the committeemen, will you?"

"Okay, Dave."

"Good." The city chairman patted the Old Man's shoulder. "Be seeing you, huh? And keep up the good work in your division; you're one of our best committeemen."

"Okay, Dave."

The Old Man walked out. The elevator operator greeted him again. When the Old Man walked outside, Michael yelled to him again, then came over to talk to him.

"Did you talk to Clarris?"

"Huh? . . . Oh, yes, yes. I talked to him. I told him what you said."

"What did he say?"

"Well, he said he'd get right on it, Michael. Said he'd talk to the mayor and the director of public safety first thing in the morning, see what he could get them to do. Said he'd use all of his influence to correct the situation."

"Good!" said Michael.

The policeman was beside them again. "Keep moving," he said, "or I'll run you in!" Michael moved with the other pickets; the Old Man walked away.

15.

IT DID NOT SEEM TO MARGARET UNUSUAL WHEN THE PASTOR, AT Sunday services, after his sermon, announced the presence of a guest speaker—"a young man of courage and dignity, who has been doing a wonderful work"—but she was pleasantly surprised to see step up to the rostrum Michael, the brother of Philip and Claude, to whom she had, previously, paid scarcely any attention. As surprising—and as pleasant—was the fact that he cut a nice figure, standing there, in a dark suit, his hair neatly brushed, his deep sunken eyes bright and alive. He seemed fresh, vigorous, sure of himself. Strange, he had never impressed her in this way before.

He spoke—spoke of violence, of offenses against dark skins, of the insolence of the law, of the dignity of men; spoke—of a hidden history, of a courage over years, of a need now for the courage to fight back. The deep-set eyes gleamed; the right hand moved, in emphasis.

Is that Michael?

Margaret scarcely heard the words—their meanings, their import, their true eloquence. But she heard the energy behind the words, heard passion, fury, strength. Like the others, she leaned forward, listening; unlike the others, she did not feel the race's indignation, rage, the bugle's blare. She felt heat: rising slowly from her stomach, spreading, touching her surface, like a hand. Michael's voice rose and fell, this she heard, the sound. She moved her eyes into his eyes, sank into them, into him. *Is that Michael?* So that was Michael.

"Yes, yes," murmured the old woman beside her, as she had murmured during the sermon of the pastor. And, yes, yes, thought Margaret, looking at Michael, listening to the beating of her heart. And where had it been, all this time, this that she heard behind the words?

Afterwards, speech over, services over, Margaret made her way through the crowd toward the stage. She waited, hovered, on the edges of the circle which surrounded Michael. She watched him shake hands, looked into his heated eyes. She waited until the crowd had drifted away. Then she stepped up to Michael. "You were wonderful! Wonderful!"

He smiled with pleasure. He had not known she was there. Did she come always to this church? Was she walking in his direction toward home?

They walked down the street. He had been wonderful! wonderful! she said. The things he had revealed—she had not been aware of such injustices; were they really so numerous?

"Why, they've been all over the Negro papers," Michael exclaimed. "Haven't you read about them?"

Shyly, and a bit shamefacedly, Margaret confessed that she did not, too often, read the newspapers, and that, when she did, she was far too much inclined to turn immediately to the woman's page. The trouble was—she got very little from a simple reading of items in a newspaper; she needed, she said, to have things explained to her.

"Why don't you come to meetings of our society?"

"I'd love to."

They walked. Drawn out by her evident interest in, evident enthusiasm for the things his society was trying to do, Michael chattered more than was usual for him. He explained all of the activities of the society, drew anecdotes, painted pictures, poured out his enthusiasm. She listened, fascinated.

They were at her door. Margaret shook his hand, and said, "And when you have your next meeting, would you pick me up, and take me along?"

"I'd love to."

"And when will that be?"

"Tomorrow night."

"That's a date."

Michael turned and walked away. She was a marvelous girl; strange, he had never noticed how marvelous she was before.

16.

LIL FOUND A ROOM IN A ROOMING HOUSE ON BAINBRIDGE STREET. Nights, she worked at the *Showboat*; through the mornings she slept. She bought an electric stove and began to cook most of her lunches, and many of her dinners, in the room, on the two burners. She did not get in touch with her parents, gave her address only to her brother, Joe.

Her room was in the back of the house, her window looked

out over the dirt yards, and through the window Lil watched the weary strong brown women at their tubs of clothes; they seemed to wash clothes all day. The yards were filled with children.

Lil relaxed in the new peace of her lonely life and breathed deeply for the first time in a long while. Slim was in New York for awhile; Lil was glad, because she wanted to be alone. Afternoons, she loved to lie back on her bed, knees up, and read popular novels that carried her off into a world completely different from this one she knew. Nights, when she had finished work, and lay in darkness in the bed, she listened to the voices through the paper thin walls: men and women, married and unmarried, talking, making love, quarreling. Mostly quarreling. *They always quarrel.*

To get to work each evening, Lil had to run the gauntlet she knew so well, had always known: the gauntlet of men, standing idle outside of saloons, outside of pool rooms or on the corners. "Hey, baby, what you rushing for?" "Hey, baby, don't you wanta stop, talk to ole pops for a little while?" And when she ignored them: "Hincty bitch!" or "Stuckup whore!"

The men were always there, on the corners, in the doorways; and they were always there, in the night club, reaching for her as she served their tables, whispering propositions.

Sometimes, for no particular reason, she lay across her bed and cried. For no particular reason. But she felt better, invariably, afterwards.

One afternoon, there was a knock on her door. "Who is it?" Her brother, Joe, walked in.

"Lil, you got any dough?"

"What for?"

"I need to borrow some. A lot."

"What for?"

"I knocked up a chick."

Lil said, "Well, why don't you marry her? Who is she? Jane?"

114 ·

"Don't talk silly," her brother said. "Look, you gonna loan me the money? I got to get it somewhere."

"For an abortion!" she said with disgust. "Well, I don't have much."

"Loan me what you got. Got a hundred dollars?"

"Not for you, Joe; not for that."

"What you got?"

"Twenty."

Her brother whispered a curse. "Okay, gimme that." She gave him the money and he left.

Lil started fixing dinner. *Knocked up a chick!* Just like that! *Knocked up a chick!* Through the wall, Lil heard a couple quarreling.

17.

THE BLUES SINGER FELT TENSE, AS USUAL, WHEN THE *Showboat* closed, so she leaned over the piano and said to the rambling pianist, "Hell, let's go do something. I'm bored."

"It's Saturday night—Sunday morning, that is. The city's pretty well closed down."

"Hell, I know a place," she said. "Come on."

They dragged along the protesting bass player, who had a car. They drove into a tiny street on the South Side and the Blues Singer knocked on the door of a house. Someone peered out, opened the door, said, "Hi, baby," to the Blues Singer and led them in. They walked through the living room and dining room into the kitchen, then down stairs into the smoke-filled cellar, where a faint light shone and men and women stood talking or moved together dancing to the music of a phonograph. "Well, it ain't much," the Blues Singer admitted to her companions. Everybody there knew the Blues Singer, all shouted greetings. Along one wall, an improvised bar had been set up; over the windows, looking onto the street, had been nailed layers of blankets, to keep the activities of the cellar hidden from roaming police.

"Whatcha know, baby?" someone said to the Blues Singer.

"Not a goddamn thing, not a goddamn thing."

They moved over to the bar. "Gimme somethin'," the Blues Singer said.

"Not for me," said the bass player. "I been drinkin' too much all night. My old lady gonna kill me."

"Hell, what kinda talk is that? Be a man! take a drink!"

"My old lady'll—"

"Waiter! A drink for the man! Hell, can't let a wife run your life!"

They drank. The man operating the records was putting on the old favorites: "Summit Ridge Drive," "Traveling Light," "Sweet Slumber." Couples were dancing and kissing in the dim light. "Hell, it sure ain't much," mumbled the Blues Singer.

"Wanta dance?" asked the bass player.

"Well, ain't that a bitch? Where did you learn to dance?"

"Hell, I'm a great dancer!"

They danced. The Blues Singer felt tense; she felt as though she had been running for ages, and as though her legs, now, could not stop churning, though she wanted them to.

"Gimme another drink," she said to the bartender. *Hell, I got over this stuff when I was seventeen!* Seventeen. Long time ago. Legs churning.

"Wanta dance?" asked the pianist.

"Ain't that a bitch!" the Blues Singer said.

And then, fifteen minutes later: "Look," said the Blues Singer, "I'm bored stiff with this place. Ain't much, is it?"

"I know a place. A kind of ... funny place," said the bass player.

"Well, why the hell didn't you say so? Let's go."

They drove far over to the North Side. The bass player kept looking at his watch and frowning. "It's really late. I really oughtn't go, see, my old lady's gonna beat the hell outa—"

"Aw, shut up whinin'!" said the Blues Singer.

The sign, in front of the little club, said *The Ray Cee.* "Ain't that a bitch?" howled the Blues Singer. "It's kind of a funny place," said the bass player, hesitantly. "Well, let's have a look." They went in. The Blues Singer saw at once what the bass player had meant by "funny." The men in the place were dancing with men, and the women were dancing with women. "Oh, one of *those!*" said the Blues Singer.

"See, I tole you—"

"Well, let's grab a seat, see what these folks is puttin' down."

They sat at the bar. The club was rather elegant, seats done in red plush, walls upholstered, lights cleverly arranged so that bulbs were hidden and only their glow could be seen. The Blues Singer looked at the passionate couples around the room, then looked at the bass player with a slight smile. She looked at the bass player, then winked at the pianist, then looked at the bass player again. The bass player became wary.

"Now, look here, baby, don't start no crap now," he said pleadingly.

" 'Course not, sugar," said the Blues Singer, winking at the pianist, "only thing, I was just wondering . . . how come *you* knew about this place?"

"Now, see there, baby, I tole you don't start no stuff. Don't start no signifying."

"Well, how come, buddy?"

"Well, somebody brought me here once, that's the honest truth, I swear it is. I come here once with a musician to *watch,* see?"

The Blues Singer winked again at the pianist. "I'll bet. And you never came back by yourself."

"Naw, I never come back, not till tonight."

"Well, you sure found the place mighty easy for somebody who was *brought* here just once."

"I just got a good sense of direction, that's all, baby."

"Heh, heh. Yeah." She winked at the pianist. "Think we got to pass the word around the *Showboat* about our boy here? Think we gotta hep the people that our boy has started to get a little funny?"

"Got to do it," said the pianist.

"Now, see there, I tole you, don't *signify!*"

"Which one of these real cute little boys is yours?"

The bass player's face was pained. "See there, see there, I tole you."

The Blues Singer watched the dancing couples. *Poor dumb bastards.* She noticed suddenly that a very pretty girl, dressed daintily and with a sweet face, was staring at her and smiling from her table in a corner. *What the hell!* The Blues Singer looked away. After awhile, she looked back toward the corner again. The sweet girl was still staring at her and smiling sweetly. *What the hell!* The Blues Singer wanted to strike the sweet face, wanted to hurt her. *Why do you want to hurt her? Look out, baby, that shit's dangerous!*

"Let's leave," said the Blues Singer.

"Good," said the bass player, "I got to get home, my ole lady'll—"

"Home hell!" said the Blues Singer. As they walked out, the Blues Singer saw the sweet girl still looking at her, following her with her eyes.

"You look jittery," the pianist said.

"I ain't jittery worth a damn!" snapped the Blues Singer. Then she laughed. "It's our boy here who's jittery."

"Aw, cut it out," whined the bass player.

They climbed in the car. The Blues Singer said, "Let's go over to New York."

"What!" shrieked the bass player.

"I'm for it," said the pianist.

"Aw, now look," said the bass player, "I got to get home. *You* two go to New York."

"Hell, you got to drive us, baby."

"Aw, I got to get home. My ole lady'll kill me sure!"

"She'll kill you for sure if we tell her how you been out pattin' young boys. Ain't that a bitch?"

"Aw, cut it out."

"Let's go. It's that way to the New York highway."

Making low, complaining noises, the bass player drove in the direction indicated. He seemed close to tears. "My ole lady gonna *kill* me!"

A faint suggestion of dawn lay on the horizon when they arrived in New York. "All right," said the resigned bass player, "where to?"

"You know the *Disc Club?*"

"Yeah."

"Let's hit it for a minute."

The Blues Singer had a key, and they went into the *Disc Club*. This was a small, two-room affair: in one room was the bar and the glass case containing photographs of famous members of the club, most of them jazz musicians; the second room contained tables, each with a burning candle on top, and a space for dancing. Music was piped into both rooms from a hidden phonograph. There were not many people, the Blues Singer spoke briefly to those who were there, and the bass player yawned and said, "Well, what shall we do now, dance?" "Don't be such a sourface!" growled the Blues Singer. "Let's sit down."

Their faces shone in the candle light. No one was dancing, and most of the tables were empty at this hour; couples were kissing at the few tables that were occupied. "Goddamn!" said the bass player, "and I'm gonna catch hell from my old lady just for *this!*"

"Got an idea," said the Blues Singer. "Let's go wake up Kate Summerfield."

"She's just about got to bed," said the pianist.

"Good. Let's get a bottle of whiskey and wake her right up."

"Suppose she's got a man with her?" said the bass player.

"Little Lord Fauntleroy in person! Hell, we'll wake him up too, junior!"

"But, if she's got a man, they might not be sleeping. They might be—"

"Oh, shut up!"

The Blues Singer bought a bottle of Old Overholt at the bar and they climbed into the automobile. Segments of New York were waking up; there were a number of cars now on the street. "She lives on Fifty-Seventh Street." Kate Summerfield was one of the country's most famous night club singers. When their car pulled up in front of Kate's apartment building, the Blues Singer was surprised to see people going in and coming out. They got into the elevator with some other people and said, "Fifth floor." "I know," said the operator.

"Are you going to the party, too?" a man asked them.

"What party?"

"Oh, I thought you were going to the party."

"What party?"

"Kate Summerfield's."

"Well, I'll be goddamned!" said the Blues Singer, and slapped the bass player on the shoulder. "Wake up, Lord Fauntleroy, we'll have a good time after all!"

Kate Summerfield said, at the door, "Baby!" and threw her arms around the Blues Singer. "All right, all right!" said the Blues Singer gruffly. "None of that! You ever meet these two bastards?" She introduced the pianist and the bass player. "Lord Fauntleroy, here, thought you might have been layin' up with a man."

"What an outrageous thought!" Kate said.

It was a noisy musicians' party; whiskey, gin and champagne were everywhere; the people were white and Negro, mostly musicians, a few actresses and emcees, all shouting to each other, a few dancing, some others making martinis at the bar. The Blues Singer knew nearly all of them. "Who's got a weed?" she asked. Somebody offered her a Chesterfield. "Christ!" she said, "what a bunch of goddamn shmoos!"

"So, what have you been doing with yourself, dear?" asked the directress of an all-girl orchestra.

"Minding my own business. What about you?"

"Oh, I've been working."

"What's his name?"

The directress' laugh had murder in it. The Blues Singer moved over to a famous drummer and said, "Hank, listen, you must have a weed. I mean a *real* one!" The drummer held up his palms and shook his head. "Goddamn! What's the world coming to!" The Blues Singer cornered a trumpeter. He led her into a bedroom, and gave her a marihuana cigarette. "Now, *there's* a man!" said the Blues Singer. "Thanks, baby."

"Don't mention it."

Alone, in the room, the Blues Singer smoked the cigarette. The world slowed down, the world slowed down. She felt very nervous and wanted suddenly to cry. *Ain't that a bitch!* She wanted suddenly to lie down across the bed in peace and cry. *Ain't that a bitch!* She went out into the main room again, sat down in a corner, and listened to the party's roar. "Anything wrong?" the pianist asked. "Hell, no. Where's our boy?" The pianist laughed. "He's in the other room, calling his wife, wants to explain why he isn't home." The Blues Singer chuckled. "He's gonna catch hell. Good old Lord Fauntleroy." Then the pianist was gone. The Blues Singer peered through the smoke and saw him dancing. She listened to the party's roar.

"Breakfast!" shouted a young saxophonist, coming in from outside with a huge bag of food. "Eggs and bacon! On the hoof!"

Three hours had passed, the morning had really arrived, and the Blues Singer roused herself to say, "Don't tell me Kate's gonna do the cooking!"

"Hell no!" shouted Kate, from a far corner of the room.

"*I* am cooking it!" said the saxophonist.

"Jesus!" said the Blues Singer.

The saxophonist scrambled the eggs, in huge batches, and people came in with plates to be served. The bacon was cooked in with the eggs. Two percolators, plus a can of Nescafe, supplied the coffee.

The Blues Singer, chewing, calling to the bass player, "Hey, sourface, did your wife forgive you for being a bad boy?"

"I didn't get no answer," said the bass player, with a long face. "That man wouldn't let her out of bed!"

"Oh, she wouldn't do anything like that."

The Blues Singer howled. "Ain't that a bitch!" She howled.

"Did anybody sleep last night?" asked an arranger.

"Don't go prying into my love life," said a torch singer.

Somebody said, "Where Madge Ellis?"

"In Europe, on tour."

And somebody said, "That's for me! Mixture of business and pleasure. Oh for the life of a celebrity!"

And somebody said, "Did you say celibacy?"

And somebody said, "*Sell*-a-bitty!"

"That's wicked!" somebody said.

The bellboy walked in with more whiskey. "Did we make much noise last night?" Kate asked. "Oh, no, Miss Summerfield." "You're a goddamn liar and here's five bucks." The Blues Singer opened the first bottle and poured herself a glass. By noon they were all very high again. "Well," said Kate, "when the hell are you people going to let me get some sleep?" "To hell with you and your sleep," said the Blues Singer, "*I* ain't sleeping, am I?" "It shows under your eyes, deary," finally got in the directress of the all-girl orchestra. "It shows under your tits, baby!" answered the Blues Singer. By two o'clock, the new batch of whiskey was gone. By three, someone said, "Let's go *do* something!" "I know," said the directress of the all-girl orchestra, "let's go for a ride in the park!" So they all went downstairs and piled into their cars.

It was a beautiful, clear, cool Sunday. "Isn't it *beautiful!*" cried the directress of the all-girl orchestra. "Wish I had a weed," said the Blues Singer. They were sitting on the grass. "You know it's *cold* out here!" said Kate. "Let's go to a movie," somebody said. "There's a jam session in Harlem. We could go there." "How about just going for a walk for a change?" "My old lady," said the bass player, "has probably called in the cops!" They walked for awhile. They were all rather drunk. They came across a pavillion. "What we need," said somebody, "is some coffee." They sat outside in the pale sun and drank the coffee and ate small cakes. They walked back to the cars; the Blues Singer felt like part of a great herd of cattle moving. They were in front of the apartment building. "Upsy daisy!" they said to the elevator operator. "Ohhhh!" moaned Kate, at first sight of the living room: shambles: bottles and glasses, broken and unbroken, ashes piled high in trays and overflowing onto tables, chairs and the floor, records thrown about on hassocks and chairs, carpets rumpled, beds crumpled, dishes everywhere with crushed out cigarettes in the hardened remnants of scrambled eggs. "Could we send for some chorus girls and get up a nude line?" asked the arranger. "Well, I like *that!*" exclaimed the directress of the all-girl orchestra. "You'd love to get naked, wouldn't you?" said the Blues Singer, and laughed wickedly. "Supper time!" someone shouted at seven-thirty. They went to a little Italian restaurant in the Village. "Hey! where's the goddamn Chianti?" "Let *me* draw off the oil!" cried the directress of the all-girl orchestra. "And afterwards," the trumpeter said, "we can all drop over to the *Baby Grand* and hear Wynonie Harris." The *Baby Grand* was beginning to be crowded. "Whisky, whisky, whisky, naturally!" they told the waiter.

Wynonie Harris was on stage. "*Good morning judge. . . .*" The audience howled. The shake dancer had three encores. "Chicken and waffles?" They sat at *Wells,* eating the chicken and waffles, with the music of the organ in the background. "When," asked the bass player, "are we going home?" "No needa hurrying to your funeral," laughed the Blues Singer. But after the fourth Scotch, she relented. "Well, we got to go. So long." "So long, baby." "See you, sugar." "So long."

Night air and the sound of a motor; for two hours. "There they are," said the pianist. Lights of the city. And when they were in the city, the Blues Singer said, "Let me off here."

"Ain't you going on home, get some sleep?"

"No. Let me off here. Good night, and thanks."

Puzzled, they drove off. The Blues Singer looked up at the cold sky. She got on the subway, rode several stations, got off again. She was nervous. She did not really believe, as she went into the *Ray Cee* again, that the sweet girl would be there, for the second night in a row. But the sweet girl was there, at her same corner table. She smiled at the Blues Singer, but the Blues Singer looked away, walked directly to the bar. "Scotch," she told the bartender. She was not quite sure just why she had come back here. "Hello." The sweet girl was beside her, at the bar. Well, she had known that, hadn't she?

"Hi," said the Blues Singer. She drank part of her Scotch. "What are you drinking?"

"Scotch." The Blues Singer ordered it. She felt very embarrassed but she had known she would. The drinking helped. "There's another room, in back," the sweet girl said sweetly. "It's much more cozy. Could we go there?"

The Blues Singer followed her into the second room. The room was small with very low lights, and the two-person sofas were arranged behind posts and in coves so that each was in semiprivacy. There were small tables in front of each sofa, on which the bartender put their drinks. They sat down. "It's nice here, don't you think?" the sweet girl asked. "Yeah," said the Blues Singer.

The sweet girl was extremely pretty with soft eyes, hair like a halo, and hands delicately tapered to immaculate nails. Her fingers caressed her glass. Her voice was an intense whisper.

"What . . . do you do here?" the Blues Singer asked. She was surprised by the hoarseness of her voice.

The sweet girl smiled. "Mostly, I think, I've been waiting."

"Waiting . . . ?"

"For . . . someone. For you, I think."

Her hand touched the Blues Singer's arm. The Blues Singer felt ridiculous. The girl said softly, "You came back for me, didn't you?"

"Yes."

"I . . . knew you would."

The Blues Singer felt a chill—whether of pleasure or pain, she did not know. She was trying as hard as she could to be casual; but she was nervous and afraid this girl could see it. Well, what did one do next. "You're shy," the sweet girl said, and laughed a tinkling laugh of delight. She put her head on the Blues Singer's shoulder; the Blues Singer could smell the perfume of her hair. The girl's body was soft, pretty. The Blues Singer's hand found the arm of the girl; she held the arm tight and then, in a trance, bent down her head and kissed the girl on the mouth. The sweet girl nearly swooned. The Blues Singer shook herself and trembled violently.

"You're wonderful . . ." the sweet girl was whispering, with her eyes closed, but the Blues Singer suddenly stood up. The girl's eyes opened. "What's wrong?" The Blues Singer trembled; shame, fear, sadness shook her. "What's wrong?"

"Nothing," the Blues Singer said, hoarsely. "I'm . . . I'm sorry, baby. I'm going home."

The girl leaped to her feet. "But *why*, darling? Oh, you can't

mean it! You can't leave me ... not like this! I ... I *love* you!"
Tears stood in the sweet girl's eyes.

"I'm sorry, baby. I'm sorry. I've got to go!"

She went out of the room, the sweet girl following her, pleading, crying. People stared at them. *Screw 'em!* the Blues Singer told herself furiously. She was outside. The sweet girl was at her side, weeping, begging an explanation. The Blues Singer shouted, "Get the hell out of here! Get out!" The girl stood sobbing. The Blues Singer walked off. The girl stood sobbing. The Blues Singer walked down into the subway. She caught a train going toward home.

She was still trembling when she got out at her stop and walked along South Street toward her room. She was trembling as she mounted the stairs and stood at her door and took the key from her bag. She opened the door. She stood there in the doorway, looking straight ahead of her. There it was again, inevitably, the room. There it was again. There it was.

18.

THEY WERE GOING, THE FOUR OF THEM, TO SEE A PLAY, AND IT had been Suzette's suggestion that they stop, en route, at a restaurant, rather than bother to have dinner at home. They were all in high spirits: Claude had been working hard, over some old articles, preparatory to their being published as a book; Kristin had been busy with rehearsals for a new recital, to be held within a few weeks in a large hall; and Dan and Suzette were their usual selves—talkative (Dan doing most of the talking) and at peace pretty much, with the world.

The play was to begin at eight-thirty, so they went to an automat, where they could be served quickly, rather than to a more leisurely restaurant. Dan, lanky, feet stretched out under the table, held forth. "You know, it hurts my heart to eat a meal in a hurry any more. Ever since I was over there in France, and saw the way the workers got two hours for lunch, and the way they took three or four hours to eat a dinner, what with the soups and main dishes and cheeses and desserts and coffee and wines and *digestifs*—well, that just about spoiled me, see? Why, man, meals are not for eating, you know that? Know what meals are? Meals are excuses for people to get together and talk!"

Suzette said, "Danneeee eees truly French now." She beamed with pride.

"The French believe," said Dan, "that there are only three fit things in life: eating, drinking, and making love. At the dinner hour, they're doing all three!"

"Eeeee eees truly French now," Suzette beamed.

People were looking at them: eyes from other tables. They were all used to that by now, and paid no attention to it.

"You're mighty quiet, ace," Dan said to Claude.

"Am I?" Claude said, with a start.

"I got a feeling, old man, you been working too hard. This book and all that stuff. You don't take life easy enough, don't relax enough, way I see it. Don't work so hard, and when you leave it, don't think about your work."

"Eeee eees truly French," said Suzette.

Claude laughed. "No, I haven't been working too hard. Was I silent? Well, it's just because ... I was away, in my thoughts, I suppose." With his fork he made a gesture toward the food.

This recent restlessness. With his wife, he was very happy. But he read, in the newspaper, of things—of violence, of Michael's new society, of picket lines and stirrings. And he looked at himself, what he was doing—writing articles from afar! It did not seem to be enough. He wanted no more, he abhorred any more!—but what he was doing did not seem to be enough.

Kristin's bright eyes were darting from table to table. With so many people in the restaurant, she was having a field day, looking at the faces. "Look!" she would cry to Claude. "That old woman! Isn't she beautiful?" Or she watched with fascination the carver at the counter wield his knife. At one point she looked suddenly at Claude, squeezed his arm, and asked, "Did I ever tell you?"

"Tell me what?"

"That I love you."

"Never." He laughed; but he returned the pressure on her arm.

He would never cease to marvel about Kristin, Claude thought. Where did she come from, this clean, pure, in many ways child-like, woman with her soaring spirit? Where was the man who had never held an ideal of a woman? And how many had been, like him, so completely satisfied? He voiced a silent prayer to whatever gods there were for the accident that had brought them together.

There were loud shouts and laughter. A group of young men, seven of them, fresh, as their conversation showed, from a base ball game, came straggling through the restaurant looking for a table. They all wore jackets and dungarees; several wore baseball caps, turned with the peaks behind. Claude was lifting a glass of water when he heard one of the men, passing the table, shout to the others, "Well, will you look at these goddamn niggers!"

Claude slammed his glass to the table and said to Dan, "What did he say?"

"Take it easy, he's just stupid," Dan cautioned.

"*What* did he say?" Claude rose in fury to his feet. "You. What did you just say?"

The man looked at Claude. He was a big man. The entire restaurant had gone suddenly silent; the man was standing close to Claude and the others were some distance away, watching. There was the brief, fleeting impression that the man did not want to pursue the point, that he wanted no trouble, but everyone was watching and it was too late.

The man said, "I said, 'Will you look at these goddamn—"

Claude had never struck a man so hard. All the strength of his body and all of his anger were thrown against the man's face. The man fell to the floor, instantly unconscious.

There was a murmur in the restaurant, but no one moved. Then the man's friends advanced menacingly. "Well, now look here—!"

"Look what!"

"Why, you black sonofabitch, we'll tear you apart!"

Dan was instantly to his feet and around the table beside Claude. Kristin and Suzette stared in fear. There were three Negroes seated at a nearby table. Claude said to them sharply: "You have black faces. You heard what these men said. Stand up!"

The Negroes were startled; they stared at Claude, hesitantly. Finally, two of them stood up.

Claude said in fury to the third: *"Stand up!"*

The Negro's face mirrored a struggle between shame and fear. He stood up.

There was tension in the room. Claude said, "Now, by God, we'll see some bloodshed this evening! Come closer!"

In the moment's hesitation, Claude said again, "Come closer! Why don't you move? Come!"

One of the men, who had been reluctant from the first, said, "Aw, what the hell."

The one who had spoken before said, "Let's beat the shit outa them!"

"Aw, what the hell, Jack was in the wrong. What the hell. Forget it, no needa starting a riot." He bent down to help to his feet the man whom Claude had struck. Most of the group agreed, with varying degrees of willingness, with the peacemaker.

The belligerent one said angrily to Claude, as they turned to walk off, "You don't know how lucky you are, brother!"

Claude stood still a moment. He turned to the Negroes who

had risen and addressed the reluctant one. "Learn how to die! The pain is quickly over!"

A man, the manager, walked over to Claude. "Please, I don't want to be rude, but your presence here might cause more trouble. The girls—the ladies—you know. Would you mind leaving?"

"Leave? There'll be no leaving. I have a dinner to finish." He sat down to eat it. Kristin and Dan were silent; Suzette exclaimed, "They were horreeeble!"

Through the meal, and through the concert that followed, none of them talked about the incident. But that evening, when Claude and Kristin dropped their friends at the door of their home, Dan said to Claude, "You know, ace, you can't go around losing your temper everytime something like that happens. If you do, you'll be mad all the time. Wisdom is the better part of valor, as the man said."

Claude said, "Damn wisdom! Choose pride instead!"

Dan looked at him for a moment, shaking his head. Then he grinned and swung a friendly fist to Claude's shoulder. "Anyway, old man, it was a great right cross!"

19.

THE MEN STARED AT LIL AS SHE WENT IN AND OUT OF THE ROOMing house: men on the streets, in the stores, in the halls. Eyes always followed her; she was always conscious of them: those and the whistles. And the remarks. "Baby." Her name.

The color of a rooming house was gray. It was not warm, nor bright, and in the halls the half-light hung like an indecision between day and night, between life and death. The in-between, the shadow world: it was what a rooming house was, and what its inhabitants were: people settled and yet unsettled, intimate neighbors but not yet friends.

Over them ruled the landlady: a shadowy, small-faced, peering woman who spoke curtly, rarely smiled. Mrs. Lucas. Mrs. Lucas collected the rent. Most of the tenants tried very hard always to pay Mrs. Lucas on time.

"Can I come in for a moment?" Mrs. Lucas asked, frowning.

"Oh, please do," said Lil. She was a bit nervous; she did not know what wrong she had done.

Mrs. Lucas' eyes looked quickly around the room, to see what changes Lil might have made. She sat down. "No, thanks," she said, without smiling, when Lil offered her coffee. "Generally," she said, "I don't allow single girls in my establishment. It don't look good. But you look all right." She looked at Lil closely. "I notice you always go out at night, and you're home all day. You ain't in business, are you?"

"Business?"

"You know what I mean." Her squinting eyes fixed Lil.

Lil looked at her coldly. "No."

"Well, I just have to be sure, you see, don't get hot because I asked you." Her eyes squinted at a spot on the floor, where Lil had spilled some coffee. "Saw a man come up the other afternoon. That your steady boyfriend?"

"That was my brother."

Mrs. Lucas looked at Lil incredulously. "Oh, yes. Yes."

Worlds which passed in shadowy hallways. A certain man, slightly over thirty, whose clothes hung on him like rags on a scarecrow, whose eyes were distant and burning with dedication. Never smiled, never spoke; but, one day, as Lil passed his door, he said, "Hello." He spoke softly and politely.

Lil looked at him. "Hello," she said.

She was walking away, but he said hastily, "Please, I . . . I don't talk to anyone else here. But I've noticed you." He was standing in the door of his room, wearing a frayed shirt into which the bones of his body jutted. "Sometimes I feel like"—he shrugged—"talking to somebody. I'm an artist." He made a gesture over his shoulder; Lil could see the canvases around the room. "Like to take a look?"

Strange paintings: elongated faces, twisted arms, lopsided houses. "I . . . hardly ever go out. I see you here frequently during the day. Sometimes, I feel like talking to someone."

Essentially, he was a shy man. Lil enjoyed listening to him in the afternoons; there was great fervor in his voice. "I want to be a great artist! That's what counts. They're nonsense, all these ordinary jobs. For ordinary people. I want to be a great painter!"

Lawrence—his name—licked his lips and stared at her through the burning, hungry eyes. "Do you think I'll be a great painter?"

"Me? I . . . how can I know? I don't know anything about painting."

"But you can *feel!* Look at them! Don't you *feel* something about them?"

"I . . . Yes, I . . . feel something."

"I'll be a great painter! A great painter!" He licked his lips.

Early evening was a gratuitous time of day. Sometimes, Lil invited the painter in for dinner. "You're too kind!" He was a very hungry man. "You're a wonderful woman! I knew it when I first saw you; it's why I spoke."

Or sometimes, on her evening off, Lil invited him in for coffee.

He told her his life story—how brutal his early life had been, how he had been mocked at school, how his parents had not understood him—"all they could think about was money! Money! Pah!"—how he had been thrown out of the art school he had attended. He burned his eyes into a distant wall, chin jutting out defiantly: "They don't know!" he whispered passionately, "but they'll see!" He seized Lil's arm. "But you . . . *you* believe in me, don't you?"

Lil nodded. He released her arm and stared back into the wall.

When finally, hesitantly, the painter made his first love advance, Lil told him, very gently, no. He sat still for a moment; obviously, he was embarrassed. "I'm sorry. I hope this won't change . . . anything."

"No."

A cold night, or rather morning. Lil came in from work rubbing her hands; quickly she put on a pot of water for coffee, then lay back, exhausted, on the bed. She said, "Who is it?" sitting up, surprised, when the knock sounded at the door.

The knob turned; the painter walked in. He had never before come so late without an invitation. It was a moment before Lil realized that he was drunk.

"Yes?"

He stood in the door, looking at her. "Lil . . ." Tears were streaming down his face.

Lil was frightened by the tears. "What is it?"

"Lil! Lil! Lil! I love you!"

She could only stare. The painter stumbled toward her, arms outstretched, sobbing, "Lil! Lil! I love you!" He seized her. "Lil, I love you!"

"Lawrence! Stop it!"

She did not want to make noise. The man's sobbing frightened her. He pressed her back on the bed, sobbing, crying, "I love you, I love you!" His hands were caressing her body. "Lawrence! Get out!" Pity left her; she was angry now. The man pressed on her, sobbing, crying his love. "Get out! Get out!" But there was no reaching him by voice, now. The odor of whiskey assailed her; memory, sharp, bitter, hate-filled came rushing like blood to her head. With all her strength she struck and kicked; her teeth sank into his face. He was off of her, tumbled to the floor. Eyes seared with tears, Lil hardly saw the man at all as she lifted ashtrays, books, and dishes from the table and hurled them at the painter. "Get out! Get out! Get out!" She lifted the pot of hissing water from the stove, about to hurl it, but the man had scrambled to his feet.

"Lil, please—"

"Get out! I'll kill you!"

The painter was gone. Lil slammed the door and fell across the bed, pounding her fists into the mattress.

When, two days later, Slim came back to the city from New York and looked for Lil at the *Showboat*, the manager told him, "Lil quit."

"*What?* Why?"

The manager shrugged.

Slim went to the rooming house. Lil called, "Come in," when he knocked and told her it was he. She was standing in front of a mirror. She was trying on a new, sleek dress which fitted her body like a glove. Slim had never seen her in such a dress before.

"Baby! Hell, no man'll be able to keep his eyes off of you!"

He circled her waist with his arms. Lil looked in the mirror at the dress; it brought out every line of her beautiful body. When Slim moved away, to sit down, she fixed her hair, newly done, so that it was back off the ears, saucily. She applied lipstick, rouge, darkened her eyelashes with mascara. Slim stared at her. "Baby, you look devastating!" But he was a bit worried. He had never seen her like this before.

"What's it all about, baby?"

"What?"

"Well, for one thing, quitting your job."

"I was tired."

Slim looked at her. What was this? "I see. And all this—this new sex appeal. What brought that on?"

Lil turned and looked at him. "Slim, I'll talk to you straight. It's got to be over between you and me."

"But why?"

"It's just got to be. Don't ask me why. It's got to be."

"Baby . . . now, look, this is Slim. I love you. You can't just chuck the whole thing and not give me a reason."

"That's what I'm doing, Slim."

He stared at her. His pride was in conflict with his love for her now. His inclination was simply to leave; he was not a man for begging. But there had been months between them. . . .

"Lil, you're makin' a great mistake."

"Then let me make it, Slim."

He stood up. He started to say something else, changed his mind, walked to the door, said, "So long, Lil," and went out.

20.

IT WAS EIGHT O'CLOCK IN THE EVENING WHEN THE KNOCK CAME at the door. Claude was searching for something in the bedroom. Kristin opened the door, and Claude heard her say, "Oh. Yes?"

"We're from the fifth precinct, lady. Sorry to disturb you, but we got reports from the neighbors that a nigger's been seen regularly roaming around here, and he seems to be interested in this place of yours. We just want to know if he's been bothering you, or if you've been having any trouble."

"What!"

"We just want to know if you've had any trouble. The neighbors figure he's out either for robbery or rape, or maybe both."

"What! What! What!"

"Well, you don't have to be too scared, lady. We know how it is, but we're gonna keep a lookout, and if the nigger gets through us and molests you, you just give a sharp yell and we'll be here before he can do any damage."

Claude stepped out of the bedroom into the living room. The policemen started; their eyes widened; one of them drew his pistol. Claude stared his hatred of them.

"What the—"

"What's he doing here?" one of the policemen asked Kristin.

"He's my *husband!*"

"Your *what!*"

"My husband! My husband! My husband! My husband! My husband! "Get *out!* Get *out!*" She was screaming hysterically.

Claude was trembling with anger.

"Get out," Claude said.

The policemen stared from one to the other of them. "Well, I'll be—" They stared in a daze. Finally, they walked out, cursing.

Kristin covered her face with her hands. Her body shook with sobs.

Claude closed his eyes tight. He went back into the bedroom.

Book Three:

FESTIVAL

1.

WITH SPRING FESTIVAL TIME CAME TO SOUTH STREET: THREE DAYS
of merriment, of celebration; three days of dancing and singing,
eating and drinking, parades, speeches and meetings. Festival
was the welcoming of spring to the neighborhood, a time when
most of the stores on South Street closed and the street was roped
off for several blocks and chairs and benches were placed along
the sidewalks. No one in the neighborhood knew exactly when,
or under what conditions, the custom of having a festival had
originated, although, each year, at Festival time, the speakers
talked of "this tradition handed down from the days of our slave
forefathers"; nonetheless, the people, who had grown up with
the yearly celebration, had come to expect and accept it as much
as they expected a turkey dinner on Thanksgiving or an evergreen
tree on Christmas.

Festival was always celebrated on a week-end—the first week-
end after the beginning of spring, provided the weather were
good—so that as many people as possible would be off work and
able to come. For weeks in advance the Negro newspapers would
herald the event; local shopkeepers would run "greeting" advertisements in the papers. Vendors, unseen through most of the
year, would appear suddenly with specialties for the occasion;
bars spruced up, doubled their orders of whiskeys and other
drinks. Up and down the length of South Street, banners would
stream from storefronts.

2.

THAT FRIDAY AFTERNOON OF THE BEGINNING OF FESTIVAL THIS
year, the early spring sun shone down as the long column of
brass bands, representing the Elks, various lodges and sundry
churches, streamed through the Negro neighborhood. The marchers wore, for the most part, incredible uniforms—gold braid
abounded, there were white bands around most hats, and the
predominant colors were purple and red. Quick-stepping, proud,
heads thrown back, they marched through the whole of the South
Side, led by the cocky, bare-legged, white-booted majorettes.
Youngsters carried floats. Discords sounded from the brass.
Many of the marchers were out of step. But there was a light
in the eyes of those who marched and those who watched—
watched leaning from upstairs windows, crowded front steps,
crowded benches, or pressing against the out-holding ropes. Festival, traditionally, was a time of joy, a time for the forgetting
of troubles.

The long line of marchers halted along the length of South
Street, where the brass bands, each in turn, went through their
favorite numbers, to the cheers of the onlookers. On a platform,
near Broad Street, sat the Mayor, the head of the Elks, the
Director of Public Safety, and some ministers of Negro churches.
The Old Man also sat on the platform. As each band played,
these "judges" marked their cards. When all bands had played,
the Old Man rose, coughed, and made a long and eloquent speech,
praising all of the bands and marchers, saluting the beginning
of Festival, and then, finally, announcing the name of the band
which, "in the opinion of these honored and impartial judges,"
merited first prize. Another cheer went up, mingled with some

moans, when the winner was announced. The Old Man held up his hands for silence, then, after introducing all of the officials seated on the platform, presented the next speaker, the Grand Exalted Ruler of the local chapter of the Negro Elks, who, after a long speech, presented the Director of Public Safety, who, after a long speech, presented the Mayor, who, in a long speech, opened, officially, the annual Festival.

There was real cheering then, and one of the brass bands struck a tune while the others disbanded for awhile and the people poured under the ropes and into the street for dancing. The people danced all afternoon. When the first band was tired, another rose to take its place; then another, in its turn, while those not playing either watched, danced, or went into the bars for quick drinks and talking and laughter.

But the evening was the real beginning of Festival.

3.

IN THE EVENING THE FISHFRY WAGONS CAME OUT—STRANGE looking affairs, portable stoves, equipped with deep fat compartments in which breaded trout and bass, fresh-caught, were dipped and fried, then tossed onto oil paper and handed over to the people who crowded around and tossed coins into the tin box. Some wagons sold fruits of all kinds; others nuts, candies, ice creams, popcorn, and melons; some sold crisp, still-steaming French-fried potatoes; others hamburgers or hotdogs; others ice-cold cans of beer. The brass bands were gone now; in their place, on the raised, big platform, was a famous dance band (for the other nights there would be other bands, which accepted no money for playing during Festival, demanded only their expenses in traveling to and from the city). The young jitterbugs were out, and in their glory; the girls wore short skirts and white shoes, the boys box coats and wide-collar sport shirts. Skirts, legs, arms—these flew as saxophonists and trumpeters and drummer made "crazy riffs"; and girls, too, flew—over the heads and shoulders of boys who felt the music, knew it in their bones, exploded mixed emotions in the dance. Between numbers, exhilarated and warm, the dancers crowded around the refrigerator wagons to catch their breath, and drink deeply of the steaming-cold beer, from cans just double-opened.

There was other music, too—for the older people. The band would shift, from time to time, into sentimental slow numbers, a vocalist would moan popular ballads, and the dancers shuffled feet slowly on the asphalt, men who had not danced in months smiling down upon women who had not danced in months— porters, handymen, waiters, mechanics, truck drivers, machinists, welders, sweepers—with wives or girlfriends.

About ten o'clock, the show began. While the band took its turn at beer, and the dancers rested, and the spectators sat on the benches or crowded in the street or leaned out of windows or stood on raised steps, Mrs. Aline Purnell led the choir of the First Baptist Church in a group of hymns. After a short break, members of the Sydney Beckett dance group, specialists in African rhythms, mounted the platform under the footlights, greased, seminude bodies shining, and danced to the beat of an African drummer. Eddie Saxon, age seventeen, a member of the junior Elks and one of the candidates for the Elocution Prize (which carried a scholarship to a leading university) stood up and recited some of the poems of Paul Lawrence Dunbar, Claude MacKay, Langston Hughes, and Countee Cullen. Time for dancing again. The band remounted the platform, and with them, this time, came the Blues Singer.

They listened, then, the audience—listened, even the young-sters, as they shuffle-danced to the music which was the soul-beat of a people:

dancing, and the old people and the young, with cold beer running down their throats, and the knowledge of the neighborhood which was the world and the people who were the universe, and fish burning tongue, and ice cream cold, and Holiday.

4.

SLIM BROUGHT HIS YOUNG NEPHEW, JOE, TO THE FESTIVAL. "THIS is great stuff; you'll have a great time!" Slim said. Little Joe shrugged. "This ain't the first time I ever been to nothin', Uncle Slim." Slim looked at him. "Hmmm. Well, no, I guess not."

The sweating band was playing a very hot jazz number. Joe stood near the curb, hands in pockets, looking at the dancers. From time to time, he shook his head, rather sadly.

"What's wrong?" Slim asked.

"Nothin'!" Joe shook his head again, looking at the dancers.

When the band shifted to something slow—a fox trot—Slim walked over to a waitress from the *Postal Card* and asked her if she wanted to dance. They moved out into the street and danced slowly, the two-step. Slim whispered something in the girl's ear, then looked over her shoulder to see Joe watching him; hands in pockets, his nephew was shaking his head in the same sad way. "What's the matter, sport?" Slim called. Joe just shook his head and said nothing.

After the dance, Slim walked over to Joe. "What're you shaking your head about, so much?"

"Uncle Slim, you're a nice guy and all that, but you sure can't dance."

"Can't dance? Sure I can dance!"

Little Joe shook his head sadly. "You can't dance, Uncle Slim. None of these cats know how to dance. You're all old-fashioned, know what I mean?" He shook his head sadly; of the mingled pity and disgust which his gesture conveyed, pity was probably uppermost.

Slim looked at Joe with one eye closed. "Hey, sport, what do you know about dancing?"

"Me? Hell, I'm a *cat*, Uncle Slim."

"A cat?"

"I can *dance*, Uncle Slim. None of this old-fashioned stuff from me. I mean, I can *dance!*"

Slim screwed up his face. "Sport, you can't dance."

"Hah!" Joe just stuck his hands deeper in his pockets and continued to shake his head. He glanced up at Slim—pity in his eyes—then said, "Watch this." He walked across the street to the same waitress who had danced with Slim; she was drinking beer from a can and talking to some friends. "Wanta dance, sweetheart?" The waitress stared at him and laughed. She went with him into the street.

Joe could dance. He did a smooth "off-time" to the too-fast band rhythm, bouncing slowly and conservatively to every other beat, alternating his step from side to side, disdaining, all the time, even to glance at the Slim who stood stupefied watching from the sidewalk. People caught sight of the kid who was leading the voluptuous waitress; mouths agape, they crowded around, forming a circle, clapping their hands; the other dancers stopped to join the onlookers; Slim had to stand on a step to see Joe dance. Standing astonished, watching, Slim caught Joe's eye for a second; Joe winked, then hardened his face into its nonchalant mask again. "I'll be goddamned!" Slim kept murmuring to himself. "I'll be goddamned!"

Joe ignored the cheers which came afterwards. He bowed to the delighted waitress, thanked her, then pushed his way through the crowd toward Slim. "Well, I'll be goddamned, sport!" Slim said admiringly. Joe did not bother even to look at Slim. He put his hands back into his pockets and stood watching the other dancers, shaking his head.

Some of the other boys of Joe's age, from the neighborhood, came over. "You were great, Joe." Joe acknowledged the compliment by a slight bow of his head. He looked up at Slim. "Hey, Uncle Slim, how's about buying us a drink?"

"Sure." Slim was leading them toward the soda-pop wagon, but Joe steered him over toward the beer wagon. Slim screwed up his face. "Now, don't tell me you drink beer?"

"Sure," Joe said.

"*All* of you?" He looked at the other boys.

"Natch!" they said.

They lifted the fresh-opened cans, tilted back their heads. Slim watched them in amazement. Joe looked at Slim with half-closed eyes, then said to the others, "Uncle Slim's a great guy, you know, but he's behind the times. He's old-fashioned!"

5.

KRISTIN'S BRIGHT EYES DANCED AT THE SIGHT OF ALL THE PEOPLE. Her eyes caught everything: "beautiful" faces, odd-angled dancers, a man in ecstasy playing the saxophone. She wandered with Claude through the crowds, danced with him, ate a hotdog, munched peanuts, drank beer. Her face shone with rapture in the presence of what she most loved: *Life!* There was *life* in the air of South Street.

The band struck up a conga. Kristin watched the twisting, snapping line. She felt suddenly what she had felt many times before: a sharp wave of pain that she was *outside* of this nation of people, a stranger looking on. They, the Negroes, never completely accepted her, could not, really, for she was outside of the common life experience which bound them all together.

Claude must have read her thoughts; he looked at her and smiled softly. They were standing near the fishfry wagon; in the street, the conga line was weaving. The Blues Singer, several feet away, had been watching Kristin's face for the past five minutes. She came over and said, "Well, what's a pretty young girl like you doing just *lookin'* at all this dancing? Come on, let's get on the line!"

Kristin leaped happily at the suggestion; she and the Blues Singer waited until the whipping tail of the line came around, then Kristin seized the waist of the last man, and the Blues Singer clutched the waist of Kristin. Off they went to the music.

Claude, watching them dance, felt, with a sharp, helpless ache of his own, the pain of Kristin. It was a pity, a pity! that she was not a Negro.

The line was going past Claude again; other people had attached themselves to it, now, behind Kristin and the Blues Singer. Kristin's face was flushed, her eyes sparkled, her head tossed from side to side; passing Claude, she shouted an excited greeting—for this moment, for this moment, she *belonged*! The Blues Singer, behind, looked at Kristin and at Claude. She winked at Claude.

6.

IT WAS A ROLE UNFAMILIAR TO PHILIP, BUT HE LOVED IT—THE role, so long denied, of *participating* with the people, of being one with those around him who were healthy and gay. Philip shouted perhaps more loudly than anyone else at the Festival; he drank the beer in great gulps, sang loudly the songs in which everyone was supposed to join, waltzed, two-stepped and even attempted, with little success, a jitterbug. It was a role unfamiliar and exciting; he was an ordinary, down-to-earth human being among other ordinary, down-to-earth human beings.

Joy! Had he ever lived before? Had that been life in the cold, lifeless retreats of living rooms? Had that been life, the immersion into books, into endless discussions, into Freud, into Kafka, into Dostoievsky?

He had never felt such strength before: moral and physical. He *felt* himself expand. Moving through the gay crowd, he seized girls whom he would have been too bashful to touch before, kissed them, held their waists (feeling flesh beneath the cloth!), danced with them. There, across from him, stood Lil, the sensational Lil, flower in hair, eyes sparkling, talking to someone and drinking a beer. Michael was beside her, his arm was around her, she was looking up at him laughing in her surprise, and he had kissed her, hard, holding it, and was away again, laughing, and she was laughing still. There, just arriving, was Margaret, looking probably for Michael. "Margaret!" He was by her side; he kissed her, and was away. ("If she knew me now, *now* she would not scorn me!") But Margaret belonged now to Michael. Philip did not care. The world was rich, and he was away, singing with the crowd.

"Claude! Claude! I have to come see you. I've been so busy, nothing like it before . . . the society, you know . . . Kristin, you look lovely! How are you?" He danced once, with Kristin; then, a drink with both of them, and off went Philip again. He sought out Michael, who was standing with Margaret. "Hey, Michael, Margaret! . . . do we take a drink?" None for Michael, but Margaret would. Philip fetched the cold cans of beer. "To everybody! To people!" Philip shouted. He and Margaret raised their cans while Michael looked and smiled.

No, Philip told himself, dancing through that evening, no, he had never lived before. No, he had been dead before. But a man

could change. Now, new-born, a new Philip moved in the world!
He was *with* people now!

7.

SLIM FELT GOOD TO BE OUT HERE LIKE THIS, ON SOUTH STREET,
with all the people! He knew nearly all of them; most were in
his district, he collected the numbers bets from them. Some
friends of his came over; Slim stood chatting with them for
awhile. The spotlights shone down on the never-silent bandstand,
and floodlights illuminated the crowded street for blocks in either
direction; banners hung from storefronts, swaying in the faint
breeze, and children, sent early, growling, to bed, leaned from
upstairs windows. The night was cooler than the day had been,
but the coat of a suit sufficed for onlookers, and the dancers
needed no coats at all.

Slim wandered among the people, feeling content. Brief pauses:
a word or two with Claude and his wife, Kristin, who faintly
embarrassed Slim, because he found it impossible to treat her
like "one of the girls" and knew no other way to treat any woman;
a chat with the ever-serious Michael, who reminded Slim of a
meeting scheduled for Sunday in the neighborhood at which he,
Michael, was to speak; a few words with the Old Man, who was
beaming as though he, personally, were responsible for Festival
and all the joys attached; and then Slim stopped to chat with a
girl from the neighborhood.

"Well, baby," Slim said, "having a good time?"

"Uh huh. Bet you ain't, though?"

"Why not?"

"Oh, don't play all innocent with me, Slim. You been seeing
the way that ex-girlfriend of yours been playing around."

"Lil?" Slim had not seen her; he saw her now, following the girl's malicious glance: Lil was standing across the street, near the beer wagon, with an oily looking man; she was laughing at something the man was whispering into her ear.

The girl with Slim laughed. "Come on, Slim. 'Fess-up you're still carrying the torch for her."

"Not me," Slim said.

The girl laughed. "Hey, Slim, you been keeping count? How many boyfriends does that make she's had in the last month?"

"How should I know?"

The girl howled.

Without coat, Lil was wearing a sleeveless dress that brought out all of the incredible curves of her body; she had put a flower saucily at the side of her hair. Slim had seen her many times in the last month or so. She had changed, it seemed to him. She wore more make-up than before—though this went well on her. She was always in the company of suave, confident men whom Slim detested, always gay and laughing in their presence, and her eyes seemed always to be whispering to them things they had never whispered to Slim. Whenever she saw Slim, she nodded a greeting, or, if she was close enough, said a pleasant, "Hello." Nothing more. Slim's own lips always gave back the formality, while his eyes, finding nothing, moved away.

Lil did not work; yet, she had a lot of new clothes, including many of the daring, form-fitting dresses she had begun always to wear. To a degree, she had abandoned South Street; her new boyfriends took her to the smarter night clubs in other parts of the city. These boyfriends were, for the most part, "sportsmen"— gamblers and petty racketeers—who drank a lot and spent a lot of money. Lil's eyes—and body—spoke to them; they fell, one after the other, head over heels; and Lil, when finally bored, abandoned them, one after the other, taking up with others, as it suited her whims.

Slim looked at her from across the street. For a moment her

eyes, wandering, met his; she smiled a brief greeting, then wen
on talking with her companion. Slim moved away through th
crowd. He stood talking to the bartender from the *Showboa*
But from time to time he glanced back to see Lil still talkin
flower singing in her hair, eyes caressing her latest conques
and once, carried away by something her escort said, she leane
her head forward, laughing, upon his shoulder, then raised h
head and kissed him, laughing, on the mouth. Slim turned awa
He talked to the bartender. The ache had never gone. The baffl
ment, always present, upsurged: *Why?*

8.

MICHAEL WANDERED THROUGH THE CROWD, A FRESH CARNATIO
in his lapel. He was not dancing like the others; he was n
shouting, he was not singing. He got into conversation with fe
of the people. And yet Michael was enjoying the Festival. He w
enjoying the dancing of the *others*, enjoying *their* laughter, *the*
songs. *They* were having a good time; therefore, so was he.

He saw Claude. Claude waved to him, smiled; Michael a
swered with a short nod, as he always did whenever, by acciden
he met his brother. To Kristin, whose anxious eyes searched h
face, Michael made no gesture at all. Michael never "saw" Kr
tin. For him, she did not, as a human being, exist.

It irritated Michael, in spite of himself, that Claude did n
seem—at least outwardly—to be affected by the coldness wit
which Michael treated him. Since the wedding, Michael had n
spoken one complete sentence to his brother; in every gestur
every regard, Michael showed his hostility and his contempt f
the "choice" that Claude had made; he made it quite appare
that he thought Claude a traitor. Yet Claude did not respor

in either of the two ways which might have been expected; he neither returned Michael's hostility, nor made any overtures showing a desire for reconciliation. He waved to Michael, smiled without strain, seemed always willing to talk, if Michael felt like it. He did not seem in the least disturbed. It was the *confidence* of Claude that irritated Michael. Michael had the impression that Claude did not take him seriously; that he regarded Michael, as a matter of fact, as a spoiled, pouting child, who would eventually come to his senses.

Sometimes, after running across Claude, Michael would turn angrily to Margaret and burst out with:

"I can't *stand* him! I didn't recognize it before; he's *arrogant!* How else can he act so smug? How could he ever have been a real leader!"

At other times: "It's that *woman* who did this to him, Margaret! She's destroyed him! Made him less than a man! What do you suppose she says to him, when they're alone? That he's no longer a Negro?"

Or he would say: "Is he blind? ... Why can't he see it? What does she love in him except his body? What does she really *know* in him except what's physical? ... what can she know, when what is to be known can only be known by another Negro? They're sick, these white people; and she's among the sickest of them all!"

Margaret listened usually in silence. One day, she said to Michael, after one of his tirades: "You love him very much, Michael. That's obvious."

"I hate him!" Michael said.

He liked to talk to Margaret. She was the only person to whom he could really talk, committing all of himself, all dreams; the only person with whom he felt completely relaxed. Even among the fellow members of the Action Society, he was not completely at ease: they had too many areas of life in which he could not participate, too many desires, too many enjoyments, which were completely alien to him. No, these people were, in a way, foreign;

but Margaret was not. She was by his side, a shadow; she could listen for hours, never stirring, never bored; into her he could pour everything that he was.

The band struck up a set of waltzes. A girl rushed to Michael: "Come along, Michael, dance for a change, be a human being for a change . . . just for tonight!" "No thanks," Michael said. "You know I don't dance." "*Try* it!" said the girl, but Michael insisted: "No, thanks." Still, there was the faint pain—"be a human being for a change."

9.

THE BAND STILL PLAYED, THE YOUTHS STILL DANCED—BUT THERE were fewer people on South Street now. The weather had cooled, and some of the people had gone to the indoor dance, at the Olympia, some few had gone home, and many others had crowded into the bars. The Blues Singer was at the *Postal Card.* A man said, "You want a drink, baby?" and she stood at the bar with the men and made a toast to love and drank the first glass down. Through the door, faintly, came the sound of the band in the street. The Blues Singer snorted. "Them people think they're musicians!" She snorted again. "Them people don't know what jazz is!"

She looked at the man who had offered her the drink; her rough brown skin glistened, her eyes were dim, and the light cast Indian shadows under her high cheek bones. "You ever hear of King Oliver?"

"Sure," said the man.

"Now, *there* was a jazz man!"

"Sure," said the man, "and Bunk Johnson and Jelly Roll Morton and Kid Bolden—"

"And Big-Eye Louis Nelson and Kid Ory—"

"Sure."

"Them was the days," the Blues Singer said. The bartender had filled her glass again, and she raised it. "I remember sitting and listening to Mary Lou Williams play 'Little Joe from Chicago.' "

"Remember 'Ain't Gonna Give Nobody None of This Jelly Roll'?"

"And 'The Royal Garden Blues'?" The Blues Singer pounded her hips. "You're all right! Where you from?"

"New Orleans."

"Goddamn!" the Blues Singer said. She looked around the bar, then sat still, eyes soft, listening to the music from outside. "Shit!" she said, "these bastards these days don't know a goddamn thing about jazz!"

"Don't know a goddamn thing!" the man agreed.

"Thing is," said the Blues Singer, "these goddamn musicians today don't *feel* nothing, know what I mean? Hell, they ain't *lived* nothing, just think about cars and ass, ain't never *felt* nothing!" She glowered into the mirror behind the bar. "Now, you take some of the *real* boys, like, say, Chick Webb—hell, them people *felt* something, they *lived* something real! Know what I mean?"

"Sure," the man said.

"Hell, born cripple, all that stuff—hell, Chick *felt* something!"

"Sure."

"Listen—" The Blues Singer suddenly threw back her head and opened her mouth and the words came out, the moaning music: "St. James' Infirmary." The bar quickly quieted. Somebody closed the second door, to further shut out the noise of the street. The Blues Singer sang and sang, then stopped. The bar was still. The Blues Singer looked at the man. "See what I mean?" she said. "That's the way the old timers used to sing it." She glared at herself in the mirror behind the bar.

She raised her head again:

She said, when she had finished, "That's the way the old timers used to sing it!"

10.

THE BARTENDER WHO WORKED AT THE *Showboat,* WHICH WAS closed tonight, was standing near the beer wagon, eating a hot-dog. He was a man of medium height and weight, with a pleasant, but rather ordinary face, and chocolate brown skin. He had, at home, a wife and three children—two boys and a girl.

The Bartender was munching the hotdog, feeling the warm, salty juices pour tingling onto his tongue. To the hotdog, he had added relish, mustard, onions and pickles, and, every once in a while, he would take a swig of beer to wash it all down. Dimly, he heard the band, but he had been hearing it all night, so that now the music was heard almost unconsciously. The Bartender was looking at the pictures in a copy of *Life* magazine.

It's a good magazine, he thought. He was not reading any of the text in the bright, uneven light of the floodlights; he was simply looking at the pictures.

From time to time, the Bartender would look up and respond to the greeting of someone who knew him. "Hi!" someone would say, as likely as not pounding him on the shoulder. "Yeah, yeah," the Bartender would say, glancing up, smiling acknowledgment. He was never too enthusiastic. No need of getting excited about things, the Bartender always said; you could get over your point without getting all excited.

He chewed the hotdog slowly and looked at the pictures in *Life* magazine and, from time to time, took a swallow of the beer.

The hotdog was a medley in his mouth: the pickles and onions and mustard and relish and hotdog changed their interrelationships: sometimes the pickles tastes strongest, while the others were subdued; sometimes the mustard dominated, sometimes the relish, sometimes the pure hotdog itself. Over all, ruling, was the roll: too strong, dominant, at the moment of entry into his mouth, it soon softened, subsided, to become the alloy for all else.

The Bartender was looking at the photograph of a woman leaping with an open umbrella, for parachute, from the top of a New York building. It was the Picture of the Week. The Bartender shook his head. The world sure was funny!

11.

THE MEN WANTED TO INVITE CLAUDE TO HAVE A GLASS OF WINE or whiskey with them, but he was with Kristin, and they were not always sure of what to say when she was around, so they did not ask him. Then Kristin walked away, to talk to Philip, and the men walked over to Claude. "Well, hell, Claude, come on and have a drink." "Sure," Claude said, "I'll get Kristin."

"Okay."

But he was aware that the men did not particularly want her. He went over to where Kristin stood and said, "I'm having a drink with some friends; would you like to come along?"

Kristin looked at him and at the men who were looking at her. "No, thanks, sweetheart," she said. "You go ahead. I'll stay and talk to Philip."

In the bar, the men all knew Claude. They called greetings, came around; they lifted their glasses. "Well, what you been doing with yourself, Claude? Ain't been seeing you much around."

"Nothing much. Some writing. . . . Nothing much else."

He loved these people.

"That so? Well, don't tell us you done gone and retired on us."

They laughed.

"Yes. That's about it."

"Well, toast, Claude."

They drank.

"How's the missus, Claude?"

"She's fine. She's outside."

A man held his glass. "Claude, wanta ask you something. Can I ask you something? You don't find it funny, do you? . . . married to a white woman?"

"No." He looked at them. He knew them, so he said, "There are incidents sometimes, you know."

"Sure, *we* know."

"But aside from that . . . there's nothing strange."

"Sure. I just . . . Look, ain't she prejudiced at all? Excuse me from askin', but you're one of the boys, you know? She ain't prejudiced at all?"

"Not at all."

"Well, how can you tell? No, I'm just wondering, see. You know how it is, the boys hang around the bars and places talking, and naturally they talk about friends and all, and some of us just was wondering about it. Most of them people's prejudiced as hell, you know how it is. What's white. She ain't prejudiced at all?"

"Not at all."

"Well, I'll be goddamned!"

"Well, now, look here," said another man, "say, for example, that she ain't prejudiced against *you*. Right? Now, you're famous, Claude, ain't no getting around that. Right? Now, but what about your friends? What about us, for example? Would she feel the same way about us?"

"Yes."

"She think of us exactly like she thinks about anybody else? . . . Exactly like she thinks about white people?"

"She would look upon anyone as a person—one person. If she liked the person, she would like him. She would not *see* the color of his skin."

"Well, I'll be goddamned!" the man said. "Well, you know how it is . . . I ain't never seen a white person who wasn't prejudiced before. See, you can understand why I ask."

"Yes."

The first man drank a little. "Claude, look, you don't mind all this? If you do, I'll shut up and mind my own goddamned business."

"No, I don't mind." Because he knew them; because he understood them; because he loved them.

"Because, you're one of the boys, and we all admire you, you know that. You got guts, see. You did a lot for all of us, but most of all you're one of the boys and never got to feel too high and mighty to talk to us and take a drink with us just because you're famous and all that, you know what I mean? Just one of the boys, and we all like you, and it's the only reason we talk so goddamn much. Right?"

"It's good to hear."

"Well, I got a question, and it's a hard one. But, see, some of the boys was around, you know how it is, and they was talking and I got in a argument and I'd just like to ask the question. But it's a hard one for you to answer."

"Go ahead."

"Well, now, you've sorta retired, like you said. You ain't going around getting in all these race fights and all that no more. You're tired of that, you want a little peace for a change, you want to live your own life for a little while. Right?"

"That's pretty much it."

"Well, good. Now, did you decide to retire *before* you met this whi . . . your wife, or *afterwards*?"

Words: razors. "She had nothing to do with it," Claude said. "I decided before I met her."

"There!" The man pounded the bar. "See, that's what I told them bastards, but they wouldn't believe me! I said, 'Hell, what you talking about, Claude's a man! . . . ain't no woman gonna lead him to do nothing he don't want to do!' I *told* them that!"

"Well, you know how people are," one man said.

"Sure, people are a bitch!"

"I *told* them that, but they don't believe me, know what I mean? They go around saying, 'Well, now ain't that just like a colored man, gets hisself a little famous, first thing he does is run off and marry a white woman! Don't never fail. And then he's no more good to his own people!' That's what they was saying! They was saying, 'See, first thing these white bitches do, they get all sweet and soft with their little darkie husbands, and they curls their milkwhite hands all over his face, and they says, 'Oh, baby, you don't wanta get all mixed up with them dirty niggers, like you was still one of them, do you?' That's what they was saying. And, hell, I got mad, know what I mean? I said, 'Hell, you can't talk that way about *Claude*, he's different! Claude's a goddamn *man*, ain't no perfumed woman gonna get him to give up his race!' So they says, 'Well, how come he had to run off and marry one of *them?* Ain't there enough good-looking colored women around for him? Hell, we got all kinds of good-looking colored women, all colors, shapes and sizes, and he gotta run off and marry one of *them!* Just like all these colored men when they gets famous!' And then they says, 'And do you know why he had to marry one of *them?* Because, he's ashamed of his race! He don't wanta be a Negro! He's been famous so long, and up among them white people so long, that he wants to be one of *them!*' Ain't that a bitch? *Claude!* Much as Claude's done for Negroes in his time! Now, they go around saying things like that about him!"

Claude said nothing. Behind his eyes, tears were forming.

"Hell," said the man, "a man's got a right to be tired, know what I mean? And he's got a right to marry who the hell he damn pleases! And if he prefers white women to colored women, that's his own goddamn business!"

"I do not prefer white women." Claude said it softly; he had to say it softly because he understood the hands that held the razors. "I did not marry white women. I married my wife. It's my wife I love. It's my wife I prefer to all the women I've ever known."

Why explain it? Why? Why? But these were friends who were proud of him, and he was proud of their pride.

"Sure," said the man, "that's what I mean."

"Sure," said another man. "People ought to mind their own goddamn business!"

"Sure. Toast."

They drank it down.

12.

BY NINE SATURDAY MORNING, SOUTH STREET WAS CROWDED AGAIN. The sun had risen bright in a cloudless sky; the day was warmer, more spring-like than the previous day had been; the sun shone brightly, blindingly, directly down, then bounced off windows, signs and shiny shoes; the sun cast shadows, too: in doorways, behind wagons, underfoot, so that the dancers, those hand-joined cardboard puppets on a string, were multiplied by shortened shadows mocking them.

Newspaper photographers had come out early to get Festival pictures: they moved around the bandstand, mingled with the crowd, stooped, stood on steps or mounted in the tenement houses to lean from windows for high-angle shots. There was a smell of distant green in the air—the smell of spring.

It was a day for festival, a festival day, and the people, all of them, felt this very strongly. Saturday: few people worked today, and South Street was even more crowded than it had been the day before.

The Old Man was in his glory. He was standing outside of the .*Postal Card*, at the most crowded part of the street, surrounded by a bevy of beautiful girls, many of whom had come from out of town. They hugged him, kissed him, laughed at his jokes, were charmed by him, were fascinated by him, allowed themselves to fall in love with him in the general good feeling of the day. The Old Man reigned as king of the women, shah of a harem. He was dressed for the occasion, in a powder-blue suit, canary yellow shirt, brown and tan sparkling shoes and an ivory-handled walking stick. His hair was brushed to a high gloss—not one loose strand stood out. He had used a good, pine-scented cologne on his face after shaving, and dusted powder over his body after his morning bath.

"Hey, how's it going old Man?"

"Well, well! Sid! Pardon me, my dears— Well, well! Sid! How *are* you? . . ."

"Hello, Old Man!"

"Well, well! Harry! Well, well! When did you drop in? . . . Pardon me, my dears—I have so many friends, you see, something awful. . . ."

Everybody knew the Old Man; everybody spoke to him; he spent the day shaking hand after hand, exchanging chatter, pounding shoulders and backs. "Well, well! Ed! How *are* you?" Toward noon, the Old Man danced with several of the "young ladies." Shortly afterwards, he bought lunch at the *Postal Card* for about six of them, who rolled with laughter at all of the clever things he said to them; later, he was on the street with them again, strolling about, introducing them, adding to their number, buying all of them beers.

What a happy life it was! he thought. Life was rich! Life was filled with people and with love and good times! There were friends, friends. friends who were always glad to see one; there were girls, girls, girls, and there were whisky, sunshine, and success!

13.

LITTLE JOE KNEW THE BOYS WERE LOOKING AT HIM, SO HE walked up to the pretty girl, who was about fifteen, and said, "Let's try a dance." She was a good dancer, but Joe did not let her know it. As he danced, he looked all around, at the buildings, the crowds, the sunlit sky—but not at the girl, who was impressed by his dancing, nor at the boys, who were watching, admiring, Joe knew, his casual attitude toward the girl. The girl was brown with black curly hair and soft brown eyes under long, turned-up lashes. After the dance, Joe led the girl over to where she had been standing, with her aunt, on the sidewalk. "Thank you," he said, bowing slightly. "Oh, thank *you!*" said the girl as Joe walked away.

Joe walked over to where the boys were standing. "Boy!" said Davy, "she's a pretty girl, Joe!"

"She'll do," Joe said.

"What did you say when you asked her to dance?"

"I just said do you want to dance."

"And what did she say?"

"She said yes."

"That all?"

"Sure. What else did you expect?"

"Boy!" Davy was looking at the girl. "I'm gonna ask her to dance!" he said with sudden courage.

Joe pretended not to look—he pretended to be listening to what the other boys were saying, or to be watching the crowds casually—but he watched Davy and the girl out of the corner of his eye. Davy was grinning into the girl's face, talking a mile-a-minute—the idiot! Davy was all right, but he certainly did not know how to handle women! You didn't fall all over yourself when you were with a woman; you played it cool, acted as though you were not interested at all, acted as though you were bored; you had to be hard to get. That was the way it was done. Maybe some day Davy would learn.

Davy had three dances in a row with the girl. Joe did not like that very much. He was watching them out of the corner of his eye.

"What are you looking at, Joe?" asked Teddy, one of the boys.

"Me? Who's looking at anything?"

"Sure," laughed Teddy, "you're watching Davy dance with that girl. What's the matter? Jealous?"

"What have I got to be jealous about? I ain't watching nothing!"

He was a little irritated by that, so he tried to make sure that Teddy and the others did not see him when he glanced at Davy and the girl. Out of the corner of his eye, he watched what was going on. Davy was talking a lot to the girl and she was talking back, looking up into his face, smiling at him as though she were really interested in what he was saying. Joe did not like it a bit.

When Davy came back to the group, he said, "Boy! That girl is really sweet!" He was starry-eyed.

"She'll do," Joe said, casually.

Teddy winked at the boys. "Know what, Davy? I think she really likes you."

"You do?"

"Sure, could see that by the way she was looking up in your

face while she was dancing with you. She was looking up at you like she was looking at something wonderful! Ain't that right, Joe? Don't you think she really fell for Davy?"

Joe shrugged. "I wouldn't know."

"Sure," Teddy said, winking at the other boys. "Sure, you saw it, Joe. She fell head over heels for Davy. Anybody could see that."

Joe deliberated whether or not he should break Teddy's nose. Davy was standing starry-eyed, believing what Teddy had said. From time to time, Davy would turn around and grin, catching the eye of the pretty girl. Dope! Joe thought. He was furious.

After a decent amount of time had passed, Joe said, "Well, guess I'll go take another dance."

Teddy grinned and winked at the boys. "That so, Joe? Well, who you gonna dance with, Joe?"

"Don't know. Maybe with that girl, there."

"You mean with Davy's girlfriend?" Teddy said. "Man, you can't go messing around with Davy's girlfriend. You ought to leave Davy's girlfriend alone."

"Davy can spare his love for one dance," Joe snapped.

"Sure," Davy said, big-heartedly.

Joe considered breaking the noses of both of them.

The girl went into the street with him. Joe knew that the boys were watching him, knew that Teddy was grinning. He jitter-bugged with as much nonchalance as he could maintain; then the band went into a slow number, and Joe moved smoothly with the girl in the crowded street.

"You dance beautifully," the girl said softly.

"Thanks," Joe said, curtly. He was not prepared to treat her decently, yet; he would make her suffer first.

The girl looked at him. "Can I . . . can I ask you something?"

"Go ahead," Joe said.

"Your friend . . . the one I danced with a moment ago. What's his name?"

Joe felt something very hot in the pit of his stomach. "Him? Oh, he's Davy. Not much of a friend, though," he added.

"No? Oh, I think he's *very* nice. Handsome, too."

The heat was spreading up through Joe's chest. "Oh, sure, sure."

"I . . . wish something. I wish he'd ask me to dance again. Do you think he would?"

"Why not?" Joe was sick of all of them. He wanted to go away to another part of the street.

He led the girl back to her aunt and did not bother even to say, "Thank you." He walked back over to where the boys stood.

"Well, how was it?" Teddy asked. "How was Davy's girl, Joe? She look even better the second time?"

"I didn't really notice," Joe said. "She don't mean nothing to me. Matter of fact, I don't even think I'll dance with her anymore. She's not such a good dancer, you know. Steps all over my feet, I can't stand that in a woman. Don't think I'll even dance with her anymore."

"She didn't step on my feet," Davy said, incredulously.

"Well, you're just as bad a dancer as she is, so you probably had your feet in the wrong place so she couldn't step on them!" Joe glared at Davy. Then he rubbed his face and said, "Well, if you like her, why the hell don't you go dance with her?"

"Maybe she wants to rest a while."

"No, go ahead and dance with her! What the hell! You sure are stupid, don't even know how to treat a woman! You've got to rush a woman, don't you know that?"

"Is that so?"

"Sure, sure. Go ahead and dance with her!"

So Davy went away to dance with the girl again.

All through the day, Davy was dancing with the curly-haired girl. Teddy made remarks and winked at Joe and Joe glared but held his tongue and dismissed the girl with contempt. Obviously, the girl was stupid—only a stupid girl would want Davy; and Joe was not interested in stupid girls. When Teddy became unbearable, Joe decided to go for a walk away from all of them. He saw his uncle, Slim, exchanged a few words, then walked around talking to some of the other boys he knew. The Festival was nice, only thing the people did not know how to dance. Joe stood listening to the music. He thought of the girl and of Davy and Teddy. He was sick of people like Davy and Teddy: they acted like infants!

"Joe."

He turned; it was the girl with curly hair; she was walking up to him.

"Where have you been?" she asked. "I've been looking all over for you."

How did she know his name. "Looking for me? Why? You were happy enough, it seemed to me."

She looked at him from under the long, curled lashes, and laughed.

"What are you laughing about?"

"Well . . ." She looked at him coyly, laughing. "Well, of course, I knew you would be jealous, but I didn't think you'd be *that* jealous."

"*Jealous!*" Her use of the word so startled him that, for a moment, he did not know what to say. "Jealous! Why should I be jealous? Of what?"

"Oh"—she put her arm in his and started walking back down the street—"Oh, I was just teasing you, Joe? Do you really think I wanted to dance with Davy?"

"Huh?"

"—But you were acting so high and mighty . . ."

"Huh?"

She laughed. "Come along. Let's dance."

14.

IN THE BACK OF THE BAR, FARTHER DOWN SOUTH STREET, THE
men were sitting at a table playing cards when Lil walked in. It
was evening. Earlier, the men had been with the crowds on South
Street; they had drunk, eaten hotdogs, even tried their hands at
dancing. They were relaxing now.

Lil came in, and one of the men said, "Well, hello, baby." "Hi,"
Lil said. She brought over a drink from the bar and stood near
the table, watching the cards turn up: the men were playing
poker.

"Give me some luck, sweetheart. Touch the deck." Lil touched
it, and a deuce turned up for the man. "That ain't no way to
behave," said the man; "I asked for *luck* baby." "Sorry," Lil said.

She stood there with narrow waist and soft round hips and
shapely legs, and watched the game. "Give me some luck, baby,"
said the man. She touched the deck and a three turned up. "Baby,
you ain't *no*where!"

The winner picked up the pot and they ordered another round
of drinks and paused for a moment before continuing. "Come sit
on my lap, baby." Lil sat on the man's lap; his hand went to her
waist, then followed gently the curve that went to her hips. "Goddam! Looka that!" He looked at the other men and they were
looking at the lines of Lil's body. "Baby, you're the best they
ever made!"

"Sure," Lil said.

"Baby, you love me?"

"Madly!"

"Till you die?"

"Till I die!"

"Well, baby, when you gonna be nice to me?"

"Why, what do you mean, sweetheart?"

"Aw, you know what I mean, baby. Don't be like that. When you gonna be nice to me?" He winked at the other men.

"Why, sugar, I didn't know you felt like that."

"Sure I feel like that, baby. Couldn't you see it in my eyes? Sure I feel like that. When you gonna be nice?"

"Whenever you say, sugar. Whenever you say."

A man said, "Deal 'em." The cards went around again.

"You know, you changed, baby."

"Did I?" said Lil.

"Sure, you changed. Got better looking somehow. Got more spirit, too, more pep, more fire."

"Well, that's what people need, isn't it? More spirit, more pep, more fire?"

"Sure. Well, you got it, baby. Don't know what happened, but you sure changed these last two months. For the better."

"Well, I'm glad," Lil said. "I'm glad you like me better."

"Love you, you mean."

"Sure. Love me. That's what I meant to say."

The man said, "Want something else to drink, baby?"

"No, I'm happy."

"Well, touch the cards again. This time give me some luck." It was a three again. "Jesus Christ!" the man said.

The man behind the bar had turned on the radio to an all-night record program. Stan Kenton was playing now. "Listen to that music! Great!"

"Deal," someone said.

The front door opened again and Slim walked in. He saw Lil immediately, and she saw him; he hesitated for a split second, in confusion, then walked to the bar. The men called greetings to him. "Hi, fellas," he said. He got a drink at the bar, then walked back to where they were. "Hello, Lil," he said.

"Hello, Slim."

They were all silent for a moment: everyone knew that Lil had been Slim's girl. Lil was still sitting on the man's lap. Someone said, "Slim, what was the number today?"

"Eight fifty-two."

"Damn! I played eight fifty-seven!"

"Well, that's life."

"It sure is. That's life all right."

There was silence again. Slim stood holding his drink and the men played cards; the men tried to make conversation, but it sounded hollow. Slim finished his drink.

"Well, I got to run along."

"What's the hurry, Slim. Stay and take a hand. Have a drink on us."

"Thanks, but I can't. Got something to do. See you."

He left.

On the radio, Billy Eckstein was singing.

"He sure was nervous."

The others nodded.

The man looked at Lil. "He sure loves you, Lil. Really loves you. Anybody can see that."

Lil said, "Nobody loves anybody." On the radio, a band was playing, "I wish I could Shimmy Like My Sister Kate." "Now, that's my kind of music," Lil said. She laughed suddenly. "Makes me want to dance."

"You can't shimmy."

"Sure I can!"

"Let's see it."

She jumped up. She lifted her skirt slightly to reveal perfect knees; her heels clicked, her legs twinkled and her hips, above all, told the music. A man shuffled the cards very slowly, looking at Lil and smiling; the rest stood staring, not moving, smiling. Lil's body became a shimmy. The music stopped.

"Well, I'll be goddamned!" said the man.

Lil was breathless; her face shone. "See!" She laughed and

stood over them, accepting their plaudits. *"Now,* I'll take that other drink you offered!"

She sipped it, standing over the men. She stood watching their resumed game, feeling exhilarated from the dance.

"Here. Try it again, baby. Touch the cards."

She touched them, and another deuce turned up.

"Damn! You're bad luck, baby," the man said with a sigh.

Another shimmy piece came on. "Dance it, baby."

15.

THE BLUES SINGER, ON THE PLATFORM, CHANTED:

Now, some people like it in the morning

"YEAH!"—from the crowd.

And, some people like it at night

"YEAH!"

But I like it any old hour
That my baby's feeling right!

The spotlight showed her. The crowd, packed near the platform, saw the white-lighted shimmering body, the upraised head, the straining neck, the upraised arms. The Blues Singer was their leader; they followed her in the song, shouting for refrain, laughing, stomping the beat along with the bass on the ground.

Hey, all you guys

"YEAH, BABY!"

Got a message for you

"WHAT IS IT, BABY?"

Look out for girls that smile at you

"WHY?"

'Cause a woman that smiles
In a certain way

> *Gonna break your heart*
> *One gloomy day*

"TELL 'EM ABOUT IT, BABY!"

Cheers, laughter, the thumping bass; the words droned on:

> *And, hey, all you girls*

"YEAH! YEAH?"

> *You better listen, too*

"WHY?"

> *I'm gonna tell you what man a will do*

"WHAT'LL HE DO? WHAT'LL HE DO?"

> *A man will cheat*

"YES! YES!"

> *He'll play around*

"YES! YES!"

> *Then come cryin' to you*
> *When the chips go down.*

"YES! YES! YES!"

Cheers, cheers, cheers and laughter; and the bass and the trumpet and the Blues Singer chanted on.

She did not love it, the Blues Singer thought, later, as she mounted the platform again; she did not love it, she thought, as she heard again the cheers, saw again the sweating musicians, saw the black-faced crowd and raised again her arms and head and voice to sing; she did not love it—any more than one loved breathing, or the beating of one's heart.

16.

FAR DOWN SOUTH STREET, WHERE THE CROWDS WERE THIN, AND where the sound of the music from the platform was not heard,

Margaret was walking when suddenly she saw Claude. Claude: he was standing next to a post, leaning on it, quite alone, looking off further down South Street, toward the area known as Grays Ferry, where the predatory white gangs lived. In Claude's hand was a can of beer, but he was not drinking from it. He was simply staring off, alone, thinking, dreaming, toward Grays Ferry.

Margaret stood still, looking at him. All that she had ever felt for him returned. What went on in that strong head? What churned beneath that outward stoic calm? There was a heat in Margaret, watching him. It was he, he, he she had always wanted!

Here, at the boundary line, where the last ropes were strung, it was rather quiet; one was more conscious here, than up the street, of the sky—dark blue, bristling with stars, with a moon low-slung—and of the air, which was cool, and of the humanity of night. Margaret stood watching Claude. He did not move. Heart in throat, she approached.

"Hello," she said softly, standing close.

He was startled by the voice. He turned to her. "Margaret. Hello." She stood beside him. She sank into his mood, floated in in it. Claude! Claude!

"Down here all alone," she whispered, half scoldingly. "Solving deep problems of the soul."

Claude laughed. "Not quite."

She tried it. "Where's Kristin?"

"Oh, back there"—he gestured toward the lights and the milling crowd—"with Philip, I think, or Dan and Suzette."

"Philip and Kristin go well together."

"Yes. They like each other."

He was silent again. Margaret liked silences. She was with Claude in the silence. What was was; the deepest was the felt; it did not need to, could not, be expressed.

"I'm not very talkative company," Claude said.

"It's all right."

"Shall we walk a bit?"

"If you like," Margaret said.

They walked slowly up toward the lights. "You . . . are enjoying the Festival, I suppose," Margaret said. She wanted to take Claude's hand, walking, but she did not dare.

"It's marvelous," Claude said. "Better than last year, I think."

"I love it," Margaret said. "I . . . I like the music, don't you? And the dancers. And all the people moving around."

Claude nodded. "Yes."

There was something going on inside of him. Margaret could feel the churning. When she had looked into his face, in the moonlight, when she had spoken to him near the post, she had seen something—some disturbance—behind his eyes. Now, her heart was beating rapidly. What was troubling him? Something . . . personal? Something . . . perhaps . . . like his married life? Something about Kristin? Was he . . . perhaps . . . tired of his marriage? Did he regret it? What else?

"Are you . . . all right, Claude?"

"All right? Yes, I think so. How do you mean?"

"Oh . . . you seemed . . . preoccupied."

He laughed. "I guess so. Forgive me. It's what I said before— I'm not very good company."

"You're wonderful company. The best. I just . . . wondered. I thought maybe something was wrong. We're old friends—aren't we? I just was worried, I just thought that if anything were wrong, you might want to talk to me."

"No, nothing's wrong."

They walked in silence.

Margaret said, "Claude, remember how we used to take long walks on South Street, and how you used to talk to me about— oh, all sorts of things—about your childhood and your brothers and your father and people you met? Things like that? Remember?"

"Yes."

"I used to love that." She was silent a moment. "I don't suppose I did much talking myself. I guess I was kind of dull to you."

"I don't think that. I don't suppose I gave you much chance to get in a word."

"No. It wasn't that. I always admired you, you know that. I still admire you, more than anyone. And then, I think, that in those days, when we used to walk, that I knew then what I still know—that I can never equal you, can never measure up. Your . . . spirit and your intelligence. You needed someone of equal spirit and intelligence. Me, I could never equal you."

Claude was slightly embarrassed. "Nonsense!" was all he could say.

"We used to walk and you used to talk and I used to listen like I was floating on air. I worshiped every word that came from your mouth, every gesture you made, everything you did!"

Claude laughed softly. "I never knew it. It sounds like a case of mild puppy love, doesn't it?"

She said nothing for a moment. Then she took his hand and looked up into his face; it did not matter, she was not thinking now, she was feeling. . . .

"Claude . . . !"

But Claude was looking away, up the street, and Margaret turned and saw Michael approaching. Michael came closer and Margaret released Claude's hand. She was trembling and she was furious with Michael.

"Margaret. I been looking for you," Michael said. He was looking at her; he said nothing to Claude.

"Really?" Margaret said. Ice edged her voice.

Michael looked at her in silence for a moment. "Yes," he said. "We'd been talking—some of the men and I—and we drew up some ideas and needed your secretarial help. You told me, if I remember correctly, that you wanted to help us."

"I—Of course." She looked at Claude. "You walk with us, Claude?"

"Of course." Claude smiled at his brother.

She walked between them. Her heart was beating furiously. She wondered if she had given herself away. From time to time, she glanced up at Michael, whose eyes were fixed straight ahead of him. They were walking toward the lights. Though they could not yet hear her, they could see the shimmering figure of the Blues Singer on the platform.

"This is silly, you know, Michael," Claude said. "This silence. You're my brother. More than that, you're a friend."

The lights, which they had now attained, shone on Michael's white carnation.

"I am neither brother nor friend to you," Michael said.

Claude was silent. They reached the bar. Michael and Margaret went in, to join Michael's friends. Claude walked toward the platform where the Blues Singer was singing.

17.

NEAR THE SAME POST ON WHICH CLAUDE HAD BEEN LEANING, FAR down South Street, Dan and Suzette were walking later that evening when the shadowy forms approached from the direction of Grays Ferry. They were white youths, six or seven of them, dressed in sweaters. Dan leaned against the post, hardly noticing them; Suzette, standing beside him, looked up at the sky. "Eet ees a beautiful night," she sighed.

The youths approached laughing loudly. In a few moments, Dan could distinguish their voices: "There it is! A whole lot of music!" Rough voices; the Grays Ferry district was a rough neighborhood.

They were paying no attention to Dan and Suzette; they were walking past; but one of the boys was in a bad mood, and it was he who happened to glance in the direction of the couple. He halted, staring, tugging at the shirtsleeves of a couple of the others. "Well, I'll be goddamned!" he said. "Look at that!"

The others looked. Dan did not move; he looked back, but he did not say anything. Suzette looked nervously at the boys, then turned her eyes back toward the sky; under her breath, she said to Dan, "What are zey lookeeeng at? What do zey want?"

"I don't know."

The boys stared. One said, "Oh, come the hell on! Let's go hear the music."

But the one who had first stopped did not like the world that night. He walked closer to Dan and Suzette, squinting his eyes to make sure of what he saw. The others watched.

"What the hell you doin' out with a white woman, sonofabitch!"

Suzette trembled. "He eeees my husband."

"Be quiet," Dan said.

"Your *what!*"

Suzette drew as close to Dan as possible. Dan kept looking at the boys; he said nothing.

"Let's take him!" the youth said to his companions.

"Oh, hell, leave 'em alone!" said another. "What the hell! Let's go down and listen to the music."

"Naw, let's take him!" The youth who said it was hollow-eyed and gaunt; he had a hungry look and an angry look: the world was, tonight, his enemy. The youth ran into Dan, swinging his fists. Dan moved quickly, swinging back. Once the fight began, indecision left the others: they leaped into the fight. Suzette screamed and kicked and clawed; Dan swung and kicked. The fight lasted only five minutes. Dan was on the ground, bleeding, and Suzette was screaming. The foot of the youth crashed against Dan's skull. Dan was unconscious. "Jesus!" one of the youths exclaimed. They all ran off, in the direction of Grays Ferry.

18.

WHEN, IN THE HEAT OF THE MUSIC OF THE BAND, LIL THREW OFF
her shoes and stood in the middle of the street and danced with
her hips to the cheers and ogles of the crowd, Slim could not
stand it—he turned away his eyes and raised the can of beer to
his lips. "What's the matter, Slim? Too much for you?" said a
woman who was standing near. The cheers grew so loud and the
crowd so thick that it was difficult to see Lil, laughing, throwing
kisses, she leaped upon the platform, where the Blues Singer had
lately stood, and danced, skirts raised, beautiful legs flashing,
soft-curved hips swaying. *She's drunk!* Slim had never seen Lil
drunk before. He could not stand it. He walked into a bar.

"What'll you have?" The bartender was surly; he was angry
because, by entering, Slim had compelled him to come inside and
miss the spectacle everyone else was enjoying.

"Whiskey. Double." Slim drank it. "Another."

The bartender was irritated. "Don't you want to watch the
dance?"

"No. Give me another drink."

Slim drank five in a row; added to the untold quantities of
beer he had already consumed, that made him drunk. *I'm drunk.
Great. We can all get drunk!*

Slim went back outside. Lil was still dancing on the platform.
The band was blowing its lungs out for Lil; the crowd was wildly
cheering. Slim cursed. He grabbed the first girl he saw and kissed
her hard on the mouth. "Hey!" her boyfriend said. "Sure, sure!"
said Slim. Across the street, near the wall, a girl was standing
apart from the others. She was not watching Lil dancing; she
seemed bored by all this. Slim stood beside her."You love me,

baby?" "Sure, honey," she said; she was not even looking at him. "No, no, I mean *really*!" Slim said. "Sure, really," she said, without turning toward him.

"Well, come have a drink with me."

"Sure. Now, you're talkin'."

Slim led her into the same bar he had just left. The bartender, standing in the doorway, frowned as Slim approached. "I'll be goddamn!" he muttered under his breath as Slim and the girl walked in.

"Two whiskeys," said Slim. "That all right, baby."

"Make mine Scotch," the girl told the bartender.

The bartender scowled as he poured the drinks.

"Here's to you," Slim said.

"Sure, baby." The girl drank it down and Slim ordered another.

The music played on; Slim could hear it, plainly, through the open door.

"Look, sugar, there's a little hotel up the street, friend of mine runs it. How about takin' a little trip there with me?"

"For fun?" She looked at him, now.

"Well, I'll give you five bucks. How's that?"

"Make it ten"—she measured him—"and in advance."

It was six dollars for the room. The girl was undressed before Slim had taken off his shirt; obviously, she was a professional. "Come on, honey," she cooed. Slim could still hear the music. He was in the bed and the girl was murmuring well-learned phrases into his ear. Her breath was bad; he moved his hand over her body.

"You don't have to go through all that, baby," she said.

It did not take long; there had been no tenderness to it; Slim had rented her body and vented his rage upon it. It had done no good; he felt no better. "For a little extra..." the girl said softly, smiling. "For a little extra, say five bucks more...."

"No, thanks," Slim said.

· *177*

He washed well, in the little bowl near the window. The music surged in through the window. "That's all, sugar."

"Well, you're certainly . . . !"

"That's all."

He was on the street again. He did not feel well, at all. *Go home, get some sleep? What the hell do you care?* He turned off South Street, heading toward home. There was a burning in his chest. *No!* He did an about-face and walked back to South Street again. The crowds still cheered, the band still played, Lil still danced. *Doesn't she even get tired?* The crowd was swimming before Slim's eyes. He passed the prostitute, who was standing near the wall, where he had first seen her; a man was standing beside her, whispering into her ear, but she was not looking at him. Slim walked toward the platform. Lil's head was thrown back, her eyes shone, she was snapping the fingers of one hand in time with the music while, with the other, she held her skirt above her knees to give her legs greater freedom for the dance. . . . Slim leaped up onto the platform and seized Lil. "What are you doing?" she cried. He picked her up, kicking, and walked with her in his arms down the steps that led from the platform. Lil kicked and scratched and screamed invective; the crowd booed. "Help me! Help me, somebody!" Lil cried, but no one moved.

Slim was carrying Lil across the street when the figure of a man—a white man—loomed in front of him. The man was heavy, squat; Slim recognized his face instantly. It was the numbers boss. "Slim, if the girl wants to dance, why don't you let her dance? She wasn't hurting anybody. Besides . . . she dances beautifully!" The man smiled at Lil.

"This is none of your goddamn business, Pete!"

"Help me! Put me down!" Lil screamed, kicking.

"You ought to let her dance," Pete said. He was looking at Lil and smiling. "You ought to let her dance, Slim, she's a nice girl, a real pretty girl, and she's a beautiful dancer."

"It's none of your goddamn business, Pete!"

Lil kicked and pushed hard, and wrenched herself out of Slim's arms. Slim lunged for her, but she ran behind the squat white man.

"Get out of the way, Pete! She's my girl!"

"It's a lie!" Lil said.

"Get out of the way, Pete!"

Pete did not budge. Slim, enraged, swung at Pete, who dodged; thrown off balance by his own momentum, Slim fell drunkenly to the ground. He struggled to his feet and tried to rush Pete again, but some of the onlookers grabbed him and held him back. "Let him go! Let them fight!" laughed Lil, tossing her head. But Slim had sobered down a bit. The men helped him home.

19.

CLAUDE HAD BEEN A WITNESS TO ALL OF THIS, AND AS SLIM WAS led away, his attention—and the attention of most of the crowd— was arrested by a screaming girl who rushed into their midst. It was Suzette.

"Help me! Help me!" she was crying hysterically. "Somebody help me!"

Claude was the first one to reach her. "Suzette! What is it?"

"Oh, Claude, Claude, sank God. Claude, eeet eeees Danneee! He eees beat up . . . there . . . by some white boys . . .!"

A large segment of the crowd took off instantly on the run down the street; and people came out of bars to stream behind them, without even knowing what had happened. "What's up? What's up?" No one had time to answer.

When they reached Dan, he was reviving. "I deeed not know what to do!" cried Suzette. "I deeeed not want to leave heeem

here but he was unconscious and I deeeed not know what to do!"
She burst into hysterical sobs. Dan, eyes opened, smiled at her.
"Take it easy, sweetheart," he said. He tried to get up. "I'm all
right." His face was bruised and bloody and there was a gash
at the side of his head. "Just had me a race war all by myself,"
he said, grinning, to Claude.

"Lie still. We'll call a doctor," Claude said.

"No, no, I'm all right. A little water, I'll be all right." He
sat up.

"Rest here for a second," Claude said. "Then we'll go to a bar
and wash you up." He had taken out a clean handkerchief and
was wiping away some of the blood from Dan's face, carefully,
so as not to touch open wounds.

"What happened, man?" asked a tall, lanky, steady-eyed youth
—a leader of one of the youth gangs.

"Well, them people over there"—he motioned toward Grays
Ferry—"don't seem to approve much of mixed marriages, old
man."

"So they beat you up!"

"Seems as how," laughed Dan.

"Zeee white boys. Oh, zey were horreeeble!" cried Suzette.

The youth said to Suzette, "Which way did they go?"

"Now, look—" Dan began.

"Which way did they go?" The tone was insistent.

Claude looked at the youth. "Why?"

"Which way did they go, Miss? That way?" He motioned
towards Grays Ferry. Suzette nodded. The youth stood up and
looked around him at the crowd. "All right, all my boys step
outa the crowd." His "boys" stepped out: tough-looking, lanky
youths wearing slouched hats and baggy coats. The youth addressed the crowd: "All right, any others of you got guts enough
to come with us, come on. We're gonna visit the Grays Ferry
people."

"Good! A man is talking! I'm with you!" They looked, and it was Michael who had spoken. He had seen the crowd running down the street, and had come out of the bar to follow it.

"We're with you!" A lot of people were speaking now.

Claude stood up. "Wait a minute!" He looked at the youth. "What are you going to do in Grays Ferry?"

"We're gonna beat some heads, man!" said the youth.

"But whose heads? You're running off half-cocked! I know how you feel; I feel the same way. But you don't know which people did the beating. You've got a thousand-in-one chance of getting the right ones!"

"Goddamn the right ones, man! We gonna beat some white heads. Any white heads gonna be the right ones!"

"Don't do it! Riots start that way!"

Michael stood beside the youth. He stared at Claude in anger. "Because you've lost your nerve, Claude, doesn't mean that the rest of us have lost ours!"

Claude looked at his brother for a moment before answering. Then he said, "Michael, you know what you're doing. You want to be a leader, you say. Part of leadership is to know when attack is futile. It's futile now. You can't find the ones who did this."

"You've lost your nerve! You're a coward now, Claude! You're finding excuses for your own cowardice!"

Claude did not bother to answer Michael. He addressed all of those who were going with the youth. "Listen! When it's time to fight, I know it! There was a time to fight fifteen minutes ago—when Dan was beaten! We were not here. It's too late to fight now. Accept that, no matter how bitter it is. Don't do anything that may touch off something for which we'll all be sorry!"

"You're a coward! You've been turned into a coward!" Michael shouted.

"Michael, you're a puppy!—and a dangerous one! Stop barking! What do you know about cowardice or bravery? I've seen brave men and cowards! There's no bravery in running off like a pack of wolves to beat up the first innocent person you see just because his skin is white!"

There was a murmur in the crowd. Most of them agreed with Claude. Some of the ones who had rushed to join the youth whispered among themselves and slipped quietly back into the crowd which was remaining.

Michael was furious. "A coward! A coward! You've turned into a woman without guts enough to fight back!"

But the steady-eyed youth looked at Claude and at Michael and at the crowd and said, "Enough of this goddamn chatter! My boys and me are going over to Grays Ferry! Them that wants to come, come along! Them that wants to stay, stay!—and watch them peckers come back and beat up some of us again!"

"I'm with you!" shouted Michael.

So were, still, a few members of the crowd.

"Then, let's go!" said the youth. They went off, in a trot, in the direction of Grays Ferry.

20.

PETE AND LIL HAD NOT RUN UP THE STREET WITH THE OTHERS; they had remained behind, among the people—including the band—who had neither energy nor inclination to go to the scene of the trouble. For those—the majority—who remained, the band again began to play. Lil smiled at Pete. "Well, thanks for helping me out of the trouble." "How about a beer?" Pete said.

They stood near the beer wagon and drank the beer while munching on hotdogs. "You're all right, baby," Pete said. "That was some dance you were doing! Whew!" He wiped his brow. "Some movement! *Some* spirit!"

Spirit! Lil smiled. "Well, thanks. What did Slim say your name was?"

"Pete."

"Well, thanks, Pete."

"You wanta dance?"

"Sure."

They were with the dancing crowd, in the street. "You sure can dance!" Pete said. "You know, I go for you, baby."

"That so?"

"Bet lotsa men go for you."

Lil shrugged her shoulders.

They had finished dancing and were standing again at the beer wagon.

"Slim your boyfriend?"

"No. He used to be, but that was a long time ago."

"He's still got one hell of a crush on you, looks like."

Lil shrugged again. She looked at Pete with a naughty smile. "Have *you* got a crush on me?"

"I told you that while we were dancing. Sure."

Lil laughed.

Pete took a long drink of the beer. "You know, Slim works for me. Does the numbers collection for me around this neighborhood. I'm the boss."

"Yeah. Slim told me."

"What did he say about me?"

"Nothing. Only, that you're his boss."

"He didn't say nothing else?"

"Nothing else."

"How about another beer?"

"Right."

They both were standing smoking cigarettes and drinking the beer.

"That Slim. You know, he tried to make trouble for me.

Among the boys. The other numbers writers. He ever tell you about that?"

"No," Lil said.

"Tried to make trouble. Tried to make me pay them more money, all that. Talking about striking or going to work for somebody else!" Pete laughed. "Well, I told him off."

"You did, did you?"

"Oh, yeah, I sure told him off." Pete laughed again. "And he knuckled under, of course. All of them did."

"Of course."

Pete looked at Lil, chuckling. "You're a smart girl."

"Sure, I'm a smart girl."

"You ought to go places, see things. How you making out? Got a couple of fur coats? Got a car?"

"No." Lil fingered the can of beer.

"How about a drink," Pete said. "A *real* drink."

"Love it."

"In my place."

Lil laughed. "What's in it for me?"

"Love."

Lil laughed loudly. Pete grinned.

"A smart girl. A real smart girl." He said, "Stick with me, baby, and life, for you, will improve. Get me?"

"I think so."

"You're a smart girl and a real girl. You need things. You need those fur coats and that car—a nice little roadster, with a boxer dog in it. Get me?"

"Sounds good."

"How about that drink?"

"Love it."

"In my place."

Lil laughed again. "You're the boss. Lead the way."

21.

THEY HAD WASHED DAN'S WOUND AND BANDAGED IT. SUZETTE HAD
driven him home. Claude sat now on a stool in a bar. The Blues
Singer walked in.

"Well! What the hell you doin' sitting here all alone when
there's music playing? Where's that beautiful wife of yours?"

"Out dancing I think. With Philip."

"And what? You ain't takin' part in all the excitement? You
ain't gone to beat the hell out of all the people in Grays Ferry?"

Claude laughed softly. "No. That's not for me."

"Them dumb bastards!" The Blues Singer sat down at the bar.
"See, that's the way *real* trouble starts. A few hot-heads!" She
looked at Claude. "Well, what're you buying me, Claude?"

"Anything you want."

"Scotch!" the Blues Singer said.

The Blues Singer stared into the mirror over the bar. She felt
tense, as usual. She did not feel like talking, but she wanted to
make contact with Claude, whom she liked, so she said, indicat-
ing the mirror: "Now, goddamn! Looka that! Ain't *that* a ugly
face for you!"

Claude said, "Stop being so modest."

And the Blues Singer said, "*You* stop being so conceited! It
was *your* face I was talking about!" They both laughed.

"How's Kristin, Claude?"

"She's fine."

"She's a good girl." The Blues Singer laughed. "Too good for
the likes of you!"

Claude smiled at his whiskey. He sipped it. He liked the Blues
Singer; he had known her for a long time. "Sometimes I think
you're right—in a certain way."

The Blues Singer did not smile. "Look here, Claude, I was only kidding. You know that."

"Sure. I was talking about—things like tonight. And other nights. Incidents. Kristin doesn't understand them. I'm sometimes afraid they might do something to her . . . well, to break her spirit."

"She loves you," said the Blues Singer.

"Yes. I'm sure of that."

"And you love her."

"Oh, yes."

The Blues Singer was nervous. "You . . . ah . . . you getting much work done, Claude?"

"Yes." Claude laughed. "Or, at least, I was—up to the beginning of Festival."

"Life's kind of peaceful for you now, huh? Not all this goddamn shouting and shooting and crap! Not all this crusading stuff! More peace—hell, living more like a ordinary human being! Right?"

"Yes."

"Well, that's great. Hell, when you get right down to it, what good does it do, all that other stuff? Know what I mean? Hell, you gonna die anyway at age seventy, and the race problem gonna still be with us. Know what I mean? Hell, you gave all your life to fighting and all that crap; it's good now, get yourself some peace and relaxation from now on."

Claude said, "In a way." And then he said, "But in a way, no."

"In what way, no?"

He laughed, looking at the Blues Singer, for he knew in advance what her reaction would be. "Well, don't shoot, sweetheart," he said, "but in a way, I feel, sometimes, a bit guilty."

"Guilty!" She looked at him in disgust. "Guilty for what? Because you decided to stop throwing all your energy into this *one* goddamn problem been with you since your birth, and decided to live a life like any other human for awhile?"

Claude could only laugh. He liked the Blues Singer. He could only laugh, and say, "Okay. Okay. No guilt!"

But the Blues Singer was off: "Goddamn it, Claude, it makes me sick to hear you talk like that! Hell, I always respected you. Hell, even if you did go around shouting all the time about this goddamn race problem, I figured, 'Well, that Claude's a goddamn *man!*' But, hell, this talk about guilt! Can that crap!"

"Okay," said Claude.

"Can it! Can it!"

"Okay. Okay."

The Blues Singer sat fuming. She glared at her face in the mirror over the bar.

22.

TWO HOURS PASSED BEFORE MICHAEL RETURNED TO THE BAR where Margaret was waiting for him. His hands were bruised, and there was a slight bruise under one eye; for the rest, he was all right. "What . . . happened?" Margaret asked. "We got some of them. A lot of them." "Got who?" Margaret asked. "Some white people," Michael said. He was tired and distant; he did not want to talk about it any more.

It was very cool now, in the morning hours. They walked along Nineteenth Street toward home.

"Was anybody hurt bad?"

"None of us," Michael said. "Some of them were."

Now, in the aftermath, he was a bit ashamed of what he and the others had done; and a bit afraid of the consequences in hatred. But he did not want to think about that.

Across Christian Street, Carpenter, Washington Avenue. Margaret took his hand. Michael became suddenly conscious of the girl walking beside him. He glanced at her; she looked up at him and smiled. He did not smile back.

"You're very . . . quiet this evening, Michael."

"Am I?"

"Is it because of the trouble? . . . or is something else wrong?"

"Don't you know?"

"Should I?"

"I think you should."

Few windows were lighted at this hour along the street. The yellow street lights burned. Occasionally, a street car rattled past.

"I'm glad tomorrow is the last day of Festival," Margaret said. "I like it, but I'm kind of tired, now. Aren't you?"

Michael said, "Margaret, have you been in love with Claude all the time?"

She kept walking, did not look at him; her hand relaxed inside of his.

"Why do you ask such a question? What makes you think that?"

"Have you?"

She said, after a slight pause, "I don't love Claude. Whatever gave you that idea?"

"You don't have to lie," Michael said, sharply.

She wept soundlessly. She wept for a long while without saying anything. Then she said, "But, I love you, too, Michael."

"That's not true."

"It is. It is."

For a moment he said nothing. "All right. Forget it."

After a few more moments had passed, Michael said, "Margaret, why go home tonight? Why don't you stay with me?"

She looked at him through the film of tears. "Do you really want me to?"

"Of course I do, or I wouldn't have asked."

"All right. If you want me to, I'll stay with you."

Michael smiled faintly. He kept walking in the direction of

her house. "No," he said, "I don't want you to. I'll take you home."

They were at her door. Margaret looked at him and said, "Michael, you despise me!"

"No."

"You do!" She stood on the step, looking at him. There was excitement in her heart. "When will I see you again?"

"You want to see me again?"

"Of course I do. Stop it, please, Michael."

"I'll see you tomorrow," Michael said. "As usual." He turned and walked toward his home.

23.

PHILIP, IN HIS ROOM, WAS FITFULLY ASLEEP. HE HAD BEEN dreaming of the night. When Suzette had run, screaming, into the crowd, crying that Dan had been beaten, Philip had been standing near a wall, talking to Kristin. He had listened to her cries, her pleas for help. But he had not moved into the circle that had immediately surrounded her.

"What is it?" Kristin had asked.

"I don't know." But he had not moved. He had known. Kristin had run into the crowd and listened to Suzette. But Philip had not moved.

And he had not moved as that segment of the crowd had detached itself from the others and went racing up the street toward the site of the violence. *I ought to go with them. There might be trouble, and they'll need all of us.* But he had not moved.

He had been dreaming, but he awoke when Michael walked up the stairs, and into his own room. He could hear Michael moving around; then, he heard him go into the hall and through the hall and into the bathroom; he heard him, in a few minutes, come out again. Michael. Brother. Foreigner.

The darkness of the room had shape, form; the darkness was a huge, inward-billowing blanket, of soft texture, all enclosed. He could reach out his hand and touch it; he had touched it, many times, before.

For some reason he thought of Keats and of summer days of youth lying on the grass in the park with volumes of poetry beside him. Reading, looking at the sky. He loved Keats. He loved Donne. Shelly? . . . Sometimes. Wordsworth? . . . Sometimes (best read in the park!). Blake? . . . Sometimes. Byron? . . . Never!

Philip smiled in the darkness. In his ear he heard delicate familiar music: Mozart's *Quintet in G Minor*. Who was playing? The Budapest String Quartet—naturally. He listened. It was not the first movement that charmed him; it was the exquisite, plaintive second. He was comfortable, warm, snug in the bed, listening. He was asleep again by the time the third movement began.

24.

SLIM, IN HIS BED, WAS ASKING HIMSELF FOR THE THOUSANDTH time: *Why?*

Why had she made such a spectacle of herself tonight? *Why* had she quit him—without explanation? *Why* did she dress in this new, sexy way, attracting the stares of every bum on the road? *Why* was she flashing smiles and running around with every greasy gigolo who flashed a big enough wallet? *Why?*

He remembered other days when she had wept tears on his shoulders because of treatment by her parents, because of remarks made by other men. Days when she had unbound to him, to him alone, all wounds; when she had given to him, to him alone, her love, and all that went with it.

Now—now she seemed to take positive delight in hurting him —in flaunting before him these new men she let pick her up. She hardly spoke to him. One would think she had never known him, except casually.

What had happened? What had happened? It was hard to sleep—wondering.

25.

SUNDAY WAS ANOTHER SUNNY DAY. BUT ON SUNDAY, THE *tone* of the Festival was changed. The morning crowds, first of all, were thinner; for many of the people were in church. But even later in the morning, when the crowds from the churches poured onto South Street, there was a difference in the faces and in the air. The people who came on Sunday were older: for on Sunday, in the city, no dancing was allowed. Too, on Sunday, the bars were closed, and no alcoholic beverages were served—not even beer. Young people, therefore, who came to Festival mainly to dance, and perhaps to drink, did not come out in such great numbers as before; and, because choirs from the churches, and soloists, were to sing, more old people than before came to South Street.

The crowds on Sunday were therefore quieter, less riotous, than those of the previous two days: they stood in orderly, chatting groups along the street and pavement, listening attentively each time that a choir went onto the bandstand. The choirs sang hymns. The Old Man, the head of the Elks and a representative from the city orchestra sat in a box just off the platform; they marked their ballots, and upon their decision the Choir Prize would be awarded.

Choir after choir marched to the platform and sang:

> *On a hill far away*
> *Stood an old rugged cross*
> *The emblem of suffering and shame*

and the audience stood rapt, listening, the old people nodding their heads, some humming—unconsciously—to the tune of the music, all familiar with each hymn and with some church pew in which, in summer, they sat and fanned themselves and rocked and hummed and listened to the music.

Choir after choir: the morning moved into early afternoon, but no one bothered to go off for lunch. Then the soloists: Sister Mary Jackson of Shiloh Baptist Church, Sister Maddie Wilson of First Baptist Church, Sister Viola Johnson of Mt. Vernon A.M.E. Church, Brother Ernest Simpson of Calvary M.E. Church. . . .

There was a faint murmur of surprise from the audience when the Blues Singer, dressed in a conservative black dress, mounted the platform and took her place at the microphone. The music was struck, and the Blues Singer raised her voice:

> *Oh, when I come to the end of my journey*
> *Weary of life, and the battle is won,*
> *Carrying the cross, the cross of redemption*
> *He'll understand, and say, "Well done!"*

When she had finished, the Blues Singer descended from the platform. There was no applause: applause was not proper for a hymn. The Blues Singer moved back among musician friends in the crowd, and winked at one of them. She whispered, chuckling: "These sonsabitches are surprised as hell, ain't they? Thought I couldn't sing a goddamn thing except the blues! Heh! That'll give 'em something to talk about!"

By the middle of the afternoon, the music was over, and there was intermission until the evening when new choirs and soloists would mount the platform. Meanwhile, tea, coffee, sandwiches and other refreshments were sold.

Some of the people, rather than simply stand around, decided to walk over to the nearby hall where there was a meeting of the Negro Action Society, at which Michael Bowers, its president, was to speak.

26.

MICHAEL BREATHED NEGRO NATIONALISM FROM THE PLATFORM. Standing behind the rostrum like a preacher in a pulpit, speaking on "The Negro—Past and Present," eyes on fire, employing all of the effective inflections he had learned so well during these months of public speaking, he said:

"We, too—we Negroes—have a history; and a proud one. They—the white men—have told you in their schools, and they tell you in their books, that when they put ropes and shackles on our forefathers, they did the black men a favor—transported them out of savagery into the sweetness and light of the white man's civilization. They have told you this—and they lie! Not from barbarism did they tear our ancestors but from high civilizations—those of the Sudanese and Guineas on the West Coast of Africa, and the Bantus of the South. Not savages these: the world marveled at, and was envious of, the wood carvings of the Congo and Nigeria, the bronzes of Benin, the brass figures of Dahomey, the intricate weavings of the Gold Coast and the manufactured implements and pottery of them all. They wrenched them from high art and civilization: from complex songs and beautiful folk tales, proverbs, riddles; from an elaborate system of courts of justice. The slavers, the real savages, tore them from these, their roots, in fire and blood, laid waste their land, yanked the heart out of their civilizations, branded their bodies like those of cattle, crowded them into between-decks too low for them to stand, the men, women and children together, living in their excrement at temperatures from ninety to one hundred degrees, pregnant women giving birth without medical aid, the death rate fifty per cent or more.

"They have told us in their books, and in their films, that the black man who worked under the sweating sun was happy with 'Ole Massa'—and they lie! The history of slavery is a history of revolt! So often did the slaves, on the ships, uprise, that the captains started something known as Revolt Insurance! Violence, violence, violence is the only history of slavery on these shores! Happy with 'Ole Massa'—with escaped slaves raiding plantations to free more slaves, with slaves going on strike, committing suicide, mutilating themselves, escaping to become guerillas, arsonists, murderers in their happiness! The names Gabriel, Denmark Vesey, Nat Turner—remember these, for these were the greatest of the rebels, these died martyrs in the Glorious Old South, these are our heroes.

"And they have told us, in their schools, that the period after the Civil War—the period known as Reconstruction—was a terrible period in the history of this country. And for *them* it was! For this was the greatest period in our particular history on these shores; this was the period when there were Negro governors of Louisiana and Mississippi, twenty Negroes in the National House of Representatives, two Negroes in the United States Senate; a time when there were black lieutenant governors, secretaries of state, speakers of the houses of representatives in the states, superintendents of education and one Negro justice of a state supreme court. Then: the Restoration: the betrayal by the North of the human gains of the Civil War! Sold down the river were the poor whites and the Negroes. The slaveholders of yester-year, a little leaner for the war, brought sharecropping to take the place of slavery, introduced shackles of economics and law in place of earlier shackles of iron. The Ku Klux Klan, unleashed, marched, and the bodies of black men, like Christmas balls, decorated the trees of the colorful South. Poor white trash was taught to turn its hatred against goddamn nigger, and Gone With the Wind, gone with the wind were all the gains bought in blood in the Civil War.

"They have told us, in their books, and in their schools, and in their newspapers, that the black man has made great and continual gains in a steady upward rise since the days of slavery; and they lie: for, all the years since Reconstruction, through depressions, social revolution and two earthquaking wars, have been but a desperate striving, continually and in pain, to reach again the human heights we occupied in the triumphal years immediately after the Civil War. So have we fought; and still we fight!"

Background: the past. Then Michael spoke of the present day, of the situation in the nation, of the situation in their own city: violence, bombings, police brutality "and all the smaller indications of White Supremacy."

"There's a backlog of repressed energy inside of all of us," he said. "We have some insulted pride, some outraged sensitivities. Let's assert the dignity, affirm the resentment, reveal the pride, deliver our insides of the things they have pent up over the years. It's time, now, to act!"

A tall, gaunt, hollow-cheeked man with strong burning eyes on the platform; his words, and the emotions behind them, moved the audience. Michael was conscious of himself and of the audience; he was conscious that, with a word, with a gesture, with an intonation, he could move them this way or that, up or down—that he could bend them, now, at will. Something inside of him rejoiced and expanded; he felt like the strongest man in the world, a giant, a leader, a king. *Command the emotions, and they obey! Say, 'Go!' and they go; say, 'Come' and they come!* Something inside him expanded, filled up with air.

In the studied pause, his eyes wandered over the hushed audience: they fell on Claude. He looked for a long while at his brother, at his empty lapel. Then he said:

"In this period of great difficulty, in which strong—often harsh—things must be done, we must beware of our so-called leaders. You all know them—the ones who purport to speak for us, the ones who purport to conduct us toward a goal. We must beware of them.

"What is the function of a leader? Put it, that in any people— any oppressed people—there is aspiration for something better, and there is energy to achieve the aspiration. The leader is the man who directs this group energy—goes ahead in the forefront, and shows the rest of us where to go.

"Now, our leaders, in this country, are subject to pressures of many kinds; for various reasons they—consciously or not— betray the energies we place under their command. Some betray us for money. Some betray us for fame. Some betray us because of fear. Some betray us through personal, internal weakness, about which we did not know.

"But the worst, the worst is the one who betrays us because he was never with us, never part of our honest hopes, our dreams, our spirit! These are the most difficult to recognize of all. For they seem to be with us; they seem to fight beside us, at our head; they seem to speak our minds, sound our trumpets, wield our swords. But all the time, secretly, in their deepest hearts, they are nourishing—unknown, sometimes, even to themselves— a hatred of the very people they profess to love, a hatred of the very race to which they belong. And their fight, their fight is a struggle only to *lift themselves*—so they think—above the other people they secretly despise!

"Hard to recognize, these. They hear, all around them, the

opinions that white people have of Negroes: that Negroes are lazy, that they are stupid, that they are dirty, that they like only to sing and to dance; and the only thought of one of these false leaders is—'*I* am not like that!' *He* is not like that—but the rest of us are! And so they seem to fight. They join our ranks. They stand in picket lines, participate in riots, travel all over the country—the world, perhaps—in the name of the fight against prejudice. But for whom, really, do they fight? For all of us? They fight—consciously or not—for *fame! And once they have fame they can extricate themselves from the general mass that is the rest of us!*

"Such, I say, are the leaders who are not with us; who have adopted the attitudes of the white world around them! What is good?—they accept the white standard! What is bad?—they accept the white standard! And what, who, are Negroes?—they accept the white standard *except* as it applies to themselves!

"Recognize these! These are the most dangerous of all our phoney leaders! Recognize these! Once 'liberated,' once having achieved their goal, they marry white women, leave our ranks, flee, fly, don't participate any more in our struggles, fight from the other side to undermine us if they can! *They become one of the whites!* Beware of these! These are the betrayers of their people and of the blood of their fathers!"

27.

THE AUDIENCE WAS FILING SLOWLY OUT OF THE HALL, CLAUDE among them, when, suddenly, there was a commotion in the lobby. "There was a fight!" Some men came in, half-carrying the bleeding body of little Joe, Slim's nephew, whose white sweater was splattered with blood.

"Call a doctor!"

"What happened?"

"A fight. On South Street, up near the other end. Some of the boys from Grays Ferry."

"Stand back! Get some water!"

"The Grays Ferry boys?"

"Angry about last night."

"What happened to Joe?"

"He was in the way. Got beat up, too."

"Many people hurt?"

"Quite a few."

"Those bastards!"

Claude was bending down over Joe. "How do you feel, Joe?" Joe tried to grin, but his face was too swollen, and the grin was a distortion.

The doctor came and bent over Joe. "You'll live, young man," he smiled. "We'll get you to a hospital."

They put Joe in the car and drove off. Claude walked slowly home.

28.

IT WAS THAT EVENING, AT HOME, THAT THE STRANGE THING occurred. They—Claude and Kristin—had decided on late dinner. Claude had told her, heavily, of the new violence during the day, and then had sat down to try to do some work—perhaps to relieve his mind. But the work had not gone well; other thoughts, feelings, had intruded, and he had gone into the living room and sat in the chair near the window and looked out at the trees that moved darkly in the half-light, and then suddenly he had turned around, and seen Kristin, and he had felt instantly strange.

She was standing in a pose Claude knew very well—beside the piano, violin at her chin, the bow moving easily over the strings—one of her frequent practice sessions.

But Claude had said, feeling ridiculous, but feeling already the beginning of that cold chill which would, in a few moments, freeze the marrow in his bones—he had said, "Kristin—sweetheart—forgive me for interrupting, but—are you touching the strings?"

Pausing, slowing, she had half-smiled and said, "Of course, darling."

She had resumed, and he had watched, and the bow had again gone over the strings, and he said, "Darling, play louder."

She looked at him really strangely then; she raised the bow again, struck hard the strings; her body swayed, her head tossed, her arm moved, while all the time her puzzled eyes watched Claude.

It was then that the cold chill really mounted; then that he felt, truly, the stabs of horror, then that he heard bells ringing, felt his stomach contract, felt his temples pound:

He could not hear the music!

Book Four:

RAIN

1.

IT MUST HAVE BEEN A TRICK OF THE SENSES, A MOMENTARY aberration, Claude thought—for, in the days that followed, he heard the music quite clearly. Strange; very strange. He and Kristin discussed, frequently, the night of deafness to the violin, and, with each discussion, he felt again, though with constantly diminishing force, the cold chill that had run in shocking waves through his body. But the days passed, the spring mellowed, and eventually they did not discuss that night any more.

Claude buried himself in work: *there*, on the pages, was a world that made sense! He found it difficult to come out of himself, in conversation or in response to the remarks of Kristin. She became aware of this, and, far from taking offense, became more gentle and loving than ever, though keeping her distance, talking only when she felt that Claude wanted to talk, and for the rest occupying herself with work, practice, household chores, reading, and listening to records.

Claude apologized. "I don't know what it is," he said, "I seem to be way down inside myself, and can't seem to push myself up."

She brushed away the apology. "I love silence; it relaxes me," she laughed. "I used to be so excitable that I was afraid I would one day fly to pieces. Peace and quiet is good for me. Thank you for it, sir."

Claude did not go out much, and, when he did, usually walked only around the block, hardly noticing the sights or the people he passed, but inside himself, thinking—mostly of the book he was working on. He had a great reluctance to go back to South Street. He thought often of Michael's speech, at the meeting during Festival; though of it, with a slight, ironic smile. He found it hard, also, to read the Negro newspapers that came weekly to his door; he would read a few pages, see stories of discrimination, prejudice, violence against Negroes; and then he would have to put the newspapers down. Eventually, he would not even look at the papers.

They had few visitors. Gordon came, to rehearse with Kristin; Philip came, occasionally; Dan and Suzette came. "Mr. Victim," Claude called Dan, with a laugh. But even when Dan and Suzette were there, talking; even when Dan, leaning back, legs stretched out, held forth on a fascinating subject, Claude found himself participating with only a particle of himself; the rest of him was off, floating—he was not always sure where.

And the daily music of Kristin's violin—yes, he could *hear* this music, all right; could hear the notes, the rises and falls. But something in the music seemed to be missing—some power of persuasion, some emotional content pertinent to *him*.

2.

KRISTIN'S WAS A WORLD OF MUSIC, LIGHT, AND AIR. SHE WAS baffled by this other, darker world of violence and strife.

Her problem was simple—she could not *understand* the great uproar that arose out of the color of a skin. The color of a skin? What had that to do with the worth of a man, his intelligence, his sensitivity, his strength, his bravery, his skill? The color of a skin? Why, that was a brown which might be obtained by, say, the most noble white man—a president or king—as the aftermath of a week at the beach! Why, brown was a beautiful color, for all that, and, looking over groups of Negroes, noticing the infinite variety of shades—of textures, even—she had often felt a positive envy that her skin was a colorless white!

She had been shaken by some of their experiences since the marriage. She had been shocked, first, by the reaction of people she had thought her friends: they now ostracized her, did not invite her to their homes, for they knew that Claude would come with her and, not wanting him, they sacrificed her. She had not been able to understand the stares of people on the street; she had not understood their inability to get an apartment in a white neighborhood. The attitude of Michael hurt her—in particular because it affected his relationship with Claude so that she had the disturbing knowledge that *she* stood between two men who had loved each other. Most of all, she had been crushed by the "incidents": by remarks on the street, by fights and near-fights, by the beating of Dan.

It would be all right, of course—or, at least, it would be much better—if she could learn to accept the situation as it was, to adjust to it; if she could say, "Yes, this is so, and it's horrible; but, it is so, and, knowing that it is so, I will live with it and understand it and expect it." But though she repeated this to herself many times, and though Cláude said it to her, and though Dan reiterated it, she *could not* adjust to and accept the fact: for her sense of *logic* was assailed.

It was all so strange, so baffling; and in the face of it, she felt so impotent! She looked at Claude in these days of his moodiness, of his silence, and she understood it and wanted to help him, but she could not because she did not know how. She would live with it; she was in love, and the man she loved was a victim of all this—her own experience of the pain was mainly vicarious. She must bear it, for it was there; but she longed, really, as Claude longed, really, not to live in this world of tensions at all; she longed to live with her husband in the realm of Beethoven, float with her husband on the sentiments of Mozart, rejoice with her husband in the cool, calm, celestial wisdom of Bach. She wanted to look up, not down; she wanted to live only among the great human emotions and humane thoughts. But here, surrounding them, impinging upon them, assaulting them, was this strange, dark, terrifying world of pettiness and animalism; and this other world intruded, jarred, made discords, shrieked, growled, broke the strings of violins.

3.

SINCE THE INCIDENTS OF THE FESTIVAL, TENSION HAD INCREASED between Negroes and whites of certain areas of the city. The tough gangs, mostly Irish, of the Grays Ferry area, in retaliation for the, to them, unwarranted raid of the Negroes on their territory, made forays into the border areas of the Negro neighborhood, notably around South Street, and the Negro youth gangs made forays of their own into Grays Ferry in return. Not for years had there been such warfare between the two sections: there were many beatings, on both sides, some stabbings and even several outbreaks of shooting. As usual, it was the innocents—those who belonged to no gangs, on either side, and had not participated in any of the violence—who were, for the most part, the victims. The Negro press, alarmed, called for action by the mayor; and the mayor's answer was to increase the number of policemen along the border areas, with instructions to arrest all members of gangs who crossed the line to start trouble. This increased the tension, far from alleviating it, since the police tended to arrest only members of the Negro gangs, while letting off, with warnings, those who belonged to the white.

The Negro Action Society was at a loss when it came to coping with this situation. What could they do—join the Negro gangs in their attacks on the white neighborhoods? Hardly. Should they merely station groups to help defend the Negro neighborhood? This seemed a negative approach; and, besides, the police would surely arrest any bands of men they saw. The Society, Michael included, was in a dilemma; at meetings, there were long debates; no program of action could be decided upon.

There had developed in the organization, since the outbreaks of violence, a general lack of faith in Michael's leadership. "You shouldn't have supported that gang that went into Grays Ferry," members insisted.

"What should I have done?" snapped Michael. "Should I just have sat still after the attack they made against a Negro? Are we supposed to sit around and just let them beat us up? Or, are we supposed to fight back?"

"There's a time to fight, and a way to fight," came the reply. "What good did it do to beat up innocent people? Claude was right. You had no way of finding the people who had done the beating. The best thing would have been to let the matter drop— no matter how bitter that was."

"You act as though *I'm* responsible for what's happening now."

"In a way you are. Just as Claude said."

Michael said nothing, but he was furious. Meanwhile, fights in the neighborhoods continued, and the Negro Action Society remained—inactive.

4.

LIL HAD LIVED WHAT PEOPLE CALLED "THE GAY LIFE" SINCE HER break-up with Slim. Men flocked around her; she went to party after party, did the rounds of clubs; cars came frequently to her door, and she had half a dozen proposals.

Most of the men declared passionately their undying love, and begged her to surrender herself to them. Lil, laughing, played a dangerous game. She never said, definitely, no; she gave always the impression that it was just a question of time; and, meanwhile, she got her new boyfriends to pay her room rent, buy her gifts, and, in most cases, to give her an allowance. When a man became too persistent, or when Lil saw she could not hold him off much longer, she dropped him. The cast-offs became bitter.

One unsuccessful suitor came one day banging at Lil's door. Lil said, "Come in." The man was in a fury. Lil had led him on! She had spent his money—extracted money from him! She had pretended to like him, perhaps to love him! Then she had dropped him, and taken another. She was no more than a common con-girl! No more than a prostitute! She was a bitch!

Lil took all of this very calmly, brushing her hair. When the man paused for breath, Lil said, "You shouldn't behave like that, Charlie darling. It doesn't become you. You're really a very dignified man, at bottom, I think. Remember how gracious you used to be in helping me across streets, and in and out of cars? You're really very dignified. You shouldn't act like that."

"You didn't seem to think I was very dignified when you threw me away like an old shoe!"

"Not like an old shoe, sweetheart. You were too serious, don't you see? And little Lil doesn't want to be too serious right now. Little Lil wants to have some fun out of life for awhile."

"Fun at my expense!"

"No, darling. That's not exactly true. Just fun. I just want to have fun. Nothing serious for awhile."

"Then why did you pretend to be serious! Tell me that. You knew that *I* was serious!"

Lil looked at him and smiled. "Were you really, sweetheart? Tell the truth. Were you really? Now, really, you weren't serious at all. You have to take it with good humor, darling. Confess— you wanted to go to bed with me. Isn't that it? And men play a game with women—they buy them flowers, and take them out, and buy gifts—they do a lot of things, and declare they're in love, and all that, and it's all a game. They're all out for one thing. Confess. Now, that's a sport, don't you see? It's like hunting rabbits or squirrels—you use traps, and all other kinds of tricks; like a game. Now maybe rabbits and squirrels decide to play some games, too. And if, once in a while, one of them outwits you, why, then, I don't think you have any right to complain. Do you? Be honest now, instead of just hurt and proud! Do you?" She used a coaxing voice with a faint drawl.

But Charlie was not in a mood to listen to reason. He raved. Lil listened for awhile, and then said finally, "Well, Charlie, you're not a sport. I'm sorry. I had thought more of you. This talk is going to get us nowhere, and I have to finish dressing to go out, so you'd better leave."

"Where are you going?" the man demanded angrily.

"Why, I don't see that that's any of your business, sweetheart."

"You're going out with another man! Another sucker! I know!"

"And if I am?"

"You can't treat me like this! Who the hell do you think you are!"

The man swung at Lil. She moved quickly, and his open palm grazed her cheek. The man turned to swing again, but stopped short; Lil was facing him, a pair of scissors in her hand. But it was not the scissors which chilled him; it was Lil's eyes. He stared; and suddenly she smiled and relaxed, narrowed eyes still on him, and put the scissors back on the dressing table.

She said, "You didn't mean it, really, did you, sweetheart? You lost your temper—went berserk for a moment. Isn't that so? And you're sorry now, aren't you?" She was looking at him and smiling. "You'd better go home, sweetheart. I don't want to hurt you; you're really sweet—and I don't want to go to jail so young."

The man left—rather quietly. But most of the frustrated suitors had sense enough not to threaten Lil.

The affair with Pete had started out like all the others. What had seemed, at first, readily available, had, in fact, been withheld.

Lil had gone home with Pete that night of the Festival, and she had taken the drink he had offered her. But when he had approached her, in his apartment, she had moved away and looked at him with mocking wide eyes. "What's the matter?" Pete had asked.

"Why, Pete! Whatever do you have in mind?" she had asked innocently.

No amount of cajoling, pleading or pressing had softened her. "Why, I'm a *good* girl, Pete!" she had exclaimed. "It's just a question of time." Pete, irritated, had finally driven her home.

Next day, Pete had come around with flowers. "What about dinner?" Her eyes had mocked him. "Just dinner, Pete? Is that all you want?"

"Cut it out, baby," Pete had said.

But it had been only dinner. Pete had been annoyed. And he had been annoyed those other nights that they had gone out together; been annoyed after he had taken her to a shop, to buy a new evening dress "for the smart spots, baby"; been annoyed after he had come around for several weeks and still her mouth, her voice, had denied him, while her laughing eyes invited. "I'm not coming around any more!" Pete had snapped one evening. "But why, darling?" Lil had cooed. "You're just a flirt; you don't mean anybody any good." "Why, Pete! You wound me!" she had said. And the eyes had invited.

Pete had stayed away for several days; during that time, Lil went out with several of the other men who were always pursuing her. At once of the clubs she visited she ran across Pete; he was sitting at the bar, talking to the owner. She had waved and smiled to Pete; he had waved back. The next day, he had come around to see her again. "Who was that fellow you were with?" "Just a friend?" "Is *he* the reason you keep saying no to me?" "Why, Pete! I told you—I'm a good girl. Can't you understand that?"

One day Pete said, "Look, baby, I'll lay it on the line. I want you to be my girlfriend; I'm nuts about you. No more of this crap, right? I own an apartment house on Pine Street. There's a vacant, furnished apartment, five big rooms, kitchen and bath— modern furniture, beautiful, the works, see. Say the word and it's yours. But no playing around. I'm the only one who can visit you there, see."

Lil's smiling eyes studied Pete. "It's a deal."

There was a bar in Lil's new apartment, and Pete kept it filled with whiskies, champagnes, wines and cognacs; and he had a girl come in to do the cleaning three times a week. In some of the town's leading shops, he had charge accounts made out to Lil, and, true to his word, bought her a small, convertible automobile.

Lil became, in every sense, his girlfriend. Nearly every night, in the beginning, Pete came to see her, frequently staying the night. "You're a great girl, a great girl." Sometimes, when he came to call on her, Lil was not at home. Pete, who had a duplicate key, would go in and wait for her; sometimes he would have to wait until three or four in the morning. "Where were you?" he would ask.

"Out. To some clubs."

"With whom?"

"A friend."

He would become furious, but, in the beginning, he would hold his tongue. One evening, however, after a long wait, Pete lashed out at Lil.

"Look, you're not supposed to be going out with other men!"

"Why not, sugar?" Lil cooed. "It's harmless. They're just friends."

"Friends! Hah! No man wants to be just a friend of yours!"

"What am I to do, my love?" Lil asked, mocking him with her eyes. "I can't just sit here, night after night. I have to have a social life; and, of course, you don't want me to meet *your* friends . . . I'm your deep, dark secret." Her eyes laughed into his eyes; she knew why he did not want his friends to know about her.

"That has nothing to do with it!" Pete snapped. "You're not supposed to be going out with other men! You belong to me!"

Lil smiled; but there was no smile in her voice as she said, "Cars and apartments don't buy me, my sweet. Lil belongs . . . to Lil! To nobody else!"

5.

TROUBLES IN THE CITY, AND QUARRELS WITHIN THE SOCIETY, dealt harder and harder blows to Michael's confidence in his own ability to lead. He wondered where he had ever gotten the idea of forming the Society, wondered why he bothered to remain its president. Let one of *them* take over for awhile; they would soon find out that it was no easy thing to lead!

He still saw Margaret frequently, but since he had found out that she was in love with Claude, his feelings toward her had changed. That she was in love with someone else was a sign that something was, in her eyes, lacking in him—and this added to the decrease in his own self-confidence.

He was in a very bad mood one evening, as they walked toward home. They had just left a stormy meeting of the Society, during which one member had gone so far as to demand Michael's resignation—"because of a do-nothing policy at a time when the greatest action is needed!" Michael had offered his resignation but the other members had not accepted it, mainly because they did not know who else could serve as president.

"What do they expect?" Michael said angrily to Margaret. "They blame me for all the troubles in the city! They act as though I'm responsible for everything that goes wrong! How can I decide what's to be done now? It's not so simple! What would you do?"

Margaret did not know.

"And I suppose," Michael said, "I suppose that you, too, have lost confidence in me? I suppose you agree with them, that all these troubles are my fault, the result of my bad judgment?"

"No," Margaret said.

They walked for awhile in silence. Then, hesitantly, Margaret said, "Michael, why don't you try to get Claude to come back? Why don't you try to get him to join the Society?"

"Claude again! That's all I hear! Claude! 'Claude was right!' That's all I hear! And you—you're just in love with him!"

Margaret was silent. The moment the words left his lips, Michael was sorry he had said them. "Anyway," he added gruffly, "Claude's finished. We've heard the last of him!"

Margaret said softly, "I don't think so."

Michael was plunged in gloom. They did not speak the rest of the way home.

6.

PHILIP TRIED TO TAKE A COLD, HARD LOOK AT HIMSELF. HE wanted to know, honestly, who he was.

He had felt a great exhilaration, for awhile, after joining Michael's society—exhilaration that had reached its zenith during the spring Festival. It had seemed to him that he had shucked off the old fears, the old timidity, the old withdrawal from the churning mainstream of life; it had seemed to him that he had emerged from the shell of a rather protracted adolescence into bright and shining manhood. He had developed a theory, even, during that time—the theory of the "purgation" necessary for every man at some time during his life: purgation, through forced activity, of ancient fears and squeamishness; purgation, that was, through forced activity *counter to*, and in spite of, the fears of yesterday. Fears, like body wastes, he reasoned, would come out through the pores in exercise.

But, either his theory had been incorrect (he thought of a story by Ernest Hemingway called, "The Short Happy Life of Francis Macomber"), or it—his earlier reticence—had not been a question of fear at all, but of something else—perhaps simply hypersensitivity, or perhaps simply a good sense of proportion.

At any rate, at the Festival, he had trembled and had not moved when the others had gone to the aid of Claude's friend, Dan. Now, thinking about that, he did not even feel guilty. And his whole being—watched, by his mind's eye, almost with detachment—had revolted, and still revolted, against the violence that had followed. "Now, ask yourself," he told himself, "ask yourself—Is this really a question of cowardice?" He could not, with certainty, answer his own question; but he did know that, to his rational mind, violence was an utter waste and an utter stupidity. He could not face violence; he could not willingly participate in it. It was futile, then, to pretend otherwise.

It was interesting, he thought, how a man could fool himself up to a point—how a man could build for himself a false personality and a false outlook—up to a point, that point being the sudden, usually unexpected "crisis" moment, when the false self was put to the test and, despite the dictates of the will, despite the strength of the illusion in the mind, shattered itself against the inner *reaction*, the real self emerging and standing naked shouting its name.

It had all been ridiculous anyway—the "gesture" of joining the Society, the new personality and outlook he had assumed. For had he had, really, any reason to be ashamed of the simple fact that he recoiled from hatred, fled from violence, lived in terror of the brutish things in life? He did not want to make excuses; but he imagined that, heretofore, he had been a victim of the "male" obsession in America—the need to be a "he-man," "rugged," "red-blooded." Was this really so important? Was it anything much, really, to close up one's hand into a ball called a fist and, with this, used as a weapon, pound another human in the face? Was this "manhood"?

Perhaps. At any rate, Philip now had the proof, in action, that *he* did not fit this he-man image, that *he* did not rush cheerfully to battles, that *he* liked peace and quiet and books and music and escape, as far as that was possible, from personal and racial tensions. Very well. He would accept that proof and accept the fact. No more vindictiveness—he removed the white carnation from his lapel. No more Negro Action Society for him. No more meetings, no more plans for violence to counter violence. Not for him. He would accept himself as being what he was. Perhaps that acceptance would, in the ultimate count, be his greatest bravery.

7.

ONE EVENING, WHILE OUT ALONE, WALKING, CLAUDE FELT AGAIN the pull of South Street—the need, if only for the evening, to go back to the old loved neighborhood and see the old, familiar faces, and the old, familiar bars.

He walked along South Street, peered into a few of the bars and into the *Postal Card*, then turned onto Broad and walked to Lombard Street, and down the stairs to the *Showboat*. Same place: smoke-filled, the people, the oval bar. Claude took a seat at the bar and ordered a whiskey from the Bartender, who was standing eating an apple. The Blues Singer went onto the platform. She sang: the same unforgettable voice, the same emotion.

Claude noticed Michael, sitting alone at a table far to his left, looking quite haggard and withdrawn. Claude felt sudden compassion for his brother, and a sudden desire to talk to him. He got off his stool and went back to Michael's table.

"Hello, Michael. May I sit down?"

Michael looked up at him; there seemed to be a struggle inside of him, for a moment, before he said, "Help yourself." Claude sat down, made a few idle remarks: How was Michael getting along? How was the organization? How was Margaret? Michael answered in monosyllables.

They were quiet for awhile. Claude laughed: "It's like a funeral. I'm not quite dead yet."

"You are to the rest of us!" Michael said.

Claude sipped his drink, lighted a cigarette. The *Showboat*. He remembered that first day home, after his trip to Africa, sitting here in this club, listening to the Blues Singer, talking to— to whom had he been talking?—Lil, the girlfriend of Slim. Also the Old Man, who was sitting now across the room, talking to three attractive girls.

Michael, across from him, was studying Claude's face.

"How did you happen to come down here tonight?" he asked Claude.

"I was out walking and I felt a sudden urge to see 'the folks' again." Claude laughed. "Can't stay away from them for too long at a time."

"It's kind of a new urge, isn't it?"

"No."

"And . . . your darling wife? Where is she?"

"At home."

"She doesn't . . . object to these urges of yours, to get back among your own people?"

Claude smiled. "Still the same old Michael."

"*I* won't change!"

"That's nothing to boast of."

Claude smoked. Michael watched his face. Michael struggled with himself before he could speak again.

"Claude." His voice was softer.

"Yes."

He leaned forward suddenly and touched Claude's arm. "Claude, it's not too late. Come back to us! Join our organization!"

Claude shook his head. "No, Michael. For one thing, your group has no focal point. It's only negative. There's little constructive to it."

"You see, you're probably right!" He seemed eager now. "The group does flounder. That's why we need you in it!"

Claude smiled. "Even if I am a 'leader' of which Negroes must 'beware'?"

Michael said, "It was . . . well, I was trying to hurt you, you know that. Besides, it's not too late for you. I have a feeling there's a struggle inside you—either side can still win. I want *us* to win, Claude. Will you work with us?"

"No. I've had enough of it. I'm tired, Michael. I accept this weariness as either strength or weakness, whichever you want to call it. But I'm tired. I want to be a plain, ordinary human being for awhile."

Michael said, "There are fourteen million of us with brown skins who want to be human beings for awhile!" Claude felt the blow; Michael saw that he felt it.

Michael pursued, leaning further toward his brother, "Claude, we need leaders. We are a people who, God knows, have had a rough time; there's a battle none of us want any part of, a war, we're under attack! We can spare no one!"

And then softer still, more pleadingly, almost desperately, Michael said, "Claude, listen—you have a name! When you speak, the people rally around you. They have confidence in you; you've won enough victories for us in the past to merit any confidence! You've learned! You have no right to withhold your experience from the rest of us. We need you!"

Softly, Claude said, "Michael, you waste your breath. . . ."

"Claude! Claude! I am no leader! I play a game! You called me 'puppy' once—well, I know it, I knew it that night, it's why

I was so furious! I play a game, I try, but I'm not a leader! You are! It's *you* we need!"

Claude did not answer. He finished his drink and stood up. "I'm going home, Michael," he said. "I hope I see you soon again."

8.

ONE BRIGHT AFTERNOON, AS CLAUDE WAS STROLLING IN THE neighborhood of his house, he passed a corner newsstand where he frequently bought his newspapers. There was an odd newsvendor there, whom Claude had frequently noticed: a short, skinny man with extremely hollow cheeks and a funny nasal voice (Claude had heard him talk to others), who made a lot of jerky, jumpy movements around his newsstand. Claude happened absently to glance at the man, and the newsvendor winked.

Claude was startled. He stopped and looked at the man; he could not believe that he had seen correctly. "Did you wink?" he asked.

The newsvendor grinned; his teeth were yellow and widely spaced; his skin was so white that the veins showed clearly through.

"Sure, you're the one lives around the corner, ain'tcha?"

"Yes."

"Sure." He sidled up to Claude. He winked again. "I always notice you." He grinned. "Look, I look stupid, don't I?"

Claude laughed. "I wouldn't say that."

"Sure, I know. I look stupid. Hell, it don't bother me, but people always take me for stupid." He winked.

Claude said, "Why do you wink?"

"Just being friendly." He frowned. "You ain't mad, are you?"

"No. I just wondered."

"Just being friendly." He smoothed over the top of one newspaper. He looked at Claude again. "You know, I never can figure out why it don't hail in summer."

"Why what?"

"You know—hail. That hard snow. I never can figure out why it don't hail in summer."

Claude shook his head in amusement. "Well," he suggested, "it's kind of warm for ice in summer, don't you think?"

The newsvendor nodded. "Well, that's the way life is, ain't it?" He was resigned to the world.

"Yes, I guess it is," said Claude.

Shaking his head, Claude started to walk away, but the newsvendor stopped him. "Hey! Don't go away!"

"Why not?"

The newsvendor looked crestfallen. "See, that's the way life is. Nobody wants to talk to me." He looked the picture of woe. "Why is that, you figure?" he asked Claude.

Claude shrugged. "Maybe people are busy. Maybe they have other things to do than talk."

The newsvendor nodded. "See, that's the way it is with life: people always got something to do. Never any time to stop and enjoy themselves, have a good time, make a little conversation, be sociable for a little while. You know?"

"It's very sad," Claude said.

"Me, I like to discuss things."

"Is that so?"

"See, people always think I'm stupid, see; but I like to discuss things."

"That's admirable."

"Bet you think I'm stupid, too."

"Not at all."

"Sure you do. I can tell by your tone of voice." He winked. "But I'm not stupid."

"I don't think you are."

"I just like to discuss."

"Certainly."

The newsvendor asked, "Do you like to discuss?"

"Yes, when I have time."

"That's the way life is. Nobody takes time for the important things, like discussions. They're very important. But nobody takes the time."

"I agree, but I have to be moving along."

"Okay. That's the way life is."

Claude started to walk away.

"Hey, Claude!"

Claude, startled, turned around and looked at the newsvendor. "How do you know my name?" he asked.

The newsvendor said, "Oh, I know lots of things. All kinds of things. We know each other, you and me."

"From where do we know each other?"

"See, people think I'm stupid. That's the trouble. But I'm not."

"From where do we know each other?"

"For example, *why* don't you want to discuss with me? You think I'm stupid."

"Not at all."

"Sure you do. Now, I like to discuss things. For instance, you take Negroes. Now, that's a subject, ain't it? Well, I like to discuss Negroes."

"That's nice."

"Sure. Now, you think I'm prejudiced. But I'm not. Not at all. I like Negroes, matter of fact." He winked. "Don't you?"

"Me? Certainly. I'm one."

"Sure. That's what I was talking about. Now *that's* a subject for discussion."

"What is?"

"For example, *why* are Negroes inferior to other races?"

"I don't happen to believe they are."

"But people are always rushing. Don't never have time for discussions. Don't like discussions."

Claude decided the man was hopelessly insane. "Well, I have to be going," he said.

"Sure, you have contempt for me."

"I told you before, I have no contempt for you."

"For example, do you believe that people inherit characteristics? Say, for example, that children inherit some of the characteristics of their parents, through the genes?"

"Certainly. That's a scientific fact."

"Well, there you are!"

Claude was completely baffled. "Where am I?"

"Standing right there."

"I have to go."

"Sure. And see, for example, there are differences between nationalities, because they inherit the traits of their parents. For example, you take the French. They have a certain kind of mentality. Now, you can say that it's the culture, but then I say how come the culture is different from the culture of, say, Germany? How come? Which comes first, the culture or the mentality? Does the culture come out of the mentality, or the mentality out of the culture. Which comes first, the chicken or the egg?" He winked.

He said, "For example, do you know that Negroes are the same the world over—no matter which culture they're in? For example, no matter where you look and find Negroes, you find them just as dirty, just as stupid . . . know what I mean? Always in the slums, always backward, always beat by every other race . . . know what I mean? I don't want to be prejudiced, but this is a discussion. You know? And what I said is scientific fact."

"It is not scientific fact, at all."

"For example, it's something you've got to think about. For example, you take South Africa. You know anything about South Africa?"

"Yes."

"Well, you have to think about it. It's a subject for discussion. For example, why are the Negroes of South Africa the only people in the modern world who permit themselves to be ruled by a nation of white people *superimposed* over their own nation? Why is that? Or, for example, why were the blacks of Africa the only people the settlers could use as slaves in America? Why didn't they use Indians? I'll tell you. Because the Indians were superior! The Indians wouldn't *let* themselves be slaves! They would kill themselves first. You have to think about these things.

"The sun was too—"

"And now, there's South America. Do you know anything about South America?"

"Yes."

"Well, now, why is that, do you think?"

"Why is what?"

"Well, naturally. Now, Argentina is the only white nation in South America. Now, why is Argentina the most advanced of the nations of South America—the most civilized, the most independent of the United States, the strongest militarily?"

"That's a—"

"You see, there's a question, Claude."

Claude said, "Are you in the habit of calling your customers by their first names?"

"Oh, let's not stand on ceremony." He winked.

"I have to be going."

"Sure, nobody likes to discuss. How's your wife?"

"My wife?"

"How is she? Charming woman. Pretty, too, eh?" He winked.

"She's fine," Claude said, walking off.

9.

MICHAEL FELT A SOARING JOY, AS WHEN A HOPE ABANDONED, OR an ideal thought destroyed, is suddenly restored. All was not over with Claude! Talking to his brother the other day—above all, watching his face—he had *seen,* as he thought, that Claude felt guilty about his retirement, that he wanted to return to the ranks of his people where he belonged!

With Claude back (for Michael saw his brother, in his mind, already returned) things would change. Claude would join the Society—become it's leader! Branches would form in other cities. The Society would become the *new* instrument for the Negro people, in the *new* age; and Claude, at it's head, would once again be the voice of his race! *He* would know what to do!

Gone, from Michael's mind, were all the bitter things he had thought and said about Claude since his marriage. Gone was all desire, to be, himself, a leader. *He* was not a leader—why fool himself? But Claude would be back; and everything would be all right!

And why had he not yet declared himself, not yet come back to the fold? One reason—*that woman!* Ah, they were clever, those pale-skinned creatures! What weapons she must use to keep Claude from his duty! . . . Tears, undoubtedly! Pleading her weakness, her need for him! Declarations of undying love! A hypocrite!

She, *she* was the obstacle! *She,* the block, the bar! *She* was the rope around Claude's neck, the shackles at his feet. As long as Claude was with her, even though he worked with the organization, he would be handicapped, have to fight a rear-guard action! *She* was the enemy! Against *her* must the battle be waged!

10.

"CLAUDE; YOU MUST LEAVE HER!"

"What!"

They had met, again by accident, at the *Postal Card.* Margaret, too, was there. Michael hesitated for a moment; he was afraid that perhaps he had been too abrupt; but it was too late, and he pursued.

"Kristin." His tone pleaded with Claude not to be angry.

"What are you talking about?"

"Claude, forgive me. But your marriage was a *mistake! That's* what changed you. You'll never be free until you leave her!"

"Hold your tongue!"

Margaret looked at both of them nervously. Michael, to ease the tension a bit, ordered three beers. But he was not yet finished; his hope, for Claude, gave him courage; he was sure that Claude would listen to reason. He had a sudden idea—wicked, but effective; any weapon that served to bring Claude to his senses was justified.

Michael looked at his brother. "Claude, do you know that Margaret is in love with you?"

"Michael!" Margaret cried.

"What?" Claude said, startled.

"Do you know it?"

"Michael! Michael! Michael!" cried Margaret.

Claude stared at both of them in astonishment.

"She loves you, Claude," Michael said, leaning toward his brother. "She's loved you all the time, through all the years you were away, all the time, all the time. Only you. She loves you even now, loved you at the time of your marriage. She can love no one but you."

Margaret was in tears. "Oh, Michael! Michael!" She got up and ran out of the room. Michael did not try to follow her, and Claude was too stunned to move at all.

Claude was silent. In his mind, things, little things, which had gone by scarcely noticed, began to fall into place.

"You never knew it?" Michael asked .

"No."

Michael leaned forward. "Claude, listen to me. Do you know *why* you never knew it?"

Claude looked at him.

Michael said, "Because you never *saw* Margaret!—not really."

"What are you trying to say?"

"Claude, Claude, please forgive me; but you're my brother. Let me say what I think. *Why* couldn't you see Margaret? *Why* couldn't you see what was so obvious—that she loved you?"

Claude looked at him, waiting; but Claude knew what Michael was going to say.

Michael said it. *"Because she's a Negro!"*

Claude started to speak, but Michael raced on. "Claude, listen, I don't want to offend you. But I want to say what has to be said. Claude, listen, let me talk—don't stop me, don't be angry, just let me talk. Will you? I want to talk about a tragedy—the tragedy of a historical accident, the accident by which we, of brown skins, flat noses and short, coarse hair were born in a society where the ideal of beauty is a cream-colored complexion, aquiline nose and long, silky hair! Do you hear me? It's a joke of fate, and there's nothing we can do about it. The movies, the television, the beauty contests, the advertisements in the newspapers—they bombard us every day of our lives with a beauty image that is not our own! In Africa the beauty standards are different, and what the white world calls beautiful would not be beautiful to an African or to a Chinese. But we were born here. And just as surely as we adopt the English language, some of us adopt, also, in one degree or another, the beauty-image of America! Don't Negroes tend to favor, even among themselves, Negro women who are fair, and who have long, silky hair? *Why?* How can we protect ourselves against this ugly distortion? You chose to marry a blond white woman with blue eyes! *Why could you see her and not Margaret?"*

Claude said, "I love Kristin because she is Kristin. I don't care whether she's white or green; I don't care whether she has blue eyes or red!"

Michael was exasperated. *Why* did Claude fight so! Michael drank part of the beer, looking at his brother. An incredible warmth, not felt since those days before the marriage, went out from him to Claude. Brothers were closer than a husband and wife! *Why* did Claude fight him so! Why could he not recognize that Michael wanted, more than anything else, to save him?

"Claude."

"Yes."

Michael hesitated; but, then, he had to go on with it. "May I ask a question?"

"Go ahead."

"In what way does Kristin love you?"

"The same way I love her—as a human being."

"Your color does not enter into it?"

"Not at all."

Michael looked at him. "All right. Now, again, I'm asking you for permission to say what I think. I'm your brother. What I say, right or wrong, is said as a brother, and is said because I believe what I am saying. Right?"

"Go ahead."

"Claude"—Michael leaned forward—"from the time of birth until the time of death, every white American is bombarded with an impression or impressions—distorted impressions—of the Negro. What do white people know about Negroes? How many come into our segregated neighborhoods? Of those few who do come in, how many get really to *see* us or know us? Where do they get their impressions of the Negro, then? From books, movies, fleeting impressions as they pass by a Negro neighborhood. What kind of impressions can they get? Books on the Old South show the Negro happy and singing in slavery. A lot of cheap Negroes, without pride, appear on the radio and television in the roles of mammies, acting stupid, for the benefit of the laughing white audience! The only time Negroes are mentioned in the newspapers is when they have committed crimes—and *then* they're mentioned all right! The white people know about jazz, and consider it the music of savages; they know about spirituals, and think of our sweet, simple faith which has 'carried us through the years'; they know about gangs and gang fights. They have an impression of us, Claude; it permeates their culture, drifts like dust particles in the air. They have an impression—it's that we're lazy, that we're dirty, that we're primitive, that we're unintelligent, that we're sensual, that we love to dance and sing, that we're passionate. . . ."

"What are you driving at?"

"Is Kristin a woman of steel? Is her spirit wrapped in some new alloy which is absolutely impervious to all the superstitions about us that are held by her society, her parents, her friends?"

"You want to say—"

"That Kristin is white, and an American! That she contains within herself, no matter how wonderful she may be in other respects, the poison that is native to her society! That she *cannot* think of us—or of you—as 'simply another human being'! That she in fact *does not* think of you, or any other Negro, as simply another human being! That she thinks of you as a Negro—and as something different from a white man!"

"And the fact that she married me? . . ."

"Lust! Pure and simple! There's the ugly part of it! Lust! You and I?—we're animals, Claude! Remember her statement, a long time ago, when I first met her . . . something about the great 'passion of Negro music'? I didn't like her at that moment! And what about the 'passion of Negro love'? Does she believe in that superstition, too? I say she does! I say she married you out of lust!"

"You're finished?"

"Yes. I'm finished." Michael watched Claude anxiously.

"Then, listen—I won't waste my breath in a futile attempt to prove that what you say about Kristin, is not true. Things like that can't be proved. As a matter of fact, what you say may be true—since nobody knows the ultimate truth about anything. I'll say only this: until I know, beyond the slightest doubt, that what you say is true, I'll assume that it's not true. Until I see the poison—see it clearly, beyond a doubt—I shall assume that there is no poison there. Michael, Kristin is my *wife*. One does not go around questioning the motives of one's wife, or even discussing her. I listened to you this while because you're my brother and because it was probably good for you to get all this off your chest. But the subject is now closed. There will be no more discussions of Kristin. Incidentally, if you're interested—I love her with all my heart and soul. And *not* because her skin is white!"

11.

KRISTIN WAS IN HIGH SPIRITS, GOING ABOUT THE STUDIO, CLEANING it. There was no particular reason for the mood, except that she had awakened in the morning feeling fresh and energetic, had had a good day's work at the office and had found a cheerful letter from her brother when she came home. She loved to clean the studio—the studio was, for her, a personality, almost another human being, in whose presence she felt cozy, at ease, in good humor.

She was dusting the piano when the doorbell rang, and Gordon, her accompanist, came in. He laughed when he saw her: she had changed into slacks and a grey sweater, which was now dirty, and wore a kerchief around her hair; and there were smudges of dirt across her face and on her forehead. "Don't dare look at me!" Kristin cried. She finished dusting the piano (more quickly than usual, the pleasure being therefore less), then ran into the other room to wash.

"All right!" she said, coming back into the room, clean and shining. "All fresh and ready! Doesn't the studio look beautiful?"

"Beautiful," Gordon said.

"This is when I love it most—right after cleaning! It's all nice and shining." She looked around with sparkling eyes at her handiwork, then turned brightly back to Gordon. "What will you have before we begin practice? Tea? Coffee? Something stronger?"

"Coffee will be fine."

While making the coffee, she sang lustily the aria to Marguerite from Faust. "Sing with me!" she shouted to Gordon.

Gordon laughed. "You know I can't sing."

"Neither can I! What difference does that make? It's the feeling that counts!" She came into the room carrying the steaming pot of coffee, and two cups and saucers. "For example, a friend of mine was with the Army in Italy, and do you know what he told me? In Italy, *everybody* sings—children, workmen, housewives, everybody!—and they don't care a bit about whether their voices are good or not. They just sing at the tops of their voices! Operas!"

They chatted while drinking the coffee. "Feuchtwangler is conducting the city orchestra next month. Have you ever seen him? You *must* go! He's *marvelous* in front of an orchestra—like a god!" Some good, new plays were coming to town; it was necessary to see them, too. And Kristin talked again about the *wonderful* thing—an agency was interested in her, and, whenever she felt ready, they would be willing to book her for concerts all over the East. Soon—in one more year, or even less, perhaps—she would be ready to start on a real concert career!

"Well, shall we begin?" Gordon sat at the piano and Kristin held the violin and bow. Gordon watched her: he was always enchanted, watching her, as she played. They practiced for an hour and a half. "I suppose that's enough for today," Kristin said.

They sat down with a glass of wine. Kristin was quieter now; she was still with the music. Gordon, who was always quiet, watched her face.

"Kristin, how are you?"

"How am I?" She came back to the room with a start.

"I don't want to intrude. But, are you happy?"

She laughed. "Happy? I'm delirious! Why?"

"I just wondered." He said nothing for a moment, then, still in the quiet voice, said, "I thought that recently I had noticed something . . . something slightly wrong, between you and Claude. I thought . . . well, I worried about you. I thought I saw shadows cross your face, and Claude's, on too many occasions. Oh, I know it's none of my business, but I wondered . . . you know how it is."

"But what could you possibly have seen?"

"Oh, just those shadows. And Claude seems . . . well, less talkative than before, as though he's worried about something, you know. And you—up to today, that is—seemed a bit quiet, to me."

Kristin nodded. "Oh, I suppose you would see things like that, once in a while. People are so cruel, sometimes! They make remarks about Claude and me, when we're together sometimes, or, at any rate, they simply stare and stare! Sometimes . . . things happen. Oh, it's ugly. I don't like to talk about it! I become *furious* when I just think about it!"

Gordon was silent for a moment. Then he said, "Kristin, I hope you'll pardon me for speaking out of turn. But, I want to say something just this once, and then I won't say it again. Your happiness means more to me than anything. And I hope with all my soul that you will find that happiness with Claude, because I like him, too. But sometimes circumstances, conditions, the unwritten social laws, are stronger than we. If you ever find that you're unhappy with Claude, if you ever find that you want to leave and resume a . . . more normal life, please tell me. You see, I love you; I'm saying that not as a suitor, but simply to let you know. I've loved you for a long time."

Kristin stared at him. "Oh, Gordon!" A wave of sadness rose up in her because of him. There was sadness in her eyes and in her smile as she shook her head slowly, looking at him. "I'm so sorry, Gordon . . . sorry for you, if you love me. I never thought of it. But your offer . . . it's an offer that's wasted, an offer I'll never take up. You speak of circumstances? Of conditions? Of social laws? I love Claude. There are no circumstances stronger than that."

Gordon said, "I'm happy to hear it. Sincerely, I am."

12.

AN EVENING, ALONE, IN THE HALF-LIGHT OF LATE DUSK: THE TWO of them, Claude and Kristin, sitting alone, near the window, in the studio.

—Kristin, how I love you is not, I swear, as other men love other women—not the dull, content emotion of a herd, empty of fire; not the habit routine, not the insipid thing unworthy of the name. . . .

No, how I love you is an all out-surging thing; the expanse of my being; the rush of all my spirit out to you.

How can a man put overpowering emotions into words, without sounding like a fool? I love the way you laugh; love every movement of your singing body; love every fiber of your lighted soul; love the music you play; love your hair, your eyes; love the music you love; love the way you hum a tune; love your sympathy. . . .

I love you with all that pent-up energy heretofore reserved for hate, and, dispensing love for you, I cannot hate, can only love, as though for all my energy there were only one small door, out of which both love and hate could not, together, flow . . . I love you. . . .

And Kristin:
—Claude, darling! Do you know what you are? You are dignity, you are courage, you are pride and strength! Sweetheart,

what can I say in face of what you have, already, said? Backtrack your words, toward yourself, and you have my love for you. I love you because you have known pain, and the knowledge of pain has enlarged your soul: knowing pains, you understand all pains; knowing longing and joy, you understand all longings and joys. Battles have taught you courage; your knowledge of the Negro people has taught you humility. You are much greater than I. You are a wider, wiser human being than I. I learn from you. I want to grow as big in soul as you. I love your greatness of spirit. I love you.

13.

THE BLUES SINGER SAT ON SUNDAY IN THE PARK AND WATCHED the children sailing boats in the pond. The sun was warm overhead. People strolled or sat on benches; couples, star-eyed, passed; the trees were full and like a ceiling overhead, the grass was like a rug; far over, on the right, beyond the neat-clipped hedges, a flower show was in progress; and beyond all, beyond and over the trees, were the tall buildings shining grey in the sunlight.

The wasteful passage of Time.

A child, a girl, came wandering across the grass and paused in front of the Blues Singer. She stood, at some distance, in front of the bench and stared into the face of the Blues Singer. The Blues Singer looked back; the child studied the Blues Singer's eyes. The Blues Singer chuckled and said, "C'mere." The child came closer slowly; she stood in front of the Blues Singer, studying her face. "Well, I guess I must look funny or somethin', huh?" The child studied her. "What's your name?" the Blues Singer asked. The child's eyes wandered to the Blues Singer's blouse; she studied a large brooch that was pinned there, and then looked again at the Blues Singer's face. The child was not at all shy; she simply stood, relaxed, at her ease, regarding the Blues Singer calmly with interest.

The Blues Singer said, "What's your name? Where's your mother?" The child did not answer; she looked away from the Blues Singer for a moment, looked toward the pool where other children were sailing their boats; her eyes were rather wistful. "Well, you're a real cute little girl!" the Blues Singer said. The child was dressed in a spring outfit: a white blouse and a blue jumper; she wore her hair in pigtails.

The sun shone warmly down. The child looked again at the Blues Singer and then, suddenly, smiled brightly, walked still closer, and sat down beside the Blues Singer on the bench. Her eyes went wistfully again to the pond and the children and the boats. From time to time, she looked up at the Blues Singer and smiled.

"Well, you're just makin' yourself at home, ain'tchu?" said the Blues Singer. The child looked at her. "Well, I don't suppose I'll make no *strong* objections, young lady. Just go ahead, take over my seat; I won't make no *strong* objections." The Blues Singer chuckled. The child looked away again toward the boats.

The Blues Singer leaned back on the bench, looking around. *Wonder where her mother is.* The child sat peaceful, hardly stirring, studying with great seriousness, and with that constant wistfulness, the boats and the children who owned them. "Why don't you go over and play with them kids?" asked the Blues Singer. The child did not look at her or answer her. "You know, you're just wastin' your *time*, baby, with an old bag like me." The child looked at the boats. Again, the Blues Singer chuckled.

The sun moved down in the sky. The child sat silently. No one came looking for her. The child sat absolutely still, without saying a word. The Blues Singer watched the child's tranquility, looked at the way her eyes followed the flights of birds, or the movements of the sailboats in the sudden gusts of wind, or the activities of the squirrels that dashed, occasionally, into view, on the grass in front of the bench. The shadows lengthened, and the Blues Singer kept watching, fascinated, strangely close to tears, the unmoving child who sat so still beside her, so at peace, so self-possessed; and the child still turned, from time to time, to look at the Blues Singer, and, sometimes, smile.

The shadows lengthened. The Blues Singer did not want to move. "Well," she said to the child, "if you don't watch out, you're gonna be here all night, little girl. Where's that mother of yours?" She laughed coarsely. The child smiled. The Blues Singer put her arm around the child's shoulder and felt the small bareness—so fragile! so fragile!—of the child's arm. She pulled the child close; the child did not resist; she looked toward the boats.

The Blues Singer whispered softly, almost to herself, "Could I take you home and keep you? Would your mother ever know?"

The child looked up at her; she looked again at the brooch. The Blues Singer unpinned the brooch and gave it to the little girl.

A woman came walking along the path, looking for something. "Cynthia! . . . Oh, there you are! Come along, sweetheart, it's time to go."

The mother smiled briefly at the Blues Singer. She took the child by the hand. The Blues Singer watched both of them walk off, down the path.

14.

ON ANOTHER DAY, AS CLAUDE WAS WALKING DOWN THE STREET, he passed the newsstand again where he had had the encounter with the bizarre newsvendor. The newsvendor was talking to someone. Claude, remembering with amusement the former encounter, stopped for a moment.

"Hello," Claude said.

The newsvendor was delighted. "Well, well! How are you?"

"Fine."

"I'm glad you stopped. I was afraid you were angry."

"No."

"We're friends, aren't we? It's important to have friends. 'Each man is an island, separate to himself'—to correct Mr. Donne." He winked at Claude. "That's why friends are necessary."

"Well, how's business?" Claude asked.

"The Dodgers won't win," the man said sadly.

Claude smiled. Well, he could do this, too. "But the Red Socks are hitless," he said.

The newsvendor nodded and winked. "You're a very wise man. Very. You think I'm crazy, don't you?"

"Far from it."

"You are a very intelligent men," said the newsvendor.

"Thank you," said Claude.

"The sources of love are the bowels."

"You believe so?"

"I know many things."

"I don't doubt it."

> *"Oh, lass mich nicht vergessen dass*
> *Ich liebe dich*
> *Und dass du liebst mich*
> *Und dass wir leben fish. . . ."*

sang the newsvendor.

"Beautiful," Claude commented.

"We have laid the basis," said the newsvendor, "for a very beautiful and lasting friendship."

"I don't doubt it," said Claude.

"You are redundant, my friend. The wages of sin is—punishment!"

"Ah, a Dostoievsky fan."

"You're very intelligent," said the newsvendor, "it's probably why I like you." He paused a moment. "Kafka was not right, you know."

"No?"

"No. Man is meant to be more than a beetle."

"Does he succeed in being more than a beetle?"

"That's material for a discussion. Would you like it?"

"A discussion? Yes."

"Man is not beetlewise. He is fishwise."

"Ah!"

"Thus, the meaning of the song."

"Aha!"

"You are a humorist, you know," said the newsvendor. "Very amusing. Have you ever considered Man's place in the Universe?"

"Yes."

"Very small."

"Very."

"For example—what the hell is it all about? You see? Baffling, isn't it? For example, if there is no God, then life is meaningless. For if there is no God, then there is no life after death. And if there is no life after death, then what the hell are all the three-score and ten about? Do you gather me?"

"Absolutely."

"You are mocking me!"

"I don't mean to."

"For example, take Man. Shall we take Man? Well, he's in a rut. Do you follow?"

"Vaguely."

"Well, he's repeating himself. Do you gather?"

"Oh, yes."

"I saw a building once. It was gray. Beautiful."

"I love beautiful things," said Claude.

"The color of a river—*ex*quisite!"

"*Ex*quisite!"

"What paper do you want?"

"The *Journal*."

The newsvendor handed him the newspaper. He looked at Claude with narrow, smiling eyes for a moment, then winked. He put out his hand and shook Claude's hand. "Claude, my friend!" he said warmly.

"My friend!" Claude said. "Well, until next time."

"Until next time."

Claude was about to walk away, but the newsvendor stopped him with, "But she's very pretty."

"Who?"

"Your wife."

"Oh. Thank you."

"We're friends, aren't we?"

"Who?"

"You and I."

"Oh, yes!"

The newsvendor shook his head. His face was very sad. "Ah, the tragedy of it all!" he said.

"Of what?" said Claude, who really found the newsvendor delightful.

"How it must end. Your marriage."

"Oh? And how must it end?"

"Well, you're so stupid."

"Thank you."

"Don't be offended. I'm talking about your pride. We're friends, aren't we? Friends may talk."

"Always."

"Why are you angry?"

"I'm not. Not at all."

"A sweet girl she is." The newsvendor shook his head. He looked at Claude. "Married to a white woman! What a pity!"

"Why a pity?"

"Oh, what I told you. That it must end. Oh, some people can make it work. Not you. Too much pride. That's always bad."

"You think so?"

"Well, it's better if it ends. Against nature, you know." He winked at Claude. "White people and Negroes—never meant to marry. Against nature."

"How is it against nature?"

"Well, it just *is*!" The newsvendor smiled. "That grounds for a discussion? For example, when did it ever work?"

"Here in America?"

"Yes."

"Well, it's worked many times," Claude said.

The newsvendor shook his head. "No pride. When it worked, the Negroes had no pride. You understand me? For example, people have to have pride. Without pride, where would we be?"

"And?"

"Well, that's why your marriage can't work. Too much pride. Anyway, it's better if it doesn't work. Against nature. Black and white." He shook his head and waved his finger. "Can't work. Negroes aren't human, *we* know that!" He winked. Negroes are animals. . . ."

"Is that so? Well, I have to be going. I don't feel much like talking. . . ."

"Oh, don't be angry!"

"I wouldn't bother to be angry. I'll see you again." Claude started to leave.

The newsvendor cried desperately, "Oh, but don't take offense! Hear? For example, once I had a dog. That was an animal, too. And the dog once saved my life. Now, that was a very intelligent animal, and a very *nice* animal. . . ."

But Claude was walking away.

15.

SLIM WAS SITTING IN A HORN AND HARDART'S RESTAURANT ON Sixteenth Street when Lil and Pete walked in. Lil waved and said

"Hi." Pete waved and grinned. Slim waved; a lump rose in his throat, and he found it difficult to swallow his food.

Pete and Lil sat at a table across the room. Throughout his meal, Slim kept glancing at them. He was on his dessert when Lil stood up and walked past his table, waving a second time, on her way to the ladies' room. The lump in Slim's throat grew bigger. He stopped Lil when she returned.

"Lil."

"Sure, Slim." She paused near his table. Slim saw Pete looking at them.

"Can I have a word with you?"

"Sure. What is it?"

"Sit down a moment."

She sat down. "What is it?"

Slim said, "Lil, it's been a long time, now. If it means anything to you, I love you. I'll keep on loving you, I guess—because I know you. I know you a damn sight better than that pig over there you're running around with." He paused; Lil looked at him and said nothing. Slim went on, "But that's not what I wanted to talk about. Lil, if you don't love me anymore, if you want to go on with this crazy life you've started, selling yourself to the highest bidder—well, I guess you know what you're doing. But I want to know just one thing. *Why?*"

There was a long silence. Then, Lil said, "Slim, I'm talking to you, now, and I know who you are, too, and I know what used to be, so I'm going to talk straight and then I don't ever want to talk to you again. I love you, Slim. I'll never be able to say that, and mean it, to any other man. I love you. Now, forget about me."

"But, *why*, baby?"

She stood up.

"Lil—" Slim's voice was about to break. But ·Lil turned abruptly and walked back to her table.

16.

LIL AND PETE WENT TO LIL'S APARTMENT. PETE DISAPPEARED
into the bedroom; Lil clicked on the radio, picked up a bonbon,
poured herself a drink and settled deep in an easy chair with
a magazine.

Pete came back in a dressing gown and slippers, and made
himself comfortable in another chair. "Well, what did your old
boyfriend have to say?"

"Slim? Nothing. Wanted to talk, see how I was."

"Suppose he don't like it, your being with me."

Lil shrugged. "He didn't mention your name."

Lil read the magazine. Pete said, "Dunno. He's a no-good kinda
bastard, anyhow. Been thinking for a long time about puttin' on
somebody else in his place, picking up the numbers around South
Street."

"What's wrong with Slim?"

"Don't like him. He's a trouble-maker. Stirrin' up trouble
among the colored numbers boys. Lazy, too."

"Not Slim," Lil said. "You've got your signals crossed. Anyway, if you fire him, you'll lose half of your customers around
South Street. They're not gonna give their numbers to anybody
except Slim."

Pete thought about that for a moment. Then he looked at Lil.
"What's the matter, you still carrying the torch for that guy?"

"Me? Not on your life," said Lil, without looking up from the
magazine.

Pete chuckled. "Naw, you got more sense than that, to carry
the torch for a no-good bum ain't got no money. You're too smart
for that." Leaning back, chuckling, Pete lighted a cigar. He lis-

tened to the mellow composition of Don Byas and the Art Simmons Trio on the radio—Byas, master of the saxophone; Simmons lording it over the piano. Pete felt content. "Pour me a drink, baby," he said.

"Pour it yourself."

Pete chuckled again, going to pour his drink. "Little tigress. That's what I like about you. You got spirit." He had the drink now, and he settled himself comfortably in the chair once again. "You know," he said, "you're not like other colored girls."

"You don't say."

"Nah. You got class. I could tell that first time I saw you. You got class. That's how come I decided, 'well, Pete, now there's the girl for you.' "

Lil kept reading the magazine.

Stretching and making himself even more comfortable in the chair, Pete said, "Always did pick colored chicks, y'know. Best thing. Keeps your business out of the street. Don't have to worry about marrying them or having kids or nothing like that. And, hell, if they're at your house, and anybody important comes in, well then, hell, they're your maid, see?"

Lil glanced up at him; in her eyes was a look of infinite hatred; but it was gone immediately, and she looked back down at her magazine, and said, "I see."

17.

TOWARD EVENING, RESTLESS, CLAUDE LEFT THE STUDIO AND wandered down to South Street. He walked into the *Postal Card* where the juke box blared and a crowd of people milled about. Finding one booth empty, he sat down and ordered a light dinner.

The waitress said, "Well, Claude, haven't seen you for a long time."

"No, I haven't been around much."

"Well, everybody says you been hidin' out since you got married." She laughed and walked away.

Claude rose and telephoned Kristin, to say that he would not be home for dinner. When he returned to his booth, he found a young man—obviously, from the text books he carried, a student —sitting in the seat opposite him. The student, startled at seeing Claude, said, "Oh, is this your booth? Sorry, I thought it was empty." He started to get up.

"Sit still," Claude said. "There's plenty of room for two of us." Claude sat down.

"Sure is crowded!" the youth said.

"It always is around this time." While Claude looked at the chart, to see what he would drink, the student pored over one of his books. The student was very frail, and his clothes were poor. When the waitress came, Claude ordered a martini to precede the dinner. The waitress looked at the youth.

"Oh," he said, and paused; he seemed to be estimating which drink would cost the least. "A beer, I guess."

"Aren't you eating?" Claude asked.

"No. I'm on a budget."

Claude laughed. "That's some budget that leaves out eating. I like company while I eat. What do you say, we'll have a couple of martinis first, then a meal together."

The student, obviously, was much too hungry to stand on ceremony. The martinis were brought by the waitress. "Deadly drinks," Claude said. "Toast." They sipped their drinks. "You're a student?"

"Yes. Studying law."

"Criminal?"

"Constitutional." The student looked at Claude with bright, intelligent eyes. He smiled, almost sheepishly, as he said, "I want to argue before the Supreme Court."

"Quite an ambition."

The student was staring at Claude. "Haven't I seen your face before? Aren't you . . . Claude Bowers?"

"Yes."

"Jesus!" The student stared in embarrassing awe. Claude was moved. "Claude Bowers! Jesus! Claude Bowers!" Then the student said, "Wait till I tell the boys! We all admire you. You know, I think it's because of you that I decided to study law. I used to read all the time in the newspapers about you. You were—you still are—a symbol, sort of, of the best spirit of our . . . well, our people. Anyway, I decided that *I* should do something, too!" He laughed.

"So you took law."

"Yes. I want to try civil rights cases before the Supreme Court. We need more Thurgood Marshalls." He laughed again. "And we can't all be the active fighters, like you—with picket lines and everything."

Claude said, "Well, I'm not very active any more."

"You're the greatest Negro living today! Do you know that?" said the student, his eyes filled, again, with awe.

Claude did not know what to say. "Toast," he said. They finished the martinis as the dinners were arriving.

Through the meal, the youth talked spiritedly about law, about the vigor and intelligence of the new students, about the great exchange of ideas at the university. During the war and afterwards, he said, Negroes—the young ones—had undergone a mental revolution. The generation now growing up was one of which they could all be proud. "You've no idea what an impact your actions and your words have had upon us. You've given us an ideal to go for. You're a symbol, as I said. And the ideas of the new generation are *your* ideas—you wrote them and we've read them."

They finished the meal and talked for awhile longer. The youth had to leave. "Homework," he said. "They work us hard in law school! But I just want to say it—meeting you has been the greatest thrill of my life! The greatest!"

They shook hands, and the youth left.

Claude walked up South Street, past the poolrooms, past the stores, past windows from which gypsies beckoned, past people who walked or stood in doors. Hollow doors and windows like gaping, toothless mouths. Sounds: of shouting, of singing of laughing.

Ahead, in a square, Claude saw a crowd. As he approached, Claude could hear their voices—they were singing. A gospel meeting: most of the participants were old, and dressed in shabby clothes. On a makeshift platform, at the beginning of the square, stood a large woman with a powerful voice that rang from the surrounding brick houses: she was leading the people in song. Claude joined them, stood on the periphery. Gospel songs:

> *I want to moooooooo-ve*
> *A little closer*
> *To my Lord*

Claude looked into the God-filled face of an ancient woman standing near him. She was singing at the top of her lungs, while tears streamed from her eyes. Claude moved away.

Lombard Street. Slums. An old man, passing by, looked like a slave, bent under the heavy sack. A hundred pounds of coal, hard-bought, for the little stove in the single tenement room.

"Can I help you?" Claude said.

The man shifted the sack from his back to Claude's. "Heavy," he grinned, "but you're young."

He led Claude up Lombard Street to one of the tenements. They mounted steps and passed through a black hallway. The man switched on an ugly, yellow light, and said, "Some stairs. We got to go up some stairs." They mounted. "Heavy, ain't it?"

The old man chuckled. "I carry that bag up the stairs all the time. All by myself."

"You're strong," Claude said.

"Two more flights," said the man. "Tired?"

"No."

"I carry that bag up the stairs all the time. All three flights. All by myself."

"Stronger than some of these youngsters," Claude laughed.

The man chuckled. "I'm old all right. But I carry that there bag."

It was a small room. The pot-bellied stove stood at one wall, its slender chimney jutting upward, then into the wall, like a bent arm. There were a table, a bed and a bureau; the bulb was small, dim, and the floor was bare. On the table was a small statue of Frederick Douglass, the slave who had been a leader of the Abolitionist Movement, and beside that was the Holy Bible. The man saw Claude looking at the statue.

"Know who that is?" he asked.

"Frederick Douglass."

"That's right." The man looked slyly at Claude, studying him. "Great man, Fred Douglass." The old man chuckled, then scowled, while going about the business of making the fire. "Don't make people like Fred Douglass anymore."

"No."

"Way I figure," said the man, "way I figure, the guts done gone out of the race."

"I don't think so," Claude said.

"Don't, huh?" The man looked at Claude through narrowed, sly eyes. "Well, I do." He was opening a can of baked beans. "You eat yet?"

"Yes."

"Well, you can take a glass of wine with me."

They were sitting at the table. The man was sitting on the bed while Claude used the one chair in the room. "See, about the generation of nowadays, see, it's too soft. Scared. Like comforts too much. Want to lean back and let the other fellow do it. You follow me?"

"Yes," Claude said. He felt very strange.

"Ain't enough guts in the race anymore. Ain't enough people ready to sacrifice. Not enough working together for the *whole* group!"

Claude sipped the wine. In the closet, through the open door, Claude saw some crumbling books. He wondered how old the man was. About eighty. Maybe more. Hundred-pound sacks of coal. Every day, in the winter. "Pour yourself some more wine," the man said. "Good for what ails you." He chuckled at the secret of his longevity. He dipped his bread into the sauce of the beans and ate with gusto. He looked up at Claude suddenly, with a sly grin.

"Ever hear of Marcus Garvey?"

"Oh, yes."

The old man measured Claude. "What do you know about Marcus Garvey?"

"He was the head of the Back-to-Africa Movement."

The man narrowed his eyes and stuck out his chin belligerently. "A great man!"

"Yes," Claude said.

The old man chuckled, dipping his bread into the beans. "Don't make men like that nowadays." He looked up slyly at Claude, waiting for him to challenge the statement. When no challenge was forthcoming, the man went back to his beans. "Used to work for Garvey," he said.

"You did?"

"That's right. Used to work for Garvey. Was a member of the Movement." He chuckled. "*Them* was the days. Used to have some people with guts around in them days. Was gonna go build us a country of our *own*, don't have to fool around with these goddamn white people." He chuckled, then scowled. "Ain't like

246 ·

that no more. Spirit's gone, guts gone. Everybody wants to take it easy, let the *other* fellow do the fightin' for the race. Everybody nowadays lookin' for *peace*, see, own little private life. Don't matter these people keep kickin' us in the face. Just some *peace!*" He scowled, then cast a sly, disdainful glance at Claude.

Claude stood up when the man had finished eating. "Don't want another glass of wine?" "No, thank you," Claude said. "It was . . . an experience to talk to you, sir."

He walked home. Kristin had left a note: she would be back shortly, she had gone some place with Philip, who had dropped by. Claude turned on the radio and sat down in a chair near the window. He thought of the old man. *Old man carrying coal endlessly up the stairs. . . .*

There was a knock on the door.

"Yes?" The young man who stood in the doorway was blonde and pleasant-looking; something about his face seemed to Claude vaguely familiar.

"I was looking for Kristin," the young man said. "You must be Claude. I'm Jimmy, Kristin's brother."

18.

HE WAS A PLEASANT, SOFT-SPOKEN YOUNG MAN, AN INTROVERT who thought more than he said, who obviously dearly loved his sister, Kristin, and took a genuine liking to Claude. He stayed only over the week-end—he had not seen Kristin for a long time, had missed her, and had flown in to spend two days, and would fly back to make his Monday morning classes.

He listened to, and was impressed by, Kristin's playing. She had improved very much since he had last heard her, he said; she would go far, to the top, she would be a great violinist. The three of them went to the theater; they took walks together; they sat at home and talked. Mostly, it was Kristin who talked: Jimmy sat silently listening, smiling his soft, pleasant smile, glancing, from time to time, at Claude. Claude wondered what was going on in the young man's mind. On Sunday, the day of his departure, Claude found out.

"Shall we go for a walk . . . alone?" Jimmy asked him.

"Yes."

They walked in the neighborhood, Claude nodding to the news-vendor (who winked), and stopped finally in a luncheonette, for a cool drink.

"You've enjoyed your visit?" Claude asked.

"It's been pleasant. Kristin wrote me wonderful things about you; and they were all correct. I have a high opinion of my sister"—he laughed—"I think she's a genius. She deserved a husband who was equal to her, and she got it." He paused, to light a cigarette. "Now, that said, may I speak to you?"

"Of course."

"You knew I would?"

"Yes."

Jimmy smiled. "We're alike in a lot of ways. That's why we can talk. It's good . . . I'm going to intrude where I have no right to intrude. I have a favor to ask of you—a very difficult favor, but noble acts are always difficult, otherwise they wouldn't be noble. I'm asking you to persuade my sister to divorce you."

Claude looked at the brother for a moment: even eyes met even eyes. Claude liked the way Jimmy's eyes did not waver, liked his self-control, his lack of embarrassment. Claude said, "Why?"

"Because unless you persuade her, she never will. She has too great a sense of duty for that; she would never want to hurt you. This is especially true because you are a Negro; that fact makes her obligation to stay with you all the more strong."

"What makes you so certain a divorce is in order?"

"Because Kristin is unhappy. Oh, she hasn't said that—I know my sister very well, and she would never say that to me; I doubt that she'd ever even admit it to herself. But I know she's unhappy, simply because she *has* to be unhappy. We'll speak logically. Of what does the ordinary life of a human being consist? The day-to-day life, the little life led from birth to death? It consists of a little world. One has one's work, one's friends, one's favorite pastimes; one revolves in this personal universe.

"Now, married to you, Kristin is denied her world. She's lost her white friends—they cut her off to cut you off. She might be all right if she could live in your world, the Negro world. But she's denied that world, too. Granted that all of this is wrong—is inexcusable—but it's a *fact*. Kristin lives in a vacuum. How long can that go on? You cannot be so vain as to think that she can feed on your company alone.

"But there's more. What I've spoken about is only passive. But what about the *active* things that result from your marriage? There have been incidents, things said, fights and near-fights, insults on the street—Kristin has written to me, in great indignation, about them. These will go on. They are wrong, but they will go on. They tear Kristin to pieces! They drive her wild, because she cannot understand them! Granted, granted that they are wrong, base, evil, whatever you like. The *fact* is that they will go on! The *fact* is that they will always rip at Kristin's heart! *How can you permit her to endure this pain?*"

"We can't surrender to the prejudices of the people around us!" Claude said. "The world is out of whack—let the world adjust itself!"

"And Kristin? Must she suffer untill this miracle occurs?"

"I love Kristin. And she loves me."

"I will grant that, for the sake of the argument, though I do not believe she loves you—I think she reacts so strongly against the wrongs done you and your people that she mistakes her *sympathy* for love. But I will grant even that she loves you. If you love her, you will free her from this torment and this isolation."

"Kristin is a woman! a mature woman! She can make her own decisions!"

"She will never make this decision, Claude—because of a sense of *duty*!"

Claude paused. He was tired. Heavily, he said, "I will promise this, Jimmy—that, if I see one sign, feel in the slightest degree, that Kristin is unhappy with me, or would be happier without me—in her 'world,' as you say—I will insist on a divorce."

Jimmy smiled and stood up. He shook Claude's hand. "That promise is enough for me. You are a sensitive man; you will feel it soon enough." He was about to leave; he looked at his watch. "I have to go. Kristin will be at the studio."

"We'll go to the station together," Claude said.

Jimmy said, "You're a noble man."

"I am not noble. Far from it!" Claude said.

19.

CLAUDE, ALONE, BY THE WINDOW AT TWILIGHT:

Why was it given to me, this double curse of skin and responsibility? I don't want it!—I did not ask for it at birth! That man who passes on the street, that girl across the way—for them no stupid rips and tears! for them no skin-deep scars!

A skin! What's a skin? Or the shape of a nose, or the texture of hair?

Infinity in Time. Infinity in Space. Death comes sweeping at the end of seventy years. A man should live for awhile!

Bach is the greatest of them all! And Aeschylus. And Beethoven? And Shakespeare? And Sophocles? But how did the Greeks arrange it? One century: the Fifth! Incredible!

"There are fourteen million of us, brother, who want to live a normal life for awhile! It's not so easy for all of us!" Michael.

Sympathy? Sympathy? I will not believe that! Of course she loves me! The brother is a white man! What do they ever know of love that pays, with joy, the price? His white skin speaks! The poison of his nation speaks! His Miami college speaks!

To hell with all old men who carry coal! Will they tell me where my duties lie? Duties? Duties? Who imposes duties? Who sorts them out, defines them, names those who are responsible? I saw an idiot on the street. What were his duties?

A man defines his duties for himself! And I'll have none!

Kristin, if you love me not, then let the race war break! Let the rock-bound hatred erupt, let the mountain moan and run red with blood! What have I to do with these things! At seventy, rain or shine, I die!

Who'll tell me what my duties are! Let each man look to himself!

I remember all those sweet dreams I used to have, about the singer of the blues. What beautiful songs!

Where is there another people like this? Where on this earth? From Slavery—God! What do I see on the shadowed faces, in the eyes behind the shadows? We know! And an old man carries coal. To Frederick Douglass. "Don't make them like that anymore!" Old woman raining tears upon a hymn. "Blow, Louis! Blow, blow, blow!" Scar on trumpet lip. "But the cats was there! That's all that counts. The cats was there!"

How I should despise it to be branded with white skin in this country! To have missed the dark experience! Not to know! Not to know! Pale pink blood! On our backs! And we look up—and down—simultaneously!

Kristin, you are not one of them! You are one of us!

Pain to Kristin? Torment? Could it be? And an absence of pain without me? I do not believe it!

Sad-eyed at the Festival. Outside, and she wanted to enter in. How sweet the Blues Singer was! The conga line. Her eyes sparkled then. Face sang.

Darling, your eyes speak more than your brother's lips!

Who said that? "There is no horrible crime, no cruelty known to man, of which I do not, at some time, feel myself capable." Goethe. That, or something like that. And Michael says that I love her because her skin is white and her eyes are blue and her hair is blonde; and that she loves me out of lust. I am her dark destroyer, her twisted passion's ideal. Nonsense! But wait—don't dismiss out of hand. You are not as great a human as Goethe; nor is she. Nonsense, yes, but do not flee from the thought. Think of it. Consider it. Then dismiss it. . . . The beauty-ideal, Michael says. Well, Marlene Dietrich is beautiful. And she is white—so? Does that mean that I am distorted, that I think she is beautiful because she is white? There are many beautiful Negro women. Ah, this is nonsense! Michael's thoughts are ugly! Has he ever read a poem?

Margaret. Sweet girl. Could not see Margaret? See that she loves me? . . . as she thinks she does? Why, because I did not return the love! What nonsense Michael speaks!

"Now, look here, what I want to ask is this: did you decide to retire before you met this whi . . . your wife, or after?" Razors from the Festival. Friends, those. Even on Negroes this poison works! How could it fail to? The hammer falls every day; and the poison is in the air. Who can escape?

Not I; nor Kristin. But she did not marry me out of lust! And I did not marry her because her skin is white!

What stupidity all this is!

Because of the color of a skin! All this is because of the color of a skin!

Listen, logically. What's all this rubbish about duty to a race? Say as well, duty to a family, to a nation, or to mankind. "Each man is an island. . . ." The newsvendor said that. Not so stupid, he. One fills the seventy years as best one can. What is the age of Man? Build an earthly paradise, say—erect it on the blood and bones of martyrs who feel "duty." What then? In some century unborn the earth will explode, and all on it shall be destroyed. Or. the rotations of the earth shall so slow that one side will be burned to a crisp by the sun, while the other side freezes over. Of what use then the paradise? To what good then the blood? What has paid for the deaths of the Jacobins? Who died defending Troy? Lay down one's life in some Peloponnesian War? Duty? Duty? Martyrs want to be martyrs! The seventy years—fill them up! That's the trick!

That student in shabby clothes! "Symbol." "Ideal." A plague on all old men carrying coal and all students with ideals!

Perhaps Sophocles is even better than Aeschylus. I don't know.

"Too much pride." That's what the newsvendor said. A stupid man!

Not stupid. That's not the word.

"We know each other, you and I." Crazy, perhaps. Surely.

One's duty is something one decides for oneself!

And have you decided?

Yes, I have decided.

What have you decided?

No duty!

None at all?

None at all! None at all! It is either all duty, to which I devote my energy and my life, or it is no duty at all, and the hearing of the music!

And you've chosen?

Yes, I've chosen.

Because of Kristin? . . . or did you decide independently?

Independently! What nonsense is this!

Don't shout. I can hear you. And what if Kristin does not love you?

She does love me! Isn't it plain?

Yes, yes, but this is a scientific discussion. If she feels, as her brother says, sympathy; if she would be, as her brother says, happier without you, in her own world—what then?

· 253

I will not consider it! Kristin!—answer it! What do you feel?

"A pain, my love. For the world, for me, and for you."

And do you hear, still, the music?

"I shall always hear the music. The music is me."

And would you hear it more clearly, would the pain diminish, if you were . . . away from me?

"Hear the music more clearly? The pain go away? Without you? But, you are the only audience, darling, for my music. My music exists only inside you. Go away? And where would my music sound? What use would it be to play? . . . Darling, I am astonished. I am a simple person, an open person; you are more complicated than I. But do you know the word 'love'? And have I used it? And do you think the word is tinsel to me? Do I bandy it about? Do I toss it to the dogs, and to all strangers passing by? Darling, you insult me. You make me cheap. I love you. I say it simply. And that—is that not enough? I love you. How often need I repeat it? What proofs will you demand? I love you. That should be enough."

Book Five:

CYMBALS

1.

THE OLD MAN WAS IN A PANIC. HIS WHOLE FUTURE WAS AT STAKE —and all because of a quarrel between two other men. He did not know what to do.

The two men were the Governor and one of the senators of the state, both of whom were members of the political party to which the Old Man belonged. The issue between them was this: that the Governor, who had been only a lieutenant of the senator (who had controlled the state party machine for a decade, and had, indeed, put the Governor in office), was now challenging the power of the senator, and bidding for party rule himself. Their struggle centered around the party's primary elections, to be held soon, to decide the party's candidate for the other senatorial seat. The Governor and Senator had named separate slates; each was calling on party members and the public to support him; each knew that the outcome would decide the question of who was to control the party, and therefore the state.

The state party itself was therefore split down the middle because of this contest at its topmost height. Every city party leader, every county leader, every ward leader, every district leader, every committeeman and every party worker, was faced with a burning question: which slate of candidates to support, that of the Governor or that of the senator.

The choice made by each individual had, for the individual, large personal ramifications, for at stake, in each choice, was the person's political future. The war between the Governor and the senator was a bitter one, without quarter. There were threats and harsh words on either side. The Governor promised that, if he won, he would purge from all party jobs those who had supported the senator; and the senator replied that he would oust those who had swung to the side of the insurgent Governor.

All politicians, and particularly those in the lower ranks who had to depend on political jobs for their livelihood, were terrified.

The choice would have been easy if, as in former years, the senator had been clearly the stronger. But the two opponents now were quite evenly matched. The senator had the great prestige born of his long political domination; he had the support of the Old Guard members of the party machine; he had heavy industrial backing. The Governor, a "reform" candidate, had the support of "citizens' groups," of the newspapers, and of small businessmen; he also controlled some ten thousand state political jobs.

The Old Man's duty in such a contest was clear: he should support the senator. This was due to the "star system"—that each politician had his particular "star," whom he followed in battle, with whom he rose in victory, with whom he went down in defeat. That was the meaning of a political machine: the man who controlled it was the supreme star, a civilian general; just beneath him were the sundry county leaders, the colonels; each county leader controlled several city leaders, the majors; each city leader controlled certain district and ward leaders, the captains; each district and ward leader controlled certain committeemen, the lieutenants; each committeeman controlled certain "workers," the noncommissioned officers, and the committeemen and the workers influenced, by their personal popularity and hard work, the votes of the ordinary citizens. The ordinary citizens were merely privates.

The Old Man's particular star was a district leader named Herb Richardson. They had started together in politics years and years ago, and Richardson, quick, brilliant, wise in the ways of power, had risen rapidly to the rank of ward leader, and now controlled the district in which the Old Man's division was located. Richardson had been a loyal friend of the Old Man: no ward leader had been able to damage the latter; no upstart youngster committeeman had been allowed to displace him; no worker, to whom a reward was owed, had been permitted to oust the Old Man from his job. Indeed, as Richardson had risen, he had made sure that the Old Man, among others, had risen with him—not in power (since power was a thing possessed in itself, which, by definition, could not be "given"), but in the importance —and salaries—of the jobs he held.

Richardson and the Old Man talked in the back of a bar. To Richardson, all was simple. "We'll go along with the senator," he said. He smiled—he was a handsome man, graying at the temples—and said, "What does this upstart Governor know about politics? He'd still be trying cases in a magistrate's court if the senator hadn't put him in office!" Richardson was disgusted. "That bastard! The senator made him—now look at him!" The Governor, like President Woodrow Wilson in an earlier period, had "betrayed" the men who had put him in power. Such treason could not be supported.

As the primary election campaign developed, it became evident that the upstart Governor was gaining ground. Editorials in the newspapers hammered every day at the "corruption" of the machine, hailed the Governor as a "reformer," urged all party members to support the new Liberalism. The citizens' groups held meetings, sent sound trucks into all neighborhoods, hung posters. Ward leaders and district leaders holding political jobs in the State, threatened with dismissal, shifted their allegiances—however reluctantly—to the Governor. As the odds changed in favor of the insurgent, many of the weaker politicians, who could not afford the luxury of loyalty, leaped from the senator's sinking ship. It became apparent, at last, that the Governor would win.

Richardson, the district leader, was sad. "We've been in politics a long time together," he said one evening. "Remember the beginning? Committeemen." He laughed. "Meeting over at Mickey's bar with the boys. How we used to fight like hell with old Ed Sawyer when he was ward leader." He shook his head. "It's sad, you know, to see the senator going down. He's done a lot of favors for us, was with us when others were against us. It's through him I rose—indirectly, but through him." He thought of the politicians who had changed to the side of the Governor. "It's unbelievable! There's a time when this wouldn't have happened; there used to be a time when politicians were loyal to the people who made them. Remember Is Durham? Bill Vare? Pendergast?" He sighed. "Those were the days!" He clapped the Old Man on the shoulder. "Well, it looks like the Boss is going to lose, but we'll go down with him—to the end. Then we'll see what happens. If worse comes to worst, don't worry. You can always take a desk job at my contracting firm—and you don't ever have to come to work!"

The Old Man smiled. Those were kind words from Richardson, and he appreciated them. It had been a long time. Richardson was loyal; the Old Man, for a long time, had known that.

One day the Old Man received a telephone call from Marty Smith, a big county leader, who was one of the supporters of the Governor. "Can I talk to you?"

"Sure."

Marty sat over a glass of whiskey in the Old Man's house. "I'll get right down to brass tacks. There's a colored group— some kind of Action Society, or something—that has been on the Governor's tail for a long time, calling him prejudiced against Negroes and all that. Now, that don't look good. So, to prove all that's a lie, we want to win all the Negro districts—or at least most of them—for the Governor in this campaign. What we'd like you to do, we'd like you to head the campaign for the Governor in the Negro neighborhoods."

The Old Man was flattered; but he said, "Well, you know how it is, Marty, I'm bound to support the senator."

Marty chuckled. "Look, the senator's gonna lose. Anybody can see that. Now, *he* doesn't have to worry about what happens next—he's got enough money, and enough reputation, to get along all right. He can afford to lose. *You* can't! You know what the story is—when the senator loses, out you go because you supported him. It's not too late. The Governor wants the Negro vote. Shift to us, and you're a magistrate when the Governor wins."

"A magistrate!"

"A magistrate."

The Old Man's head was swimming. A magistrate! He looked at Marty. "Give me some time to think about it."

"We don't have much time."

"I'll tell you tomorrow."

All that day, and all through the night, the Old Man thought: A magistrate! What he'd always wanted! He saw a picture of himself on the bench, saw himself dispensing justice, saw himself with power over the police, saw his picture in the newspapers. A magistrate! Young girls around him, calling him "Judge." A magistrate! A magistrate!

The next day he gave Marty Smith his answer: Yes, he would head the campaign for the Governor in the colored neighborhoods.

The announcement of the Old Man's change of support appeared in all the Negro newspapers, along with a picture of him. Nothing was said, because nothing was known, about the projected reward of a magistracy.

The Old Man's telephone rang, but he did not answer it. He knew it was Herb Richardson on the other end—Herb Richardson, incredulous, unable to believe that what the papers said was true.

At the political club, many of the politicians would not speak to the Old Man. The Old Man stayed away from the political club.

After all, he thought, Marty was right: the senator doesn't have anything to worry about! But *I* do! My whole future is at stake! I can't just throw it away! Besides, the machine *is* corrupt! It *does* need to be reformed!

But over and over again, what he was really thinking was: A magistrate! A magistrate! The realization of all my dreams!

2.

LIL LIKED THE APARTMENT. SHE BOUGHT BOOKS, BOOK, BOOKS— all the books she had ever heard about, all of the famous books she had always wanted to read. She stacked them on the shelves and, during the idle afternoons, took them down, one by one, and lay across the bed to read them. She finished very few of them. She laughed to herself and said that perhaps the books were too intelligent for her. She bought magazines and cheaper adventure novels. These she could read.

She loved reading lying on her back on the bed.

She thought, sometimes, of her parents and her brothers. Her father—a mild shiver. Her mother—a faint smile. Her brothers. *Knocked up a chick!* Rex, probably, was still in jail. Lil never got in touch with her family.

She thought, sometimes, of Slim.

There were trees along the street on which she lived. The weather was warm and she liked to go walking under the rich rustling leaves. This street was clean. There were men on the street, men passing, and they, like all men, stared at Lil as she walked. But this was a different kind of neighborhood—the men did not whistle or call her baby.

Lil loved those evenings that Pete did not come. She felt calm and happy when she was alone. She liked standing in the evening at the big window, her knee on the window sill, looking out at the shadowy buildings and the lighted buildings beyond and the sky with stars.

Pete loved money. Money was all he had. Pete thought that everything and anything could be bought with money. To have money was to have everything.

Pete was in other rackets besides the numbers lottery. He controlled, also, the narcotics trade and all prostitution in his area. All of the "girls" of the area had to hand over part of the money they made to Pete's representatives; and the narcotics traffic flourished among teen-age school children. Lil despised this; but it was none of her business, she thought. This had been going on for a long time.

Another thing Lil despised was Pete's ruthlessness and brutality. He loved power, she discovered, and acted sometimes as though he were a god. His favorite expression was, "I'll fix that bastard!"—meaning that he would send his sadistic strong-arm men to give the unfortunate victim a beating. Sometimes Pete had his men beat people in the Negro neighborhood. He beat people who crossed him, or people whom he accused of trying to "muscle in" on his rackets. Pete loved to watch the beatings. He grinned and his eyes lighted up as the beatings took place, or as he told Lil about them afterwards.

He loved also to "handle" Lil: loved to put his hands on her arms, or her bare shoulders, or her legs. At every opportunity Pete touched her. His hands were hateful to Lil—they were clammy hands, with the blood of his victims on them. But when he touched her she did not move. Her body became loose, lifeless —she let him do what he wanted with it. It was strange when he touched her; it was as though he did not touch her at all, as though her body did not belong to her, was something unconnected really with her.

Pete came to the apartment in a fury one day. "That bastard Slim!"

"What's the matter?"

"He quit! Imagine that! He quit!"

Lil's heart leaped. She was glad. Good old Slim. It was time he quit. She smiled and said nothing as Pete ranted and cursed Slim.

Walking along South Street one evening, Lil started to go into a bar. Through the door she saw Slim—he was behind the bar, the bartender. Lil laughed softly. Slim the bartender. So that was what he was doing. A bartender, chatting and laughing with the customers. Good old Slim. He was in his element when he worked with people. Something warm flowed inside of Lil. She would not go in. Her presence might disturb him. Maybe not. Anyway, she would not go in.

She returned home. Pete was there, sitting in a soft chair, drinking. "Where have you been?" he asked. She did not answer; she went into the bedroom with a magazine and lay down across the bed to read.

One night Lil felt the need to have some fun. She went to a club, to which Pete had once taken her, and stood at the bar. Rye on the rocks, she told the bartender. The band was playing.

Beside her, at the bar, sat a soldier, obviously alone. He glanced at Lil and, when she met his eye, looked shyly away. Inside herself Lil smiled. A shy soldier—wonders would never cease. On week-end pass, probably. Away from home. Lonely. "Would you like to dance?" Lil asked him.

The soldier was delighted. His soft, pleasant face lighted up. He was a good dancer. Afterwards they talked, at the bar. The band played a rhumba and Lil danced with her hips. People stared, marveling at the movements of her body. Lil felt good. She was beginning to warm up. She took another drink and talked to the lonely soldier. I ought to go to bed with him, she thought. What difference did it make? He was a nice man, and lonely. As well him as Pete. But she said nothing to the soldier.

By two o'clock Lil had had a lot to drink and was feeling

wonderful. She danced now with her dress above her twinkling knees and her free hand snapping the beat; she laughed silently with head thrown back. People stared. It was a show. The soldier, her partner, stood in front of her, watching happily, his feet and his hands in time with the music. He embraced Lil after the dance.

Lil did not know at what point Pete had come into the club; her first knowledge of his presence was when he shouted furiously at her. "What the hell are you doing!" He was burning. Lil tossed her hair. "Don't shout at me!" Pete turned to the two strong-arm men who were with him and pointed at the soldier. "Fix him!" Lil charged to block the ruffians, but they tossed her aside. The soldier fought well, but they beat him, though Lil scratched and kicked. The soldier lay bleeding on the floor. The club was in panic.

"That'll teach you!" Pete said to Lil. "That's what happens when you feel like flirting! If you don't care for yourself, you'd better start caring about the men!"

3.

CLAUDE COULD NOT SHAKE OFF GUILT AND CONCERN FOR KRISTIN. Both made mental and emotional peace impossible, and interfered with his work. Violence in the borderline areas, between Negro and white neighborhoods, continued, and was the subject of nearly all conversations among the people whom Claude visited on South Street. Claude, who had always been a man of action, felt uneasy—guilty—when he overheard, or participated in, such conversations. Negro newspapers, each week, were filled with stories of incidents. Delegations from Negro organizations went, again, to call on the mayor. Claude tried to block his ears to the things that were happening; but the sounds came through.

More acutely than ever, he was aware of Kristin's isolation—the thing to which her brother had called attention. Because of the incidents (which never ceased to occur) Kristin became tense: now, when they went out together, Claude could feel her *waiting* for something to happen, expecting it, fearing it, her whole evening ruined because she could not relax and enjoy herself unconsciously. For Kristin's sake, Claude had made the supreme effort to control his temper. People stared at them; Claude tried to ignore this. Passing them, on the street, people frequently made comments: "Well, look at that! Salt and pepper!" Claude held his lips together tightly, feeling Kristin go tense. Police stopped them frequently, on one pretext or another; usually, they seemed to assume that Kristin was a prostitute. "We're married," Claude would say, keeping his voice as calm as possible. The police would snarl and send them on their way.

Eventually, Kristin became reluctant to go out; she preferred to stay at home, where she knew there would be no incidents. But at home was isolation: for the most part, only Dan and Suzette, Gordon, and Philip.

Claude could not escape the guilt and the uneasiness, no matter how he tried.

4.

WHENEVER HE SAW HIM, MICHAEL PRESSED CLAUDE TO "COME back to your people, and join in the activities of the faction-ridden Negro Action Society. Claude steadfastly refused; but Michael felt that his brother was weakening.

"Soon he'll come!" Michael said to Margaret. "And once he's back with his own people, that wife of his will be on her way out!"

Sometimes, after talking to Claude, Michael had a touch of remorse. But when he felt such remorse, walking, Michael no-

ticed the tenement houses of the Negro ghetto—blackened out-
rages. And, seeing these and other things, Michael hardened his
heart again. *These* people had no rest; *these* people knew no
retreat!

5.

CLAUDE AND DAN WENT WALKING.

"Claude, may I say something, will you forgive me? I can't
help noticing what's happening. You and Kristin don't go out
much any more. When Suzette and I suggest that we four go out
someplace, you and Kristin always find excuses." He looked at
Claude. "You're finding it hard, aren't you, ace?"

"Yes."

Dan shook his head. "It's a goddamn shame. See, I know how
you feel. And Kristin—well, she's extra sensitive, these things
upset her even more than they do Suzette, I guess. But what're
you gonna do?"

"I don't know."

"It ain't funny"—he laughed, as though to ease the tension
inside himself—"but you can't just hang around the studio. Man,
you *got* to go out once in a while! I'm stickin' my nose in, but
you're my ace, I got to talk to you."

"It's all right."

"Look, me and Suzette are married, right? Now, we have
exactly the same kind of things happening with us that happen
with you—people saying things, people staring, all that kind of
crap—right? Now, we don't let it kill us. We think these bastards
are dumb as hell, and we laugh at them. So we don't stop going
out, and we still enjoy ourselves. Right?"

Claude's eye was fascinated by a bird soaring in the air. "The
trouble is," he said, looking at the bird, "the trouble is that

people are different. Maybe I don't have a sense of humor; anyway, I can't laugh when things happen. I get angry. And Kristin is bewildered."

"You gonna let these people wreck your lives? That gives *them* the laugh."

"I know."

Dan said, "Look, Claude, do me a favor—let the marriage work. Right? I'm talking serious, now. I'm scared as hell of what I see. The way you're heading, well, there's only one end. You know what I mean. Your marriage *can* work—if you let it! All you've got to do is this—recognize the society for what it is, and tell the society to go screw itself! You've got to live *in spite of* the society! You can't change it; don't you change either. All you need is self-control and common sense."

"That's all?"

"That's all."

"Self-control. I knew a man—a young man—in France. He told me that the Germans had come into his house and raped his wife and mother. He said he knew they wanted to kill him, and that they would have killed him if he'd tried to fight them off. So he stood by and did not move. The thing is that I would have died in that moment; that young man lives. Common sense? Do you know how groups of three or four Japanese, holed up in caves in the jungle, fought to the last man, holding off battalions of American troops? They died in the end. Common sense would have been to surrender. I admire their lack of common sense."

Dan said, "Claude, you mean you're not going to *try*, even, to save your marriage."

Claude said, "Yes. I'll try. I'll try very hard."

"Claude, it *can* be done! Try to control yourself. Try hard to get Kristin to adjust to *what is!* We're friends. I love you both. Try . . . try hard, for me."

6.

PHILIP HAD TAKEN A JOB AS AN ASSISTANT IN A LENDING library. He made out file cards and learned to handle the Dewey Decimal System. The new position, really, was ideal: there were plenty of books to read.

He knew a great relaxation, and a return to his "normal" self, after he decided to stop deceiving himself, and quit work with the Society. Michael had been furious, of course; he had denounced Philip as a "traitor." Philip did not care. He was relaxed and content, now.

He began to see his old friends in the discussion groups again. He liked them; he was really one of them, he decided. Were these, his friends, isolated? Yes. Were they in a sort of ivory tower? Yes. But the world had driven them into isolation, into the tower; there were times—historical moments—when the social brutality and insanity reached such a point that they could not be lived with by sensitive people, by people not yet completely brutalized. These people, his friends, could not "adjust" to a monstrosity. They could not adjust to wars and the threats of wars, to inane mass destruction, to hysterical rantings, to race hatreds, to crusades, to stupidity, to the running wild of the mob.

So they met in their little groups, in the living rooms of their homes, and, over coffee, discussed books and art and music and ideas.

At the library where Philip worked was a very fresh and very pretty girl, whose name was Raye. Raye had been to college and was now getting her master's degree at night school. Nearly every day—since it was convenient—she and Philip took lunch together, at a luncheonette not far from the library. They talked about books. Raye wanted to be a writer.

Philip took her with him, when she was free, to some of the "sessions" with his friends. They liked her immediately: she was one of those charming, quiet persons whom all people seem to like. During the conversations—or, rather, the shifting mono-logues—she listened quietly, sitting fresh and attentive in her chair; she preferred listening to talking, but, when finally she put in her points, they were usually well made. Philip found that she had a marvelous sense of humor (this, too, quiet, however) and that though she was pleasant and usually cheerful, this was no sign of emptiness, for she was, at bottom, serious.

Weeks went by. Philip and Raye became increasingly fond of each other. Finally, one day, Philip asked her if she had ever thought about getting married.

She laughed . . . and blushed. Of course she had thought about it, she said. What woman had not?

Philip laughed, too. It would be a good idea, he thought, if they became—well, without too much rigidity or officialness, of course—engaged.

So they became engaged. Philip even bought Raye a ring.

7.

BUSINESS AT THE BAR INCREASED ONCE SLIM HAD COME TO WORK there. The numbers writer was an institution: all the people along South Street, and its environs, knew Slim. Slim was *real!* So the bar was crowded every evening.

Slim liked the job; he liked working around people. Mr. James, who owned the bar, was a sensible man, and more or less let Slim run the bar as he saw fit; this meant that Slim could laugh and talk and give free drinks to people when he felt like it, which, in turn, changed the atmosphere of the bar from that of a business establishment into something more like a club. Late in the evening, when the "tourists" had gone home and only the hard core of steady customers were left, there were bull sessions at the bar. Favorite subjects were two: women and the Army. About women: women meant trouble, they meant heartbreak, they meant cheating and gold-digging, and they were necessary; about the Army: all officers had been lousy bastards, all sergeants had been lackeys for the officers, all foreign cities had been romantic and all other privates had been great guys.

Naturally, Slim knew the police who had the South Street patrol, and he took them aside one evening and said, "Look here, give us a break, will you? How's about it if we close the doors and put shades in front of the windows and keep on having the club open past two o'clock?" The cops said all right, and so each night, at two, the doors closed and the lights were blocked off and the initiated still had a place to go.

The Blues Singer came in frequently, after she finished work at the *Showboat*. She chuckled, seeing Slim in an apron. "Ain't that a goddamn sight!" Sometimes, if the mood hit her, she sang a song or two for the people gathered there. She took drinks with Slim. She liked Slim. He was a dumb sonofabitch, but she liked him.

During the day, and in the early part of the evening, there was a cute little waitress working the tables in the bar. Slim began to take her out on his nights off. She was a bit naive, and rather shy of the men who cracked dirty jokes and made harmless passes at her. She liked Slim, however. She became his girlfriend.

8.

CLAUDE TALKED TO KRISTIN; IT WAS ONLY FAIR TO DO SO, HE thought. He had been moody, lately, he said; and Kristin had a right to know the reasons, since they affected her as much as him. There were other things—things happening in the Negro neighborhoods—but he was disturbed by her isolation and her pain. "Marriage to me means, inevitably, certain things—unpleasant things. It means a certain kind of pain and tension. I see it in you, and it worries me."

She nodded. She had known—or thought she had—what was disturbing him. It was true that she had not yet learned to take calmly the things that happened when they were together. "But I'm trying, darling. Please be patient with me."

"Patient? There's no question of that. But I've wondered about a lot of things, my sweet. I don't know . . . don't be shocked when I use the word . . . but I've even thought about divorce."

"Divorce!"

"Not because you don't love me, or I don't love you—but because you're being hurt, inside, by this situation. These pains, these incidents, this isolation, this inability to relax. They're *damaging*, to the soul. And they will go on, and on, and on. Without end. I don't like to think that you'll have to face this forever. You're too sensitive—"

"But *you* face it!"

"Yes. But I've been conditioned through a lifetime; I remember nothing else. There's some kind of shell—not too strong, I'll admit—that covers my sensibilities. But you have no shell, Kristin. You're naked, and each blow causes pain—I can see the bruises appear. How long can this go on?"

"I'm your wife. I love you. I'll learn about these other things."

Claude said, "You'll never learn. I'm not sure I want you to learn. That shell I spoke of—if you get it, it will block some things from *coming out* as well as going in."

She kissed him softly. "Don't talk. You speak of pains; but let me tell you of a greater pain, a far greater pain. Life without you. That's the pain from which I could not recover."

One Saturday afternoon, while in town shopping, Kristin had a sudden desire to hear the music of the Blues Singer again.

Lombard Street was not far away; she walked down the stairs into the dimly-lighted club where, on Saturday afternoons, jam sessions were held. She was looking around, trying to decide which table to take, when she saw Margaret sitting alone.

"Hello," Kristin said. "Oh, hello," said Margaret.

"Are you alone?"

"Yes. I'm to meet Michael in an hour. I decided to hear some music in the meantime. Sit down. What . . . brings you here?"

"I just wanted to hear some music. I love the music here."

"Yes. So I . . . remember."

A three-piece combo—piano, bass, and saxophone—were playing tricks with "Flying Home." Kristin listened to the incredible, interwoven tunes and rhythms: the musicians were holding intricate conversation, laughing and talking, shouting, interrupting, cracking jokes—and the audience, as well as the musicians, understood all this. Incredible! Kristin stared, entranced.

Afterwards the thick-hipped Blues Singer went onto the platform and the lights went dim and the room was quiet and the Blues Singer sang. *How beautiful! How beautiful she is!* Kristin cried inside. She looked at the Blues Singer's rough-skinned, high-cheeked face, watched the cords move in her throat, listened to that voice which was a wail of infinite strength and pain. *How beautiful! How beautiful she is!*

During the intermission, afterwards, Kristin ordered a lemonade and talked to Margaret. "Well," said Margaret, "it's strange to see you here. Were you in the neighborhood?"

"Near by. I'd been on Market Street, doing some shopping, buying things for dinner." She laughed. "My lord and master loves good food, and *fresh* food—not stuff from cans."

"I see," said Margaret. And then she said, "And how is he? . . . your lord and master?"

"Fine. Under a lot of pressure, though. Work and things."

Margaret was silent. Kristin said, "You've known him a long time, haven't you?"

"Since before he went away. For years. For years. We . . . used to go walking. He used to talk to me. He used to tell me what he thought and what he felt. I listened. He taught me a lot of things."

Kristin said, "You're lucky, knowing him so long. I envy you."

Quietly, but with acid in her voice, Margaret said, "Envy me? Do you really? And what do you envy?"

"Why, that you've known him so long."

"Because I've known him so long. And do you envy that? Why should you envy that? I've known him a long while; but you have everything else."

Kristin looked quickly at Margaret. "I suppose you're right." She laughed, and tried to make it sound light.

Kristin looked at her glass, but she knew that Margaret was staring at her. And Margaret knew that Kristin knew that she was staring at her, and Margaret could hold it back no longer. "Do you think you love him?" she said.

Kristin raised her eyes to Margaret. She felt sad. "I know I love him."

Margaret's soft voice was filled now with bitterness. "How can you love him?—you with your pale white skin and blonde hair and thin blood and pale painted lips! How can you know what it is to love a Negro? How can you say you 'love' a man whose emotions you can't reach, whose depth is beyond you, whose pain was branded on his skin at birth?

"How many floors have you scrubbed in the homes of people who despise you because your skin is not like theirs? How many rats have come crawling in your tenement house? How many hymns to unhearing God have you sung? How many slaves were your fathers? How many outcasts were your children? To love needs emotions, and to love a Negro needs emotions tempered with rage, with bitterness and with pain!"

Kristin did not know how to answer Margaret because there was no argument, only an emotion to be answered.

Kristin said softly, "Margaret, I'm sorry. You . . . love Claude."

Tears of anger and frustration streamed down Margaret's face. "No! I hate him!"

Kristin tried to touch Margaret's hand across the table, but Margaret brushed it away. Margaret stood up. She had stopped crying now, though the traces of the tears remained on her face. "I have to go meet Michael," she said.

Margaret left. Kristin sat for awhile, thinking. Shortly afterwards, she left too.

9.

THERE WERE TEARS IN KRISTIN'S EYES WHEN SHE ARRIVED HOME at the studio. She had tried to wipe them all away before walking into the house, but, though they did not flow, the tears still filled her eyes; she did not want Claude to see them, but he did.

"Kristin. What's wrong?"

He was close to her; his hands were on her shoulder. So close, so close—she could not resist; she leaned her head against the comfort of his chest and cried softly. She could not help it, she could not resist. Claude was silent. He let the deepest pain subside. Then he asked: "What's wrong, my sweet?"

"Claude"—she looked up at him with the tear-filled eyes— "Claude, Claude, Claude, this is such *nonsense!* Such *stupidity!* A skin! A skin!"

"What is it?"

"I can't tell you. I can't. I can't." She searched his eyes. "Claude, darling, don't I love you? Do I love you? Am I worthy to love you?"

"Yes. A miracle. Am I worthy of your love? . . . there's a question."

She held him tight.

"Why do you ask the question? What happened?"

"Claude, I can't tell you. Really, I can't. Please forgive me. Only, say again that I love you. As you should be loved."

"More than I should be loved."

She held him, as though for life.

She fixed dinner, then, while Claude sat in the living room, pretending to read. During dinner she smiled, and tried to make light conversation. Her eyes were red. After dinner, and after doing the dishes, she stood by the piano and picked up the violin and started to play, but her eyes filled up again; she put down the violin. There was a knock on the door; it was Gordon, her accompanist; he had come for evening practice. Kristin tried to play with him, but finally gave it up. "I don't feel much like playing," she explained. Gordon looked at her eyes.

Claude was tired; he went to bed early, urging Gordon to stay for awhile and talk to Kristin—perhaps persuade her to practice a bit. He was tired, but emotionally and mentally, much more than physically. He saw Kristin's tears, heard her tearful voice; what had happened? But, then, what did it matter, the *specific* thing that had happened? Many things happened. It had simply been something else, this time—something else that had caused Kristin pain. He thought of his love for her, and of hers for him. What was best for her? What was best for them?

He was suddenly aware of Gordon's voice: "Kristin, you've been crying."

"It's nothing," Kristin said.

A moment of silence; then Gordon said, "Kristin, I promised not to speak of this any more, but I want to remind you of my offer. No, more than remind—I want to *urge* you to do something. I know you love him; but you must leave. You must come away. You'll destroy yourself."

"Gordon, you have no right to speak. You promised you wouldn't speak again."

"I know, but I must speak. Kristin, I can see how miserable

you are. Your music, for one thing, will suffer. You *must* leave!"

"Stop it!" Kristin said. "I will not have you speak to me this way. I'm serious, Gordon. Don't drive me to say something for which we'll both be sorry."

"I'm sorry, then. I really won't say any more."

"Don't. Please don't."

Claude thought: *Your music will suffer.* He was ashamed of having overheard. He turned on his side and tried to go to sleep.

Sleeping, Claude dreamed of a tall dark man who walked along a road whistling a happy tune. It was dusk, and the man was alone, and the evening was warm, and the man walked whistling with eyes shining and a heart beating and a soul light with pride. For the man was alive.

And the faint shadows of the trees, formed by the early rising moon, suddenly uprose and hemmed in the happy man. "What is it?" And the shadows whitened, and their words were animal sounds, and their teeth were jagged fangs.

And they killed the man—swung him from a tree. And they laughed and were happy. And these were countrymen.

Father in a grave! Claude murmured, waking: I love you, too!

10.

THERE WAS ONLY ONE WAY, THEY BOTH DECIDED, TO OVERCOME the thing that threatened them—that was to face it head on, and *compel* themselves to deal with it as they must. Their enemy, if one could call it enemy, was the world immediately around them. Staying at home and hiding, as it were, from that enemy did not lead to victory; they must go out and do battle.

With Dan and Suzette, therefore, they went out, one evening, determined to enjoy themselves and not permit themselves to be affected by the people around them.

They rode the subway, rather than take the car, since the subway provided a greater test. Kristin was slightly nervous, though she tried not to show it. People on the subway stared at them. Dan, to distract, as much as possible, the attention of Kristin and Claude, held forth on the nature of love. "There are three kinds of love," Dan said. "There are intellectual love, spiritual love, and sensual love. Now, any one, without the other two, is pretty boring, and generally doesn't last for long. Any two, without the other one, is fairly good, and about the most men can usually expect. But all three!—now, *there's* a bonanza, rarely found, and worthy of three salaams when it is!" People stared. People stared.

"How maneee have you found?" asked Suzette.

"All of them, baby. All of them."

As they walked along the street, people stared at them; some people, passing, turned to stare at them until they were out of sight. Husbands nudged their wives and wives nudged their husbands: Look at that! The stares were accusations. A crime was being committed.

They created a sensation, entering the small restaurant where they would dine. Everyone looked up from his table: eyes followed them until, and after, they were seated. "And have you heard the one about the mouse who played the piano?"

"No!" Kristin said, brightening.

Dan told the story and they all howled.

In the lobby of the movie theater people stared at them, and one man said to his wife, loud enough for them to hear, "Now it's things like this that make me think maybe this here democracy's gone too far!" Kristin became a bit nervous and Dan glanced at Claude. "Then there's the one," he said, "about the sleeve job."

"*Don't* tell that one!" Claude laughed.

"What eeees a sleeeve job?" asked Suzette.

"That, cherie, is the whole question."

Afterwards, when they went to a night club, the doorman told them, "I very sorry, sir, but we have no more tables."

"What?" Claude said. Through the door he saw many empty tables.

"All right, all right," Dan said hastily. He led Claude away. "Now, don't blow your top, old man. You know as well as I do that this is what happens in the twentieth century of Our Lord."

They went to another club, to which they were admitted, and again created a sensation. The manager's eyes almost popped out as he led them to a table. There was a dance floor and a band. When the waiter had served them, they went out on the floor and danced. The band members watched them. The customers watched them and whispered among themselves. Not all of this, Claude knew, was hostile—but he was always annoyed by the stares, none the less.

"Now, it's not so bad as all that, is it?" Dan asked.

"No."

Kristin laughed nervously. Whenever she looked around the room, there were eyes, eyes, eyes watching her.

The air was pleasant; they would walk home. As they started down Pine Street, a police patrol car cruised by and flashed a light on them. The patrol car came to a halt. "Hey!" called a policeman, stepping out.

They halted, and the policeman approached them, while the other sat in the car. "Now, hold your temper," Dan whispered to Claude.

The policeman stopped about fifteen yards away from them. "C'mere." He beckoned with his finger. He wanted *them* to walk to *him*. Claude burned inside, but, when Dan glanced apprehensively at him, he walked, with the others, toward the policeman. The policeman shone his flashlight in their faces.

"Can't you see us with street lights?" Claude snapped.

"What?" said the policeman, scowling.

"Nothing," Dan said quickly. "What was it, officer?"

The cop looked at Claude for a moment; then he looked at Dan and Kristin and Suzette. "What're you doing?"

Claude was burning inside, but he held his tongue. Dan could do the answering.

"Just coming from a night club, officer," Dan said.

"Well, what's this?" The policeman motioned, with his night stick, toward Kristin and Suzette.

"They're our wives."

The policeman looked at them incredulously. The second policeman had now descended from the automobile to stand behind his comrade with his hands on his hips, looking at the group.

"What's happening?" the second officer asked.

"These guys claim that they're their wives."

"I don't believe it?" said the second policeman. "Where's your wedding licenses?"

Claude said, "Do most people have the habit of carrying their wedding licenses around with them wherever they go?"

"What?" said the cop, sharply, looking with hostility at Claude.

"We don't have them with us," Dan put in. "But they're our wives, all right. Look at our hands. Rings."

The policemen looked at their hands. They looked at the girls and scowled. "You Americans?" They looked at Kristin and Suzette.

"I am French," said Suzette.

"French, huh?" The policeman spat; he looked at Kristin. "What about you?"

"I'm American." She was trembling.

The policeman looked at her for a long while, with extreme distaste. "What night club you coming from?"

"The *Garden*," Dan said.

"Where do you live?"

"Mason Street," Dan said. "Number 685."

"And where do *you* live?" He pointed a finger at Claude; he was writing down the addresses in a book.

Claude stared hatred at the policeman.

"He lives on James Street. Number 922," said Dan.

The policeman looked at Claude and cleaned his teeth with his tongue. "Can't you talk for yourself, boy?"

Claude saw red; but he held it in; he had to. "Yes, I can speak for myself," he said hoarsely.

The policeman looked at him for awhile, then turned back to his book. "Nine-twenty-two James Street," he murmured, writing. He looked at the other policeman. "Well, what shall we do?"

The other policeman shrugged.

The policeman turned back to them. Before he spoke, he looked a long while at Claude, as though trying to decide something. Then he said, "All right, you can go." The policemen got back in their car. They drove off.

Kristin took Claude's arm as they walked on; she was trembling, and he could feel the tremors flow down into her hand.

"Well, those bastards," Dan laughed, "they're dumb as hell. See their eyes pop when I said they were our wives? They're dumb. You've got to have a sense of humor, I guess."

For awhile, then, there was peace as they walked along. Dan held forth on one subject after another; Suzette tried, in vain, as usual, to get in a word or two. Neither Claude nor Kristin talked much.

They were not quite sure at what point they got their "escort"—the group of young men in shirt sleeves who followed close behind them. They had passed several gangs of boys, standing on street corners; then, suddenly, they had been aware of a following, as it were. The youths, behind them, were talking loudly, making threatening remarks.

"Should we beat the shit out of them or not?"—that was the

question their escort was debating, loudly, so that they, in front, could hear.

"Don't pay any attention to them," Dan whispered. "Just keep walking like they weren't there."

Kristin, by now, was crying softly.

Claude was dying inside.

"Well," said one of the youths, loudly, "we could hang them, if we could find a tree."

"And some rope," laughed another.

"Well, let's see—how many teeth will *you* knock out?"

"Four," said one.

"Seven for me," said another. "Seven's my lucky number."

"Leave some for me, what the hell!" said still another.

And they all laughed.

They walked, walked, and walked. The youths, following them, made no attempt to catch up to them. "Don't be impatient," the youths behind shouted up to them, "we'll get there by and by. We just want you to *think* about it first."

And they all laughed.

"Just keep walking," Dan whispered.

Kristin was holding tight to Claude's arm. She made no attempt to stop the sobs, now.

"How," asked one of the youths, "do you suppose these niggers got such pretty white chicks?"

"Long dicks," answered one of them. "You know niggers are like horses."

"Well, shall we cut them off?"

Memory of a father! It struck Claude like a flash of white light.

"Sure, let's cut 'em off!"

"And the girls?—hell, they're no better than the niggers."

"We could work them over, too."

"We could cut off their tits."

"One tit from each of them—that'll make them lopsided."

And they all laughed.

Claude whirled; he cared about the "test" no longer. And, seeing that Claude had whirled, Dan turned also.

Kristin's head was down; tears poured from her eyes. Slowly, slowly, she shook her head.

"Whew! Looka this!" one of the youths said to the others. There were nine of them: husky youths, over whom Life had, in the early years, constructed a brittle armor. Little that was human went into or came out of these.

One youth scratched his head; he was pondering a deep problem: "Which one shall we beat first?"

"Let's beat the big one first."

"Well," said another one, "that's too simple. See, I got a idea. We beat 'em both, but not so they're unconscious—just enough to take the wind out of their sails. Then, we holds them on the ground, see, while some of us work over the bitches. That way, they watches. After we get finished with the bitches, well, hell, then we go back."

The others applauded this suggestion. "Harvey," one said, "you're a genius!"

"Nothing to it," Harvey said.

But another police patrol car suddenly passed, and, seeing the group assembled, halted. The two policemen got out.

"What's going on?"

The youths looked at the policemen. "Well," one of them said, "we was looking out for law and order, officer. We was gonna save the cops the job of punishing two prostitutes going out with niggers."

The policemen looked at Claude and Dan, and their wives. "That right? These girls prostitutes?"

"They're our wives," Dan said.

The policeman rubbed his chin. "Your wives, huh? Can you prove that?"

"Not here," Dan said, "except by our rings. But we've got licenses at home."

The policeman studied them for a moment. He turned to the youths. "All right, go ahead back where you came from."

The youths scowled; they looked at each other.

"Did you hear me?" said the officer. He reached for his club.

The youths glared at Claude and at the policemen. They turned and walked, reluctantly, toward home. "Fine white men you are!" one yelled back at the police.

The policemen turned back to the two Negroes and their wives. "All right, you'd better let us drive you home. It's not very healthy for you out here, it seems."

"We can walk," Claude said.

The policeman said, "No need of being brave. You're just looking for trouble. Besides, I want to take a look at those marriage licenses you talked about."

"Sure," Dan said.

The policemen drove them to their respective doors. "About the license," Dan began.

"Forget it," the policeman said.

Nor did he care to look at the license when he and his partner had deposited Claude and Kristin at their door.

11.

IN SILENCE THEY WENT TO BED. BUT NEITHER OF THEM SLEPT.

To Claude, it was clear that this could not go on. He was sorry; but life was full of sorrows. This could not go on. He could not look, much longer, into Kristin's eyes, and see those tears of pain. Nor could he look, much longer, into hate-filled eyes of hoodlums, and remain what he was, a man retired. It could not go on.

Because he saw it clearly, and was tired, and was convinced, the pain was less than it might have been. God knew he loved

Kristin!—with all the strength of his being. But, more, he loved his own dignity and self-respect that said: You cannot go on, watching this pain, being the cause, indirectly, of this pain; you cannot adjust silently to injustice; you cannot be insulted, and retire.

Had he known these things all the time?

Kristin sighed, beside him. *Poor creature! You were not made for the insanities of man! Your life is in the stratosphere. You don't know it; but I do.*

He thought of that incredible walk—so important in his life—when he had, with Michael, gone past the church and heard the violin. *All this from that!* And the first recital, and then the meeting after the recital. *My darling wife. You thought then, and think now, that music can cure everything.*

Well, music could not. If only it could!

It was necessary to fight. Whether one wanted to or not. While these things went on, all around, it was necessary to fight back—in self-defense! Duty? It was not really a question of duty. It was a question of pride.

Pride.

Your music will suffer. How true that was. That evening, she had not been able to play.

Brothers were a scurvy lot: they loved their brothers and their sisters!

But that was a strange thing: that not hearing the music that evening. But I don't believe in rot like that!

A police escort home! *And do I need protection from jackals and snarling rabbits? Has it really come to that?* No! That would not be!

It came to this: that the music was a discord, where he was, and he had been used to the discord, and could go on hearing it. But Kristin could not; for her, there must be golden melodies. He would, as first her brother, and then Gordon, had said, free her to hear her music—whether she willed it or not. For the pain of separation would be only temporary; after a year, she would hardly feel it; but the pain of togetherness would last forever, and drown the singing in her throat.

In the middle of the night, Claude sat bolt upright. Kristin, startled, touched his arm.

"What is it, sweetheart?"

He stared at her in the darkness. "Kristin! I've got it! The solution for us!"

"Solution? What?"

"We can go away!"

"Away?"

"Away! Away! Away! We can go away—to Canada, for example! The poison's not yet spread there! Why, you can study there, as well as here; and I can write! Why couldn't we live in Montreal? We'd make new friends! There'd be no isolation. There'd be no wars around us! No hatred on the street!"

"Darling! That's wonderful!" She, too, was excited.

"It's *stupid* that we never thought of that before! Stupid! Stupid! All this worrying, all this tension—is for *nothing!*"

The great weight lifted from both of them. Like children, they embraced, kissed, chattered. Already, they began to make plans. Stupid! Stupid! that they had never thought of this before! They would begin to make arrangements immediately; they would leave as soon as possible for Montreal.

12.

"LOOK HERE, BABY, THAT STUFF AIN'T NOWHERE," THE MUSICIAN had said. He had made a grimace toward the marihuana cigarette.

"What do you mean?"

"That ain't the kick. You ought to try the real stuff. The needle."

"None of that stuff for me!"

That had been four weeks ago. But the Blues Singer had tried the needle of heroin—"just this once." She had liked the cool, floating deliciousness; now she carried a needle with her, all the time.

The Blues Singer went from her home to the *Showboat* and from the *Showboat* to some other club and from the other club home. She rose and washed and cooked and cleaned and worked and laughed raucously at clubs and parties and slept.

Sometimes the Blues Singer took a long look at herself. She was not getting any younger. Sometimes she tried to see the direction of her life, tried to draw a line from the point which was her childhood through the point which was the present, and then, by extending the straight line, see what her future would be. She never completed the line; she shuddered at the thought of it.

The Blues Singer had no friends. She knew a lot of people. She knew mostly musicians, liked to joke and talk with them, liked to play with them; she knew, also, sundry racketeers and customers who came to the club to hear her sing. But she had no friends. For conversation, there was only her dog, Lilac.

When she had been young, the Blues Singer had found out that life was tough. It went like this: if you were a man, you went out and worked your head off for some no-good bitch of a woman with painted lips who was playing around with a young smart aleck while you were away, and you knew it, and you had to take it, because you loved that woman even if she was a bitch; if you were a woman, then you went out and cleaned house for some no-good white woman, then came home and cleaned your own house, and had kids by the dozens, and washed clothes, and cooked and worried about the bills for some lazy, no-good bum of a husband, who would not get up off his rear to go out and find work. And life went like this: even when you thought you were in love, it was all a lie, nothing but a need, the artificial filling of a vacuum, because, when you got right down to it, there was nobody worth loving, anyway. Life went like this: everybody in this world longed, and longed, and longed for something, longed for the something with all his heart, longed with sad eyes and with tears at night, longed with pains in the lungs, longed with sweat and tired feet; and the something for which one longed could never be found. Because the something did not exist. And the nonexistence of the something: that was the Blues.

Before going to the *Showboat*, the Blues Singer put the needle in her arm. She sat in front of the dressing table, leaning on her elbows, looking at herself in the mirror.

You're an ugly bitch! And then: *I ought to go back to the Ray Cee. What the hell, might as well try everything once.*

But she knew she would not really go.

She stared into the mirror hating herself and all the world. Tears came briefly to her eyes; she brushed them away. *Ain't that a bitch!*

I hate all the daughters and sons of bitches in this world!

The world was a lousy place to live!

"Get out of the way!" she told Lilac, the poodle.

Lilac whined.

"You're just like everybody else, Lilac! Whining, whining. The whole goddamn world whines. A world of whining sonsofbitches."

Everybody ought to go jump off the bridges, she thought.

She went into the *Showboat* and stood just inside the door hating all of the bastards who had come to hear her sing.

Like I'm a goddamn circus act!

She would quit this goddamn kind of work, one of these days.

A customer said, "Hey, baby, I got a request number for tonight. 'Black Coffee.' "

"Go screw yourself!" the Blues Singer said.

The bass player·was walking past. The Blues Singer stopped him.

"Look, stupid, tonight try to play *with* me, huh?"

The bass player looked at her in surprise.

"I always play in time, baby."

"The hell you do! *I'm* doing the goddamn singing, not you. Play *with* me!"

She walked between the tables and the bar. She was sorry she had yelled at the bass player. Oh, what the hell! People were too goddamn sensitive anyway! Might as well toughen them up.

"Well, my dear, you look lovely today, lovely. As gorgeous as ever." The Old Man was talking. The Blues Singer scowled at him, and at the girls who were at his table. *Stupid bitches.* "Yes, yes, yes. Lovely, lovely. Care to sit down? What a lovely dress. Yes, yes."

The Old Man ran his hand along her hip. The Blues Singer whirled angrily and slapped his hand away. "Keep your goddamn hand to yourself! I'm sick of all this crap!"

"Why, my dear—"

"My dear, hell! You're full of crap. You're too old for all this shit. Why don't you cut it out, stop acting like a goddamn bald-headed idiot!" She was beside herself; her eyes blazed angrily as she shouted at the Old Man. "What the hell do you think you are? Don't you know everybody laughs their head off about you? Don't you know it? Don't you know everybody feels you're full of crap, a sucker, somebody they can take for a ride or laugh at like you were a goddamn clown? You think these bitches here with you are here because you're handsome or something? They take you for the ride of free drinks like everybody else. And they laugh at you behind your back!"

"Well, I'm sorry if—"

"A lie! A lie! You're a goddamn lie! Can't you hear me? Are you so full of crap that you're deaf? You're a lie! A lie! Your whole goddamn life's a lie! Open your goddamn eyes! Face it!"

The Old Man, flustered, tried to laugh it off. But the Blues Singer would not listen. She walked off toward the platform.

13.

ON SUNDAY MICHAEL LEFT THE HOUSE AND WALKED DOWN THE
street to the home of Mrs. Adams. The old, slow-moving woman
was ready for church. "How you been, Michael?"

"Fine, thank you, ma'am."

She walked leaning against him and talking slowly to the
church. Michael listened to the sermon of Reverend Kirkland
and then to the singing of the choir. "You been makin' quite a
name for yourself, Michael," Mrs. Adams whispered to him. "I
heard some of the sisters talking the other day about a speech
you made somewhere." She looked at him knowingly. "And they
tell me that the young ladies of the church have taken quite a
fancy to you." Michael laughed softly and winked at Mrs. Adams.

He loved this old woman.

Afterwards, they stood outside, talking to some of the members
of the congregation; then Michael walked Mrs. Adams home.

He wondered what to do now.

The sun was hot; he walked slowly in the shade. People were
strolling down the street in their Sunday clothes. At Christian
Street, he decided to turn and pay a visit to the Negro branch
of the Young Man's Christian Association. In the game room,
people played checkers, shot pool, and a couple of members of
the Negro Action Society were playing ping pong.

"Hello," they said to Michael.

Michael watched their game. The two young men who were
playing had taken off their coats, rolled up their sleeves and
taken off their neckties to open their collars at the neck. They
ran back and forth, swinging at the ball; they alternated smashes
with chops; they laughed when they made good returns, groaned
when they missed. Michael watched them.

They rested after the game. "Well, what's happening, Michael?"

"Nothing."

One of them turned to the other. "That girl was really sharp I saw you with the other night. The steady?"

"Naw. You know me," his partner said.

"Are you going to the Omega's dance Friday?"

"Natch."

Michael said, "Friday? There's a meeting of the Society on Friday."

The two players looked at each other. "Oh. Yeah. Well, what the hell, Michael, we can miss that one meeting. The Omegas don't give a dance every day."

"It's not right to miss any meeting," Michael said. "Especially now, when we're having all this trouble. It won't hurt to miss a silly dance; that meeting will be important."

The two players looked at each other. "Yeah. Sure. Yeah."

"Are you coming to the meeting?"

"Sure, Michael. Sure."

Rather self-consciously, the two went on talking about the girl one of them had been out with the other night: how good-looking she was, and how much fun. They talked, too, about a party they had been to, the preceding week-end. Michael was bored by such talk. He stood up. "I'm going into the magazine room."

"Okay, Michael. Sure. See you."

In the reading room, some men were sitting in front of the television set, watching a baseball game. Michael looked through the magazines, to select one he wanted to read. Something happened on the television screen, the sound of applause came from the baseball field, and the people in the room shouted and cheered and slapped their knees. Michael shook his head. It was amazing how excited people became over a game involving a little ball! He did not understand it.

He found the magazine he wanted—a Negro magazine, called

Crisis. He settled back in a chair to read an article on the fight for the vote in the South.

Later, on his way out of the YMCA, Michael stopped for a minute to chat with the director. "Well, haven't seen you around here for sometime, Michael."

"No, I've been busy. With the Society."

"And with some young lady probably, eh?" The director chuckled. "All the boys getting married, settling down, having children. When are you going to take the plunge?"

Michael laughed. "I don't know." Marriage? He had never thought about it.

Once outside, Michael did not know what to do with himself. He walked slowly, toward no particular place. Young couples passed him. People in front of houses, or in the doors of drug stores, laughed and talked. Old people came from afternoon services at church. Children, in Sunday frocks, ran by. Michael looked with a tender smile at the children. *For you we'll build a better world!*

An old woman sat in a chair near the wall at the corner of Carpenter Street, selling shoe strings and chewing gum. "Buy some chewing gum from an old lady?" she pleaded. Poor woman, Michael thought. He bought several packages of gum, though he never chewed it. "You're a kind young man," the woman said.

The woman pointed at her hat. "You see this hat?"

"Yes." It was a small hat, with a feather in it.

"Hats are very important," the old woman said. "They're good for rain or for the sun—as protection, you know."

"Yes."

"This is a new hat. That's why I like it. I'm very proud of it."

"It's a very nice hat," Michael said.

"I love hats. You can get them all colors: gay or somber. And there are so many kinds! I get so excited, you know, pardon me. But you can get them broad-brimmed and narrow-brimmed, peaked and flat, tilted and straight; you can get them with feathers or without feathers, with bows or without bows, with artificial flowers or without artificial flowers. It's wonderful!"

"Yes." Michael was baffled.

"Kings and queens wear hats. They call them crowns."

"Yes."

The woman busied herself arranging the shoe strings. She was humming a tune. Michael walked away.

He wandered about until the evening, when he ate alone at a small Negro restaurant, with bright, pleasant curtains at the windows and bright cloths on the tables. He had told Margaret he would stop by her house after dinner. She had just finished dishes, and felt like going for a short walk. Because Margaret had missed the last meeting of the Society (something of which Michael strongly disapproved), he brought her up to date on the latest activity—or, rather, inactivity—of the organization.

Margaret nodded from time to time, as Michael talked. She said little herself. Michael talked about the increase in violence, about the ineffectiveness of the police, about the tragedy of the dissension within the Society. Margaret listened. When Michael had finished talking about these subjects, he did not know quite what to say.

"Michael," Margaret said, "don't you ever laugh?"

"Laugh?"

Margaret smiled softly. "Don't you ever dance? Don't you ever let yourself go? Don't you ever play?"

"Well . . . I don't know."

"You don't think I'm saying this harshly?"

He hesitated a moment. "No."

"I'm not. But you're so serious, Michael. You have a lot of . . . energy; but it all goes into one thing. Why don't you just laugh, about . . . nothing? Why don't you ever just do the simple, silly things that other people do?"

The words pained Michael; he knew that they struck truth. "It's not so easy as all that," he said softly.

"No. I don't suppose it is."

Early, he returned with her to her home. She stood in the doorway, hesitantly, as though waiting for something. Michael felt a bit awkward. He kissed her lightly on the mouth.

"I'll pick you up tomorrow, for the meeting," he said.

She smiled. "All right, Michael."

He was not sleepy, so, again, he walked. He found himself suddenly down near the river. He stood on the bridge, leaned against the rail and watched the barges slowly pass. Their horns sounded eerie in the night. The water was still. On either side of the river were the shadows of buildings. Overhead was a moon. Michael watched the barge disappear at a bend in the river. He walked back toward home.

Walking, he passed a church, a familiar one, and heard, from within, the sound of people singing.

At times, he wished that he, too, could sing.

Philip was not home; the house was empty. Michael undressed and went to bed.

14.

PHILIP AT THAT MOMENT WAS AT THE HOME OF RAYE, HIS fiancée: a two-room apartment in which she, a student away from home, lived alone. The room in which they sat was pleasant, though sparsely furnished, since Raye had little money; there were more hassocks than chairs, the bookshelf was made of orange crates, and Raye, herself, had made the cabinet for the record-player.

Beethoven's *Sixteenth Quartet* was playing. Philip sat next to Raye, on the studio couch, eating some sandwiches she had made for him and drinking a glass of beer. They had had dinner early, at a restaurant, and afterwards they had seen a good play.

Philip, leaning back, was extremely contented.

"I've just read a book," Raye said. "*If He Hollers, Let Him Go.* By Chester Himes. He's very good."

Philip nodded.

"Oh, how I long to write novels!" Raye said.

Both of them listened to the music. Beethoven, in this quartet, was pure mathematics.

Philip sighed happily. "I wonder what our marriage will be like."

"Reading!" Raye laughed.

"And writing—at least, for you."

"Yes. Writing."

Philip looked darkly at Raye. "Hmmmm. And what, may I ask, will our wedding be like?"

Raye bowed her head and held her hands and looked at Philip in mock shame. "Please," she said, "may we have a big one? I've always thought that, if I got married, I'd want a big wedding. I don't know why, it's a lot of nonsense, it's silly, but please let me be silly just this once."

Philip scowled. "Just this once. Well, all right, I'll suffer through it. They say one should always grant the last request of a dying man—or woman."

"Is marriage death?"

"The death of your freedom!"

"Ah, you'll be a *tyrant*, won't you?"

"Absolutely!"

"And I'll love it! I make a good slave."

"You make a lovely slave," Philip said.

Philip chewed on the sandwich like a contented cow. He drank the beer.

"Philip, will we travel?"

"Absolutely. That's one of the joys of life."

"Good! Where?"

"Well, to Europe, to South America, maybe to Africa."

"Wonderful!"

"Maybe Mexico, too. I saw a story on Mexico in a magazine—in *Ebony*, it was—about King Cole's honeymoon. Maybe we'll go there on our honeymoon."

"Marvelous. Willard Motley's there."

"Yes."

"And Philip, do you want children?"

"Yes."

"Lots of them?"

"Lots of them. All girls."

She frowned. "I want all boys!" Then she laughed. "We'll compromise. Half and half. Then the girls can be yours and the boys will be mine."

"That's good enough," Philip said.

Raye paused and looked at him. "Philip."

"Yes."

"I love you."

In the moment that they looked at each other, Philip said nothing. But a great warmth and happiness flowed through him.

"And I love you," he said finally.

"And it's so wonderful!" she said. "Because do you know what?—I sometimes used to think that I'd never love anybody. And do you know why? Because I never thought I'd find anyone who would satisfy me. I always thought I wanted too much—someone who was intelligent and sensitive, someone who understood the things that were important to me. And here, just look! I've found him. And I can't believe it, yet. I still think I'll wake up one day and find that it's all a dream."

Philip was moved and grateful. He touched her hand. He kissed her, and both of them trembled.

He had never been with a woman before. Nor had she been with a man.

They went cleanly to each other. They were gentle; they were tender; they were romantically in love.

Afterwards, softly, rather shyly, Philip said, "Raye . . . are you sorry?"

"No," she said.

They kissed again. Lights out, they went to sleep.

15.

THAT SAME NIGHT, PETE CAME INTO LIL'S APARTMENT, DRUNK and in a rage. The number writers, he said, were out on strike! "Those goddamn niggers!" He caught himself quickly, looking at Lil. "I'm sorry, baby. You know I'm not talking about you. It's *those* bastards!"

He sat in a chair, cursing. "It's that goddamn Slim! Him and his talking led to this. He started all this. That bastard!"

Then he chuckled. "Well, he's fixed!"

Lil looked at him quickly. "Fixed? What do you mean?"

"Ah, fixed, baby, fixed!" Pete chuckled. "Some of the boys. You know, the old treatment."

"What?" She stared at him. "Slim? A beating?"

"Sure, sure," Pete said, "Don't nobody mess with old Pete and get away with it. *Nobody!*" He looked, smiling, at her. "Not even you, baby. Nobody. Old Pete don't let the world mess with him."

"Slim? Slim? A beating?"

"Whatsa matter, what's it mean to you?" Pete said. "You still carrying the goddamn torch for that sonofabitch? To hell with him! You just sit here, tend your onions, let me handle the people what cross me!"

Lil was out of her seat. She was going toward the door. Pete jumped up and blocked the door. "Where the hell you think you're going?"

"Get out of my way!" Lil said. Her voice was hoarse with anger.

"Why out of your way? Where the hell do you think you're going?"

"Get out of the way, Pete! I'm going to stop those goons of yours!"

"You still carrying the torch for that sonofabitch?"

"Get out of my way!"

Pete laughed. He stood in front of the doorway holding his stomach and laughing at the top of his lungs. Lil tried to push him from in front of the door. "What the hell—!" Pete said. The laughter stopped. As she tried to push him, Pete swung his open palm at Lil, striking her hard on the face. Lil was knocked to the floor. She stared up at Pete, startled, not quite aware of what had happened, for a moment. Then her eyes blazed. She stared, stared at Pete from the floor. She smiled slightly, and the blaze left her narrowed eyes. Slowly, she rose. She looked at Pete and smiled, with the narrowed eyes. She said nothing.

Pete said, "Well, anyway, ain't no need of getting excited, baby." He chuckled. "It's too late. The jobs over. The boys have already worked old Slim over. Did a good job, too." He chuckled again. "You ought to know I'd be there to see it. Told you before. I never liked that bastard anyway."

Lil looked at him. Her eyes remained narrow and the faint smile curled the edges of her lips.

Pete softened. "Aw, come on, baby," he said coaxingly, "don't be like that. I know he used to be your boyfriend, but what the hell, that's all over, ain't it? 'Bout time he got taught a lesson. Nobody messes with Pete and gets away with it."

He came close to her, put his hands on her arms. She did not move. Her eyes lowered. She was unresisting as Pete pulled her close to him and kissed her. Her soft body rested against his. On his breath she smelled alcohol.

"How 'bout it, baby? You love old Pete?"

She was silent. Faintly she sobbed, leaning her head against his chest.

"What the hell, baby," Pete said, "you know how it is. A man can't let people get away with crap like that, he's got to fix the people who cross him." He stroked her shoulder; her body was soft beneath his hand. "Good old Lil. Good old Lil. Sorry I hit you, but you like to be treated rough, don't you? I figured that when I first met you. Man got to take you in hand." He stroked the shoulder. "Good old Lil. Good old Lil." Then he said, hoarsely, "Let's go to bed, baby."

She followed him into the bedroom. He took off his shirt. "Hell, we coulda done worse to Slim, y'know. We beat him—knocked out a few teeth, I guess—but, hell, we coulda pistol-whipped him or killed him. I told the boys, no, that's not necessary, just work him over a little." He chuckled. "Tried to be a hero, fought back. The boys sure fixed that soon enough."

She had taken off her dress. Standing on one leg, she took off a shoe and stocking, then stood on the other to take off the mates. The outline of her body was clear under the slip. Pete looked at the legs and bared shoulders and the way the body went in at the waist. She went into the bathroom to wash, then returned. Pete's eyes followed her movements. Something hot rushed inside of him. He was close to her; his hands held her shoulders, he felt the bareness; he pulled her near again, liking her presence; she was limp in his arms.

"Gimme a little kiss," Pete said.

She raised her head and looked at him. The blaze had gone from her eyes now; they were soft and surrendering. She put her arms around his neck, locked the arms behind his head.

He lowered his lips to hers. Her lips parted. There was a razor blade between her teeth.

Pete screamed. Lil's arms were locked behind his head. She held him tight. Her eyes shone hatred. Holding him tight, she moved her head from side to side.

16.

THEY WERE, THE TWO OF THEM, LIKE CHILDREN IN THE NEXT FEW
weeks, as they packed, put some things in storage and arranged
for the sale of the studio. Kristin bowed low, and kissed every key
of the piano, before she would permit the storage men to take it
away; with a sigh, she watched other cherished properties bound
with ropes, then disappear. Claude, for his part, assumed the air
of profoundest grief as his writing desk was removed. And in
both of them there was the wish that they could cart the entire
studio to Canada with them.

"And to think," Kristin said, with a laugh, "how you reacted
when I first brought you to the studio. You were appalled; you
didn't like it at all!"

"Nonsense, nonsense," said Claude.

Kristin kissed him. "And do you know what? I'm so happy we
couldn't find an apartment after all, when we got married. Tell
the truth—would an apartment have been as nice as this?"

"Not at all!"

"There! You see?—you married a wife with taste!"

The great load lifted from both their minds; and it was suddenly as though the load had never been there. Now, with their
marriage beginning new and clean again, they found it easier to
talk about all the things that had disturbed and threatened them.

These things had been complex. Claude had wanted, and still
wanted, to live not as a Negro, but as a man. His skin was
brown—that pleased him well enough, but he wanted to live a life
in which that would have little more importance than the color
of one's hair. A human being—emotionally, spiritually and intellectually—had range; there were many keys to the piano, and
it was a poor melody that was played only on the lower end.

Poverty, afflictions, the ordinary human lot—let these come, they were nothing, they were part of the universal human experience. It was the universal human experience that he sought.

But there was more than this. Even had he wanted to continue to fight, even had he wanted to continue in the role of "champion," he would have found the paucity of means maddening. For, as he had thought many times, the race struggle in America was a contradiction—*how did one wage war for the victory of love? How did one fight to gain social acceptance? How did one, out of bitterness and a sense of injustice, struggle, not to overthrow the dominant group, but to be embraced by it and welcomed into its midst?* By taking cases to law courts? By getting into fights, following insults, on the streets? By election campaigns or lobbies? These were hardly satisfying.

Then, Kristin, to whom all of this was completely foreign. Both she and Claude were now resigned to the fact that, emotionally, she would never be able to adjust. Every incident, every insult, every mere stare was as shocking and painful as the first had been; and, psychologically, she was even worse, now, because, even when no incident occurred, Kristin found herself *waiting* for the unseen beast to spring.

Finally, the other, attendant things had done their work. Their isolation from both the Negro and white worlds was insupportable. Claude could not escape a nagging sense of guilt, brought on by its inactivity—even though, intellectually, he had convinced himself that there was no reason why the guilt should be felt. Petty things: Claude knew that he could not accept in silence insults that greeted Kristin and him on the streets—and yet, his intelligence rebelled against the inanity of pointless street brawls with hoodlums hardly worth the bother.

Conflicts and contradictions, then, had, emotionally and spiritually, been tearing both of them to pieces.

Kristin admitted, now that the danger was over, that she had, against her will, become convinced that their marriage had been doomed—not because either of them willed it, but because of what she saw and felt was happening inside of Claude. Eventually, she knew, his own guilt, and his concern for her happiness, would have driven him to urge divorce. "I felt a terror," she told Claude, "because I saw it coming, and didn't know what I could do to stop it."

Claude said, "I saw it too."

Dan and Suzette were, naturally, sorry to learn that Claude and Kristin would be leaving. But Dan said, "Maybe what you're doing is right. Anyway, it's right for you." He smiled, pounding Claude on the shoulder. "You're too proud to make the compromises you have to make," he said. "You lose your temper, you're too passionate. Your marriage would have gone on the rocks here. Mine won't. It's a difference in people." They would go with them to the station, Dan said; and, when vacation time came, perhaps they would visit them in Canada.

They had a piece of extraordinarily good luck: a musician friend of Claude, presently in Montreal, wrote in response to a letter from Claude that he had found an apartment for the couple in that city, and at a word from Claude would put up the money necessary to hold it. "Wonderful!" Kristin cried. Claude sent off the letter. From other friends, he got the names and addresses of people he knew who were in Canada at the moment, for one or another reason.

Kristin wrote her brother about the pending move. She received a prompt reply: her brother was overjoyed to hear the news, he confessed that he had had no hope for the marriage, but believed, sincerely, that, on foreign soil, there was no reason why their union could not work.

Michael provided the one sour note: he was furious when Claude told him of his plan to live in Canada. "Why, you're running away! You're running away completely from your people and the fight!" He stormed away from Claude shouting that there was "still one of the brothers who remains faithful to his father and his race!" Still one of the brothers who wore with pride the white carnation.

Claude, and Kristin when he told her, did not care. They were floating on air. Life, for them, was beginning all over again. It would include music and new friends and—a new thought—children, brought up free from color pains!

17.

PHILIP WALKED WHISTLING DOWN THE STREET, NEAR THE NEIGHborhood of Grays Ferry.

The stone was in the air.

The youth who had thrown it, the stone, did not dislike Philip; did not know him, as a matter of fact. But several months ago, at the beginning of spring, he had been standing, with some others, on a street corner, minding his business, when a group of Negroes had come running up the street, from the neighborhood of South Street, and fallen upon them. All of the white youths had been beaten savagely—for no reason, as far as they could see. And this youth—rather a shy youth, with red hair and freckles—had never forgotten or forgiven it. Today, standing alone, again minding his own business, he had seen Philip—a Negro—come walking down the street. Memory and hatred had shot through him; memory and hatred had stared out of his eyes. From the gutter, he had picked up a large, jagged-edged stone; he had waited until Philip was opposite; then he had thrown it with all his strength.

The stone struck Philip at the temple. A jagged edge cut through into the vein. Philip fell. Blood poured from the vein.

The youth, across the street, was frightened when he saw the blood. He had not really expected the stone to strike its mark; he had thrown it as an expulsion of energy and resentment. He saw the blood and, frightened, looked around to see if anyone had seen him. Seeing no one, he ran around the corner and home. "What's the matter?" his mother asked as he raced panting into the house. "Nothing, nothing," he said, trying to control his breathing. His heart was pounding with fear. "You seem in a mighty big hurry," his mother said. "Just a little exercise." He picked up a newspaper and sat down in a chair and, hands trembling, tried to read.

Philip lay on the pavement, his face in the pool made by his own blood.

18.

ALL ARRANGEMENTS HAD BEEN MADE. THE STUDIO NOW WAS AL-most completely empty; they would spend the night in a hotel, where they had already booked a room, and leave for New York early in the morning.

Kristin felt nostalgic in the empty room. "Oh, look at it, Claude! So bare. Even my poor piano!" They would decide, later, whether to have that sent to Montreal. Several trunks were being shipped to their new address; as immediate baggage, they would carry only two large suitcases, a typewriter, and Kristin's violin.

There was a knock at the door. Claude and Kristin looked at each other: it was strange, but a chill went through them both. The knock came again: urgently. Kristin opened the door; there stood a panting dark youth. "Pardon me, Miss. I came to see Claude."

Kristin stepped aside. Claude, for a moment, simply looked at the youth; he did not want to ask the question. "What is it?"

"I was sent here by your brother Michael, Claude. I got a message. It ain't a pretty message. I was sent to tell you that your brother, Philip, is dead."

"What!"

Kristin gasped.

"Killed. By one of them cracker bastards—pardon me, Miss—from over in Grays Ferry. Killed with a rock when he was walking down the street. One of them cracker bastards."

"Philip? Philip?" Kristin cried.

Philip dead? *Dead? Philip?* Claude could not grasp what he was hearing.

"The body's in the morgue," the youth went on. "Michael went down and identified it right away. He sent me over to get you."

Claude stared. Those were cymbals he heard ringing in his ears. He said, "I'll come right with you."

19.

IT WAS EVENING WHEN HE RETURNED, AND MICHAEL WAS WITH him. Kristin had been waiting nervously by the window; she ran to the door as Claude and Michael came in. "There's no mistake?" she asked.

"No."

She had made coffee; the three of them sat down to drink it. There had been no dinner; sandwiches sufficed. Philip. Claude thought over and over: Philip. There was an irony there: that *he,* of the three, had been the one to be killed!

"There's been some trouble," Claude told Kristin. "Some fights; some bloodshed. When they found out that Philip was dead, some Negroes lost their tempers. There might have been a riot—"

"But Claude stopped it," Michael said. He looked, with the old admiration, at his brother. "I tried to stop it," he said, "but no one listened to me. They listened to Claude. They always listen to Claude."

For one brief second, Claude shut his eyes. Then he said, "But the danger's not over. We'll have to go back. We'll have to prevent a repetition tonight. Some hotheads . . . you know how it is."

Kristin nodded. Her eyes were searching Claude's face.

"Claude," Michael said hesitantly, "things haven't been so good between us recently. But our brother's dead; we've had a brother and a father die from violence. Us—well, it's a sort of blasphemy for us not to love each other. Will you take my hand?"

The light shone on Michael's white carnation. Claude's own lapel was empty. He took his brother's hand.

Michael finished his coffee. There was silence, in the room. Awkwardly, Michael stood up; he stood slightly embarrassed in front of his brother and his brother's wife.

"Well, I've got to be going back. I'll see you there later, Claude." He looked at Kristin. "I've never been very nice to you, Kristin. I . . . I might have been wrong. If so, forgive me."

"Oh, Michael," Kristin said, "there was never anything to forgive!"

He left. For a long while, neither Kristin nor Claude spoke. Then Claude broke the silence.

"Kristin—"

"Don't say it, Claude! Don't say it!" There were tears in her eyes.

"Kristin, Kristin I love you! But I can't go away."

She was silent, weeping.

"What an irony!" Claude said softly. "As though Life watched laughing, waiting to play it's final practical joke. A joke on us!" He said it bitterly.

"Claude, and afterwards? And afterwards, we flee? Tell me that afterwards we flee!"

He shook his head. "You know I can't do it."

She wept, but she nodded. "Somehow, I knew that the flight was a dream; somehow I knew it could not, really, be. Perhaps it should not be. I don't know. This is all so—stupid. But I'll try to learn to understand."

"No, sweetheart, you'll never learn to understand. And I don't want you to. For you, there must be music and green things. There must be light and violins. You'll be a great musician, a great violinist—if you're given a chance. If you stay with me, you'll be nothing."

"Claude! Claude! Don't talk like that! Without you, there is no music!"

"Perhaps it seems so now. But that's not true."

"I will not hear it! How dare you talk to me like this. I love you! Don't talk to me like that! Music! Music! I don't *care* about the music!"

Claude smiled, standing up. "Even as you say that, you know that it's not true." He picked up the suitcases. "I'll drive you to the hotel. I have to go back to South Street for awhile."

"Claude, you're cruel!"

"All inevitable painful things must be done swiftly—brutally, perhaps."

"*You* have decided this! Without me!"

"I have decided this because I know myself, and know what I must do; and because I know you, and what you will never do yourself. Your brother was right."

She was standing in front of him. Her arms were around him and her face was buried in his chest. Claude thought: What have I done to deserve the love of this loveliest of all women?

He held her tight.

"Shall we go?"

She dried her tears now and looked at him. She stood looking at him for a long time.

Claude thought: Maybe Life invents these moments to strengthen and purify us.

They were in the car, driving toward the hotel. Both of them were silent, and Kristin wept no more. At one corner, not far form the studio, they halted for a red light; the newsvendor at his stand suddenly caught Claude's eye and winked and waved. Claude looked at the newsvendor. With a slight smile, he waved back. He remembered, now, from where it was that he knew the newsvendor.

20.

LIL WAS ON A TRAIN SITTING IN THE STATION. SHE WAS GOING TO California. She would not decide, until she got there, which city she would stay in; probably, Los Angeles or San Francisco. She was reading a magazine, waiting for the train to depart.

A man got on the train and sat opposite her. The man was middle-aged and slightly bald. He looked at Lil. Lil kept reading her magazine.

The man coughed. "Er, pardon me, miss, but—do you know what time the train leaves?"

"In five minutes," Lil said.

"Thank you." A pause. "Er, are you going very far, Miss?"

"Pretty far." She did not look at him.

"The weather's nice, isn't it?"

Lil read the magazine.

The porter came by. The man leaned toward Lil. "Er, pardon me, miss, but would you care to take a little drink here with me?"

"No, thanks."

"Well, a gin and tonic for me," said the man. The porter went away. When he came back, the balding man reached in his pocket and took out a huge roll of bills. He peeled off one from the top. The porter whistled.

"A twenty! Don't you have anything smaller than that?"

"No."

"Well, I'll have to bring you back your change," the porter said.

The man sipped his drink. "I'm a businessman," he said to Lil. "Going to Chicago for a convention, then I'm gonna stay for a month and take a look at the old town. Need some relaxation. Nothing but wine, women, and song." He coughed. "Where did you say you were going?"

Lil turned the page. "Chicago," she said, without looking up. She crossed her legs, so that the tight skirt slipped up to her knees.

21.

JOE HAD A NEW FIXED IDEA—HE WANTED TO GO UP IN AN AIR-plane. "You can hire them by the hour, see," he told Slim, as they sat in a booth in the *Postal Card*. "The pilot takes you up. Hell, it ain't dangerous at all."

"Danger? I ain't worried about the danger," Slim said indignantly. "But where do you think money grows?—on trees?"

"Aw, it's not expensive, Uncle Slim. You ain't worried about the money, don't try to kid me! You're scared. You think that thing might fall down out of the sky. Well, it won't. People been riding them for a while, now."

"I ain't scared!" Slim protested vehemently.

"Well, you gonna take me up?"

"Well, maybe."

Joe said, "Good! When? Saturday?"

"Well, for Christ's sake!"

"Look, Uncle Slim, I know you, and I don't want no crap about this. Saturday?"

"Well, maybe."

"Good! Saturday. Now, that's definite, understand?"

"Well, for—"

22.

WALKING ALONE, LATE THAT NIGHT, WHEN SOUTH STREET WAS relatively still, Claude felt a great calm and only a slight sadness. Occasionally, someone passed—an old man with white hair; couples chuckling, despite the world, alive, living, conscious unconsciously of the wind and the moon and the stars; a youth, with pork-pie hat and wide-legged trousers, fighting with clothes and a tone of voice his private universal battle against fear and hatred and the white-humped whale from which all evil sprang.

Claude breathed deeply, walking, and thought of an old man endlessly carrying bags of coal and a youth with law books and an ideal and people singing gospel songs and a brother, harmless, who had died. He thought of South Street, great blood vein of a people; thought of gaping dark doors and narrow halls and children who must one day grow up; thought of a hundred years and the years before and a slave who had died and a lie that had been born; thought of laughter and sad eyes, of lidded pain and rage, of dances in youth, of life lessons learned; thought of a million unsung deeds of bravery; thought of community; thought of love.

He felt now, walking, not sad at all; and not happy, either—but alive, and strong, and part of a wonderful people, and with something in this life of use to perform. Which was enough. Who, on earth, had more? And those other things? those mocking stars overhead? . . . endless, baffling Time and endless, terrifying Space? One could, should, be aware of them, in wonder and in awe. But one could not live in their contemplation; one could not live according to their all-paralyzing commentary. One lived—whether one wanted to or not—in the bounded time and the bounded space of one's own life and one's own world, within the bounded nature of one's spiritual core. The thing to do was to accept this, without tears, with strength, dignity and, sometimes, defiance. Man was and always had been only Man; for him, there were crosses to bear, and pains to endure, and seemingly pointless struggles to wage—while the almighty stars laughed overhead. And the thing to do was to laugh back at the stars. The thing to do was to laugh with upraised shaking fist and head held high. The thing to do was to feel with all one's fibers the charging wonder and mystery of Life, to confront both the hard and the soft, and to wrestle straining with the Angels and wrestle with the self. Battle lost or battle won: this had no importance. The thing was to wrestle; the thing was to feel; the thing was to laugh with the upheld head.

Give back, then, to the beloved Kristin, her necessary world of music, of the song. For him? This was his blooded world, his cross, his love, his challenge—South Street.

23.

AT THE SHOWBOAT THERE WAS SMOKE, THERE WAS MUSIC, THERE was noise all around; there were faces that told stories; there was laughter and there was pain.

The Old Man, at his favorite table, in the company of five charming young ladies, was in an excellent mood. "Congratulations! . . . congratulations!"—these were coming from all around. The Governor's faction—*his* faction—had won the primary elections. The Old Man was home a winner. He would be a magistrate before long!

"Congratulations! .... congratulations!" People kept passing by. And the girls still laughed and kissed him. There was money in his pockets, and he was alive.

Scores of friends. Dozens of young ladies. Physical well-being.

Life, thought the Old Man, raising his glass, is a beautiful thing. A beautiful thing to me.

At the bar, the Bartender stood eating an apple and reading a copy of *Look* magazine. In it was a picture story on San Francisco. Funny streetcars: *people have to get out and push at the top of a hill!* The Bartender chuckled, biting into the apple, feeling first the delicious red tension of the skin, and then the mushy substance moving slowly in his mouth. He finished the article. It was a good article. It was a good magazine.

The lights were dimmed. The Bartender, reluctantly, put down his magazine. The people became quiet. The Blues Singer mounted the platform, under the spotlight. The light flickered from her sequins.

The Blues Singer threw back her head and opened her mouth and began to sing.